BEING THE STEEL DRUMMER

Liz Bradbury

LESBIAN MYSTERY BOOKS

ALLENTOWN, PENNSYLVANIA

TO WONDERFUL
BECKY,
THANK YOU
SO MUCH FOR
YOUR GENEROUS
PLEDGE AND
THE GREAT AND
SWEET AND
FUN THINGS
YOU MAKE
HAPPEN!

I LOVE YOU!
YOUR COUSIN! LIZ! 10/10/14

BEING THE STEEL DRUMMER

Copyright © 2012 by Liz Bradbury
Cover design by Liz Bradbury

LESBIAN MYSTERY BOOKS

**Lesbian Mystery Books
is an imprint of Boudica Publishing Inc.
Allentown, Pennsylvania**

Visit our web site:
www.boudicapublishing.com

ISBN: 0-9800549-4-X

Printed in the United States of America
First Edition

Maggie Gale Mysteries
By Liz Bradbury:

Angel Food and Devil Dogs - A Maggie Gale Mystery

Being the Steel Drummer - A Maggie Gale Mystery

and coming soon:

C-Notes and Ski Nose - A Maggie Gale Mystery

Books Illustrated by Liz Bradbury

Sam's Stories Volume One
by Samuel J. Ernst

THE AUTHOR WISHES TO ACKNOWLEDGE:

Catherine M. Wilson for help in many ways, not the least of which is her full support with the creation of the Kindle files and her amazing editing abilities, Miriam Lavandier for Spanish translations, Vanessa Ferro for insight into police rank and duties, Gail Uhl for firearms insights, Jean Rubin for always being there when I have a grammar question, Hannah Mesouani for copy editing, Larry Storch for inspiration (see author's notes), Kate Mulgrew for inspiration, and all the extensive help from beta readers: Genevieve Goff, Gail Eric, Catherine M. Wilson, Gail Uhl, Sheryl Schulte, Hannah Mesouani, Don Kohn, Melinda Kohn, Gary Gaugler, Kelly Nansteel, Robin Riley-Casey, Anne Huey, Laura Gutierrez, Marc Freligh, and MaryEllen Elizabeth. And Patricia Sullivan who has supported and helped with the creation of every page and idea in this book and every moment of our wonderful life.

For Patricia J. Sullivan,
with whom my heart springs upward
like a palm...

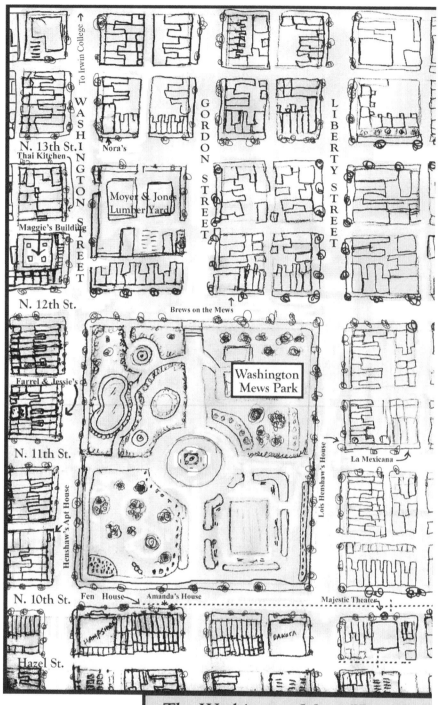

The Washington Mews Historic

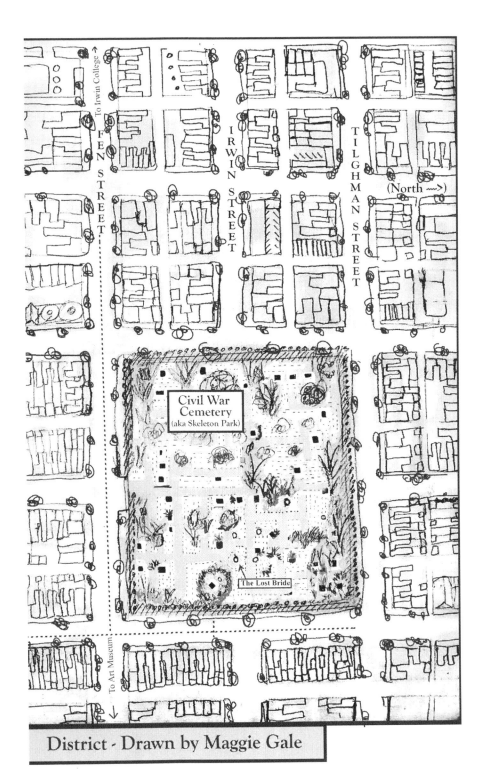

To Irwin College →

FEN STREET

IRWIN STREET

TILGHMAN STREET

(North —→)

Civil War
Cemetery
(aka Skeleton Park)

The Lost Bride

To Art Museum

District - Drawn by Maggie Gale

CHAPTER 1

"I've heard that lust is one of the gateways to hell," said Kathryn in a low voice.

"Good, let's go there right now," I whispered back.

I'd just given Dr. Kathryn Anthony, the beautiful auburn-haired woman who'd been sharing my bed for the last two months, an amorous glance in the mirror above the old stone fireplace.

The Washington Mews Neighborhood Association had gathered for our monthly meeting in our friend Amanda Knightbridge's small living room.

"People could be killed! I want you to investigate, Maggie. That's the long and the short of it; we need to send them packing!" Gabriel Carbondale said as he folded his arms and scowled like a five-year-old.

"*Gabe*, calm down," I said firmly. "Yes, there's vandalism in the cemetery, but it could just be a few kids with too little to do."

"It could be gangs!" shouted a woman from the back of the room.

"Who was that?" asked my best friend Farrel Case, twisting impatiently in her chair to peer through the crowd.

The meeting was unusually contentious this month. Fear was trying to overbalance art and I seemed to be the fulcrum.

My name is Mehitabel Arrabella Gale. I was named after a rich aunt who turned out not to be—rich that is. My creative mother, who died suddenly when I was eight, had saved me from endless schoolyard taunts by using my initials to begin a name a little easier to rock, Maggie.

I'm a former cop turned private detective with a college art school education. This might seem incongruous, but making art doesn't pay much and crime-solving benefits from creativity and also my incurably snoopy tendencies. I have light brown hair and green eyes, will turn thirty-six next Friday, and I'm an out and proud Lesbian. I live in Fenchester, Pennsylvania, a college city in the eastern part of the state. My office shares the second floor of a small converted factory building with Martinez and Strong, Attorneys at Law.

I happen to own the building, which I got in payment from a grateful client in exchange for nearly losing my life. I live in the third floor loft with my hot new...um...she might have been called my *inamorata,* in old time movies. I think Kathryn and I are beyond the *girlfriend* stage, but not quite up to more formal labeling. She's an English professor at Irwin College. The campus is just a few blocks west of Washington Mews.

Gabriel Carbondale strode to the center of the room again, taking a deep breath for another bellow.

"What an ass," muttered Jessie Wiggins, seated at Farrel's right.

I whispered in Farrel's ear, "Jessie said ass!" This rated a major headline. Farrel's beloved partner Jessie, who is ten years older and generally much more sedate than Farrel, rarely swears. *Ass* was a significant expletive. Farrel reached for Jessie's hand.

Gabe Carbondale went on triumphantly, "I have a plan! We have to cement up the fronts of the crypts! Gangs are using them as headquarters. We must cover the entire entrance of each one. *And I'll pay for it!*"

Carbondale lifted his hands as though the silent people in the room were trying to talk him out of it. "No, no, don't worry about the expense. Saying good riddance to these criminals is meat and drink to me. Coming home across the pond just a few weeks ago, I decided that I'd..."

"Gabriel, this is quite preposterous!" stated Amanda Knightbridge in a tone that halted Carbondale's rant. Amanda was the head of the Art History Department at Irwin. Her long white hair was pinned in a neat bun, her block-like body sat rigidly upright. She continued in her precise voice. "The Washington Mews neighborhood, including the Civil War Cemetery, is part of Fenchester's Historic District. We cannot destroy the historically significant sepulchers of over sixty Civil War veterans! After Gettysburg, this is the most significant cemetery in Pennsylvania. Don't be absurd," she said with finality.

Lois Henshaw waved for a chance to speak. In her rather strange outfit of mismatched items she looked like a redheaded Pippy Longstocking. Lois said, "If you ask me, and I know you didn't, I think we should round up all the horses and pee on the campfire."

"Huh?" said Farrel.

The room fell silent. Lois turned beet colored and sat down.

"But the gangs!" shouted a woman in the back. Several people, including Kathryn, sighed in frustration. Farrel grunted like Marge Simpson.

Amanda Knightbridge was preparing to waylay another of Gabe Carbondale's monologues, but someone interrupted him even more effectively. A woman walked to the center of the room with hands raised and miraculously Gabe shut up.

She was about Kathryn's height and had shoulder length black hair, with a white lock brushed back from her hairline. Her skin was carefully made-up. She was wearing a designer suit. She looked fit and was showing it off.

"I'm Piper Staplehurst. Perhaps I can help. I'm doing a residency at the Fenchester Art Museum, cataloging the collections and working on funding and development. I have a possible grant that could pay for historically accurate wrought iron gates for the crypt's entrances to deter crime. Need has to be established by a licensed expert."

Piper Staplehurst smiled at me in a flirty way. "A report from a detective would certainly prove the case for the grant."

Kathryn cleared her throat. I caught another view of her in the gilt-framed mirror. She was wearing a hunter green turtleneck and a soft tweed blazer. Her jeans fit perfectly. I didn't consciously decide she was more attractive than Piper Staplehurst; I just felt it throughout every cell of my body.

Farrel whispered, "I read about this in the museum news. She arrived in late December to help them sell off some of their extra inventory."

Piper Staplehurst was saying, "The iron doors would be similar in design to the high 19th century fence that surrounds the cemetery. Of course, we'll have to be careful moving the heavy gates in, but I believe we can guard against any truck damage..."

As she unfolded her proposal most people were obviously pleased, but Gabriel Carbondale seemed annoyed.

"I don't know if that will solve the problem..." he began.

"We think it will," said one of the other neighbors. "Look, none of us wants to spoil the architectural features of the cemetery, but we have to fight vandalism. And if it's paid for by a grant... Let's let Maggie do her job and talk about this in the next meeting."

"I say we begin tonight!" thundered Carbondale, as though it was all his idea. He wheeled on me. "Maggie, I'll cover your rate out of my own pocket." That made everyone nod.

"Well, I suppose I could," I began.

Farrel said, "I'll help you."

"OK, Gabe," I said. "We'll stake it out tonight."

Kathryn whispered, "Rats."

I turned toward her. She smiled slightly and shook her head. Everyone stood up to leave. Both Farrel and Kathryn took a few moments to introduce themselves to Piper Staplehurst. Jessie and I carried plates into Amanda's kitchen.

Ten minutes later, Farrel, Jessie, Kathryn, and I stood outside Amanda's house on 10th Street, biting back the February cold.

"Gabe Carbondale gets more insufferable each day," said Jessie with surprising bile.

"He's always been that way. It just shows more since his wife Suzanne left and he got back from that lecture series he was doing in England," said Farrel looking at her watch. "Maggie, we should hit the specter's hector soon. "Kathryn," went on Farrel, "we're doing the antique markets in the morning, right? I'll pick you up at 6:00 a.m."

"Then we'll all have brunch. And I also wanted to ask you two to dinner tomorrow evening," said Jessie. "Did Farrel tell you we're cutting back on meat?"

Kathryn slipped her arm through mine. "I wish I didn't have to tell you this, but yesterday the new head of the English department came up with the *brilliant* idea to have a departmental retreat. It's all afternoon, through dinner. He even wants us to stay overnight on campus."

"When?" I asked, hoping against odds.

"Tomorrow afternoon," she said sadly.

****

"Why didn't she tell you about the retreat yesterday?" asked Farrel.

We were in my stake-out car. Medium sedan, nondescript, dark tinted windows, and right now, very cold. We'd been at the entrance of the Fenchester Civil War Cemetery for four hours. The wrought iron fence around the rest of the four-block graveyard was eighteen feet high and kept everyone but pole vaulters out. All visitors had to get in here by passing through or climbing over the three-foot gate that was in place across the entrance to keep cars out.

"Kathryn wasn't sure about this tiresome retreat until she got an email during the meeting at Amanda's. Do you think Kathryn and I moved in together too soon?"

"Life a little rocky with your luscious new love?"

"No, actually she's indescribably delicious."

"Well yay! Let's talk about that!" said Farrel. "Maybe it'll warm it up in here."

"*Indescribably* means I can't describe it," I explained patiently. "Why is Jessie cutting out meat? It's probably much healthier and then there's the ethical implications..."

"No, no, don't change the subject. I want graphic details. Kathryn must be hell on wheels in bed."

"Given this a lot of thought, have you?" I asked laughing.

"If you don't mind me saying, Kathryn is very easy on the eyes, once you get by that academic seriousness that scares students away."

"I doubt it scares *all* her students away," I mused.

"She has that great voice, too. Maggie, you've slept in the same bed since the night of your first kiss. She gave up her apartment four weeks ago... Um... What was the question again?"

"You're worse than Gabe Carbondale." I paused to remember. "I'm just wondering if other people think we've kind of rushed into this."

"You've never given a Swedish fish for what other people thought. What do *you* think? Is there a problem? Did something happen when you were away with her in January at the beach?"

"We had a wonderful time. She's challenging and sympathetic. We talk about everything. I even met her mother, which was kind of dicey."

"Have you found something out about Kathryn that scares you? Religious right? Social Conservative? Gets her news from Fox?"

I snorted. "No, she's more liberal than I am, if that's possible."

"Has she turned out to be less sharp than the stiletto she seems to be?"

"No, she's really brilliant, funny, savvy. Did you know she's written like fifteen books? Everything is different with her, better, more interesting."

"Sex OK? Is that Ice Queen monicker that the grad students call her true, or is she... What was it that Alfred Hitchcock called Grace Kelly? 'A snow covered volcano'?"

"Oh baby, I'm with Hitch."

"I thought so. I've heard her laugh."

"Laugh?"

"I have this theory that women who occasionally laugh with reckless abandon have a special appreciation of the bedroom."

I thought back to my first date with Kathryn and the unbridled way she'd laughed at a malfunctioning computer program. Until that point she'd been so controlled. I became lost in an interesting fantasy and then realized Farrel was talking again.

"So she's flawless, yet you're worried?"

"OK, there's one thing. She drives like a bat out of hell, set on fire, being chased by a T-Rex. You know that Steve McQueen movie *Bullit?*"

Farrel snorted. "Well maybe it's her Mini Cooper. You didn't take that to Florida did you?"

"No, we took the mini-van, but right before we left, one of the other college profs gave her two tickets to the *Cezanne* show in Philly. She drove... Um, let me put it this way. It's sixty miles and we got there in forty-five minutes. Including parking."

Farrel whistled in awe, then asked more seriously, "That's all it is? The driving?"

"No," I considered, "the driving doesn't matter. It's just... Since we got back from the vacation we've both been so busy, we haven't had much time to connect. But that isn't it. I think she wants *me* to figure out something, but I'm not sure what it is."

"Jessie says good relationships are a combination of luck, hard work, and a lot of compromise. Look, Kathryn's a good match for you. You just have some residual fear from that quirky break-up with Carrie," said Farrel in her college prof lecturing voice.

"From Carrie? That was years ago!"

"Have you and Kathryn used the "L" word?"

"Lesbian?"

"Lesbian! I think that's already been established," Farrel said sarcastically. "No, *love* you idiot! Have you said, *I love you,* to her?"

"Not quite there yet," I mumbled.

"You want it to work out with Kathryn, don't you?"

"Yes, I really do." I laughed at my own intensity. "I certainly don't want to mess this up. For one thing, she's made the bathroom smell so nice. Did you know a little bottle of Chanel costs like, a hundred dollars?"

"Tell me about meeting her mother."

"OK, I..." Something caught my eye in the darkness. "Look over there!" I'd heard a faint noise and seen a pinpoint of light under the cold February moon. I slipped out the driver's side and vaulted over the low decorative gate with one hand on metal so cold I felt the shock through my glove. I sped into the darkness as Farrel climbed over the gate more slowly.

I wove my way through the field of stones halfway into the cemetery. There was no snow on the paths, only a few small patches of ice under the trees. The stiff brown grass was frost-tipped; the dirt underneath was as hard as concrete. I didn't want Farrel to trip over a gravestone onto the unforgiving ground. Jessie had calmly explained to me years before that she would kill me if Farrel ever got hurt helping me on one of these little anti-crime escapades. We were careful. We even wore bulletproof vests, but we didn't tell Jessie about that. It was too foreboding.

When Farrel caught up to me, we paused to still our breathing and listen. A dry cold breeze rustled pine needles and swayed bare branches.

Farrel zipped her jacket higher. The chill seeped like an icy liquid through the seams of my clothes.

"BooOOOK," Farrel sang softly.

I tried not to laugh.

Farrel said, "And I thought my fear of spooky cemeteries late at night was just irrational paranoia."

"Will you shut up. You'll scare the zombies away," I whispered. "There!" We heard two thuds, one right after another.

"C'mon," I said, moving toward the sounds. The eerie graveyard ambience surrounded us. Darkness, stillness.

We left the shadows of the trees, crunched over a gravel road, and came upon two granite headstones lying on their backs in the moonlight. They were old but their supine positions were new. Two frost-lined rectangles on granite bases showed where the headstones had stood for 150 years, until just a few moments ago.

"Listen," I said softly. A muffled rumble underscored the shiver of the wind in the leafless branches. We moved toward it, inching along the outer edge of a block-shaped burial tomb, pressing against its cold concrete surface. The night seemed to fold in on us as a cloud passed in front of the moon. Crouching low, I leaned to look around the corner. Farrel peeked over my head.

Farrel gasped, and I stiffened.

The freezing breeze died, letting a gentle herbal scent fill the air.

A ray of moonlight sliced through the darkness, revealing a ring of tombstones. In the middle was a ghost. A woman in a white gown floated high above the ground about thirty feet away from us. Her face was eerily familiar. She was looking right at us with her hand outstretched.

"It's the Lost Bride," said Farrel in a hushed voice.

CHAPTER 2

"I wasn't scared," I insisted to Jessie Wiggins as she checked a pie in her oven.

"Uh huh," she nodded. I've known Jessie for many years and while the white highlights in her hair halo her face, she's not angelically credulous. She does, however, have unbounded energy in her compact little body. She uses it to help Farrel run their part-time antique business and to make the best food in the northern hemisphere.

"There was this shaft of moonlight. The statue was up so high, it looked like she was floating in space. We could barely see the dark granite pedestal," I said, carrying a basket of biscuits to the table.

It was Sunday morning brunch at Jessie and Farrel's row home in the heart of Washington Mews. Cora Martin, the diminutive antique dealer who lived next door, was already there. Her short, plump frame was seated in a chair by the dining room window. She was wearing a beige sweater and slacks outfit and shoes that even I could tell were Prada. Her soft blond hair was styled to make her look younger than her seventy years.

Cora's husband Raymond had passed away almost eight years before, but though she missed him, sometimes terribly, Cora's solo life didn't slow her down. She visited her adult children and traveled to antique shows all over the country. A few weeks ago, Cora had welcomed Mickey Murphy into her home. Mickey was an adult who had the capabilities of a sweet eight-year-old, but also savant-like talents that got him into trouble. Cora helped him avoid that trouble and cooked for him. Mickey carried Cora's groceries, helped her at antique shows, and changed the light bulbs.

"A Jewish mother is exactly what Mickey needs," Cora had said. "We're a perfect match."

Jessie's cell phone rang.

"Maggie, could you get that? It's on the counter."

It was Judith Levi. She'd been Farrel's college English teacher many years ago. They'd become friends and Judith had moved to Fenchester to teach English at Irwin College when Farrel began teaching woodworking there. Now in her seventies like Cora, Judith was retired. She spent much of her time reading, writing, and reviewing books.

"Jessie? Oh, Maggie. Dear, please tell Jessie I shall be a bit late. The men from the City are here to inspect the water pipes."

I paused, then said slowly, "Judith, did you call them to come? Just answer yes or no."

"No."

"They came to your door and showed you a badge and then came in to check the pipes? Just answer yes or no."

"Yes."

"Keep talking on the phone as though there's someone on the line. Can you do that? Start now."

Jessie looked up in alarm. "What is it?"

"I'm going to Judith's." I sped out the door, grabbing my shoulder bag and pulling my jacket on on the fly. En route I fished my handcuffs from my bag and tucked them in my back pocket.

Judith lives less than half a block behind Farrel and Jessie's, in a condo apartment on the second floor of a converted carriage house.

In minutes I was at the base of Judith's outdoor stairs, looking up at her door. It opened and a muscular bald man in a winter jacket, rushed down the steps. I stood in his path. He didn't slow down. He just put his hand up like he was about to sing, *Stop in the Name of Love*, and barreled at me.

I'd been right. Most people don't haphazardly push other people over unless they're thieves or rushing to a Black Friday sale.

Twenty-five years of martial arts training comes in handy now and then. I grabbed the man's extended wrist with a two-finger vise-like grip, pressing right on the nerve points as I pulled my handcuffs from my back pocket. He fell to his knees in wailing pain.

"I'm making a citizen's arrest," I growled twisting his hand around his back, deftly cuffing him to the railing. I pushed his head back and stared into his eyes. "You keep quiet."

He nodded, trying to rub the pain out of his wrist.

I squeezed past him up the steps and slipped in the front door of Judith's cozy three-room home. She was in the living room, still on the phone. She saw me out of the corner of her eye in the vestibule, but I made a *keep talking* finger twirl. She continued chatting in a remarkably natural way.

I peeked around the door frame and saw another guy standing with his back to me, idly looking at a bookcase. He was wearing a green coveralls uniform. He looked official, but he wasn't. Fenchester water department workers wear blue.

I quietly stepped deep into the room and tipped my head back towards the door. Judith faded back with the phone.

"Hello," I said in my stern cop voice.

The man looked up sharply, surprised to find someone a tad more spry than the senior citizen who'd been there a few minutes before. He was shorter than his partner, had styled hair, a carefully shaped goatee, and the beady eyes of a B-picture con artist. The name Willie was embroidered over his front pocket next to a laminated ID badge. And he was smart enough to know when to scram. He headed for the door.

"Nope," I said reaching for him. But it was Judith who stopped him by sticking an umbrella between his legs. He lurched forward and fell on the floor. In a second I was on top of him with his arms behind his back.

"Cue, help!" shouted Willie to his partner. But Cue was tied up at the moment.

"Judith? Would you call the police, please?"

"I already have, Maggie," Judith said.

Willie grunted. "I'm with the water department."

"Yeah, sure," I said dryly.

Judith looked at me sitting on Willie's back and said, "Oh dear."

****

Rapid response is the motto of the Fenchester Police Department. They were there in five minutes. The first thing the officer said was, "Big bald guy and short guy with pointy beard! This is great. These guys are part of a band wanted for four other home invasions."

Cue had Judith's pearl earrings, her gold necklace, and about $100 of her cash in his pocket. She'd kept these items in her jewelry box on her dresser and hadn't seen Cue snatch them on his way to check the bathroom pipes while Willie kept her busy. The police bagged the evidence, gave Judith a receipt, and hauled the perps away in a squad car in record time.

"Maggie, how did you know these men were up to no good simply from our phone conversation?" Judith asked as we walked back to Farrell and Jessie's.

"City workers don't make cold calls on Sundays. They would never have just shown up at your house unless you'd reported an emergency. Criminals often pose as utility workers." I didn't add that they also often prey on old people.

"I feel foolish. I suppose Farrel will scold me."

"You stopped the thief, Judith. You're a rock star."

"Rock star? Don't be silly," she insisted. "Will they go to prison?"

"Probably, for a while."

Judith sighed. "It was poor judgment to let them in." She shook her head as we came through Farrell and Jessie's door. Judith complimented Jessie on the wonderful aromas, got herself a cup of coffee, and sat down next to Cora.

I heard Cora exclaim, "Oh no, dear, that's terrible!"

"Is everything all right?" asked Jessie, collecting serving platters and utensils.

"Everything is fine. Judith will tell you about it later."

"She seems to be having a good time telling Cora now. Oh, there's the garage door," said Jessie happily.

Farrel and Kathryn wiped their feet on the backdoor mat and pushed through the kitchen door. They were laden with full canvas sacks.

Jessie took Farrel's bags as Farrel shrugged out of her heavy jacket and pulled off her wool cap. Jessie kissed Farrel and smiled at her with a moment of joy so pure that it showed the depth of their love.

"You look like a Steiff hedgehog. Why didn't you tell me about the ghost?" said Jessie looking up at Farrel.

Farrel pressed down her staticky gray-blond hair with both hands, but it popped back up. "I wasn't scared, really, Jessie, I wasn't," insisted Farrel.

The warm kitchen flushed Kathryn's face pink at her cheekbones. She was wearing a soft gray sweater with a Sabrina neckline and a dark green scarf that was just the right shade to flatter her auburn hair. She was perfectly in style, which she seemed to achieve effortlessly and which I never seem to achieve at all.

Kathryn and I were still at that point in our relationship where everything about her—her voice, the way she moved, the look in her eyes—made me yearn for her. The intensity of it wasn't waning. Her steel-blue gaze focused on me. It held the promise of erotic things to come.

I'd gotten home so late she'd been fast asleep when I crawled into bed. This morning before dawn I'd barely felt her leave for the market.

"I've missed you," I said, taking Kathryn's canvas bag. She put one arm around my waist and we kissed.

"Have you already eaten everything?" asked Kathryn. "As though that would be possible in Jessie's kitchen!"

"I haven't had a thing. We were waiting for you."

"Uh huh, and that bacon-flavored kiss was just your new toothpaste?"

"Pigsodent?" I suggested.

Farrel said, "Hogs of Maine?"

"Sens-o-swine?" I asked.

"Can you get swine flu from that?" asked Farrel.

"I read about it in *Porks Illustrated.*"

"STOP!" groaned Jessie and Kathryn in unison.

Then Kathryn said, smirking, "Really, it's a bore... a wild boar."

Farrel and I both snorted.

Jessie said to Kathryn, "Oh no, not you too! Besides, it's soy-bacon," as she handed Farrel a pitcher of juice and waved her toward the table.

Farrel glanced around the room and asked, "Where's Amanda?" just as the front doorbell rang.

Amanda Knightbridge, the host of yesterday's neighborhood meeting, asked, "Am I late?" as she unwrapped her long woolen scarf. "Are your sister and her partner coming this morning, Maggie?"

"They both said they were too swamped with work."

Amanda unbuttoned her camel hair coat. She was wearing a multi-shade purple wool sweater and a long brown skirt that came to the top of her boots. Amanda was quite a bit taller than Cora Martin, but an inch or two shorter than Judith Levi. Though her figure was imposing, she seemed to float when she walked, like a nun in a Fellini movie.

"Will Mickey be joining us?" Amanda asked Cora.

Cora shook her head. "Mickey watches cartoons on weekend mornings. To him, it's a religion."

Amanda said, "What a shame Kathryn's new department head has called a retreat for later today. I'm sure you wanted Kathryn all to yourself this afternoon, Maggie."

Amanda went to sit next to Judith, who told her the story of the bogus water company crew in a low voice. When Farrel came to the table, Judith said to Amanda in a louder voice, "Farrel was out late with Maggie in the cemetery endeavoring to thwart vandals, *and* she left at the crack of dawn this morning to scour the antique markets with Kathryn!"

Kathryn yawned. "It was quite a bit *before* dawn."

"But did you get anything great, girls?" asked Cora Martin in the standard fashion of antique dealers.

"I got a very nice porcelain pug dog I think you might like, Cora. Oh, and two very old spoons made of coin silver. One with an urn on the back of the bowl and the other has the image of a bird flying out of a cage. Quite interesting and in fine condition," Farrel said in Amanda's direction.

"Show me the dog, dahling," said Cora in a businesslike way.

"And I'd like to see the spoons, Farrel. As you knew I would," said Amanda happily.

I sat down at the table, knowing that negotiations take precedence over eating. Kathryn sat beside me. She lay her hand in mine. For the next few minutes our fingers did their own subtle erotic dance.

Cora pulled a multi-lens jeweler's loupe from her handbag. Farrel carefully unwrapped and handed her a foot-tall ceramic dog figurine with flashing glass eyes.

Cora examined the dog expertly, holding it in the sunlight, as she and Farrel discussed price in low voices.

I leaned to Kathryn's ear and asked, "How much did Farrel pay for the dog?"

"She got it in a booth full of things tumbled together in cardboard boxes. She made an offer of forty-five dollars and the dealer took it after asking if she'd pay cash," whispered Kathryn.

"Really? Hmm."

"What's Cora paying her for it?" Kathryn asked.

"I think I heard $350."

Kathryn quietly gasped in surprise. "Why? What is it?"

"It looks German, mid-1800s, maybe Dresden, and it's very fine. Cora loves this kind of thing. Don't worry about the mark-up. Cora doesn't begrudge Farrel a profit. Cora never buys something unless she can triple the price. It may take her awhile but she'll make a lot more money than Farrel did. And Cora didn't have to get up before the freezing February dawn to find it."

Amanda fished a large magnifying glass out of her copious bag to inspect the fragile-looking silver spoons. Amanda was a collector, a very different animal than a dealer.

"Quite early, are they not, Farrel?" she said, tracing her finger over the figural designs on the backs of their bowls.

"Shall I look up the maker?" asked Farrel.

"There's no need. I recognize the marks of the silversmith. Mannerbach, about 1820. Made just about sixty miles from here. The urn is very distinct and the bird is lovely. I can clearly see the cage."

Kathryn asked me, "Why is it called coin silver?"

"I don't know as much about this as Farrel, but in the United States, real silver spoons are always marked with the word 'sterling' if they were made after 1865. Sterling literally means 92.5% pure silver. Before 1865 in the US, silver pieces were made in the same standard as silver coins, about 90% silver, and they only have the maker's name and sometimes the town where they were made. Right now, sterling is at a very high price per ounce. So spoons like these, even though they're real antiques, are at risk. Somebody might sell them for 'melt' just to get a quick return."

"Isn't the art museum selling some old silver things that were donated to them in the past? Didn't you tell me that, Farrel?" asked Judith.

Farrel looked up; her negotiations with Amanda were apparently finished. "Yes, they're selling some of the works they never show, from their stockpiles in storage. Mostly duplicate items. I asked Piper Staplehurst about the sale when we were at Amanda's. Piper's in charge of the liquidation. She said I could make a bid on some of the lots."

"I'm not sure selling off the museum collections is a wise idea," said Amanda.

But the antique dealers in the group firmly disagreed.

"Oh no, dahling, museums have tons of pieces they never show. The Metropolitan Museum in New York has ten blocks of underground storage with thousands of pieces that haven't seen the light of day for a hundred years. It's good for the Fenchester museum to thin. And money supports the museum much better than a full closet," said Cora.

"I'll get a box for these spoons, Amanda," said Farrel.

Amanda dug in her handbag for her checkbook.

"Was the bird escaping the cage to celebrate America's Independence?" asked Judith looking at the small design on the back of one of the spoons.

Amanda nodded, and Judith passed the spoons to Kathryn so she and I could see the intricate designs. Amanda said, "Good show, Farrel. You know just what I like, and I'll be a happy pauper by the time you're through with me if you keep bringing me lovely finds like this."

"I'm glad I could rescue these little pieces of history from the scrapper," said Farrel.

"Do antique dealers often sell to each other?" Kathryn asked me.

I said with a laugh, "Don't you know that old joke? It goes, *Five antique dealers were stranded on a desert island... And business was brisk!*"

Kathryn responded with an unbridled laugh. I glanced over at Farrel, who was watching Kathryn. She raised her eyebrows at me. I felt a tingle and hid a smile.

I cleared my throat, then asked Kathryn, "Did *you* find anything interesting at the market?"

Farrel said, "I think Kathryn found some things that were really good. I'm dying to hear what you all think."

"But we should all eat first!" said Kathryn.

"Yes, please, everyone eat," said Jessie, sitting at the head of the table. Conversation was lost to food consumption for the next ten minutes. The warm scratch biscuits with Jessie's homemade peach jam from the peach tree in their backyard were a runaway hit. The main focus was a corn and potato pot pie with a flaky crust. Haute comfort food for a cold February morning. The appreciation for it flowed like the peach jam.

"We have a lot to talk about this morning. I had one of those... A brush with fame. But later for that," said Cora. "Ghosts in... what do the old-timers call it... Skeleton Park? Yes, tell about the ghosts."

Judith and Cora had missed the neighborhood meeting at Amanda's, so first I filled them in on what had happened.

"Wouldn't the descendants of the departed be unlikely to support cementing up their family crypts? Was there *anyone* who supported Gabriel Carbondale's plan?" asked Judith.

Jessie grunted. Judith looked from her to Farrel. Farrel shrugged. "Jessie doesn't like Gabe."

"He has that lovely big dog," said Judith and Amanda, nearly in unison.

"We were friends with Suzanne and when she left Gabe we tried to be supportive to him, but... well..." Farrel trailed off.

Jessie grunted again.

"Why did Suzanne Carbondale leave?" asked Amanda.

"Because Gabriel Carbondale is an arrogant jerk," said Jessie flatly.

"Such strong language, dahling!" said Cora with surprise. "You know it takes two people to end a relationship, just like it takes two people to start one. But tell about the ghosts."

"We heard a noise and found toppled headstones. The vandals who pushed them over must have run. Then we saw *The Lost Bride* in a shaft of moonlight. She was ghostly. We doubled back to the entrance but didn't see anybody. I'll go back in the daylight to look around."

"For clues?" asked Kathryn, partly teasing. "*The Lost Bride* sounds like it must have a romantic Victorian story," said Kathryn as she passed a bowl of homemade apple sauce.

"The story of *The Lost Bride* is indeed quite a romantic one, Kathryn," said Amanda in a professorial voice. "Before Judith retired, she and I taught a course on the history of Washington Mews Cemetery. A trifle late in the 19th century for me, but the Victorian memorials were right up Judith's street. You know the Carbondales wrote a book on Fenchester history that covered all the local figures. You may have encountered it: *Fenchester — A History of Love, Loss, and Generosity from the Civil War to the Roaring Twenties,* by Gabriel and Suzanne Carbondale? Maggie, you and Kathryn really must read it."

Jessie grunted and got up to clear some of the dishes. She muttered, "Suzanne wrote the book."

"We have a copy of it here; you can borrow it," said Farrel.

"Evangeline Lavender Fen was the great-great-niece of Elias Fen, for whom Fenchester is named. She was also a direct descendent of the founder of Irwin College, Walter Irwin, and the College's first President, James Clymer. All these old families had close ties," Amanda explained.

"Evangeline was betrothed to General Merganser Hunterdon. He was a decorated Civil War hero. Hunterdon was a coarse, self-made man who may have been the wealthiest in the State. He was a ruthless capitalist, yet he ultimately balanced his wicked ways by becoming a generous philanthropist."

"Evangeline *Lavender?*" I said. "This may sound silly but, I think I smelled lavender in the cemetery when I saw *The Lost Bride*."

"Not silly at all, Maggie. I believe General Hunterdon had lavender planted all over the Mews, and even the dried-out winter plants have a noticeable fragrance when disturbed," said Amanda. "Evangeline was quite educated for a woman of her time. She studied art at Irwin College. She traveled to Europe and lived in Rome in the late 1860s and early '70s, but she returned to Fenchester and moved into her mother's home," said Amanda.

"Her engagement to Hunterdon was perhaps a strategic move, don't you think, Amanda?" said Judith taking up the yarn. "You see, her father died fairly young and her mother was quite destitute, having lost their money in the *Panic of 1873*, when major banks collapsed and thousands of businesses failed. There were also two younger sisters who would not have been aptly described as *comely*, and a young brother. Really quite like a Jane Austen plot. Evangeline's only hope was a good match."

Amanda agreed. "It's all in the Carbondales' book. As a matter of fact, Evangeline and her family lived in the house Gabriel rents, and I think Suzanne Carbondale was distantly related to Evangeline, though the house belongs to the college now. It's just two doors south of my house. Those were tradesmen's tiny homes overlooking the Mews stables in the 1860s. Not quite suited for Fen family lineage, but it was all they could afford. The smell of the... uh... *horses*... must have been very unpleasant."

"Luckily," went on Judith, "Evangeline was quite beautiful, though in her late twenties. There are several daguerreotypes of her in the Fenchester Historical Collection. One of them is reproduced in the Carbondales' book, I believe."

"The photographs of General Merganser Hunterdon are not so flattering. Rather an unfortunate-looking man," said Amanda.

"Yes, quite," said Judith.

"Maybe that's why they named him after a duck," said Jessie quietly.

Judith continued, "They were engaged in the 1870s for quite a few years. But... she died."

"How sad," said Kathryn. "What happened?"

"She was riding her horse in the foothills and fell."

"They found Evangeline's body in a ravine. General Hunterdon was distraught. How did you say it in the lecture, Judith? He became a professional mourner?"

"Merganser Hunterdon donated a great deal of his money to community projects. He also committed a significant part of his fortune to building monuments in Evangeline's honor. They were commissioned to an important sculptor of the day—surprisingly a woman, Victoria Willomere Snow. She came to Fenchester just a few years before Evangeline died to do a commission for the College."

"*The Lost Bride* sculpture and many other commissioned pieces were paid for by General Hunterdon at a retainer rate of twenty dollars a day for life. Snow created five Evangeline works for the cemetery alone. She lived into her nineties in Fenchester and so did Hunterdon. The commission turned out to be a record sum," said Judith. "Very little is known about Victoria Snow other than the quality of her work, because she was quite reclusive. Not unlike Emily Dickenson."

I'd avidly studied women sculptors of the 19th century when I was in college. Victoria Willomere Snow was a favorite. She had sometimes used found objects in her sculpture, which was considered very avant-garde for the day. She'd studied in Rome with Harriet Hosmer and was probably part of Charlotte Cushman's circle. Cushman was a famous actor who was notorious for her Lesbian affairs, but little was known about Victoria Snow's personal life.

Amanda was saying, "As time went on, General Hunterdon became a bit of a roué; dueling, womanizing, although his grief for Evangeline was apparently genuine. Hunterdon eventually ran for State Senate, but after he won the primary he withdrew, insisting that his grief for Evangeline kept him from going on. He lived austerely because his money all went to civic projects—bridges, parks, the original library downtown, which is now the art museum. He had the Mews park designed and built as a gift to the city. His money set up some foundations to support widows and orphans. It all was dedicated to Evangeline. He established a scholarship fund for women at Irwin."

"You mean the Fen Scholarships? Those are named for Evangeline Fen?" asked Kathryn.

Amanda nodded. "Yes, I was granted some money from the fund when

I was a young professor, to finish my doctorate. Of course that was years ago. I've heard the fund is rather low now."

Kathryn mused, "And there are five statues of Evangeline in the cemetery. That's interesting."

"I think it's about to get *more* interesting," said Farrel. "Tell everyone about our buys today, Kathryn."

"Well, Farrel was buying Cora's dog in a booth set up in the field behind the main antique mall. I'm sure that field is packed with booths in the summer, but it was frigid tundra out there today. Only a few people bothered to set up," Kathryn said, as she lifted a canvas bag from the floor and reached inside.

She put several objects wrapped in paper on the table. Kathryn pushed back the wrapping on the largest object, revealing a lyrical clay figure of a woman reclining on cushions with her hair swirling around her shoulders. The area between her legs was covered, but full breasts and the perfect angle of hip and thigh were fully exposed.

"Well, I would have bought that! May I see it?" I asked.

Kathryn handed it over as Farrel unwrapped a similar figure she had bought and set it on the table.

I carefully turned the sculpture over in my hands until I spied a small stylized VWS within an impressed snowflake design. "It's by Victoria Willomere Snow; here's her mark," I said in a hushed voice.

"Really? There's a signature? I didn't even see it. I just recognized the other pieces and hoped," said Kathryn.

"Either it's a Snow or a very good fake," said Farrel frankly. "Show them the others."

Kathryn unwrapped ten small ceramic faces each decorated with sea shells. "I knew she perfected a mold process that helped her make faces like this. I'd never seen any with shell decoration before, though," said Kathryn.

"I've seen some of her found object faces. But I've never seen any full figure nudes, and believe me I would have remembered. But I've seen this woman before," I said looking at the face. *And very recently.*

Farrel moved around the table staring at the statues.

I said, "You see it, don't you?"

"Yes. Yes, it's Evangeline Fen," said Farrel. "The same face as *The Lost Bride.*"

Judith Levi asked, "Did the two women even know each other? Perhaps Victoria Snow studied death masks to create these accurate features?"

Ew, I thought. I'd seen dead bodies when I was on the Fenchester

Police Force, but there was something about making a mold of a dead person's face that was not only divorced from art but downright creepy.

"We don't even know whether they're really by Snow," I said.

"Perhaps you should take them to the Fenchester Museum tomorrow," said Amanda. "The woman who came to the meeting last night is cataloging the museum's holdings, including an important collection of Victoria Willomere Snow's work. Perhaps she could authenticate these."

"Yes, Amanda, we should do that. Maggie, shall we see the statue of *The Lost Bride* in the cemetery after brunch?" said Kathryn with an aesthetic urgency that shone in her steel-blue eyes.

"Sure, I want to see *The Lost Bride* again in the daylight. Besides, it'll give me a chance to *look for clues*."

Kathryn's smile was so erotically charged, I barely noticed what anyone was saying until Jessie brought a luscious black raspberry compote to the table and handed out small plates.

Conversation quieted until Cora Martin said, "Well this isn't nearly as exciting as Kathryn's luck at the market, but dahlings, I went into the city for an auction at Sotheby's."

"Sotheby's? The prices must have been terrifically high! Did you purchase anything?" asked Amanda, who was unaware of Cora's frequent dealings with the international auction house.

Cora winked and said, "I was selling, dahling, and I did very well! But guess who I saw in the subway. I always take the subway. I'm a New Yorker originally."

Farrel snorted faintly because Cora's New York accent was thick enough to stop a rhino.

Judith said, "Yes, dear, we know that," without a hint of sarcasm.

"Well, I got off the Lex and transferred to the Shuttle. And I saw that actress... married to that Kevin, who is always at sixty degrees?"

Judith and Amanda both looked blank.

Farrel leaned over to explain who we were talking about as Jessie rushed back to the table.

"Did you talk to her?" Jessie asked in an animated voice.

"Well, as a matter of fact..." Cora paused for effect, "she got up and gave me her seat. Ha! It's good to be old!"

So the Sunday morning game of *Brush With Fame* was afoot.

"The theme this time is *Transportation*," said Farrel.

To herald the beginning of the game, twin black cats appeared in the dining room doorway. Griswold and Wagner wove their way around all our ankles.

Griswold said, "Merf."

Wagner said, "Ow."

We moved to more comfortable chairs in the living room and I added wood to the fire. Jessie took out her knitting and Griswold and Wagner draped their lithe black bodies over her feet. They began to snore like people. Kathryn sat on the couch and patted the place next to her for me.

We went around the room and each woman told a *Brush With Fame* story. The older women spun the best yarns because they'd had longer to gather these chance encounters. Farrel had invented this game to entice her dear friend Judith to tell some of her best stories.

Judith began with, "Well, I have to tell you something later, Farrel. Remind me."

"What?" asked Farrel.

"Later, dear. It's my turn for a story now. Let me see... Oh yes, did I ever tell you about the writer I met on the ship coming back from France just after I was in college?" Judith unfolded a story about meeting a young Truman Capote just before he wrote *Breakfast at Tiffany's*.

He'd asked her to explain the New York bus and subway system. She ended with, "But when we finally got off the ship, I saw him simply hailing a cab. I suppose it had all been too much for him."

When she was finished, I saw Farrel lean over to her, and they had a short conversation the rest of us couldn't hear. Farrel exclaimed, "Judith!" at one point, then shook her head in dismay.

This happened as Amanda recounted a chance encounter on a waterbus with a legendary movie star whom everyone in the world knew. "I was a graduate student at Accademia di Belle Arti of Venice," she said, "and he decided I should go out to dinner with him." I took a moment to consider that in her youth Amanda was probably quite a babe and that she was censoring that part of the story.

I told a story about giving a ticket to a well-known senator, when I'd been on highway patrol.

Jessie passed; she often did after she'd given us a big brunch.

Kathryn told about sitting next to a recently knighted English pop star on a red-eye from LA. "He didn't wake during the entire flight," she laughed. "I considered taking a picture of us together with my phone... What does your sister Sara call those photos, Maggie? A *monkey arm*? But I didn't have the nerve."

"I have a subway story!" said Farrel, who had recovered from the shock of Judith's earlier tussle with criminals. "Years ago I was taking a course at the New York Glass Studio and staying with a friend uptown. One day I got on the subway; the car was pretty empty, so I sat down. At the next stop, Larry Storch and a blonde woman got on. Larry Storch, the actor. He was on that 1960s show *F-Troop*. It reruns on *TVland* now and then, an odd little slapstick sitcom about an army fort in Indian Territory just after the Civil War?"

"White hat?" I said.

"Yes!" Farrel laughed. "That's right! He did a lot of work; movies, cartoon voices. When I saw him on the train, he was doing a play on Broadway..."

"He was the voice of Phineas J. Whoopee on *Tennessee Tuxedo*!" I added.

"I can't believe you know that," said Kathryn incredulously.

"I pride myself on my ability to retain useless knowledge."

"You and Farrel should start a club," said Jessie.

"Wait, there's more," Farrel said. "Larry Storch and his lady friend sat down and we started to move. Minutes later a staggering drunk pushed his way in from the previous car."

"The drunk began shuffling up to people and yelling that the Bible said they were whores or sinners or whatever. He staggered over to Larry Storch and his girlfriend and shouted they were fornicating slaves of the devil.

"Suddenly the door between the cars burst open again and a big man in a bright Hawaiian shirt carrying a steel drum made his way to the center of the car. He dropped a coffee can on the floor that was already filled with folding money and used his mallets to wail out a beautiful and loud ringing melody.

"The music drowned out the Bible spouter, who staggered back into a seat and stared at the steel drummer angrily. Everyone in the car was so relieved they focused on the drummer with pure admiration. The drunk man finally hauled himself to his feet and swayed through the doors toward the front of the train."

"What happened then?" asked Amanda thoughtfully.

"Well, we all tossed money into the drummer's can. I did, Larry Storch did... everybody. After a few minutes, the steel drummer stopped playing and went into the next car. He was a musical hero!"

CHAPTER 3

It was nearly noon by the time we'd said our goodbyes. Farrel lent me their copy of the Carbondales' local history book and I put it in my bag. Kathryn carried it as I lifted the bag of sculpture onto my other shoulder, and we made our way to the door.

Before we left, Amanda took me aside and said, "I have a feeling that I cannot explain that you should read Suzanne and Gabriel Carbondale's book as soon as possible, Maggie." I said I would and made a mental note to do so in the next day or two.

Outside Kathryn said, "You should have dinner with Farrel and Jessie."

"I'm full of brunch! I won't be able to fight crime if I can't fit into my superhero costume. And tonight I'll be busy missing you."

"It does my ego a great deal of good to see you crestfallen about not spending the rest of the day together." She faced me. "I know we haven't... uh... mmm... since we got back from the beach. And I'm aching to be with you, but," her voice dropped an octave, "I swear I'll make it up to you."

This erotic promise stirred my desire.

"How?" I asked provocatively.

"Use your imagination," she said, giving me one of those looks that could melt the snow off the roof.

"Do you guarantee satisfaction?" I was about to suggest we go straight back to the king-sized bed in the loft but we both heard her phone playing Beethoven.

"That's a department ring; maybe the retreat is canceled." She pulled her cell from her bag. "Yes, I know, Bolton... I hope it's a good idea; this retreat has become quite a pain in the... OK, I'll see you there."

"One of my fellow department members who was cryptically telling me that he had some kind of plan," she said to me.

We took Washington Street to 11th and turned left through the middle of the Mews. The tall wrought iron fence that enclosed the burial ground was two blocks north. We walked swiftly against gusts of February wind, then entered the open cemetery gate and took the gravel path.

Kathryn said, "We're moving very fast."

I knew she wasn't talking about our stride. "Is it too fast for you? Do you want to slow down?" I asked her sincerely.

"I'm concerned that it's too fast for *you*. I've invaded your space. I'm building onto your home. I made you meet my mother, and God knows I can barely stand her *myself*," she said emphatically.

"I like it," I said honestly.

"Does anything scare you?"

I smiled and shook my head a little. It wasn't that nothing scared me as much as I wasn't quite ready to tell her what did. The clingy pathetic part of me that I try so hard to hide began an internal monologue about how I had abandonment issues. But that was all way too co-dependent and not the thing a tough Private Eye should share.

She looked at me seriously for a long moment and then said, "We have to talk."

"Oh crap," I tried to say evenly, "you're going to break up with me."

"What? No, no, where did you get that idea?"

"Well, you said, '*We have to talk.*' It's the classic prelude to a *Dear John Letter*. Nothing good ever comes after those four words."

Kathryn looked carefully into my eyes for a moment, then said evenly, "Calm down. I'm not breaking up with you. I just think we should talk about *rent*."

"What do you mean *rent*?" I asked. "You mean like a place you want to rent or *Rent, the musical?*"

"I mean that, if I'm going to live with you, then we need to talk about finances. I should pay you something for rent and a portion of the utilities."

I was totally caught off-guard. We'd already agreed on her rent payments for her office on the fourth floor, but I hadn't even considered rent payments for our living space. I had to wrap my brain around it. *This is a good thing. Grown-up, serious, equal.* After a few moments I mentioned a figure for the monthly rent and said we could split the utilities on the loft.

"And could we have a year-long lease?" she asked softly.

"Really? Sure." This made me profoundly happy. I tried to act adult about the whole thing but I had an urge to grin. Good thing I was wearing a scarf; I could muffle it. Of course if she bailed on living with me, she could move into her office, but still...

Kathryn said with a sigh as we walked on holding hands, "I've always hated the beginning of the semester. Nobody knows where their classrooms are, or anyone's name. Schedules are all new and confusing. Everyone feels lost. It's so easy to misstep or say the wrong thing."

"But it's also an adventure. You learn delightful new things. The tension is exciting and full of surprises. Sometimes you discover worlds you had no idea you'd enjoy. And there's so much future to look forward to. There are always risks when you're starting something new, but..."

Kathryn stopped and hugged me so hard it took my breath away.

When I'd first met her I'd found her sexy and beautiful, but she'd seemed aloof and almost unapproachable. She'd opened her vulnerable side to me. It was a secret part of her few people knew. But I couldn't take it for granted. Her stern, intense academic personality that could be both icy and fiery was part of her nature and never far away.

Kathryn shifted back in my arms. I could see a burning glint in her eye as she said, "Maybe I can sneak out of the retreat at about ten and come home tonight." It was the first time she'd called the loft *home*.

"At the moment, I can't imagine anything more magnificent," I said. She smiled and leaned against me as we walked on.

The graying sky seemed thick. It fought the light of day. A cold wind stirred up the smell of snow in the air, freezing our cloudy breath. The skeleton fingers of leafless trees reached toward each other. Wind stirred them and they became spider legs flailing toward a trapped fly.

"This is a perfect place for an Edgar Allen Poe recitation, maybe *Annabelle Lee?*" I said.

"No, I don't like it," she said shaking her head. "That line: *I was a child and she was a child.* He was writing about his thirteen-year-old wife, whom he married when he was twenty-seven. If he'd written, *She was a child and I was a pedophile,* it would have been more apt. Scholars are so desperate to excuse Poe's immoral behavior that some insist they never had sex. It's as absurd as insisting Lesbian poets in *Boston Marriages* didn't have sex or that Oscar Wilde wasn't Gay because the word Gay hadn't been coined. No, that's wrong, because it's comparing Poe's improper behavior with a child, which would have sent him to prison today, to someone's sexual orientation that would be perfectly legal and morally acceptable today."

This was Kathryn's analytical side, which I liked just as well as the erotic one.

"I wrote a paper once," said Kathryn, "on Poe's poor choice in life companion. Virginia Clem was not only too young for him; she was the exact opposite of the kind of person who could have supported his work."

"You're committed to this anti-Poe position?"

"His words are interesting, but I can't separate his life from his work. It's part of my *Coordinative Biography* thesis. It's a theme I've been writing about for a long time. It's the basis of my new book and the theory on which I'm basing the Women in the Arts major. I've told you about this before, haven't I?

"It was the subject of the lecture you did when we were in Florida. You were brilliant."

Kathryn snorted.

"No really, Kathryn, do you ever really look at the faces of the students when you're speaking? They were hypnotized by you. It was remarkable. I was paying attention, too. Coordinative Biography simply contends that people's lives are inextricable from their work. I've always thought that, but the way you were explaining it was fascinating. The examples were so creative and yet exactly on point. I can see why you have so many fans."

"Shall I take that to mean you aren't just interested in my body?"

"Uh huh."

"It amazes me how many people, usually straight male WASPs, who routinely fall in line with the antiquated theory-system of normative standards that excludes even the most logical variations of relationships. I'm tired of having to defend the obvious."

"Shall I recite a Lesbian poet whom you don't have to defend?"

"Yes, yes, please do!" she smiled. "Maybe Anne Whitney; she was part of the Harriet Hosmer-Charlotte Cushman crowd, wasn't she? *Dim Eden of delight. In whom my heart springs upward like a palm.*"

"Yes, she was, but I was thinking a little later. How about:

I caught sight of a splendid Misses. She had handkerchiefs and kisses. She had eyes and yellow shoes she had everything to choose and she chose me.

In passing through France she wore a Chinese hat and so did I.
In looking at the sun she read a map. And so did I.
In eating fish and pork she just grew fat. And so did I.
In loving a blue sea she had a pain. And so did I.
In loving me she of necessity thought first. And so did I.

How prettily we swim. Not in water. Not on land. But in love.

How often do we need trees and hills. Not often.
And how often do we need birds. Not often.
And how often do we need wishes. Not often.
And how often do we need glasses not often.

We drink wine and we make well we have not made it yet.

How often do we need a kiss. Very often and we add when tenderness overwhelms us we speedily eat veal.

And what else, ham and a little pork and raw artichokes and ripe olives and chester cheese and cakes and caramels and all the melon. We still have a great deal of it left. I wonder where it is. Conserved melon. Let me offer it to you.

Kathryn clapped her gloved hands. "*Love Song of Alice B*! You know," she laughed, "the first time I heard that Gertrude Stein poem I was a vegetarian and I was thoroughly repulsed because I thought she really meant eating veal!"

"It still kind of ruins the euphemism for me, too."

"Maggie, how did you ever find time to learn all these poems?"

"It's a little early in our relationship for honesty. It could spoil the effect, but I'll chance it. I had a job in a furniture factory during college. I had to power-sand panels. I wore a dust mask and earmuffs. It was dull, so I learned a new poem each day. I'd recite the lines over and over as I sanded until I knew them by heart. Each afternoon I'd practice the poems I'd already learned. It made me happy to go to work. I did it when I was on the highway patrol too. Does that spoil the romance for you?"

"No, it *is* romantic. I like to think of you studying love poems all day." Kathryn's voice turned curious. "And were you doing this to impress some specific woman?"

"To impress *you*. I hope it's working."

"Oh, it is!" said Kathryn laughing.

"So how did you learn your poems?" I asked.

"Catholic boarding school."

"Wait, you're not Catholic."

"My mother felt it would be a good influence on me. She was wrong. It was a prison. My father liberated me after a year."

"That must have made you angry at your mother."

"Uh, yes. You know the movie *Bambi*? That was my favorite movie in my teen years."

I snorted. "It's good that you can make jokes about it now that you're all grown up? Isn't it?"

"Is it?" she asked dryly.

"But you learned all those poems."

"The only bright moments had to do with a rather serious crush on the beautiful young nun who taught poetry."

"An ounce of perversion is worth a pound of cure."

"It certainly is," said Kathryn in a provocative voice. "I promise I'll tell you about it some time, late at night, as a bedtime story."

We left the road and zig-zagged past plots toward the place where Farrel and I had seen *The Lost Bride.*

Kathryn looked up at the sky and then turned slowly around. She said, "So many emotions have been expressed on this little piece of ground. Historians find it so simple to presume that emotional life was vastly different 140 years ago. It's a tribute to Evangeline that Merganser spent a fortune on beautiful sculpture of her for everyone to see, but to put it in this mournful spot."

I could feel what she meant. The cold steady breeze that rustled the branches over our heads carried the echoes of deep sorrows and fleeting joys. The loneliness, the relief, both cruelty and freedom, even the need for revenge were all such a part of this place.

I sighed. "Of course, trying to frame love in the context of today and apply it to the past is tricky, but I agree, it's just as dangerous to presume today's context doesn't apply." I reached for Kathryn's hand and we walked together glove in glove toward the east along a gravel-covered path.

Kathryn asked, "Do you think Cora was right about couples?"

"You mean when she said that it takes two people to end a relationship?"

"Yes," Kathryn said softly.

I thought about my two previous committed relationships. Both had lasted a few years and had ended because we'd each gone our separate ways. But then there was Carrie, short term but remarkably intense. I'd thought it was the beginning of something lasting, but I'd woken up one morning to find her gone. The brief good-bye note had no explanation.

Long before that, when my mother died, I'd felt the dark cloud of abandonment paralyze my emotions until they were unfrozen a few years later by my father's new wife, Juana Martinez, and my new sisters, Sara and Rosa. They'd made me laugh and love again. But Farrel was right. Years later, when Carrie left, I tried to be tough, but it made me shy about giving my love away. At least I could understand that, even if I couldn't talk about it.

But Kathryn had done much more than unfreeze the heart of a lonely little girl. She'd lit a flame in me that I'd never known. Once Farrel told me that when she fell in love with Jessie she was able to look into her future and see Jessie with her. I didn't understand at the time but now, with Kathryn, I knew exactly what Farrel meant. Still, it didn't make this any easier; it made it harder. Because it mattered.

I squeezed Kathryn's arm. I said, "When Suzanne Carbondale left Gabriel he was totally shocked. Suddenly she was just gone. And I guess that's why Jessie is still so angry. Suzanne didn't just leave Gabe; she left everyone. It sure seemed like a one-sided break-up."

Kathryn nodded a little bit and then said simply, "There must not have been much communication between them. Or do you think there was someone else?"

I shrugged. "You never really know what's happening between two people. Sometimes the two people themselves don't know," I said looking steadily into her eyes.

"We'll have to be sure that doesn't happen to us." She smiled and stroked my cheek again with her gloved hand.

"OK, so next time don't wait until the last minute to tell me you have to go to some meeting, when I'm counting on an afternoon of hot erotic thrills! I wouldn't have been annoyed at you."

"You *sound* annoyed," she said with a touch of amusement.

"But not at *you*. I can coast on anticipation."

"Maybe we can think of something to tide you over... other than just anticipation," whispered Kathryn close to my ear.

We were passing the tomb that Farrel and I had peeked around the night before. There in front of us was the monument of Evangeline Fen. It was blue-white in the waning afternoon sun. On the high granite pedestal, the figure was almost as ethereal as it had seemed in the moonlight. It wasn't just a beautiful lost woman, it was a moment frozen in time.

"It's such a familiar face. No doubt about it," I said. "Your little figure has the face of Evangeline Fen."

Kathryn was speechless. She moved closer, looking up at its gentle curves. Evangeline was fully draped in an off-the-shoulder cloak. Her delicate feet and ankles were bare. She was poised to run, with her head turned slightly to the side, one bare arm back, and the other slightly forward with a hand extended in a beckoning gesture. The features were still crisp and clear, though more than a hundred years of the city's acid rain had tried to dull them.

Kathryn turned and spied the recently toppled headstones. "This statue shouldn't be out here exposed to vandals. At least no one can reach her head," she said. We'd seen a number of lower statues with their heads broken off.

"She seems kind of at home here, though. She was very beautiful. Amanda and Judith were certainly right about that," I said. A gust of wind stirred some dead leaves at the statue's base. I looked at my watch. I said, "It's ten after twelve."

"Twelve-thirty is just the check-in. I'll call and tell them I'll be late. Let's see if we can find some of the other Evangeline statues."

She turned in place, searching for other figures in white stone. To the south, at the intersection of two major paths, was a small tomb with another statue of Evangeline Fen in front of it. We went to it. The sculpture was half the size of a real person, but also on a high pedestal. She was seated with her head tilted back, wearing a traveling cloak wrapped around her body in graceful folds. Her left arm was draped across her lap. Her right hand pointed gracefully with all her fingers toward *The Lost Bride* statue less than thirty feet away.

Kathryn walked around the statue to view it from all angles while I stepped closer. The face was so realistic she seemed about to speak.

"She looks like she knows a secret," I said.

"Mmmm, yes, and kind of smug about it, isn't she," said Kathryn.

Kathryn paused and looked around. "It's so quiet here; there's privacy with all these yews," she said in a low voice. "So, Maggie, do you think it would be unseemly if we found a little... um... satisfaction, here?" Kathryn firmly pushed me against the wall of the block building.

"It's twenty degrees and we're in a cemetery," I said incredulously.

"We'll keep our coats on. And really, Maggie, in this garden of souls' 200-year history, I'm sure we won't be the first moonstruck couple to find a private corner in this otherwise hallowed ground," said Kathryn, giving me a look that was so hot it could have melted the wrought iron fence and brought a few of the corpses back to life.

"Maybe making love in it actually *makes* it hallowed," I suggested, setting the bag of sculptures next to the wall.

"You say the most inspirational things!" said Kathryn, slipping my glove off and drawing the back of my hand to her warm lips.

The logic that usually controls my brain was draining away. I found myself ignoring the freezing cold, ignoring the public place, ignoring the kinkiness of doing it in a boneyard. *Carpe Diem.*

I moved Kathryn back into a niche in the tomb wall that was sheltered by yew branches and slipped my hands into her coat and under her sweater as I kissed her throat. I undid the clasp of her bra.

"Oh!" gasped Kathryn as I cupped her freed breast and brushed her nipple with the cold pad of my thumb.

"Officer, I swear I wasn't going over fifty."

"You still have to be searched." My mouth found hers; she gently bit my lower lip. I could feel her lips curve into a smile as I undid the top button of her jeans and unzipped them. I wrapped one arm around her as my other hand moved under the silky fabric and into the increasingly moist place between her legs. She stiffened as I explored.

"Oh, mmm," she murmured, pushing down her jeans for more access.

And then we heard the distinct noise of a dog-collar tinkling. Gabriel Carbondale was walking Buster, his huge Harlequin Great Dane.

"He'll notice us," sighed Kathryn regretfully.

"Maybe not," I said, pressing her further under the branches.

Gabe Carbondale passed unseeing just feet in front of us and Buster only turned his head for a second to meet my eyes. He did a Scooby head tilt and then went on.

"Good dog!" I mouthed soundlessly, nodding like a bobblehead. Carbondale was beyond our view when I drew Kathryn from the yew branches to resume the course of her promises.

And then an echoing shot rang out. A slug ricocheted off a grave marker with a ping-zip and a puff of rock dust. Then another shot, this time louder, and then the low rumble I'd heard the night before. Gabe Carbondale screamed like a frightened boy-band fan. Before reality even registered in Kathryn, I'd spun her around and pressed her down into the protected hollow. She crouched, grasping the situation.

"Stay here. Don't move," I said in a low voice.

I reached up and chinned my way over the building wall, flattening myself on the roof in one smooth movement. The slate shingles were the definition of *stone cold* against my bare hands. I'd pocketed my gloves when I'd begun to touch Kathryn. I pulled out my cell phone and called 911, gave the 10-13 code for shots fired, and my name and location.

I peered over the roof edge, scanning the cemetery for the shooter. Carbondale was kneeling with his hands on the ground, shaking his head and gasping. About twenty feet ahead of him, near the base of *The Lost Bride,* was a body in a blue down jacket. A moment later, a person in a maroon hoodie ran up to the body, looked at it, then stood straight when the police sirens blared up the street. The person ran east behind a tall stand of yews.

I glanced back over the edge of the mausoleum and called softly, "Kathryn, stay where you are. Please don't move."

She looked up at me and nodded.

I rolled to the other edge of the roof and dropped down silently, wishing I'd brought my Beretta along. I hesitated, acutely aware that someone with a gun was nearby.

The body groaned. It was the start of a death rattle. I sprinted to the person on the ground, pulled off my scarf, wadded it up, and pressed with all my might against blood flowing from the front and back wounds.

"Don't die! Fight!" I yelled urgently, pulling out my phone with one hand to shout for an ambulance to come with the police.

Twenty feet away, Gabriel Carbondale threw up.

CHAPTER 4

"Yes, it's cold, but you see, I'm a professor at Irwin College and I was reviewing the historic art and architecture here."

Kathryn was giving her statement to the police. She hadn't really seen anything, just heard the shots. The officer interviewing her was trying to figure out why anyone would be in a cemetery on a day like this, unless they had to bury somebody.

The first police car arrived four minutes after I called. Two minutes later the ambulance pulled up. The EMTs took over for me, but it was too late. They cleaned the dead man's blood off my hands, but my jacket was ruined. That seems to happen to me a lot. One of the EMTs loaned me a hoodie. I transferred the stuff from my pockets, and the EMTs bagged my blood-covered jacket and scarf and gave the bag to the crime scene team.

I'd given my formal statement already, so I went back to the spot in which Kathryn and I had been rolling in the pine boughs and retrieved the bag of sculpture. Then I drifted toward the crime scene. The cop let Kathryn go. She waved to me and sped off to her meeting.

One of Fenchester's finest, Ed O'Brien, was leading the investigation. He'd been my boss in my previous life. He was balding and had the ruddy complexion of a guy who drank a lot of beer. He was smart and hard-working but lacked imagination. He patted me on the back.

O'Brien spoke as though the crime scene itself was the first half of his sentence. "Carbondale couldn't have done it. No gun, no powder burns, wrong position." He reached into his lined black raincoat to offer me a stick of gum. "You see anything?"

I passed on the gum and said, "Lieutenants don't investigate crime scenes and I thought you retired?"

"It was a deal I couldn't refuse, Maggie. I retired from being a Lt., and got rehired as a sergeant. Means I get my pension, I get to investigate crimes again, I get my salary as a sergeant too, and if I live long enough, I could actually get another pension."

"You're kidding."

"True. I'm saving the city money. Less paper work, more action, and now my wife's gone, gives me something to do." O'Brien turned back to the crime scene. "The other guy. Tell me again."

"He came from the right, stopped to look at the body, then kept running east behind those yew trees. He had a maroon-colored hoodie, dark blue jeans, and dirty white sneakers. The hood was up, so I didn't see a face, but his hands were white. Could have been a woman but I'd say from the posture it was a man. About five feet eight inches tall. 150 pounds. Fast runner. I heard a rumbling sound, then the victim moaned a few times and I hurried over to him."

O'Brien nodded as he took notes.

"What does Carbondale say?"

Gabe was sitting a few headstones away, shaking his head.

"He's a basket case. He saw the dude in the blue jacket, heard the shots, saw blue jacket fall down. Saw blood, started to freak, and he's still freaking. Didn't see the second dude; probably had his eyes closed by then." O'Brien took a deep breath and looked around the cemetery. "So where's the shooter? Might have been a gang banger, maybe hiding in one of the crypts. But my team checked all the open buildings and they're all clean. Small. Barely room for one person to turn around."

"ID on the victim?" I asked.

"Nothing I could see. No tattoos or gang symbols either. In his pockets was about $500 cash, disposable cell phone, and a set of keys... um... Chevy key, standard house key, brass skeleton key like they use in row houses. It's a load of cash for a guy like this. You're really not supposed to be in on this but want to see him?"

I nodded.

We looked at the stark white face of a young man who'd woken up this morning with no idea that this day would be his last. His brown eyes were fixed in a death stare and becoming cloudy. He had a fringe of beard, pale white skin, a brown scarf, and red chapped hands. Under his open blue down jacket was a thin red sweater over a white tee shirt. He had new baggy jeans and black sneakers. A bullet hole and a big red stain made the outfit horrible.

I took out my phone and snapped a picture of his face.

"What does the Medical Examiner think?" I asked.

"One shot, medium caliber. Ten to fifteen feet away, to the back. Went through the heart, exit wound in the jacket front."

"And Carbondale didn't see the shooter?" I asked.

"No, he says he only saw the vic fall," said O'Brien.

"Any other witnesses?"

"Little girl down near the entrance saw the shooting from outside the fence over there but didn't see anyone exit the gate."

"I'm not sold on the guy in the maroon hoodie doing it. Have the guys checked for trees or buildings near the fence that someone could use to climb over?"

"Why the hell don't you like Hoodie for this?" O'Brien asked.

"He didn't have a gun in his hand and your guys haven't found one. *And* he came from the wrong direction. If the vic was shot in the back, This suspect was in the wrong place to do it, and Ed, don't call grown women girls. It's so '70s."

O'Brien snorted, then looked up at the overcast sky. He sighed. "Look, Maggie, unless this was a gang thing you know we suck at this. If you can help..."

"Sure Ed. It was my job to be looking out for crime in this place, so I'll do what I can, but right now I don't know any more than you do. I want to talk to Carbondale."

I moved over to where Gabe Carbondale was sitting.

"Gabe?" I said gently.

He looked up, unseeing.

"Gabe!" I yelled to get his attention. "Did you see anyone?"

He shook his head. He was shivering.

"What were you doing here?"

"Walking Buster. Oh crap, where is he?" He shook his head and gagged. "I'm going to be sick again." He leaned over and dry heaved.

"Buster's over there." I pointed to the giant Great Dane sitting on a toppled gravestone.

Gabe saw the coroner's crew taking the body away and retched again.

"You can go now. Sergeant O'Brien arranged for someone to take you home." Gabe called Buster and they lurched into a squad car.

I walked over to the place where the body had fallen.

Cops were still combing the leaf-strewn ground to find the spent slug of the ricochet. I was glad it wasn't my job to look for it. Gray skies were darkening and it was bitterly cold, though still early afternoon.

At a distance, a uniform officer was talking to a young woman. She was wearing layered sweaters, a navy plaid skirt, and heavy woolen tights. She wore a light blue wool cap pulled over black hair, and from what I could see she had an attractive face. She nodded. The officer left, and she walked directly across the street.

I wanted to talk to her, so I followed her. It's something private eyes do. She walked south on 11th, crossed the Mews, turned right and went up

Washington past the Moyer & Jones lumber yard, to the corner of 13th. She entered the front door of a big row house that had been divided into apartments.

Lights in each of the apartments were on except the one on the ground floor. In a minute a light came on in there too. I could see her through the window talking off scarves and then going into another room.

My cell chimed. It was Gabriel Carbondale.

His voice was high pitched. "Maggie, can you come over? I'm so confused, this is all... I was only talking about gangs and vandals, but this is... Can you come right now?"

I walked back down Washington to Gabriel Carbondale's house on 10th Street. After all, he was the paying client.

****

When Gabriel and Suzanne Carbondale lived together in this historic row home, two doors south of Amanda Knightbridge's, Suzanne had been responsible for their home's decor. I'd been there a couple of times, but not since Suzanne left six weeks ago. At that time, the place was bright and comfortable with beautiful details. Suzanne liked subtle art that made you think and laugh.

She had a number of abstract paintings by local artists. She'd even bought and framed one of my sketches of the Mews and hung it in the kitchen next to a lovely Matisse collage print.

Gabe Carbondale answered the bell. His face was gaunt and his eyes were hollow from shock and hurling. He seemed relieved to see me and agitated at the same time. Though indisputably pompous, Carbondale was fairly handsome, but right now he had a mean-old-man face. He looked as though he was going to yell, "You kids get outta my yard!" at any second.

The house had totally changed. Instead of light airy colors, the living room was the dark green of Jaguar sports cars. There was a pair of 19th century hunting prints over the fireplace and duck decoys on the mantel. The leather sofa was still in place, but there was a huge plasma flat screen on the wall.

The room looked so self-consciously masculine that the word *overcompensating* was ringing in my ears. Nothing of Suzanne remained, as though Gabe was trying to erase her. But then I guess if I'd been dumped the way Gabe was, I also might want to *wash that gal right outta my hair.*

Buster woofed hello from behind the closed kitchen door.

Gabe said, "Samson's here. The police told me I shouldn't be alone and Samson was walking by."

Samson Henshaw, former architect now realtor, sat stonily in an arm chair. He lived in the Mews with his wife Lois, the one who had been at the neighborhood meeting and spouted her incongruous comment.

Henshaw was tall and craggy. Straight women would probably find him ruggedly handsome. He had regular features and a good head of dark brown hair, but he seemed terminally sad, like a Basset off his Prozac. His general *Squidward* aspect had intensified since he and Lois first moved to the Mews.

Washington Mews has a gossip network that moves faster than rabbits on Red Bull. According to Cora Martin, one of the linchpins of communication, Samson's problem was *domestic*.

And right now the scowl he was giving Gabe behind his back was verging on pure loathing. *Since when did Samson hate Gabe?*

Gabe grunted me back to the present. He said, "Look, Maggie, I need to tell you about something." He glanced at Samson, hesitating.

Gabe's cell phone rang and he literally jumped into the air, hunching his back like a startled cat. He picked up the phone and held it to his ear. Then he remembered to say, "Hello?"

He paused listening for a long time as if he'd forgotten how to speak. Finally he cleared his throat and said, "Yes, it, uh, made my hair stand on end. I'll not sleep one wink. Yes, she's here now." He listened again staring at the floor and finally said, "Yes, thank you, good-bye." He clicked it off, turned, and focused his eyes.

"Who was that?" I asked at the height of nosiness.

"That Staplehurst woman from the museum. She heard about the... *you know*... I guess it's already on the newspaper's web site. She wants you to stop by her office with a copy of the crime report and you can sign something, and then she can submit the grant. She's on deadline."

It seemed a little insensitive to me that less than an hour after the murder Piper Staplehurst jumped on it as the proof she needed for the grant. Of course, maybe the streaming news hadn't touched on Gabe as the prime witness.

Gabe looked at his cell and then turned to me. "Maggie, I could have been shot." He cleared his throat again. "Dead as a doornail. If I'd gotten there earlier, it might have been time for me to shuffle off this mortal coil." He shrugged, and sweat beaded on his forehead. He put his hand over his eyes and took a deep breath. Gabe Carbondale's shocky face had turned as white as *The Lost Bride*'s. He dropped his cell. The cover cracked and the phone bounced into Buster's water dish by the hearth.

"Crap," he said, reaching for it.

"You'll have to get another one now. They never work after they've been in water." Samson snorted grimly.

"I have another one around here somewhere," Gabe said vaguely.

"Gabe, most murders happen between people who know each other. This wasn't aimed at you," I said, trying to be reassuring.

"Murder! It wasn't murder. It was a gang thing."

"No, it was murder. An unarmed man was killed by another person with a gun. That's kind of the definition of murder, Gabe," I said.

His face went even whiter.

Samson slapped his hand on the chair arm impatiently. He'd gotten roped into playing nursemaid and he didn't like it.

I said to Gabe, "Do you want me to keep working on the crime in the cemetery? Things are a little different now."

"Huh? Oh, no, don't go on. Crime has been established surely, so the game is up. You can just send me a bill for last night."

"OK, but I think I'll continue to look into it on my own a little."

"Huh? Why?"

"Because murder messes with my feng shui. I don't like it when someone is killed on my watch. Tell me again what happened from your perspective."

Gabe Carbondale paused to think, then took a deep breath and said that Buster had wanted to go out. "So I put on his leash and walked him over to the graveyard. We went up the main trail then turned right to loop around and, just as I got near the fence, I heard a shot. I looked up, saw someone in a blue down jacket running, then another shot and he fell down as cold as any stone. I didn't see anything else."

He'd skipped saying, I screamed like a twelve year old girl, closed my eyes, and fainted. But I couldn't blame Gabe. No matter how macho you are, you never know how you're going to react when faced with blood and fear. At least once a year, one of Farrel's burly male woodworking students has an eyes-roll-back moment after a careless slip of a chisel.

I'd seen some horrific traffic deaths while I was on the highway patrol in Indiana after grad school. I was the first woman on the force in that part of the state, so a slew of unwelcoming veterans turned up to watch me fall apart at my introductory pile-up. I didn't, though. It took all my concentration but I was able to remove myself from the bloody scene and view it as though it was a painting. It was a valuable skill.

"Did you hear anything? Think carefully. You heard the shots and the sound of someone running and...?"

He shook his head. "Wind in the trees?"

Samson Henshaw said, "Look Gabe, I really have to go. You're OK right?" Without waiting for an answer, Henshaw went to the door and jumped ship.

Gabe was still shivering. He should have called someone like Cora Martin for support. She'd have made him tea and cookies, covered him with a warm blanket, and had him watch some classic movie on TV.

"Gabe, see if there's a game on. I'll make you something to eat."

I went down a little hallway, passed a half-bath, and turned left into the kitchen. One of the biggest indoor pets in the world shuffled over to me. I petted him lavishly. He was black and white like a Holstein cow. Suzanne named him Buster, not only because his huge wagging tail busted things, but because his markings were like Buster Brown saddle shoes.

Yet this Buster was way too big to *live* in a shoe. In fact, he was almost too big for this kitchen. Great Danes are the couch potatoes of large dogs. They like to relax and be petted. They love people. I guess that doesn't describe *all* Great Danes, but it describes Buster. He was a very loyal dog. Loyal to Suzanne. Suzanne had walked out on Buster too. I wondered if Buster was as pissed off about that as Jessie.

Buster woofed quietly, then lay back down on the floor. I stepped over him to find some beer and something with which to make a few sandwiches.

Buster got up and went into the laundry room, which also served as the back vestibule. He barked.

"What?" I asked.

He looked at me, tilted his head, then swung his doggy butt around knocking over a stack of cardboard boxes. I felt a gust of cold air as he went out his dog door into the fenced backyard.

The kitchen was in order, but my sketch and the other framed art pieces were gone from the wall. This room had also been *de-Suzanned*.

Buster padded back in and settled in the middle of the floor. I filled his food bowl in the laundry room and picked up the cardboard boxes his tree-branch-sized tail had spilled. One box's lid had come off. In it I spied my framed sketch, the Matisse collage print, some of Suzanne's kitchen tools. Nothing she really needed. Gabe had just packed up what she'd left and pushed it out of sight, if not completely out of mind.

Peanut butter and jelly sandwiches were the best I could do. I found a tray and carried the food and a bottle of beer into the living room.

I sat down and asked him to go over the shooting one more time. He told me the same story.

"You said you wanted to talk to me about something? What was it?" I asked. Maybe it was that he was still frightened or needed me to make him a sandwich.

"Oh, well, just that this shooting makes crime in the cemetery a foregone conclusion. And so I won't be..."

"You won't be paying me any more. I get it."

CHAPTER 5

I went home to the loft.

This small factory building was payment for what turned out to be a very dangerous job. At the time real estate was low, and the value of a quarter-block-long factory building in a residential area was pretty scant. Still it was a fascinating, mostly raw space, so I dove in.

I'd put a tool-belt-load of sweat equity into making the loft livable. The bright, comfortable space was mostly one big high-ceilinged room that served as a living and dining room with a fancy open kitchen on one side. There were two bedrooms—a bigger one where Kathryn and I slept and a smaller one for guests. There was also a fabulous master bathroom, a well-designed laundry room, and a smaller bathroom next to the guest room. The huge floor-to-ceiling windows offered panoramic views of the Mews and the city beyond.

On the top floor of the building, which is reached via a spiral staircase in the loft's living area or by the main stairs or freight elevator in the hall, is a large open space roughly divided into four quarters: an extensive gym for working out, an art studio so as not to let my art school education go to waste, a storage area, and a large corner that was rapidly becoming a two-story office for Kathryn.

I enjoy it all, but right now it felt empty. So I went down to the second floor office of my step-sister Sara and her law partner Emma Strong.

Attorney Sara Martinez was sitting at her desk in her office, flipping the pages of a bound brief. Her dark chocolate hair was drawn back in a pony tail. Her skin tones looked even and healthy as always. She was stylishly dressed for work, but still seemed comfortable.

I'm such a contrast to my younger sisters Sara and Rosa. With light brown hair and green eyes, my skin is so pale white that at the beach I have to steep in 100 sun block. Kathryn and I have that in common, which made our choice to vacation in Northern Florida in January, where the temperatures are moderate and sunny days are short, a perfect one.

Sara said without looking up, *"Buenas tardes, querida hermana."*

"¿Quieres ir a la Cocina Thai a cenar? Estoy loca del hambre."

"¿Dónde está tu novia habañera? ¿Por qué ella no come contigo? ¿La estas tratando bien o es que ella está disponible ahora? ¡Dame su número y yo le mostrare un buen tiempo!"

Sara looked up and wiggled her eyebrows but then stared at me. *"¿Qué paso?"* she asked me seriously.[*]

My poker face has served me well in the detective trade, but Sara has always been able to tell when things were wrong with me. When her mother married my father, we became instant friends, even though she was younger. She'd decided to teach me Spanish, and my new stepmother Juana agreed wholeheartedly. I committed to the hilarious lessons and soon was able to share secrets with my new family that my sweet but seemingly befuddled father couldn't understand.

Knowing something that a grownup didn't know was enormously attractive to a child who'd felt her life was out of her control. It wasn't so many years later that I realized my father was faking his inability to understand us for my sake. Which made me love him and miss him all the more, once he was gone.

In those days, when something was heavy on my mind, Sara could tell. Just as she could tell now.

"What is it?" she asked more softly.

"Someone was shot in the cemetery today. I was there," I said simply. "He died."

"Did *you* shoot him?"

"No, but I couldn't save him."

"You can't save everyone, querida," said Sara softly.

****

"Forget the menu ladies. We have a curry to die for and fresh roast pork. And spring rolls, just made. Be right back."

We handed back the menus and gave over our appetites to Mrs. Sakda. It was 6 p.m. Sara and I sat across from each other in a booth at Thai Kitchen, just a few doors from our offices.

"I love this place," I said to Sara. I loved that the family who ran it knew

---

[*] "Good afternoon, beloved sister."

"Do you want to go over to Thai Kitchen for dinner? I'm starving."

"Where's your habañero girlfriend? Why won't she eat with you? Are you treating her right or is she available now? Give me her number and I'll show her a good time!"

Sara looked up and wiggled her eyebrows but then stared at me. "What's wrong?" she asked sharply.

us and made us special things. I loved that it was in my neighborhood. I even loved that Mrs. Sakda and the network of women in the Mews had gossip honed to a fine art.

"Tell me the rest of what happened at the cemetery. Were there other people there?" said Sara.

I filled her in on all the players, then added, "And there was a witness. The police talked to her."

"How did Carbondale take it?" asked Sara.

"Fell to his knees, screamed like a macaw, barfed a week's groceries."

"No way he could have done it?"

I shook my head. "No gun. Not the correct angle. And his squealing like a piglet was pretty convincing. He seemed genuinely flummoxed. He was too busy heaving his lunch and being scared witless. He'd really have to be a Shakespearian actor to feign those reactions."

"Don't say flummoxed. Real people don't say flummoxed."

"I do."

"I know. You've done that since we were kids, and you're getting worse. I think sleeping with an English professor is rubbing off on you. Wait, what were you and Kathryn *doing* in the cemetery?"

Before I could explain about the statues of Evangeline Fen, Sara exclaimed, "Oh my god, you were doing it! Sex in the cemetery? Was Charles Addams there to draw it?" Before I could confirm or deny, Sara paused to consider and then asked, "Was it fun?"

I laughed but didn't bother to respond. Finally I said, "Well, it wasn't fun after I heard the shot."

We both thought about that for a moment. Finally Sara broke the silence. "Evie is leaving."

"What! When? Why?" Evelyn Quaid had been their office manager since Sara and Emma set up their lawyering shop two years before I'd gotten the building. She was a bit scatter-brained, but very sweet and earnest.

"Her mother's sick. Her father called from Pittsburgh. She's leaving right away."

"She could come back," I suggested.

"I don't think so. She's already cleaned out her desk."

"Huh," I said taking it in. "We'll have to advertise for someone new. Do interviews, train."

"Yeah, it's a pain, and Emma wants two people—an office manager and a paralegal for the law firm."

Before I could calculate the added cost, Sara said, "We'll pay the paralegal. You can split the manager with us like we did with Evie."

"What if I need to use the paralegal for some cagey court angle?"

"We'll see. Let's talk about something else. We can worry about staff tomorrow. What about that witness you mentioned?"

"I'm going to interview her."

"How're you going to find her?"

"I know where she lives."

"How?"

"Followed her home."

"Really?" Sara said wryly. "Pretty?"

"From what I could see."

"And you are going to see her this evening? While your beautiful new squeeze is working?"

"I'm not after anyone else."

"Actually, I wasn't thinking about someone for you. I was thinking about someone for me."

"Oh sure, like you'd just go on a blind date."

"I would!"

"Pon farr?"

"Not exactly. It's just that I'd rather *play the field* occasionally than spend all my days working the fields 24/7. So I'm throwing caution to the wind and *carpeing* the diem."

"That's what I said to myself in the cemetery and look where it got me."

"Different situation, and you'll be checking her out for me," said Sara.

"OK, if she seems interesting and age appropriate, I'll signal you."

"I'll take my food back to the office. I have to have this brief finished by 9:00 p.m.," said Sara. "I just have a little more to do, and then I have to fax all the pages. Maggie, everything's all right between you and Kathryn isn't it?"

I told her honestly that we were having a wonderful time and I was sorely hoping to see Kathryn soon.

"I bet!" Sara winked at me and smiled.

Mrs. Sakda brought the food to our table herself, brimming with pride over the dishes she knew we'd love. The spring rolls were lightly fried and stuffed with fresh vegetables with a hint of shrimp and egg. I spooned a red curry stew over my bowl of whole grain rice. The delicately flavored sauce spoke of ginger, cilantro, and lemon grass. The chicken was perfectly cooked, slivers of fresh carrots and green beans added interesting color and texture, toasted almonds gave it all a rich crunch. Sara sniffed the wonderful aroma, filled up some take-out boxes and left to finish her work.

****

"You're a detective, really?" asked the young woman answering the door. She spoke with a light Scottish accent as she eyed my investigator's ID, then she glanced over my shoulder into the darkness. "And a wee bit of a night owl. Well, come in then. It's a snell night."

After dinner I'd walked up Washington Street to the corner of 13th and rang the bell for apartment number one, and she'd let me into the tiny place.

She had a pleasant, interesting face. Very white smooth skin, alert dark eyes, dramatic features and a head of short curly black hair.

"Did I see you at the cemetery when I was keeking through the fence? When the place was hoaching with police? Bit of a shock. Let's sit down, shall we?" She pointed to a couch that was covered with a patterned bed sheet. I took out my small laptop.

"Let's start with your name."

"I have a long series of first names, which ends with Eleanora, so Nora is fine."

"Last name?"

"Hasan."

"Student at Irwin?" I asked conversationally.

"A grad student." She considered me with a wary look. "Not from INS, are you?" I shook my head. She relaxed a little.

"You're from Scotland?"

"Well, no," she said simply. It sounded a little bit like *nae*. "Actually, I grew up in Morocco. My mum is from Scotland." There was clarity in her accent, precision and melody, but with a slight undertone of discontent.

"What are you studying?" I sat back for what I hoped would be a long, detailed explanation in a *Highland lilt.*

"*Theatre History From a Feminist Perspective.* I'm on an international fellowship. And now I'm in Fenchester." She sighed, as if she'd told this to dozens of people who hadn't cared very much. She added, a bit mechanically, "I'm working on a thesis on women in the theatre, with a focus on those who played male Shakespearean parts in the 19th century."

"Charlotte Cushman?" I suggested. "I was just talking abut her with some friends."

"Yes, oh my, brilliant! How do you ken her?" And then Nora Hasan smiled, and her interesting face became radiantly beautiful. It was kind of startling. My artist's soul gasped inwardly. It took me a moment to recover.

Finally I laughed. "I studied Charlotte Cushman, along with the women artists who lived in her house in Rome—Emma Stebbins, Edmonia Lewis, Victoria Willomere Snow—when I was in art school. I found their stories so interesting." I paused thinking it was funny that Victoria Snow kept popping up. Nora nodded without responding so I carried on. "Um... so you grew up in Morocco? And you learned English from your mother? Did you ever live in Scotland?"

"No, Mum's living in Scotland now. She just moved there a wee bit after I came to the States. I'm going to have a cup of tea. Fancy some?" she said, standing up. She smiled again, but I was ready for it this time.

Now I understood why her accent was so charmingly Old World, sort of like dialog from a British mystery. Nora was using the vocabulary and inflection of a middle-aged woman who'd grown up in Scotland decades before, but she'd never actually been there herself.

Nora moved to the kitchen area. From what I could see through a half-open door, the bedroom barely had space for a twin mattress. The bow window that took up most of the apartment's front wall was uncurtained. Darkness made the windows black like Nora's eyes. The window glass reflected the warm apartment. All I could see through it was a glowing row of streetlights.

Nora reached for a canister of tea bags from the cupboard. Her wooly blue sweater had a wide plunging neckline that showed an expanse of smooth shoulder and throat.

I thought to myself, *She must be cold in that low neckline.* Then I realized that this was an atypical reaction for me when regarding low cut sweaters on other attractive women. My inner voice repeated, *Other attractive women. Other than Kathryn? Yes, other than Kathryn... Huh!*

As much fun as having tea with a pretty grad student should have been, all I could think about was Kathryn's brief suggestion that she might sneak out of her retreat to come *home* around ten. But it was still before eight. I didn't need to rush this interview, though I did want to speed up the clock.

Nora put two cups of water in a tiny microwave and pressed *Start.* "I know you're supposed to boil tea water, but I'm a wee bit lazy," she said.

"Tell me what you saw at the cemetery."

Nora Hasan sighed and then became surprisingly confidential. "Since you came chappin' at my door, I think you should have to share a bit of my

misery. You see, I was set to have a rather hot date. It's been yonks since...
but I got stood up, which has me low." She automatically wrapped the tea
bag string around the bowl of the spoon and the bag, squeezing the last
few drops into her cup. A dimple appeared in her cheek. She added, "And
thereby hangs a tale."

"I'm sorry your date didn't show. I hate when that happens."

She rewarded me with another smile, saying, "A ministering angel
shall my sister be. Really you're just what I need, a mate I can tell my
troubles to. Do you mind?"

I shook my head to show I didn't mind and smiled.

She said, "I was not paying attention when you showed me your card.
What was your name again?"

"I have a set of first names too. Mehitabel Arrabella Gale, but Maggie
is fine."

"I don't ken that I've ever heard those names before. How did that all
come about?"

I briefly explained and she listened intently, asking a couple of questions
to help the story along.

"Well then, Maggie... em... here's my little yarn. You see, I was hoping
for a nice dinner and a wee bit more than pudding. Oh dear, I tend to wear
my heart upon my sleeve. I suppose that's what put my date off?" Nora
went on with the story while I listened and nodded encouragement.

It didn't take Nora long to tell her cryptic but standard tale that began
with flirting and ended with nothing, not even a phone call. When she
finished, it was clear she felt better having told it, but not clear whether she
was talking about a male or female antagonist.

It doesn't take a seasoned detective to know that straight people very
rarely hesitate to identify themselves as straight. That's why being in the
closet never really protects you from someone who wants to pry. A straight
person would never avoid gender pronouns when talking about a date. Nora
had been jilted by a woman but was a little uncomfortable being completely
honest. Not really surprising considering being Gay is illegal in Morocco.
The threat of fifteen years in prison would make anyone reticent.

I smiled and said, "She should at least have called."

"Well, now, you *are* a detective, aren't you," she said with her head
tilted to the side.

I shrugged gently. "About the shooting..."

"Fair enough. All right then. I went along 10th Street to the corner
market at 10th and Fen. When I came out, I went back up Fen. Then I heard

something of a pop. Screwed my courage to the sticking place and skelped right up to the bars of the fence to *keek* through the trees. I heard a wee girl scream. I could see the statue of the woman in the shroud. Very white it is. Like a wraith. Then I saw someone come from the left into view. When I heard another pop, he froze and turned round in all directions. He was wearing a dark red hooded jumper and denim jeans. He had his back to me so I couldn't see his face, but he was a ginger. Then he flipped up his hood, covering his hair.

"Are you sure it was a man?"

"Hmmm, it's my impression. Might have been a woman, but I doot it." She sat considering for a moment then went on, "I could see beyond him. Farther away, there was a large splash of blue on the ground. The soldier said it was a dead man. I saw the person in the maroon jumper stop and look at the blue coat and then he turned and ran behind some bushes. Then I saw a man farther back, kneeling on the ground, boaking like a sick cat."

Nora took a sip of tea and considered. "In a tic, police sirens. I saw them drive up Fen Street. Then running. And in a wee moment I saw you talking to a man in a mac. I thought the game's afoot, so I went round to the gate to give my bit to the police."

"So the person in the hooded sweatshirt had red hair and was fairly thin. Was he white?" I asked.

She nodded. "Aye."

"Good, let's call him Red. I don't like that the police are calling him Hoodie. When you heard the second shot, you could see Red, right?"

"Aye."

"Could you see both his hands then?"

Nora paused to recall the scene. "Aye, both of them. He turned with his arms out a bit. He didn't have anything in his hands. Certainly not a gun. Besides, the sound of the shot came from farther away."

I read back what I'd written on my laptop. "You heard a shot, Red ran into view, you heard another shot, Red looked around, you could see he was empty handed. He ran up to the blue jacket, looked briefly and then ran behind the big yew bushes. And you could see the other man on his hands and knees throwing up directly beyond him?"

"Aye."

"You're sure you saw Red go *behind* the bushes?"

"Aye."

"So did I." I thought for a minute. "Ever seen this person before?"

"No, I would have remembered the ginger hair."

"Did you hear anything else?"

"Hear anything? Well, em, I heard the shot, the scream, the sirens... em... might have heard a wee grinding sound at some point, like someone running on gravel, but with the wind in the trees." She shook her head.

I typed this into my laptop. "The sound was before or after the shot?"

"Both, I think. But it could have been a lorry."

"And did you see anyone on Fen Street?"

"Not until the police came."

I looked over the notes, then sat back and changed the subject to something more conversational.

"Do you act in plays, too?"

"The Bard shows, doesn't he? The lines keep slipping into my vocabulary. I can't help it. It happens to every actor. I've been in a few productions and now all the world's a stage." She laughed out loud, then sighed. "I bet Charlotte Cushman wouldn't have stood me up. Tell me what you know about her."

"Um, well, very famous in her day, certainly more famous than Laura Keene and her troupe, but both were nearly household names. You're the one who's studying her. Do you agree with scholars that Cushman lost her place in history because loving women was more severely frowned on in the early twentieth century than in her day?"

"Well aye, that would explain it for Cushman, but not Laura Keene. She was straight, but she's not remembered for her acting ability either."

"No, she isn't," I agreed. "Keene is only remembered these days for holding Lincoln's head in her lap as he died. It must have stung when she realized there was no way to avoid that being her claim to fame."

"Did you know that Laura Keene played the Majestic in 1866? Of course I suppose she played just about every theatre in this part of the country." Nora considered. "I think Cushman was forgotten because all stage actors are, unless their work is preserved."

"Explain."

"Well, 100 years ago everyone knew of Sarah Bernhardt," mused Nora as she stirred her tea. "She played every town, but when the people who saw her died off, so did her reputation. Live performers only began to enjoy immortality with sound recordings. The women who played those 19th century 'breeches parts' were too early even for silent pictures."

"Breeches parts." I smiled. "Women in male roles? Daring for the day."

"And a wee bit dodgy for polite society. Sexy, too. Tight pants showing off hips, thighs, and calves, instead of floor length dresses with hoop skirts and bum rolls. Those unfettered nether curves didn't go unnoticed by the blokes in the audiences. Or some of the women, either." Nora winked.

I nodded. "Women certainly did find Cushman attractive. Sort of a female 19th century Hugh Hefner. She must have had a thrilling personality. All those artists and writers so devoted to her."

Nora laughed lightly. "Personality? Really? Well, I suppose that's one word for it."

I adored this topic but was distracted by the possibility of Kathryn's return to the loft. I stole a glance at my watch, then said, "Did you know that a number of pieces by a woman artist of that day stand in the cemetery?"

"Aye, Victoria Snow. I've only just arrived this semester. I may not get to study the collections of women's art until later in the year. It's rubbish that women's works fall into obscurity."

"Like Edmonia Lewis's Cleopatra? Lost for 120 years and then finally found, restored, and placed in the Smithsonian? I see what you mean about immortality. Her work is still around to appreciate, even if it was lost for a time." I glanced at my watch again, then said, "It's been very nice talking with you but I have to go."

"I appreciate you letting me whinge and whine. Maggie, em... you're not interested in taking me for a nosh, then?" She smiled again in that dazzling way. She really was charming, but I had somewhere else to be.

I said, "Maybe another time you could come to my place for dinner. It's just half a block down the street. I'd like you to meet my partner. She's done research on these... Oh, you probably know her, Dr. Kathryn Anthony, at the college?"

Nora visibly shrank. She whispered, "*Crikey,* Dr. Anthony is your partner?"

I nodded.

"Yes, I know her," said Nora reverently. "I came here in hopes to study with her; she's brilliant. You're very lucky then, aren't you?"

She hadn't made it a question but I answered it anyway. "Yes, I am." I smiled. "Here's my card. If you remember anything else or see the man with the ginger hair, please call me."

I paused, then said, "I think I know someone else who might like to take you out for a late supper. Shall I call her?"

Nora had managed to recover from the mention of Kathryn. She said, "Fancy, that. Friend of yours? Nearby?"

"My sister. Her office is just down the street. Shall I text her?"

"If she looks like you," smiled Nora.

"She doesn't." I reached in my bag for my phone and scrolled through some photos, then held up a fairly hot one of Sara for Nora to see.

Nora smiled and nodded after a two-second glance. She poured herself the last of the tea and then got up to take the pot to the sink.

I texted Sara, < Have u eaten yet? >

And got back, < Have hot date for me? >

< 4 a late supper? on u btw >

< Smart? funny? interesting? >

I answered, < Yes 2 all >

< Send photo. >

I subtly snapped a picture of Nora and sent it to Sara's cell.

Sara texted back, < If I take her somewhere nice will I get lucky?>

Nora called across the room, "If she's asking if taking me for more than a bap and a banger might increase her odds, tell her we'll have to see, but it certainly couldn't hurt!"

I told Sara to drop by Nora's in about an hour. That would give them each time to get ready but not too much time to obsess about it.

"Maggie," said Nora, "you've been a delightful guest. And we'll see if I'll be thanking you tomorrow." Nora gave me another dazzling smile and I wished her good night.

In the foyer I zipped up my jacket and pulled on my gloves to meet the frigid February night.

My eyes adjusted to the darkness as I walked down the stone steps outside. There was someone standing on the sidewalk watching me. It was Kathryn.

CHAPTER 6

"Dr. Anthony," I said when I got to the bottom step. I reached to sweep her into my arms, but then I got a good look at her expression. She wasn't pleased, she looked... well, I wasn't sure. Annoyed? Frustrated? Sad? Jealous? Kind of all of the above. Sweeping was not an option.

"What's wrong?" I asked simply.

Kathryn smiled a little but didn't speak, then she shook her head.

I turned and looked at the clear view into Nora's apartment from the spot where Kathryn was standing. There was Nora, rinsing the tea cups. Kathryn turned toward the loft and began walking. I managed to keep up, but we were out of step.

Kathryn said in a low voice, only half teasing, "Was she worth it?"

"Whoa," I said reaching for her arm. I turned her to face me. She wouldn't quite meet my eyes.

"Kathryn, you can't be serious."

She shook her head at me in a *tsk tsk* kind of way.

"Kathryn," I said frankly, "I have no idea how long you were standing there, but if it was for any length of time, you'd know I didn't touch that woman. I didn't even shake hands with her. She was a witness to the murder this afternoon. The police interviewed her and I did too."

Kathryn looked slowly up into my eyes and for just a moment she focused on me with that searching stare that bores right into my soul. Her expression shifted again. "Oh, Maggie," she said, then she sighed. "I'm cold."

"Then let's go home," I said simply. When we got there, she waited while I punched in the lock code and disarmed the alarm.

The foyer was much warmer than outside. The freight elevator doors were open. Kathryn turned to take the stairs, which is faster than the lift, but I took her hand and led her into the elevator. I pulled the strap and the massive doors came down from the ceiling and up from the floor, clanking together in the middle like a giant eyelid, shutting out the view of the foyer and enclosing us in the small space. I reached for the chain link safety gate and pulled it down into place, then turned to face Kathryn squarely.

"Talk to me," I said gently.

She sighed and leaned against the wall with her eyes closed. "Maggie, I'm going to express this as intellectually as possible, but it's really a lot more visceral than I could have imagined." She seemed surprised by this confession. She sighed again and put her elbow on the wall shelf. "At the risk of sounding like a insecure bitch, I'm tempted to point out that I did fairly well at ignoring that overly made-up woman with the dramatic hairdo when she was flirting with you."

"Don't waste your energy being jealous of her. I barely remember her name."

"You never forget anything. Her name was Staplehurst, Pepper Staplehurst."

"Piper," I said drily, folding my arms.

Kathryn raised both hands over her head, then dropped them to her sides.

"Oh Kathryn, is this going to be one of those formulaic Lesbian romance plots? They meet. They're attracted to each other. They have flaws. They have a big fight and nearly let the whole thing spiral down the porcelain. Finally they get back together and have wild sex. If so, could we just skip to the sex part?"

She snorted, fighting down a laugh, but she was still agitated. Finally she leaned back against the wall and relented.

"The retreat went badly. Half the English Department wouldn't stop arguing off subject; the rest sat in silence waiting for it to end. Suddenly, someone I'd thought was far more stable began to rant loudly about some past issue I didn't understand. Nobody did, as a matter of fact. And then, just like the steel drummer, Dr. Bolton Winpenny, who teaches expository writing and actually works with this hysterical woman, walked into the middle of the room with his hands raised, saying that the meeting was getting repetitive and stressful and suggested we call it a night."

She paused recalling the scene and shook her head. "I could have kissed him. The department chair wasn't pleased about ending it, but he was so uncomfortable with *Professor Panic Attack* he agreed with Bolton and we all fled."

"This guy's name is *Bolton Winpenny*? What a great name!" When Kathryn nodded, I said, "Well, then how do I thank Bolton the Steel Drummer," I asked, "for getting to be with you tonight?"

Kathryn paused, regarding me for a few moments and said wistfully, "I was so pleased to be coming home to you early."

Then she crossed her arms and her voice unmistakably changed from narration to indignation. "There I was, innocently walking through the dark streets, and then in that brightly lighted window I saw you with that woman. Sitting on the couch, chatting, laughing, good grief, she was pouring tea into your cup. It was like a Freudian dream!" Kathryn paced across the small space, kneading her shoulder unconsciously. "It was like a scene in one of those reality shows. Where they film the philandering partner, flagrantly meeting the other woman in some sordid..." She stopped and turned, apparently realizing her description was becoming comical, but there was still something in her eyes. Something visceral, just as she'd said.

"Kathryn, I can see why it may have been a shock to see me in that window with another woman, but it also gave you a chance to see exactly what I'd do if I *were* with another woman. *She* was chaste; *I* was innocent. And *you* could see that." I thought a moment. "You know her, don't you?"

Kathryn closed her eyes. She'd gotten up before dawn to run around the antique markets with Farrel. Lack of sleep had shortened her fuse.

She said, "Nora Hasan. She's one of my graduate students but so far we've only spoken briefly. She's very smart and she's a Lesbian and..."

"*You're* attracted to her, aren't you?"

"No! Well... Oh," Kathryn paused. Then she laughed. "I hadn't thought about it. She's attractive, yes, but I'm... uh... I'm," Kathryn blushed lightly.

"Hopelessly devoted to me?"

"That isn't exactly the way I'd put it, but that gets to the gist of my feelings, yes."

"When I was with Nora all I did was hope you'd come home soon. I'm not interested in anyone but you. I want... well, I find I want you all the time." Kathryn took a step toward me, shaving a few miles from the distance between us.

"That young woman reveres you," I said.

Kathryn smiled a little and took another short step.

"I should be the one worrying about *your* fidelity," I suggested.

"Do you?" she asked.

"Should I?"

She shook her head no, emphatically, then put her arms around me. I held her tightly with one arm and ran the elevator up to our floor.

At 3 she let go and opened the elevator doors to the loft.

Kathryn shrugged off her coat and wandered through the middle of the large open space, absently touching the keys of the grand piano that a grateful, wealthy friend had given her for Christmas in exchange for putting her in serious danger. She went to the window facing the Mews.

"You're unsure of me? Is that what it is?" I asked.

Kathryn put her hand on her forehead and leaned it against the glass. "No, no, I'm sorry Maggie, this isn't about you. It's about me, um.... oh dear... I just need a little time... to... uh..."

Kathryn was usually so controlled, so confident. Now she was faltering and it was making her very uncomfortable.

"How about if I go work out for about an hour? Would that give you enough time to feel comfortable about talking?"

She was nodding. So I crossed the loft to the spiral staircase that leads to the top floor without saying another word.

The fourth floor of the building is nearly 3000 square feet. It's unfinished but has lots going on. My art studio space was idle, but in the other large corner, the construction of Kathryn's office showed rapid progress. Wiring snaked through the open two-by-four walls and the pipes for the office bathroom were all in place. Farrel's crew had already attached some of the drywall. The framing of the open second story that would be Kathryn's library area bisected the distance to the high ceiling. A neat little spiral staircase to it was already in place.

I went to the west side of the building that was reserved for some very serious gym equipment, including a high bar and a large area with mats for martial arts practice. I needed to get past that look that Kathryn had flashed me on the street. Apparently Kathryn did too. She was hammering out something Wagnerian on the Steinway. I began with a Tai Chi routine, then spent a half hour on the elliptical, and did some heavy weight sets.

She'll come to me when she's ready, my inner voice chanted. Kind of simplistic, but at least it wasn't telling me to save Paris. Kathryn's fury seemed to have lessened; she was playing something lighter but still in a minor key. *The Teddy Bear's Picnic?*

I started a set of 100 push-ups, doing them to the rhythm of Kathryn's music. I was warmed up and fluid, my muscles pumping me up off the mat smoothly as I counted to myself and focused solely on my physical actions. Soon I realized it was quiet downstairs.

I felt someone else in the space. I could smell her perfume even before I sensed her footsteps. The scent stirred me.

I could just barely see her in my peripheral vision. Kathryn was standing in the shadows near the top of the spiral stairs.

"Ms. Hyde turned back into Dr. Jekyll? Shall we talk?" I called to her softly, continuing my silent count down... *eighty-one, eighty, seventy-nine.*

"No... I'm watching you."

"Are you stalking me?"

"Yes," she said in a deep voice, taking a step closer.

"Any special reason?"

"I was hoping that you'd let your defenses down, then I'd pounce."

"I'm all sweaty. *Seventy-two, seventy-one...*"

"I'm undaunted."

"Well, your plan sounds like fun, but you've lost the element of surprise. Tell me about the first time you stalked me," I asked hoping for an interesting story to distract me from the strain of sixty more reps. *Fifty-nine, fifty-eight, fifty-seven....*

She had her arms folded and was staring at me. She moved again into the darkness. She said steadily, "I was driving home to the Hampshire. I saw you shoveling snow in front of Farrel and Jessie's, and since I'd been introduced to you I decided I might just happen to walk by and maybe we could speak."

"Speak? Is that all you wanted, just to speak to me?" I loved the sound of her voice. It was smooth and dark, like hot fudge on rich vanilla ice cream.

She made that purring noise that punctuates her most provocative sentences. "Mmmm, I wanted to see you up close, to find out what you were like. I hoped you'd remember me."

She was circling me, fading in and out of my line of vision like a panther in the night, slipping from shadow to shadow.

"But what did you hope would happen? Did you hope you could talk me up into your parlor? Spider v. Fly fashion? *Thirty-two, thirty-one.*"

"No, no," she sputtered in surprise.

"Not a convincing protest, querida. I bet you had a whole series of possible plans. Didn't you?" I laughed. "Really, what did you want to happen that night?" *Twenty-three, twenty-two, twenty-one.*

"Walking and talking with you in the park so late that night was better than I could have imagined.

"I'd like to know more about your erotic imagination, Kathryn. Will you tell me some time? Tell me now... *eighteen...*"

Kathryn walked over to the weight machine, looking at the accessories hanging on pegs on the wall. She said, "What if I started a weight lifting program? May I use your equipment?"

"Sure," I said, "anytime."

"What are these for?"

I looked up to see her fingering some bars and velcro cuffs.

I said, "You clip the bar on to that lower chain and pull on it with both hands while you're sitting, like rowing a boat. The cuffs go around your ankles to increase resistance, for leg lifts and kicks."

Kathryn came closer and stood at the edge of the mat. She was quiet for a time. She whispered, "So you didn't stalk me?"

"Of course I did. I went right home and ran your name through every system I have. I know your entire history. I know you got a speeding ticket when you were in your twenties. I even know your credit score."

She laughed deep in her throat. "I'm not sure if I should be flattered."

"You better get used to it. I snoop for a living. It's in my genes." She took a step closer, watching me count down the last ten push-ups. "Would you still be able to do that if I sat on your shoulders?"

I laughed. "Probably not. Might have at the beginning." She'd totally avoided the subject of her sexual fantasies. Talking about sex seemed to make her shy, though she certainly wasn't shy about doing it.

"Shall we try it and see what happens?" she suggested curiously.

"OK, but...."

She stepped over me, and when I dipped down to the mat she dropped to her knees before I could begin to push up again. Soft blue denim rested heavily just below my shoulders. Her added weight held me down.

I grunted and strained, "*Arrgh*. Nope, can't do it." I tried once more, straining to push both my body and hers off the floor and then gave up.

"So, then I have you? You're pinned down?" she teased, gripping the backs of my upper arms to hold me firmly.

She was straddling me, her knees and shins flat on the mat. "Have I finally captured you?" She made that low humming sound again. She trailed her fingers up over my shoulders and traced down the straps of my sports bra to the clasp at the back and undid it, spreading it open slowly. She lightly tickled the back of my neck with the tips of her fingers, then shifted again to find more responsive places to tease.

"Other than lust, do you have some symbolic reason for doing this?"

"Are you helpless now?" she asked with just a hint of growl.

"No, I'm not." I twisted a little, drawing my arm up, reaching over my shoulder to grab her wrist in one quick movement. Then I pulled her arm under me as I held her leg against my body with my other arm, keeping her off balance. I pushed her on her back. It happened so fast she didn't have time to do more than squirm. My body was now pinning hers to the mat. The sweat from my chest made a damp place on her shirt. She shrieked at the speed of it and then laughed.

"How do you always do this to me?" she said in exasperation. "One minute I have you pinned down and the next... I don't even know what happened!"

"See what I mean about the element of surprise? You can't beat me at this game, Kathryn, and I'm not always doing this to you. I'm just teaching you a lesson. Controlling me isn't that simple." She was wriggling, trying to get some kind of footing.

"At least I have your attention now. Oh, mmm." My mouth pressed against hers and she began to put her arms around me but stopped. "You *are* all sweaty!" she complained.

"*Quien con bebés se acuesta, cagado amanece levantarse*," I said.

"And that means?"

"If you play in the barnyard, querida, you're going to get dirty," I said, sitting back on my heels.

"It means that literally?"

"It's something my stepmother Juana says, and it more literally means *one who lies down with babies, rises covered with shit*. But I always thought that verged on pervy, so I prefer the barnyard analogy."

"Because there is nothing *pervy* about barnyards?" she laughed. "I'm sorry about the way I acted. I had a long talk with myself and I'm over it now. Really, I don't suspect you."

"Would you like to have some more attention right here on the floor or shall we go downstairs and pay attention in the nice soft bed?" I leaned down and kissed her again, holding her head in place with both my hands. I traced the contour of her mouth with my tongue.

"Let's go downstairs," she whispered after the long kiss. Then she said pointedly, "And you can take a shower."

****

On the way I'd suggested to Kathryn that we could *both* take a shower, but she said she'd taken one right after I'd gone upstairs.

"I needed to think about things and I seem to think very well in the shower... I love that shower," she had said.

It really was a wonderful shower. A large tiled space with multiple jets and a hand-held shower head with enough water pressure to make any woman happy. But I was banking that Kathryn would take the edge off my ardor herself, so I passed on dialing to *pulse* and hurried to dry off and get back to her.

A crackling fire burning in the bedroom fireplace made everything warm and inviting. Kathryn was already under the covers. Clearly desire had trumped lack of sleep. Her bare shoulders told me that ardor release was on her to-do list as well. The near misses we'd had earlier that day sparked a tension that rushed back to me with a roar. She added to my rising lust with a carnal smile that stoked me like a coal furnace. She put her arms over her head and stretched like an agile cat in the sunlight, straining her muscles in an all consuming way.

"That was a sex stretch!"

"What's that?" she said provocatively, flipping the covers open.

I slipped out of my robe and slid in beside her. She rolled on top of me. Her lovely body pressed against mine.

"One of those fully involved stretches fueled by sexual desire."

"I'm sure you're right," she said. "Maggie, I do want to explain why I'm wary, but don't you think it's a little early in our relationship to bare all our past angst?"

She was running her fingers lightly over my throat, caressing my shoulders, working her way toward my breasts with both hands. I grasped her wrists and held her hands away, making her sit back.

"It's important to talk about things if they're getting in the way."

She sighed. "What if I flirted with a woman right in front of you, to hurt you? How would that make you feel?" She waited for my answer.

"If you flirted with someone to *hurt* me? To hurt me on purpose? That's not what happened."

"I know that's not what you did. But what if... *I* did it?"

"If someone who claims to care about you does something to hurt you on purpose, yes, you have a right to be angry. Would you do that? Hurt me that way?"

She shook her head no.

"Has someone done that to you?"

She sighed and rolled to her side. "Do you really want to hear this?"

I nodded.

Kathryn paused for several moments.

Finally she took my hand and looked into my eyes. "I told you before that my last relationship was with a woman who'd been one of my professors in grad school. I became involved with her after I finished my doctorate and was teaching. It's been a while since we broke up." She paused, counting the years in her head, but didn't say how many.

"I was such a classic case," she laughed. "I was so impressed by her. Maybe you've read her work? Her first name is pronounced *Ashling,* but it's spelled A-i-s-l-i-n-g. Aisling Philips-Von Trapp. Ash has written several books and a number of really fascinating papers."

Kathryn's voice held a tiny but unmistakable note of admiration that I was surprised to find made me jealous. I tried not to show it. A green-eyed monster is especially unattractive in someone who actually has green eyes.

I'd heard of Aisling Philipps-Von Trapp. I'd read some of her articles in grad school. I'd found her research excellent but her theories pretentious. Some of the students in my study group who had worked under her at Radcliffe as undergrads found her insufferable as a person. One of my friends referred to her as *Ass-sling Filled Up With Crap*. This probably wasn't the best moment to tell Kathryn that though.

Kathryn went on, "We lived together in Ash's house during summers and vacations. We took some wonderful trips. We wrote and talked on the phone. During that time I was teaching at Central Western University, on the Colorado campus, and she was in Cambridge."

"When were you at Radcliffe?"

"I researched part of my dissertation there and we met when I helped to teach a course... Her course, in fact. I did all the preliminary research for it. But we didn't start our relationship until after I'd finished there."

I knew Kathryn's academic credentials were stellar. Smith for her BA, Yale for her doctorate. Heck, she'd even done some time in Oxford, but I hadn't known she'd rolled around the halls of Harvard as well. Another reason she was able to make it to full professor at such a tender age.

"I guess I told you before that what ended our relationship was her lack of concern about my fidelity. I was meeting quite a few other young women who were, well... willing."

"I bet," I snorted.

Kathryn said with mock indignation, "I didn't stray."

"But?"

"But *she* did. It wasn't so much that I found out. I figured it out." Kathryn rolled onto her back. I could see by the firelight that she was staring at the ceiling. She sighed. "I'll try to keep this from becoming a histrionic narrative."

"Don't worry about it. Go ahead and tell me."

"All right. Well, here it is."

One day we went out to lunch. It was during a winter break and I'd gone to Boston. We sat together and I felt happy being with her, though I'd felt uneasy most of the time we were apart.

Ash glanced around the restaurant, then she said casually, "Have you been seeing anyone?"

I got that strange feeling, the way your stomach feels when an elevator goes down. I said, "Ash..."

But before I could say anything else she said, "Because you know, my dear, it would be all right. I know how hard it is to resist beautiful young women, and you're still very attractive. I'm sure you have all sorts of invitations."

So I said to her, "But I wouldn't be unfaithful to you!"

And she replied candidly, "Well, Kathryn, we don't really have that kind of a commitment. You've always known that, haven't you?"

The world suddenly turned on its side and the room twisted. I couldn't speak. I just sat there seeing five years spin by and all the times we'd been together, as though I was looking though the wrong end of a telescope. I nearly fainted.

Aisling seemed very surprised I was taking her simple little comment so theatrically. Meanwhile I was having one of those 'ah ha' moments of clarity that comes to you quite easily once all the fog blows away. Suddenly I realized why our relationship had always seemed so tilted.

I said to her, "You've been seeing another woman all along, haven't you?"

Aisling said to me, "This isn't something I felt the two of us needed to discuss. I was apprehensive that it would make you uneasy."

I remember jumping up and sputtering out something like, "Apprehensive? Uneasy?"

And then I had another sudden insight. I said, "It wasn't just one, was it. How many?... No, don't tell me."

She just sat there innocently. I walked out of the restaurant, back as fast as I could to her place, grabbed my suitcase, flung it into my car and drove all the way back to Denver without stopping.

Kathryn looked back at me. She said, "I only cried for about 300 miles and then I began to go over every moment of the previous five years. That took me about 700 miles. I couldn't help noticing she'd said, *You're still attractive*. That hit me like a lightning bolt. I was nearing thirty then and obviously that was too old for her. She was at least twenty years older than

I, by the way. I realized everything had been wrong about that relationship, no real commitment, no communication, no honesty, and..." She paused in mid rant.

"And what?" I asked gently.

Kathryn smiled. "And, no passion."

"In the bedroom?" I asked with my eyebrows raised.

"Yes, and in general too. Well, that little forty-eight hour drive of mine gave me a long time to think. I made some decisions about my future."

"You decided to swear off women?"

"No, I decided to swear off bad relationships. I'm gun shy and a bit reactionary. You know, what you said about hurting someone intentionally? Aisling surely had done this to other women, once they too had *aged-out* of her interest zone. She dumped me by making me leave her. So calculating. So hurtful. And it's left me with a suspicion I find hard to ignore sometimes."

"Were you angry at her for a long time?"

"I felt relief more than anything. I remember sleeping for hours and finally waking up and feeling lighter than I had in years. I was most angry with myself for asking so little of a relationship. She never said explicitly that we were exclusive." Kathryn paused.

I took the hint. "Kathryn, it's my understanding that we are in an exclusive relationship. And only until we may mutually express otherwise. That means that neither of us will be sleeping with, kissing, holding hands with, or, as the Andrews Sisters so eloquently sang, *sitting under the apple tree with anyone else* but each other. OK?"

She smiled that lovely half-smile and looked deeply into my eyes. "OK," she said.

We kissed. I could feel Kathryn's mouth curve into a smile. It was a deal-sealing kiss. She gently touched my face when we drew apart. And then we hugged and held each other again for several minutes in an unspoken conversation that said a thousand words.

"Do you ever think about Aisling?" I said when we finally parted.

"Every now and then I wonder just how many young women have shared Ash's bed, and I feel a little sorry for them," she said.

"Because she cheated on them, too?"

"No." Kathryn laughed. "Because I know what a dull time they were having!"

"So that's my cue. No pressure, huh?"

"I like a certain amount of pressure!" said Kathryn, rolling back on top of me. We kissed hotly and then she sat back.

I caressed her thighs, then urged her up the bed until I could reach her with my mouth. She stretched out and steadied herself by grasping the top edge of the headboard. I looked up at her as I found her with my tongue, then slipped my hands under and behind her to hold her tightly to me as I explored and then found my mark. She let go of the headboard, arching her back. It all happened very fast. She let the pleasure wash over her like a swollen creek swirling over rough stones. She moaned deeply in satisfaction.

Then she moved to kiss her way down my body. Soon, she was at the foot of the bed working me into the frenzy I'd been holding back since right after the brunch. She reached up to tease my breasts at the same time. She brought me to climax swiftly, realizing just what I needed.

As the moments of perfect pleasure flooded through my body, they chased a fleeting thought that this was a very intimate way to communicate. Kathryn seemed to agree, because after allowing me a few minutes to recharge she found me with her tongue again and brought me to another lovely climax. Slower this time, with more attention to detail. She had a way of watching as she did it that made me want to keep my eyes open.

When I was sated, I moved to satisfy her again. She responded to slow rousing strokes until she came with a long shuddering moan that surprised me with its primitive tones.

"Lordy," she groaned into my shoulder, "how can you manage to do this to me when we're both so tired? Neither of us had had more than four hours sleep."

"You have a point. Next time we should just let the trained seals do all the work." I yawned.

She laughed and put her arms around me.

As we fell asleep, I parsed our earlier discussions. Control, trust, fidelity, commitment. How do we prove ourselves? Where do we find the steel drum to drown out our insecurities and doubts.

CHAPTER 7

The next morning I awoke before Kathryn and slipped out of bed to shower and dress before she'd even stirred. When I came back into the bedroom she turned and smiled at me, then reached her arms over her head in a feline way and groaned.

"I see what you mean about stretching," she murmured as she opened her arms to me and I went to kiss her good morning. "You did wonderful things to me last night."

"I'm flattered you think it was all me, but it takes two for a tango like that, querida."

She stretched and then swung her legs over the edge of the bed. "If I can make an appointment around lunch time, would you be able to go to the museum with me? I'd like to take my alleged Victoria Willomere Snow sculptures over there to get that woman's opinion. What was her name?"

"Funny, I can't remember."

"Piper Staplehurst," said Kathryn pointedly, leaning out of the bathroom. "I should google her to see what she's published. You can give her your crime report."

Minutes later I was staring out the window as eggs poached, trying to recall a dream I'd had in the night. Dreams have always played a significant part in my life. When I was a child, I'd dream whole scenarios with me as an observer. My dreams often helped me figure things out, and now and then they could be prophetic. I could only get the tail of the one I'd had the night before. It was Red disappearing as he ran toward the yew bushes."

Suddenly there was Kathryn, elegantly dressed in tan linen pants, cashmere top, and a soft gray kimono style jacket with mauve silk lapels.

"Coffee," she said, turning for a cup from the maker on the counter.

I was dressed in my typical private eye uniform, black jeans, dark gray sweater, polo shirt (blue this time), and black running shoes.

Toast popped up. She buttered both pieces and put them on plates. We ate at the little table by the window in companionable silence.

"What are you going to do about that person who was killed?" she said.

"Mm," I said, putting down my coffee mug. "Carbondale fired me."

"What?"

"Well, he didn't really fire me; the case is over. Someone being killed in the cemetery pretty much confirms there's crime in there. The whole thing seems, I don't know, strange somehow. I don't like it. I'm going to work on it anyway."

Kathryn said in an amused voice, "We've established that trust is one of my issues. Perhaps not wanting to give up control is one of yours."

"I think that's one of yours too. But shall we call it tenaciousness? Then it's more like a virtue."

****

"Hi, Maggie," said Nora Hasan waving.

When Kathryn left for work, I'd commuted downstairs to my office, and there was Nora at the front desk on the landline phone in the shared reception room of Gale Investigations and Martinez and Strong, Partners at Law. I did a double-take, smirked, and waved back to Nora, then went directly into Sara's office.

"¿Tuviste suerte, eh?" I teased as I closed the door. Sara was dressed for court in a dark tailored suit and white silk blouse. She swiveled toward me in her chair and smiled.

"No tuve suerte en el sentido que tú piensas, cerebro de cisterna."

"Ay hombre, ¿ni siquiera la besaste?" *

"Well, yes, I kissed her, but we decided after that we'd be better as colleagues."

"So you hired her? So much for an equal decision."

"Emma likes her. She met her before she had to go to court."

"And then there's Gale Investigations."

"Seriously, Maggie, you like her, don't you? She's very smart. She fixed the fax so that it doesn't jam; she reorganized the billing system so it sorts by a dozen categories. She speaks Arabic fluently, and French too. She figured out how to enhance the picture on the surveillance cameras. And she can type faster than I can talk. She can take client statements."

"That's a reason to hire her in itself, but I'm seeing some problems."

"What?"

---

* "Get lucky, did you?" I teased as I closed the door.

Sara was dressed for court in a dark tailored suit and white silk blouse. She swiveled toward me in her chair and smiled.

"Not lucky in the sense you mean, potty brain."

"Oh c'mon, you didn't even kiss her?"

"Well, she's a grad student. If she's working on an advanced degree, that's going to take all her time."

"She isn't really working on a degree. She's more like a part-time fellow at the college, working on research. So we hired her from 9 a.m. to 2 p.m., and then she has the rest day to work on her other stuff. She says she can handle it."

"*We* hired her," I said dryly.

"Pending your approval."

"I think we better ask Kathryn if Nora really has time for another job." *Oh, geez, Kathryn,* I thought, *What's she going to think about Nora working as my assistant?* I wasn't enthusiastic about having to face Kathryn's suspicious ire again even though the make-up sex was fun.

"I had Nora call Kathryn and I asked her. Kathryn seemed fine about it. By the way, do you fully understand how Nora feels about Kathryn?"

"Kind of in awe?" I asked.

"Yeah, there's an understatement," said Sara.

"I'm more worried about you sexually harassing the employees. I can see the headlines: Local Law Firm Sued by Student — Secretary Says Solicitor Solicited Her."

"She's too good an assistant to lose for a quick roll in the hay. Maggie, she understands Evie's filing system!"

"OK, OK, we can give her a try. But no more kissing her and she doesn't have a green card so that might cap how much she can earn."

"We're done with kissing. Its just business now. Maybe we can sponsor her. I'll look into it," mused Sara.

"We'll have to check her references. Let's have a little probationary period before you start calling in favors from senators and the INS."

"OK, fine, you check. We'll start the paralegal search once she's trained. It can be Nora's job to set up the ads and interview schedule. Meanwhile I gave her one of the office cell phones with all the bells and whistles on it so she could keep in touch and manage things when she's off-site."

I liked Nora and she was smart. It's not easy to find someone for a position like this. There are so many skills involved, and frankly, while Evie was very good at some things, she was dismal at tech. I was confident that Sara wouldn't hit on Nora once we'd hired her, but how Kathryn was really going to react to this might turn out to be a little more complicated than a phone call.

I went back into the outer office and sat down in the client chair next to Nora's new desk. She was on the phone ordering some printer toner. She hung up and said, "Hoist by your own petard?"

I said,

> A darting fear—a pomp—a tear—
> A waking on a morn
> To find that what one waked for,
> Inhales the different dawn.

"Em... crikey, I'm rubbish at anything other than the Bard."

"It's by Emily Dickinson."

"And she's meaning I might not find this job to my fancy?"

"Aye," I nodded.

"But then again, I may."

"Aye to that, too."

"Are you going to give me the nod then or have me naff off?"

"Yes to the nod, but we'll have to check your references."

"Well, Sara said she'd pay me by the hour for a wee bit and then we'll see. And Dr. Anthony said it would be all right." Nora stated this as though it should seal me on the deal.

I nodded and smiled and sorely hoped this all wasn't a major mistake. *Oh crikey, indeed!*

"You won't be sorry," insisted Nora. "Look, I've already taken a message. You had a ring this morning from some lady who wants to see you later today. I didn't have your schedule so I said I'd ask you when you came in. Shall I ring her back for you?"

"Yes, please call her and then put her through to my office. Nora... I have a feeling you'll work out fine here."

I showed her how to access my appointment schedule on the office phone she was now carrying and gave her all my contact numbers. She smile-dazzled me, and I went into my office thinking she was probably going to be a good addition to our work team, hoping that this wasn't going to tax my love life, and marveling that Sara wasn't really that attracted to her.

****

"Lois? This is Maggie Gale returning your call."

Lois Henshaw's brassy voice echoed over the phone so loudly that I had to hold it a foot from my ear.

"I don't want to talk about it over the phone. Little pitchers has big ears." she said obscurely.

"There's a child there?" I asked.

"No... my cat, he has big ears, and his name is Little Pitchers," she strained a laugh and I agreed to meet her in a half hour.

The Mews Gossip Network had postulated that the problems at the Henshaw digs were domestic. The network is seldom wrong.

Infidelity is the reason private investigators have steady employment. After I'd "retired" from the Fenchester police force, and figured out I still wanted to be in the superhero crime-fighting biz, I trained to be a P.I. by working with an already established company called Discreet Investigations. The only thing I learned from the head dick, Seamus A. McFinn Jr. (Yes, his name really was Seamus and yes he really called himself the "Head Dick."), was: *Being a private investigator is much more like being a therapist than being a cop.*

****

A gust of wind swirled frosty air around the Mews like a dry ice demonstration at the science museum. I zipped my jacket to my chin and yearned for the warm days I'd spent in Florida with Kathryn. At the moment I'd gladly settle for a few hours in a warm bed... with Kathryn.

Chez Henshaw was an exceptional example of Queen Anne Style architecture. Clearly this house was "born" in about 1890, when the Mews was losing the last vestiges of its stable yard roots. The little brick row houses at the east end of the Mews, where Evangeline Fen had found cheap lodging for her family and where Gabriel and Suzanne Carbondale, and Amanda Knightbridge lived now, had been built *back-alley-size* for servants, tradesmen, and stablehands. They'd faced the stables while the mansions, with their landscaped front lawns, had faced eastward toward growing downtown Fenchester. But by the end of the 19th century the mansions were gone to fire and the neighborhood of new, stately brick row homes had turned inward to face the Mews Park.

The Henshaw's row house at 11th and Liberty had bay windows and a rounded tower crowned with an ornate copper lightning rod. It was even fancier than Farrel and Jessie's place on the other side of the Mews.

I walked up the steps to the wide porch with its heavy doric columns and glanced in the broad front window but the shades were drawn. The entryway was a jewel. Both the door and its flanking windows featured ornately cut glass in a swirling arc pattern. When the afternoon sun shone through, it must have cast a thousand rainbows around the living room. But today was too gray to even flicker a sun dog.

Lois Henshaw answered the bell key before I'd finished one twist. A little white cat with the biggest ears I'd ever seen wove around her legs.

Lois often insisted that she was not the brightest bulb in the string of pickle lights. She'd found her place in the neighborhood pecking order in the role of class clown. But at the moment she was an incongruous cross between the dictionary illustration of stress and a young Carol Burnett.

Lois's thick red bangs framed her animated face. Her movements were broad and exaggerated. She smiled and greeted me, but there was a brittleness in her tone. Though she was giving it everything she had clown-wise, the best she could muster was Emmet Kelly.

"What a beautiful house," I said a second before I had a chance to get a full gander inside. The interior architecture was delightful. Dark oak moldings with fascinating structural details. The furnishings, however, screamed, *What was I thinking?* It was an ebay nightmare.

The Danish Modern motif couldn't have clashed more with the house's style. The most serious problem was the colors. The orange and avocado would have rocked a 1970s retro but were a design school bad joke in this space. I suddenly had a craving for a Tab.

On the walls were three large specimens of the worst mass-produced dreck I'd seen in a long time. *Wishing-Well Scene* over the fireplace, *Venetian Gondolas* over the couch. And I swear I'm not making this up,— *Clown Portrait* over a blond-wood sideboard in the dining room.

Lois saw me looking and sighed. "I know, everything's ghastly. These gosh-awful paintings! I picked them on purpose at one of those parking lot tent sales. I figured, choose something that makes a sensitive person barf and maybe Samson would notice and help me."

Or cringe, I thought. "Did it work?" I asked.

"Nuh uh. Um, let's go in the kitchen."

It was magnificent and therefore uncommon to Queen Anne row houses. In that era, inconvenient kitchens were built unsympathetically for the help, but this space would have thrilled Jessie Wiggins. It was spacious, tiled, and had everything a serious cook could ever want. They could have shot a promo for the Iron Chef in there.

Little Pitchers the cat ran into the kitchen and played frantically by herself the entire time we talked. Lois watched her rather than looking at me.

Lois said, "Samson's really the chef. I'm... Would you like a snack? I just took these out of the oven." She pushed a plate of dark brown cookies across the counter toward me. "Go on, I just made them."

I dutifully took one. I'm rather devoted to good cookies, but this one was as hard as dried clay and amazingly tasteless. As though it was made solely of water and some kind of fiber-heavy grain. Actually, I couldn't tell if it was grain or burlap. No, burlap would have more flavor.

"You hate 'em, don't you?" She bit into one herself and shook her head. "Oh geez, I do too. I must have left out some of the ingredients. Honestly, if I'd been the cook for the Donner Party, they *still* would have eaten each other. I'm clueless about food; I thought Edith Piaf was a rice dish before I met Samson. I'm better at the cleaning up." Lois snagged the cookie plate, fiercely dumped the cookies into the garbage can, and went to the sink to scrub the plate.

As she did I noticed that any lingering cooking aromas were masked by the odor of cleaning products. They made the place smell like a swimming pool... in a hospital.

"There are worse obsessions," I suggested.

"Maggie, I'm kind of the obsessive type, but I don't have any illusions. I'm not smart. Like, when they started doing opposite side of the street parking all I could think of was that *both* sides are the opposite side. I'm a goof, but..." She turned to me and said sadly, "I love him."

"You're being kind of hard on yourself, Lois, and you're being hard on that plate too. You'll wash the flower pattern off it if you keep scrubbing like that."

"Oh!" said Lois speaking to the object in her hands. "I'm sorry little plate." She began patting it dry. "I have a report from another investigator I guess you should see." She was still talking to the plate but she meant it for me.

I said, "Why don't you just tell me about it."

"Well, it's just that I want to know why he's always out."

I said, as gently as possible, "Have you considered asking *him*?"

"Every one of the investigators says that," she whined.

"Every one? How many have there been?" I stood up and took a step back. "Lois, I'm not trying to be rude, but you're going to have to answer a few questions if you want to employ me. That's the way I work. It doesn't make much sense for you to pay me to ferret out information from *you*."

Lois nodded silently.

"Usually when a woman feels this way about her husband it's because she doesn't trust him. Or is it communication? Maybe couples counseling is a better choice than a P.I. with a big magnifying glass."

"I asked him to go to counseling, but he says there's no reason to. He used to be an architect, but that kind of dried up. We have rental properties. We live off those. We used to work together fixing them up. But he says he doesn't need me to help any more."

My mind ran over a variety of reasons a middle-aged man might not be spending every waking hour with his wife. There were even a number of innocent ones.

I opened the yellow envelope that held reports from two other investigators and scanned them quickly. "These say Samson is just working and walking around the Mews."

A folder of photos showed Samson driving his pick-up truck, carrying tools into a rental property, fixing the hinges on a door, carrying paint cans. There were several of him drinking coffee in the window of an empty apartment, standing on the sidewalk with his hands in his pockets, sitting on a park bench staring into space, walking the Mews streets and back alleys. There were no photos of him going into any inexplicable buildings or talking to hot women.

"Well, Lois, you wanted to know where Samson was during the day and this file details the answer."

"I don't think... This isn't conclusive," said Lois shaking her head.

"You expected to find out he was seeing someone? Or was it something else?"

"Maggie, I'm not pea-brained. It's not about *where* he goes; it's about *why*. There's something distracting him. Right now he wouldn't notice me if I drove through the living room in the Oscar Meyer Weinermobile. I want to know why."

"OK, I might be able to find out why he stays away. But if you're banking on me getting him to come back, you'll need a different kind of help."

"A head shrinker?"

"Yes."

"Oh Maggie, I don't want to go to rehab. No, no, no," said Lois.

CHAPTER 8

I tried to convince Lois Henshaw to just ask Samson what was going through his head. I was guessing she may have known and just didn't want to hear it coming out of his mouth. This wasn't the kind of job I enjoyed.

Back at Gale Investigations, Nora Hasan was hard at work creating an automated billing system. It was amazing to me that a young woman so apparently dedicated to the theatre arts was so skilled at computer data management. In short, *YAY!* Now I won't have to do any of this stuff.

Nora smiled. "Did you meet with that woman? So... em... do I get to discuss cases with you? Like a side-bloke?"

"Did Sara explain the confidentiality rules?"

"Aye, she did. Discretion is the better part of valor, and all that."

"This isn't really a case yet, so there isn't much to discuss. But it's still confidential."

"Shall I keep all the files in code? We could assign everyone secret drag queen names. Let's see, we could file her under a dodgy last name like... em... Lois Common-d'Nominator?"

I laughed. "Oh geez, now I'm going to think that every time I talk to her. She might actually like that name. I think she likes to make people laugh. Yes, we could do that, but we could also just use her real name and keep the file cabinet locked."

"Not as fun."

"We could compromise by just referring to all of us in the office by drag queen names. I could call you Miss Lenderbee."

"Brilliant. Nora Lenderbee. Apt too, I'm usually out of dosh, and it's a good thing, because I'm a wee sook when it comes to giving it away. Who will you be?"

"I've always liked Hellena Handbasket."

"Ha! But nae, not right for you."

"Don't tell my friend Farrel about this. She'll give up her day job just to make up new ones."

"Farrel? I haven't met her?"

"No, but you will."

"Good. You have rather good taste in friends," said Nora, nodding.

I went into my office and made a hard copy file of the contract agreement that Lois Henshaw signed. Then I pulled out my laptop and began an e-file of Lois's information. Lois had given me a copy of the other investigators' reports. I read carefully through all three. They'd been watching Samson over the last six weeks and they all came to the same conclusion. Samson wasn't doing anything Hester could win another "A" for. He wasn't doing much at all. Maybe that was significant in itself.

So now I had two jobs to do. One for Lois Henshaw re: Samson, and one for myself re: the shooting in the graveyard. I sat back and had a blinding flash of Amanda Knightbridge talking about the Carbondales' book. I pulled it out of my bag and leafed through it, randomly reading the captions under various historical photographs of Fenchester.

The book had a center insert of black and white photos. Shots of the Civil War Cemetery and other Fenchester landmarks took up the first few pages. Next came the portraits, including General Merganser Hunterdon in full uniform on a white horse. The horse looked bored. Amanda and Judith were right. Merganser had an unfortunate face. The uniform and his apparent youth in the Civil War era photo lessened the impact of his unappealing features. On the opposite page, however, a tintype of Hunterdon in coat and vest, with a gold watch chain and a stiff collar, was an image of an ugly man.

Like the earlier photo, he had mutton-chop sideburns, but in 1876 his face was stouter, with a large nose, squinty pig eyes, and a protruding lower lip. Yet it wasn't the features that made him so revolting. A big nose and small eyes don't necessarily make someone ugly. It was his expression. He looked egotistical, belligerent, condescending, and paranoid all at the same time. He was a cross between the bartender in *The Shining,* Scrooge, and any hypocritical far-right Republican. Yet Evangeline had become engaged to him.

Maybe General Merganser Hunterdon just didn't photograph well. Maybe he had some kind of inner strength or kindness that didn't show in the stark photographic images of the late 1800s. In those days, one had to sit still for a long time while an image formed on a treated photographic plate. Photographers even had clamps that held people's heads in one place while ten or fifteen minutes ticked slowly by. That's why everyone in old photos looks so stiff and staring, because they were.

I flipped the page and there was a beautiful portrait of Evangeline Lavender Fen. Her features were lovely, and there was no sense of stiffness at all. She seemed alive and vibrant. Her vitality was infectious even though she'd been dead for way more than a hundred years. She had high cheek bones, bright dancing eyes, and a haunting smile. Her graceful throat and perfect skin were fully exposed by the low-cut ball gown. She held a fan in one hand; her other hand waved the viewer toward her. She looked like her sculpture.

"No wonder Merganser mourned her for the rest of his life," I said out loud.

The phone on my desk rang. I could see Nora though the open door winking at me as she put the call through. I picked up.

"Is this Gale Investigations? Do you check up on errant girlfriends?"

"Why Dr. Anthony, how very nice to hear your voice. But why didn't you call my cell?"

"I wanted to hear the way Nora would answer the office phone. I can't believe the intoxicating Miss Hasan is working less that fifteen feet from your desk," said Kathryn's enchanting tones.

"Is this going to bother you? I told Sara that it might be... uh..."

"Yes, yes, Sara called me. This is quite a textbook example of karma isn't it?" Kathryn laughed deep in her throat. "What do you suppose I did in my sinister past to deserve this cosmic punishment?"

"Maybe it was something significantly deviant? Something particularly kinky?"

"Hmmmm, well, at least your imagination is focused on me and my sexual past, rather than the nearby present."

"Let's talk about the future, like tonight when we get home?"

"Let's talk about something sooner than that. I made an appointment with Piper Staplehurst for about a half hour from now. Are you free? Can you gather up the sculpture and meet me at the museum? Then maybe we could share a late lunch?"

"There is nothing I'd rather do. Well, nothing I'd rather do with you that doesn't involve being horizontal. I have a notion that perhaps we could work *horizontal* into this day before it's over?"

Kathryn exhaled deeply. Then she said, "I'm intrigued by this notion. Shall we talk about it later?"

****

Piper Staplehurst's office in the Fenchester Art Museum was in the sub-basement.

"I think my ears just popped," I whispered to Kathryn as we climbed down the last of the broad marble steps into a dark echoing hallway. Bronze sconces glowed just enough to see the numbers on the doors. Piper

Staplehurst's card had said room 10 SB. It was at the farthest end of the hall.

"Maybe the SB means 'Sea-level: Below,'" I suggested.

"What's the point of having a corner office if both windows face dirt," murmured Kathryn as she knocked.

We heard a voice say, "Come in."

On the phone, Kathryn had told me she'd checked a number of academic data bases and googled some newspaper articles for Piper Staplehurst's credentials.

"Really nothing in any of the higher education searches but the newspapers say she's worked in a variety of museums on development and restoration projects in the last three years, mostly in small cities like Fenchester. There's no mention of where she got her Ph.D. In fact, there's no mention of her having a Ph.D. Hmmm."

"You're an academic snob," I said with amusement.

"I try not to be too obvious about it," she said wryly.

Kathryn and I had agreed to meet at the Art Museum at 1 p.m. So now, I was carrying the carefully repacked bag of what we sorely hoped was Victoria Snow sculptures into the museum office.

"Dr. Staplehurst, thank you so much for seeing us on such short notice. We'll try not to take up too much of your time," said Kathryn, extending her hand.

"There's no need to be formal. Please call me Piper."

Piper was wearing a black suit, with a white silk blouse and black high heels. Her dramatic jet black hair with the white lock was brushed back and held in a clip. Her make-up seemed heavy for that time of the morning. In fact to me she seemed overdressed. Maybe she had a major meeting or presentation or something. In the corner I noticed a rack with a burgundy winter coat and scarf, some coveralls, some work shoes, and some fashionable snow boots,

"Here's the report about the crime in the cemetery, for the grant," I said, handing her a manilla envelope. "Is there anything else you need?"

"Excellent. I'll just add this to the grant application materials. I think this is everything I need. I can send off the application today. I already have a preliminary OK in writing to proceed. So we measured some of the openings; the first gates will be installed next week."

"My, that's the fastest grant turn around I've ever... How did you manage it?" asked Kathryn in awe.

"Oh, well there was some money left over from a similar project another town that I was able to apply to this. It will take a while to get the rest of the funds, but I had to use this money up before it disappeared."

"I see," Kathryn nodded, who had worked within the intricacies of grant writing for many years.

There was an efficiency about Piper Staplehurst's manner that was probably one of the keys to her success. Her desk was neat and the books on the shelves were even. On one table, plans to restoration projects were laid out. There was a carefully rendered schematic of the Civil War cemetery showing every stone, crypt, and elevation. The large work surface also held a collection of faded blueprints of the city's infrastructure. Several groups of carefully aligned artifacts drew my attention most of all.

"I'm sorry the office is such a mess. I may have gotten here the morning after the Winter Solstice, but I'm so busy I'd swear the days are getting shorter. I'll just clear these away," said Piper. Over her shoulder I saw Kathryn make a brief scoffing expression in response to the word *mess*. Except for some dust tracked on the floor it was one of the neatest offices I'd ever seen.

While Kathryn helped Piper stack the papers and old plans of the city on a shelf, I noticed the room's extraordinary 19th century architectural details. Nothing like it could have been built today. There was a beautiful Greek key pattern on the wall, a foot below the ceiling. Built-in marble benches skirted the room. There were four oval faux windows with glowing green glass in them that looked like they came from a hall in the Emerald City. I went to one of them, touching the frame of carved slate.

"It's a light-shaft all the way from the roof. White polished marble reflects the light through the iridescent glass. It's really an amazing effect isn't it?" said Piper smiling. She turned to Kathryn. "I have the picture catalog of Victoria Snow's work here, if you'd like to look at what the Museum has in its collection. There are a few pieces she did in Rome when she was not much more than an apprentice to Harriet Hosmer and there are photos of all the large pieces, including the Evangeline statues."

Kathryn looked at the book as Piper recited some V.W. Snow facts we already knew. I couldn't help but notice that Piper skipped over the part about Victoria knowing many of the Lesbian artists of her day.

When Kathryn got to a photo of some found-object heads, she pulled one of the little casts she'd bought at the market out of her canvas bag and unwrapped it. Kathryn had ten of the cast faces in all. The shell decorations seemed even more wild and exciting to me today. I made a mental note to try my hand at this kind of form as soon as I had a couple of free hours.

Kathryn took the nude Evangeline sculpture out of the bag and placed it on the table with the other pieces.

The sight of the collection mesmerized Piper Staplehurst. A snake sliding over the table in front of her wouldn't have diverted her attention.

After several more long moments of silence, Kathryn cleared her throat a little impatiently. "Any thoughts, Dr. Staplehurst?"

"Piper, please," she murmured, still rapt by the works.

"I'm sorry. What do you think of these, Piper?" said Kathryn.

"I... Oh well, yes, yes, even without the clear snowflake insignia, the style is hers. The media... Where did you get them?"

"At a sale."

"Really? Really? Where? When?"

I tried to read Piper Staplehurst's expression. It certainly was animated, but I couldn't tell whether she was thrilled at the possible new find or frustrated by the looming amounts of research she'd have to do to catalog these new pieces.

Kathryn explained she'd bought them from a dealer at an antique and flea market.

Now it was Piper Staplehurst who was impatient. "This statue really is a significant piece, but if there is any possibility that these works were obtained from *illegal sources...*" She stared at Kathryn, waiting for a response.

For the briefest of moments, it seemed as though Piper Staplehurst was intimating that Kathryn had received these little objects as stolen goods. But then the moment passed. It was an absurd suggestion. After all we'd just brought them directly to the museum for verification. This was not something a thief would do with stolen property.

After a beat Kathryn said disarmingly, "You take this all very personally, Piper?"

"Well, yes, yes I do." Then she laughed. "Yes, well, I suppose I do. I'm sorry. It's just that... Well, I had believed all of Snow's work was fully cataloged, and to find all these works, these unknown works..." She waved her hands over the little collection. "I just can't imagine where they came from. Where do you suppose the flea market dealer got them?"

"I heard him tell one of the other buyers that he cleaned out houses," said Kathryn.

This was entirely possible. Salvage people typically buy the entire contents of a house. Sometimes distant relatives inheriting far-away estates hire salvage teams for speedy clean-up to accelerate property sale. It's an interesting business, because while old house contents are mostly nameless flotsam and jetsam, some items can be cleaned up and sold, and sometimes there is priceless treasure. Of course, *I found it cleaning out a house* is also a fairly plausible cover-up for more nefarious ways of procurement. It's often a euphemism for burglary.

Piper Staplehurst shook her head. "Which antique market was it?"

Kathryn told her exactly where in Adamstown she's gotten it, but added, "I don't think he sets up there regularly, yet who knows. He may be back. Is there anywhere we can look *these* up?" asked Kathryn. "I'd love to find out more about them."

"There's no record of Snow using shells, and this nude statue, really, take my word for it, you won't find anything written about it. Snow must have done these when she was working in Fenchester, because obviously this is Evangeline Fen. Though it's unlikely she posed for this. A Victorian lady of the day wouldn't have posed without clothes, and besides there is no record of them ever meeting. All the larger statues were done after Evangeline Fen was dead."

"You're sure they're original Snows?" I asked.

"Yes, she did these; no questions about it. I don't even have to microscopically inspect them. I can tell by the unique color of the clay and the cast marks. Any expert would stake their reputation on it. Really, her work is very easy to identify. Forgers aren't exactly flooding the market with copies. They aren't *that* valuable."

"Do you know where her personal papers are? Are they archived somewhere?" asked Kathryn.

"Papers?" Piper Staplehurst's gaze drifted to the left as she considered. "I'm not an anthropologist so I haven't researched Snow's personal life, especially since all her work had already been identified and cataloged. Well..." She looked back at Kathryn's collection again. "That's what I'd thought, anyway. We'll have to catalog these."

"We'll bring them back as soon as the museum photographer is ready to shoot them," I said. I gave her my card and Kathryn did the same.

Kathryn paused to shake Piper Staplehurst's hand and thank her warmly for her time. It was a trifle too warm for my green eyes, but I reined in my little monster. Kathryn caught my eye over Piper's shoulder and covertly winked at me. I winked back.

While Kathryn wrapped everything back up, I examined the group of exquisite museum pieces of art and craftsmanship on a table against the wall. It included an Egyptian ushebti, some Asian porcelains, a bronze figure of a horse, and a late Renaissance miniature portrait.

"May I touch these?"

"Yes, go ahead. Your friend asked me about the things the museum is letting go. Tell me her name again," said Piper.

"Farrel Case. She mentioned she was going to bid for some of them."

"I have some other things too," Piper drew some items out of a shoulder bag on her desk. "I just took these into Philadelphia to see if Retman's Auction House would handle them, but they won't bring enough. Your friend Farrel might like them. She said she sold old silver. Really, it doesn't matter to me who buys the objects as long as the museum gets its price. I've taken things all over this part of Pennsylvania to find buyers—antique stores, consignment shops, the flea and antique markets, all sorts of auction houses."

Piper spread a pile of silver flatware on the table. I separated the pieces and picked up each one for a closer look. There was a large ornate fish server, a wide Victorian serving fork with a stag horn handle, an 800 silver punch ladle in an art deco style, an early American sucket fork, and a Georgian marrow scoop.

I picked up the hammer-formed two-tined sucket fork that had a hand-rounded spoon bowl on the other end, because it looked like the oldest piece and was in excellent condition other than some flakes of something brown on the tines. But when I turned it over there was the *Williamsburg Reproduction* stamp in the silver handle below the bowl. It was "new," and not really of any significant value.

Before I could say anything, Piper said apologetically, "Oh, I'm sorry, that doesn't belong to the museum. It's something I bought when silver was cheap, just to carry in my handbag when I have to eat a meal on the fly. These other things are all authentic though. And do feel free to look at the ancient items on the other table."

I inspected the long narrow marrow scoop. I could see by the early English marks that it was made in London by a silversmith named Hannah Northcote in the 1700s. Farrel and Jessie have an extensive collection of women silversmiths' work from that period. This was an important piece that surely Farrel would want for herself. I didn't want to tip Farrel's hand, but I knew she'd buy anything by a Georgian woman maker for a collector's price.

On the other table I gently lifted the little ushebti. Egyptian ushebtis are funerary figurines that were considered magical objects; they look like little statues of people. They were supposed to help do the work of their owners after they are deceased. This one was made of white clay. It was about ten inches long and glazed blue. It was in excellent condition for something that was two millennia old. It had hieroglyphics on it that were probably the words to the prayer that would bring the figure to life. The ancient Egyptians believed that dirt and clay had life-giving properties.

Kind of eerie that 2000 years ago the percentage of the population who strongly believed that if I recited this Egyptian prayer out loud this statue would come to life is the about same percentage of people today who believe just as strongly that God will answer their prayers.

I said, "Yes, I'm sure Farrel would like to see all these things, but..."

"But can the museum afford to part with items from its collection? Frankly, it can't afford not to," said Piper. "The museum has at least twenty similar ushebtis and a great deal of more significant silver flatware. It has more than three dozen Renaissance miniatures and only room to exhibit two or three at any given time. But to keep its doors open, what the museum needs is cash, not items in storage that will probably never go on public view."

I nodded, understanding the point.

Kathryn finished looking at the Snow catalog and readied to go.

I noticed a door at the far end of the office and asked, "Is that a way out?"

Piper said, "Well, it's sort of an old-fashioned fire escape."

"Can we use it?" I asked.

"Uh, well, I don't recommend it. Frankly, it stinks. It's tied into the sewer system somehow."

"Maggie, we should use the..." Kathryn began as I turned, lifted her canvas bag onto my shoulder and reached for the huge brass door knob. The door was heavy. I had to lean back to open it.

"The stairs are to the right. The other direction is sealed off," said Piper.

We called out our last thank-yous and plunged into the dim hallway.

The light shaft provided little illumination. Decades of city dust and grime filtered the rays of pale February daylight to a minimum. It was cool in the hall but not as cold as outside. I could feel a slight breeze coming from the left. As our eyes adjusted, we could see another light shaft about 100 feet to the left. There, a pile of rocks and concrete debris effectively blocked the way except for a dark space a foot from the ceiling; that must have been where the air movement was coming from.

To the right was the staircase. We went for it.

Kathryn's eyes darted swiftly to every surface, checking for sewer creatures. Her shoulders relaxed when it was apparent the tunnel-like hallway was not only tight and dry, but vermin free.

"It doesn't smell too bad," she said.

"Kind of dusty, but it certainly doesn't reek of shit," I said.

"Why did you want to come this way?"

"I'm drawn to doors people rarely use. I have an insatiable thirst for knowledge."

"I think it's that you're a snoop, but I'm willing to say you just like taking the less traveled path."

"You're right about that, that I'm a snoop. It made me a good investigator, but it also cut down on dinner invitations when my hosts found me peeking in their cabinets." I stopped at the foot of the stairs and looked back along the hall. "It is kind of fascinating, isn't it, that this perfectly built hallway was put here decades ago and now no one uses it. There's probably a door to every office down here."

"When I was at Central Western, some grad students told me they'd found a whole network of underground passageways that linked every building on campus. They said each door that led to the passages in the buildings was marked with a yellow and black sign that said something like: DANGER RADIOACTIVE."

"Did you investigate?" I asked.

"Would you have?"

"C'mon, it sounds like so much fun!"

"Well the doors were alarmed from the outside," Kathryn laughed softly. "It's funny, now that I really think about it, those passageways were probably marked with the *radioactive* signs in the early '60s when seeing a sign like that would strike fear into anyone's heart. But it's absurd to have dangerous radioactive material lying around that someone could accidentally stumble across. Of course the signs were a sham."

At the top of the stairs, Kathryn pushed open heavy swinging doors and we found ourselves in a lighted marble hallway. We finally reached the ground floor after another long set of broad stairs.

"I'm very excited that Piper authenticated the sculptures. I'm so glad I bought them," said Kathryn.

"So you're not going to say more negative things about her hair and make-up?"

"That was very rude of me. I was emotionally distraught," she said smiling. "If she wants to wear a lot of make-up and dye her hair in dramatic shades that's her business. I don't really understand why though. It must take her an hour to apply and it doesn't enhance her face. Perhaps she has some sort of skin condition she's covering. That doesn't explain the bright eye shadow though. Doesn't go with her Gucci coat."

"Really, Kathryn, it's not that overdone. It's not as though she was going to kill Batman," I laughed. "She was certainly sure about the sculpture. I can't wait to tell Farrel about it and about the marrow scoop too. Shall we go for a late lunch?" I said, as we got our coats from the museum checkroom.

Kathryn looked at her watch. "All I have time for is something quick. Then I have to rush off to another meeting that's going to carry into the evening. I don't think I'll be back to the loft until after 9 p.m. I'm sorry. And then tomorrow I have things all morning and afternoon, and then in the evening I told Farrel I'd work with her and the crew on the office."

"You know it's my birthday on Friday," I said archly.

"Hmmm, I like that tone of voice. Shall we celebrate your birthday all weekend?" Kathryn ran her fingers up the collar of my jacket, making a pretense of arranging my scarf. She used both hands. She looked into my eyes deeply and said, "Not that we won't see each other until then. And I won't be *too* late tonight. But Friday will be a special date, OK?"

"OK, I'll look forward to Friday, but I'm distracted by the thought that you won't be too late tonight," I said, appreciating her own provocative tone. "And of course I'll help tomorrow night on the office construction. I'm good at taping drywall. How did you know it was Gucci?"

"What?"

"Piper's coat?" I asked.

"I saw the tag... well... I looked at the tag. I can be a snoop too."

I shouldered the heavy bag of sculpture and we hurried out against the cold winter wind. We went west toward our neighborhood, while icy gusts blew the speech from our mouths. Snow was in the air, and from the looks of the darkening sky it would soon be on the ground.

Five blocks later we ducked into Brews on the Mews. We slid into a booth and put our coats in the corners of the red leather seats. I always enjoy this little cafe and not just because it's warm.

Mews old-timers still called it Pop's, its drugstore soda shop name through most of the 20th century. Its stool-lined marble-topped counter, pattern-tiled floor, brass and glass pastry display cases, and large front windows still made it seem ready for a bobby-socks rock 'n' roll teen movie. But the smell of rich coffee, fresh pastry, and soft jazz music quieted the ambiance and made it more welcoming for the coffee shop culture of the current age.

Shelly, the server who had worked here for decades, greeted us like old friends. "We have great clam chowder today. Fresh clams and everything," she said.

"Sounds lovely. I'll have that, and a Caffelatte," said Kathryn.

"I'll have the soup too, with... Would it be wrong to have root beer with clam chowder?"

"Yes," said Shelly and Kathryn in unison.

"With hot tea."

"Better," said Shelly. "Say, have you heard about Samson and Lois Henshaw? Breaking up, maybe. Well, no surprise. He's been acting wacko for a while now. Poor Lois. She's a good egg. You know she comes in here for coffee every morning like clockwork, weekdays and weekends, hasn't missed a morning in years. We chat every day. I'll get your soup."

As Shelly padded to the kitchen in her old-style waitress shoes, Kathryn said, "She's talking about the Henshaws when there was a murder yesterday? Is the Mews gossip hotline breaking down?"

"Perhaps the Henshaw story is cutting edge."

"And this Henshaw business is something *you* know firsthand?"

"Confidential," I said with a smile.

"I see. Well, then we'll talk about something else. I bet the college has Victoria Snow's papers. I want to see them."

"Would they let you take them out of the archives?"

"I doubt it. They're very strict about removing things from there, but I'll see. It depends. The bigger problem is that I just don't have the time today."

Shelly brought two bowls of chowder to our table along with our drinks. The soup was exactly what I'd wanted, piping hot, rich and satisfying, and there were even saltines to crumble in it.

We ate in silence for a few minutes, letting the warm liquid raise our core temperatures. I was nearly done when I said, "I could go to the archives. I have some work I want to get done today, but it probably won't take too long."

Kathryn looked up at me for a moment. "Yes, you could. I could give you a letter of introduction. The archives are restricted to professors and graduate students, but they also let research assistants in, and underclass students with special permission from their advisors."

"So you could be my advisor?" I said as though it was a double entendre.

Her face transformed and she became feline. She looked at me darkly, with a half-smile. "No, you could be my research assistant," she said in a tone that would easily have verged on sexual harassment if she'd said it to any real student.

"Are there perks to this job?" I parried. "Would you care to outline them?"

"There's a compensation package. We could have a meeting at 9 p.m. this evening to discuss it."

"That's amenable to me, Dr. Anthony. I follow directions without question."

"No, I don't think you do, but I have some strict teaching strategies that could improve that."

I exhaled steam. Kathryn's eye were bright.

"Yes, well," she said. Kathryn took a notebook from her bag and wrote a few sentences outlining what she wanted from the Irwin College Library Collection Archives and that I was working as her assistant in this project and should be given access.

"It's very unlikely they'll let you take anything out of the building, but each professor has a lockable shelf compartment. I'm supposed to get the new combination today. You could call me if you think you need it." Kathryn finished writing and glanced at her watch. "I'm so sorry. I really have to get going."

We paid the bill, muffled up, and hit the frigid streets of Fenchester yet again. We walked together to the campus. We stopped at the back entrance of the English Department building.

"My meeting's in here," she said through the soft scarf covering the lower half of her face.

We kissed goodbye, not very effectively through scarves, but her eyes warmed me with a smile that promised much more effective kisses later. I still had to go another block to make it to the library. I immediately missed her, and then my mind wandered to what our date might hold on Friday night and I missed her even more.

Geez you're sweet on that girl, said a voice in my head. *So what are you going to do about it?*

"What indeed."

CHAPTER 9

"Could you tell me how to get to the archives?" I asked the young man who finally appeared behind the information desk.

"What?"

"Can you tell me how to get to the archives?"

"Which ones?"

"The ones in this building?"

"This building? You mean the library?"

"Yes, the library." *Why does this kind of thing always happen to me at information desks? It's like someone just turned off the universal translator so the person I'm speaking to can't understand my alien language.* He looked at me blankly while I considered what to say next. And then I was rescued.

"Good afternoon, Maggie," Amanda Knightbridge said in her most authoritative tone. "Mr. Sellers, are you helping Ms. Gale?"

Amanda Knightbridge was wearing a long burgundy wool skirt, a heavy pullover sweater, and an imposing expression that required compliance. After all, she was the head of one of the largest departments at the College.

"Oh yes... uh, er, Dr. Knightbridge... yes..." He looked back at me. "What was it you wanted again?"

"I'm Dr. Anthony's research assistant and..."

"No need for that," said Amanda briskly. "I shall escort you to the archives. Please give Ms. Gale an assistant badge, Mr. Sellers. Maggie, you can check your canvas bag here at the desk. Mr. Sellers will keep it in a locked cabinet and he will give you the key. You may take your shoulder bag with your computer in it, along with you."

Sellers gently stowed the bag in a locker and gave me the key, then fumbled up a badge. I clipped it on. As Amanda whisked me toward a pair of glass doors, I thanked her for cutting at least a half hour from my quest.

She stopped briefly by a display of reference materials that was marked 'Irwin Professors' Publications,' and waved her hand over a row. "Did you know that Kathryn has written a number of books?" she asked. "Rather an impressive body of work, you must admit."

I began to say that I knew about Kathryn's books, but when I saw them there all together in a long hard-copy row in real time, I felt a surge of possessive pride. I smiled and nodded.

"So now you are researching the Victoria Snow sculpture. That's the task Kathryn has assigned to her new research assistant?" Amanda said with amusement as we began to walk again.

"Yes, we took the sculpture to Piper Staplehurst at the Museum this morning and she told us there was no record of any of the works Kathryn bought. So Kathryn thought of looking though the papers Victoria Snow left to the College."

"Ms. Staplehurst confirmed the figures were by Victoria Snow though, did she not?"

"No doubt in her mind. She was shocked by the find. Have you seen any of the Snow papers, Amanda?"

"I do believe she donated everything to Irwin College, including her personal papers, but I'm ashamed to say I haven't reviewed them. I have read the Carbondales' book of course. It tells a bit about Victoria Snow's life. Have you had a chance to look at the book?"

I felt like a kid in fourth grade who'd been called on to give a report on a book I hadn't finished. Luckily I'd at least opened it.

"I read some parts of it this morning. Evangeline certainly was beautiful."

"Yes, she was. You know, so much in Fenchester can be traced back to the incredible wealth of Merganser Hunterdon. But then I suppose that's true in any town where one person controls most of the money."

I nodded and added 'Read the Carbondales' book' to my To Do list.

Glass doors opened into a large space that held a group of work tables. Beyond them were rows of stacks so long I couldn't see their end. To the right were a few empty glassed-in research rooms with doors that stood open. Only one of the tables in front of us was strewn with books and the papers from three acid-free archive boxes. A young woman was perched on a stool at the table, her eyes swinging back and forth from a dusty pile of papers to her laptop screen, as though watching a slow game of tennis.

"Now," said Amanda, "the archives are quite extensive... In the back of the building there is a separate elevator and stairs that will take you to one of the four other archive floors."

"There are four more floors like this upstairs?" I asked incredulously.

"Oh no, Maggie, the four floors are underground and to the east. And each of them is much larger than this. The College tour guides say each is over a city block in size, but I'm not sure that's accurate. Nevertheless we start here." Amanda led me to the information desk. It took several moments for a librarian to come out of a back room to the computer station to talk to us.

"We would like to see the Victoria Willomere Snow papers," Amanda Knightbridge said to a young librarian.

She peered through thick glasses and a long fringe of dark hair to see exactly who was speaking, realized who it was, and rapidly tossed her magazine under the desk. "Oh, Dr. Knightbridge. Uh, yes, of course," she said whirling toward her computer screen.

The librarian clicked keys and scanned data. After a few minutes, she said plaintively, "I'm sorry Dr. Knightbridge, but I don't see a file that has that kind of title." She clicked a few more times, then shook her head and said, "Is there anything else I can get for you?"

"Are you sure there is nothing in the system? Try *Fenchester Sculpture*, or say... *Women Artists*," said Amanda.

"The system is very carefully cross-referenced. If the name Snow was anywhere in the system. Um, I could ask..." She looked over her shoulder toward to an older man who saw Amanda and rapidly joined us.

His name badge read *Senior Librarian* with the single name CURTIS under the title. He looked like a cross between Johnny Depp doing Ichabod Crane and Don Knotts, complete with extra large Adam's apple. Amanda told him what she wanted and he turned immediately to the computer screen and entered all sorts of codes.

After nearly five minutes of rapid key work he gulped and said, "Dr. Knightbridge, are you sure this is something the library has?"

"Quite sure, Mr. Curtis" said Amanda. "I happen to know the book on Fenchester history by the Carbondales cites the library's addition of the Snow papers to its collection."

I reached in my bag and pulled out the book on Fenchester history by Gabriel and Suzanne. In the reference notes at the end, it cited the donation of the papers in 1938 by the library's notation number. Amanda turned the book around and pointed to the citation triumphantly.

Mr. Curtis looked at it carefully, then nervously entered the notation number. And nothing came up.

Dr. Amanda Knightbridge's features became rather fierce. I'd seen that look before. Bright focused eyes, like a bird of prey. She said in a quiet but somehow frightening voice, "Is Isabella Santiago here?"

Senior Librarian Curtis looked nervously around. The younger librarian with the fringe visibly blanched. Curtis stage-whispered in a shaky voice,

"I believe she's always here, Dr. Knightbridge. But she doesn't like to be disturbed."

"Maggie, I'll be back in a moment." Amanda stalked off far more stiffly than her general floating gait. I could faintly hear Amanda calling out, *"Isabella,"* far back in the stacks.

I stood there with the two librarians, who were rapidly transforming into cowardly lions about to meet OZ. Mr. Curtis tugged at his collar, looked at his watch, mumbled something about having to help someone, and then sped off so fast I could practically hear the *Roadrunner* sound effect. The young woman librarian seemed terror stricken to be left alone and disappeared without explanation.

So who was this Isabella Santiago, who could strike fear into the hearts of librarians everywhere?

Seconds later, Amanda came out of one of the study rooms down the hall, followed by a female Yoda. She was tiny, wrinkled, and very old. She looked kind of bald, but it was just that her white hair was the same color as her skin. People have told me that I am freakishly pale, but this woman made me look like a San Tropez ad. She was so white, she kind of glowed. She wore a long loose robe of brocade material tied at the waist with a silk sash. Under it she had on some kind of layered white dress. She had huge owl-like gold-rimmed glasses, even bigger than Judith Levi's. She could have been a hundred years old.

"Isabella, please meet Maggie Gale. Maggie, this is Dr. Santiago. She knows this library very well."

Dr. Isabella Santiago advanced on me with swift baby steps. She tipped her head up to peer at me through huge owl corneas. I said, "Very nice to meet you, Dr. Santiago. You've worked here for a long time?"

She said, "Pffft." She turned toward Amanda and said in a surprisingly loud and clear voice, "What does she want?"

"Maggie would like to see the Victoria Snow papers."

"Ask..." She waved her hand toward the space where the small herd of librarians had been before they'd sensed danger and scattered.

"She did so, however, they could not find the reference to the papers in the system."

"System," she muttered, flicking her hand to the side. In a clear but creaky voice she said, "I'm working on a treatise on 16th century building materials and I do not have time to... Oh never mind. Follow me and hurry up about it!" She darted toward the stairs and rapidly descended three flights, then zipped toward the stacks like a cockroach heading under the refrigerator when the light comes on. She zig-zagged down nine or ten aisles and came to an abrupt halt in the middle of a row so dimly marked I couldn't read the tag. She nodded toward a high shelf.

In the middle of a series of brown archive boxes was one labeled Snow, Victoria Willomere. I had to get a kick stool to reach and slide the heavy box out. By the time I stepped down, Dr. Isabella Santiago had scuttered back to the 16th century, leaving me and Amanda alone.

As I carried the archive box back to the study area, Amanda said, "You know, Maggie, Isabella Santiago doesn't talk to people very often. We were lucky to draw her away from her work. It seems to help a great deal to be the head of the History Department. She never spoke to me when I was just a professor. I've worked quite hard to establish communication with her."

I looked back at Amanda and in the dim light of the stacks I could see she was smiling to herself.

"But now you know her?"

"I don't really know her, but I've found that if one has a good reason to seek her she'll come out of hiding. She certainly knows everything about the collections."

The way Amanda Knightbridge was talking was giving me that feeling you get when the eerie background music comes on. I wanted to ask more but Amanda said, "I'm afraid I have a meeting soon. You can use this research room here. Let me know what you are able to find out."

Amanda reminded me to wear gloves when handling any of the papers and indicated a box of white cotton ones on a shelf.

She said, "You know, Kathryn could request the research department make digital files of these papers for her. I believe there is a young woman there who has developed quite a devotion to Kathryn."

"Swell."

"Nevertheless," said Amanda with a hint of amusement. Then in a more serious tone she went on, "Maggie, have you told Kathryn how you feel about her?"

"Um, I care for her very much."

"Yes, that's evident. May I say that I don't think you should worry about convention. There are stages in a relationship and many feel that a certain amount of time should go by."

"Yes."

"But I'm not sure one of the many is Kathryn and I feel somehow that you do not fit into that group, either... Ah well, this is not my business. But, I have known Kathryn for some little while. She will give you cues, and I hope you take heed of them. I have great faith in you. I have great faith in you both."

On that prognostication Dr. Amanda Knightbridge turned on her heel and floated from the room. She left me wondering more about Kathryn and me than about the archive box on the table. I really didn't think that just *telling* Kathryn I cared for her... would be enough to make us both feel as though we were... hmmm... well, I guess Farrel and Jessie would say, as though we were a team. It wasn't about words. The total willingness to trust and to yield—we just weren't to that point. But if we didn't get there soon I feared it would create a wrinkle in our relationship that we might never be able to smooth out.

"Oh crikey!" I sighed.

I slipped on gloves, removed the cover of the archive box, and gently drew out the acid-free folders. I set my laptop up next to the folder piles.

I sorted the items carefully. The first group were legal papers. I gently went through each of the piles dividing them by type. In the last stack was a small thick leather-bound book with the initials V.W.S. on the front.

I opened it carefully. The first page was inscribed:

Dim Eden of delight,
In whom my heart springs upward like a palm;
Loving your morning strength, your evening calm,
Your star-inspired Night --
A sweeter breath blows upward from the sea,
Like a fresh hope from God's eternity; --
Latest and best, are you then coming?

Nay — shadow is not here;
Save of the rocks upon the gleaming sands,
And that which moves beside me with clasped hands,
A suffering shadow, drear
With watching, it would seem, the endless swell,
Great, white-faced waves, sent ceaselessly to quell
The stern and silent shore with thunder.

To Victoria on the occasion of her 30th birthday, May this present help you record your morning strength and evening calm and everything in between!
-from Anne and Abby. Feb. 1st, '75.

I whistled out loud. Journals are treasure and this one was gold.

And *Anne and Abby...* were Anne Whitney and Abby Manning. This was Anne Whitney's poem Kathryn was quoting in the cemetery. Wow, this was really something. I couldn't wait to look through it.

The book looked like it was part of a set. I looked back in the box, but it was the only one in there.

I took the Carbondales' book from my bag, found Victoria in the index, and read the brief account of her life. She had traveled and had shows of her work in several cities, but after 1876 always came back to Fenchester where she lived a rather solitary and very long life in Fen House. She had died in 1938 at the age of 93. Interesting, I hadn't known she had lived in Fen house. She must have bought it after Evangeline died. Now that I had a little context I went back to the papers.

Among them were Victoria's will, passport, birth certificate, some deeds; there was even a driver's license. There were catalogs documenting all her shows with pages listing all the works exhibited. These could be helpful. I put them aside.

Piper Staplehurst had said there was no record of the works Kathryn bought at the flea market, so that would mean there was no mention of the works in this box, because certainly the college and museum had already cataloged the information in these papers when they were originally placed in these archives.

I turned back to the journal and carefully turned to the first page. The writing was tiny and in a flowing artistic script that was hard to read. I finally discerned that the page described a trip Victoria was taking on a ship. I clicked on a bright extension arm lamp and swung it over the page; then I squinted at the minute letters.

March 15th, 1875:

Leaving Liverpool for New York on the Bothnia. One of Cunard's newest ships. I must say it has every convenience. My stateroom on the spar deck is spacious. Would that I had had such a room when I was in Rome.

As it turns out I know several of the other 1st class passengers and I hazard to guess quite a few of those riding steerage, though I do not see a way in which one in 1st class could venture to even converse with someone in that part of the ship. Totally blocked off.

I find this trip so different from my voyage on the Scotia ten years ago. Truly a maiden voyage for me, if not the ship itself. In fact, that ship seems quaint to me now, with its huge paddlewheel.

Of all the crossings I've taken, that really was the most memorable. For the ship itself, if not the company. I suppose the sails are about the same even now, and they say the speed is as well, but the coal dust and noise are definitely reduced and the plain fact of hundreds of other people on board below decks feels decidedly different. Not frightening as some of my more timid friends would suggest, but as though we all share a similar adventure into the incalculable future.

We will all arrive in New York eleven days hence. I am eager to land.

I was amazed that in 1875 you could cross the ocean in a steamer in just eleven days. I looked back in the box for other travel papers and found her college diploma. She went to Oberlin. She must have known the artist Edmonia Lewis there. Lewis had been at Oberlin during the Civil War period and they were both sculptors.

Victoria's handwriting was difficult to read. You barely see anyone's handwriting anymore, much less flowery 19th century calligraphy from the point of a quill. But as I continued to turn through the pages, I got used to her style.

April 11th, 1875:
The delivery and installation of my newest piece at the Vanderbilt's is done. One of Cornelius's older sons has suggested it may go to the new college the family is financing. As always, everyone is charming to me and the attention of the young men is almost comical. Yet my heart pines, but I feel I cannot hope. I wish Anne was here to advise me. Perhaps I will go to Boston to see her on the pretext of helping with her newest commission. Then I could ask her or Abby what would be my best course. But alas, I must first take Edmonia's work to New Orleans.

She's talking about Anne Whitney in this passage. She and her partner Abigail Manning lived in Boston. I turned to my laptop and found some entries on Anne Whitney's life. She was indeed working on a preliminary study to enter in a commission competition for the statue of abolitionist Clark Sumner in 1875.

And it must be Edmonia Lewis's work Victoria is going to deliver. I skimmed for another reference to Edmonia and found one.

April 23rd, 1875,

Have finally reached New Orleans to deliver Edmonia's work. Though it has been ten years, one can still see the devastation of war. Amazingly, the trains are running well.

Though I am grateful that my trip was fully financed by my longtime college friend and colleague, and proud to be emissary of her work, there is grimness everywhere that pains me. Illness and loss. Yet, when I find sympathy in my heart for the current lives of struggling landowners, I then feel a kick of reversal when they speak of the blessed old days. They seem to have no awareness that their easy lives years ago were genteel due to the forced labor of human beings. A moral outrage, still.

The fact that I am delivering a monumental sculpture made by a woman of African, Haitian, and Ojibwe descent pleases me. Particularly so when white men disparage my role (as a woman) in conducting this important work to its destination!

I gasped inwardly at this passage and then my eyes widened at the next sections that were clearly referring to Charlotte Cushman and Emma Stebbins! I skipped through them.

April 29th, 1875,

Must rush back to Boston to see Charlotte do one of her readings at the Globe Theatre. Emma suggests in her latest letter that it may be Charlotte's last performance. And unlike her many final performances as Hamlet, I suspect Emma may be accurate.

May 16th, 1875,

Charlotte's performance last night at the Globe was moving. I was in tears, not just from the words she spoke, but for the look on Emma's dear face as she watched her.

I was whisked to a party at some fine restaurant after the show in a private room that looked much like Delmonico's.

Charlotte and Emma are going on tour through New York State and then will rest in Newport. They implore me to visit.

I clicked my laptop for some quick research to confirm the timelines, then flipped ahead looking for more interesting entries:

July 4th, 1875,

The City of Philadelphia and whole of the country is already in preparation for the Centennial, even this one year in advance. Pavilions, memorials, and monuments are already in production. I am in the running for a work in the main American Pavilion. This commission should cement my reputation so I am in hopes that I will not face unfair treatment because I am of the fairer sex.

Edmonia is already at work on what is surely her most ambitious piece. The Cleopatra sculpture will be hailed, no doubt, as a huge success at the exhibition. Indeed Edmonia has amassed so much money she is already speaking of retirement somewhere in France. Perhaps I envy her... and yet, I feel alone and in need of affection.

September 1st, 1875,

These weeks in Boston with Anne and Abby have been idyllic. They dote on me as loving aunts. So much like Rome where sisters of my own heart followed their true desires. I should have done so then. At least I would have known if the flame could burn in her as well.

Of course Anne is furious that the commission she won for the Sumner monument has been revoked because the authorities have realized she is of the female sex. Some nonsense about a 'woman could never sculpt a man's legs.' Absurd! Anne vows to do the sculpture anyway and already has some interest.

Anne and Abby encourage me to follow my heart. The heavens know I want to, as does the devil. But my better judgement cautions. I do recognize, with no little amusement, that if my declaration is spurned, Anne and particularly Abby will devote themselves to finding me a new object for my affections. Indeed they have invited several extraordinarily beautiful young prospects to dinner, who all seem rather remarkably eager.

Yet I received a gentle note yesterday with tender if non-enlightening words, which renewed my desire. I have written back and hope for an invitation to visit.

Will go to Newport to see Charlotte and Emma, then should consider returning to Rome to begin work again... if no other invitation arrives.

Yeah, this was getting good. Victoria was after a woman, just like all those other hot lesbian artists, actors, and poets in Rome in the 1860s. I was willing to bet the farm that it was Evangeline, but the only thing I had to go on was the way Victoria had modeled the nude sculptures of her.

The journal was beginning to read like a hot romance novel and I couldn't put it down. The problem was, I was acutely aware that this was real life. It might not end the way romance novels always do. Victoria could be kicked in the head by the painful revelation that the object of her affection was *not that kind of a girl.* Or perhaps worse yet, that she wasn't ready for commitment.

I sighed, *It keeps coming back to that, doesn't it?*

There was a small drawing labeled *Home of Charlotte Cushman* in the journal margin. It was a beautiful house on the coastline. Below it were these enlightening entries:

October 1st, 1875,

Newport, Rhode Island. Magnificent house, yet quite different from the piazza in Rome. Excellent and well appointed studio for Emma, which she never uses. Several other 'sisters of the heart' also here visiting Charlotte. In that respect it mirrors Rome!

Charlotte's nephew Ned has married the lovely Emma Crow, who is now pregnant with his child. I have to say I had always suspected that Emma C. was devoted in the most intimate ways to Charlotte herself and was surprised to hear that Emma S. allowed the charming young thing to follow them to Italy and then back here to Newport. But then, what Charlotte wants, she wins. Both Emmas are devoted to her and seem to tolerate each other. And thus Charlotte has achieved her role as sultana, a role she has been rehearsing for with various results for many years.

October 5th, 1875,

Late last night, Charlotte found her way to my room, which is far in the east wing of the house, distant from anyone else. I supposed that was her idea. For suddenly I found her sitting on my bed with a small lantern. Though Charlotte is certainly not in the bloom of youth, being well over fifty, the lamplight softened her features and brightened her eyes.

She asked me if I was comfortable and if there was anything I wanted. She caressed my face and then drew her fingers, without undue haste, along my throat to the softness of my bosom where they rested as she began to compliment me in words I frankly found enchanting. She has a magnificent voice, and after all she is master of the craft of compelling speech.

Among other things, she said, "You are remarkably fair of face, but I find your strength very attractive."

I must admit that I was not repelled. In fact it had been so long since I have enjoyed a woman's affectionate caress that the depth of my breathing spoke its own encouragement. Clearly the meaning of it was not lost on her.

She said simply, "Shall I kiss you, Victoria?"

A rather considerable part of me spoke emphatic yeses in my mind, but then I remembered the two Emmas in another part of the house and marveled at Charlotte's incredible roguery.

"Charlotte," I laughed, "just how many women do you need?"

She laughed too. "Victoria, my dear, I need all of them! But I see I may not be having you? Not tonight? Ah well, more fool you."

"How does that make me a fool? I can't help but worry that the women who love you will be very angry with me," I asked her.

She replied, "My little lover is with child. Her husband, my nephew Ned, does seem to find his way to her far more than I. And my dearest heart Emma is simply too tired. They put you in this far away room so they could sleep, not so that I wouldn't find you. I believe they think that while you are following the scent of lavender you should consider that when you woo her, you'll be all the better lover if you had the benefit of my... experience. Many women honor me for the things I've taught them, as do their current lovers. But, my dear, I think perhaps my teaching days may soon be over. My Emmas feel this too. I know it. That's why they have directed me to you." She laughed lightly. "A farewell performance of its own kind."

I laughed again, as if to deflect her words, but I was feeling deeply moved by her offer of mentorship in these delicate arts. Deeply moved in urgent physical ways. I had the need to minister to a pain I hadn't felt in some years.

Charlotte continued, "You know, I've met her. I'm sure you will win her. Don't you want to please her in every way? I'm an excellent teacher, and in the waning days of my life I find it better to give than to receive. Especially in these days when my body fails me so grievously. Now, as the Bard said, 'Come give us a taste of your quality.'"

I could resist no longer. In acquiescence I drew down the sheet to expose my silk chemise. I confess it was my very best nightdress, the one I had made in Paris. Just a whisper of fabric. And I admit I had worn it this night in vague hopes that I would be visited by one of the many women in Charlotte's house.

Charlotte admired my nightgown and what she could see through it with a lingering glance. Then she kissed me deeply, as the overture to her next acts. She easily slipped the gown down my shoulders and her appraisal of what was revealed was more than a glance. After all, I am rather blessed in proportion and though it is not a boon to me personally, I have found others were delighted by my abundance.

Indeed Charlotte paid worthy tribute, with both her hands and her mouth. And rather more thoroughly than others have done, yet without asperity. To my surprising delight, this ministration caused me to find my first of many spendings of the night. When she found her way below, her attention became more focused, and she was able to do more than assuage my needs. There seemed to be a constant rekindling of them and then relief, repeated in waves as though crashing on the shore.

When I heard the hall clock strike 2 a.m., I became aware that this edifying interlude was at an end. Yet Charlotte left me neither besotted nor disaffected. Indeed I was hazy from pleasure, but I found myself shedding indolence to attend to her words.

She said, "Take your skills to your angel, my dear, and make her happy, for in her you will find happiness too."

I will heed this advice, and I told her so.

Charlotte had been quite true to her words. She taught me several important things about the delights and needs of my own sex and how to slake, then prime for more. I learned more to enhance these important skills in this one night than I had learned to increase my skill at carving stone in a full year at Harriet's studio. I now see why so many women have been devoted to Charlotte Cushman and I confess that I will always be grateful for her mentoring in this doss classroom, after the hall clock had struck midnight.

When I was done reading that passage I was literally sweating. Not only was it a hot little real-life love scene but it was history. Charlotte

Cushman teaching Victoria Snow the subtleties of the bedroom while
Emma Stebbins and Emma Crow were down the hall. Jiminy Crickets!

But what about the lavender scent Victoria was chasing. Surely that
confirms Evangeline Lavender Fen was the angel of whom Charlotte
spoke. I skimmed through the next few pages of the journal. Victoria had
gone to Boston with Emma Stebbins and Charlotte Cushman and had then
received a telegram from the Centennial Exposition committee asking her
to come to Philadelphia to confer about her sculpture for their exhibit.
Victoria was thrilled that they had accepted her. She set up a small studio
in Philly to begin work on it, rather than going back to Rome. The next fifty
or so pages described the studio and her work. It was interesting to me, but
didn't contain clues about the object of her affection. Victoria seemed too
nervous to mention her. She didn't want to press anything in case she was
rejected. Sometimes it's easier to live in the fantasy than try to play it out
and find it was just that—a fantasy.

I read on:

October 20th, 1875,
    *Charlotte has not come to my room hence. She has complained
of illness, and the Emmas and I convinced her to go to Boston to
seek medical treatment fearing a recurrence of the cancer that
gripped her several years ago.*

And then skipped to the last entries in this section:

February 5th, 1876,
    *I have rushed to Boston to be by Charlotte's hospital bed
and to give Emma S. as much help and comfort as I am able. I
can't describe how I feel, short of feeling that it is impossible for
someone as full of life as Charlotte Cushman, to...*

The rest of the line was unreadably smeared by what looked like tear stains.
Lower on the page in a slightly different color ink Victoria wrote:

    *In the last moments of her life Charlotte, numbed by morphine,
took my hand and told me to seek my passion.*
    *She said in a voice still rich but weakened, "She will never
be yours unless you go to her and tell her you love her. Why wait
when you know your mind? Go to her, Victoria. I have heard by the
most recent post the barest hint from Evangeline that her financial*

situation is poor. She has a young brother and sisters and a mother to support. I'm sending her some gentle sum to help her carry on.

And, my dear, I shall arrange for you to have a commission there. Yes... I shall do that, I have already decided. I believe there is a college that educates young women in the Arts..."

Charlotte turned in her bed and waved Emma to her. Emma was never absent when Charlotte needed her.

"Emma, please check with my solicitors on the arrangements." Then she turned back to me. "It will be my gift. My gift to you, Victoria."

Emma dutifully left the room to send telegrams making the arrangements.

Charlotte said, "You must go as soon as the commission is confirmed." And then she smiled. (More tear stains on the page.)

I was tearing up right along with Victoria just reading about it. In her last moments Charlotte was using all her resources to help her friends. And that was certainly a worthy scene at the end of her or anyone's life performance.

In the next few pages Victoria chronicled Charlotte's rapid decline. She described Emma Stebbins sitting by Charlotte's bed with a cool cloth, holding Charlotte's hand and keeping her free from pain with some kind of morphine brew. Victoria even drew a sketch of this tableaux in the journal. It was a simple line drawing, but I could read the profound emotion Emma was enduring by her posture and the angle of her head.

I stared at it for many minutes, losing track of the present. I was transported back in time into the role of the artist herself, considering the effectiveness of each line before me, feeling their meaning. Suddenly I *was* Victoria Willomere Snow. I was pleased with the drawing for the most part, but there was one line that seemed a bit out of place, the tilt of Emma's head needed a slightly stronger jaw line. I looked up expecting to see Charlotte Cushman in her last hours, ministered to by Emma Stebbins. But there on the other side of the glass partition I saw nothing but a brief glimpse of Isabella Santiago looking back at me and then gliding off to the stacks with a huge leatherbound reference.

When she got to the edge of the first bookcase, Dr. Santiago turned to glance at me again. She gave one simple head nod and disappeared behind the first row of ancient architecture references.

And then just as suddenly I was back in the present. I stared down at Victoria's drawing, then turned the page.

On February 25th, 1876, Victoria Snow wrote:

Charlotte died on Friday the 18th. I attended her funeral, which was a rather wonderful affair of dignitaries, actors, artists, and all mode of women who loved her.

And then the notification of my commission came.

Just as Charlotte wanted, I find myself on the way to Fenchester, Pennsylvania, by way of New York, to try my hand at wooing. I can only hope.

I looked at the clock and realized the hours had flown by. It was almost 9 p.m., which meant that Kathryn should be done with her meeting soon.

I texted her, <Archive gold Vic had sex with C Cushman>

Literally five seconds later my cell played *Save the Last Dance for Me*, which I'd programed in as Kathryn's ringtone. I snorted. Now I knew exactly how to get her out of a meeting.

"Read it to me..." she said, before I even had a chance to say hello.

"Are you out of your meeting?"

"No, I got your text and told them I had to go to the restroom, which is where I am. Read it to me. Now."

"The whole passage?"

"Do it."

"OK, this is from Victoria Snow's journal circa 1875." I read her the passage straight through, without comment.

When I got to the end there was a long silent pause. I thought I'd lost her signal, but then I heard, "Oh Maggie, I'm really enjoying having you as a research assistant." She exhaled. I could feel her heat and excitement over the phone.

"Yeah?" I said in a low voice.

"Yes!"

"About that compensation package you mentioned..."

"It's increased."

"Yay!"

"I could write a book from this little tidbit."

"So are you done with your meeting? Come over here and see the journal. Then we can walk home together."

"Oh dear," she sighed.

"What?"

"This meeting isn't even half over and it's not something I can leave. It has to do with the funding for my women's history program. If I'm not here, I'll get stiffed. I can't..."

"I understand."

"Do you?"

"Yes, I really do. I used to work for the government, you know. One time I was in a union meeting that went on for three days."

"You're a gem."

"I know." We both laughed. "Do you have any idea when it might end?"

"I'm hoping about two hours. Bolton can give me a ride home."

"Who?"

"Bolton Winpenny. I told you about him. He was at the retreat.

"The steel drummer? The one who got you out of the retreat early?"

"Yes."

"I'm indebted to him. By the way, this journal seems to be part of a set, but there's only one in here."

"I can't wait to look at it all tomorrow. Put everything on my shelf in the locked part. I got the combination. It's 6...6...6."

"What luck, you'll never forget that."

"Why didn't anyone know about this journal? This should have been researched years ago. I don't understand it."

"Well, it's very hard to read. Also box was mis-shelved. No, that's not right; it wasn't in the data system. It didn't contain the reference."

"But how could you find it? The archives are huge. The college boasts that there are over three hundred thousand archived collections."

"Well, I saw Amanda and she..."

"Oh, Amanda helped you. But how could she even..."

"She got Isabella Santiago to help us. Dr. Santiago went right to them."

Kathryn laughed out loud. "Very good! No really, so Amanda found the archive box?"

"No," I explained again, "she got Isabella Santiago to help us, though she seemed pretty pissed off about it. She's a riot, so tiny and pale and kind of interesting looking. She must have been very pretty when she was a younger woman."

There was a long pause, then Kathryn said, "You saw her? You really saw Isabella Santiago? Really? You're not teasing me?"

"Yeah, haven't you seen her?"

There was another long pause, then finally Kathryn said, "Maggie, no one has ever really *seen* Isabella Santiago, well not in the flesh anyway. She isn't a real person. *She's the library ghost.*

CHAPTER 10

Kathryn insisted she wasn't joking about the ghost in the library and I insisted I really had seen Dr. Isabella Santiago. We ended by being amused that we were both so positive.

"You haven't eaten, have you? I just called Fen-Ultimate Pizza to deliver some supper because we were all starving. By now you must be too. I'm paying, so I think you should come over and have a piece while we're on a break." Kathryn added gently, "Would you? I want to see you."

"Be there in five minutes."

When I got to the English Department Building on the quad behind Administration, I met the delivery person from Fen-Ultimate Pizza outside. I could smell the oregano before I even saw her. I paid and tipped her and carried the pies and other bags of drinks and side dishes to the meeting so I'd be all the more welcome as the bearer of brick-oven ambrosia.

In a large third-floor classroom, various professorial types slouched on chairs and leaned on tables in break mode. They were all so academic that if you'd put black graduation gowns on them they could have played a revival of *Good Bye Mr. Chips*. Of course Kathryn would be in the hot Mrs. Chips role.

When Kathryn saw me her eyes brightened.

"Everyone," she called, "please meet Maggie Gale. Not only the bearer of edible gifts, but the charmer of ghosts!"

They swarmed the pizza as only college faculty can. Kathryn put an arm around my waist and propelled me pizzaward as we argued gently about who would pay the check. She won and gave me cash.

"Maggie, this is Dr. Paul Ericson. I think you two met at the college holiday party," said Kathryn.

Paul Ericson was opening a box of salad. He was blond, fair-skinned, and had a full beard and twinkling eyes. He had on one of those tan corduroy jackets with leather patches at the elbows. He waved to me because his mouth was full.

"And this is Dr. Bolton Winpenny."

So this was the steel drummer from the retreat. Winpenney had close-cropped reddish hair and a beard that mirrored the color of the sweater under his camel hair blazer, also with leather patched elbows. Unlike Paul, who was wearing khaki pants, Bolton was wearing straight legged blue jeans that fit him well. He looked younger than his name.

"Bolton," he said shaking my hand.

"And," said Kathryn, "you know Daniel Cohen."

Dan Cohen crossed the room and bear-hugged me. Two months before, he and I had shared a high adrenaline fifteen minutes in an emergency, as we risked our lives to save another. It was one of those things that cements a friendship even though I'd only seen him a few times since.

Kathryn introduced me to several other people who were too busy with the food to do anything more than nod.

Paul Ericson, with pizza slice in hand, said, "Did I hear Kathryn say something about ghosts?"

"Maggie tells me she saw Isabella Santiago earlier this evening," said Kathryn.

"In the library?" asked Paul.

I nodded.

"Seriously?"

"Yes, Dr. Ericson, I really did." I smiled, nodding.

"Huh! Call me Paul."

"Wait, I thought she wasn't real. Don't people on campus refer to her as the library spirit?" asked Bolton Winpenny.

This time Kathryn nodded.

Dan Cohen was staring at me.

I said to Dan, "Do you believe she's a ghost?"

He shrugged. "I don't use the library archives much. I've never seen her. I thought she was an urban legend. But if *you've* seen her Maggie, then..." Dan nodded his head but didn't quite finish the sentence.

I turned to Paul Ericson, who was saying, "About four years ago I saw a woman in a white flowing dress hovering around the end of one of the stacks. I went after her, but she disappeared around a corner and when I got there she was gone. When I asked one of the librarians about her, he said nervously that she shouldn't be disturbed. Did she actually talk to you?"

I thought back. "Well, no, she just made a dismissive sound and waved me off. Amanda Knightbridge was there. She spoke to her."

"Oh, well, Amanda," said Paul knowingly. "What did she say to Amanda?"

"Something about researching 16th century building materials."

"Really? Huh." Paul shrugged moving back toward the pizza. "Maybe I should try to talk to her sometime."

Kathryn was looking at me thoughtfully. She said, "Are you sure this wasn't a dream?"

"No, no, it wasn't a dream. Do these people really think she's a ghost?"

Kathryn raised her eyebrows.

"But I *saw* her."

"On campus it's the people who haven't seen her who don't believe in her," said Kathryn.

"Do you believe in her?"

Kathryn leaned into me. "I didn't until tonight," she whispered. "Maggie, you better get some pizza before it's all gone."

Another committee member came in from outside, reeking of tobacco smoke.

"Maggie Gale," said Kathryn in introduction, "this is Carla Zimmer. Carla's in the Architectural Design Department. She was Rowlina Roth-Holtzman's grad assistant, but she's just been hired into the Department."

I covertly eyed Carla. She wasn't unfortunate in appearance. Dark hair pulled back, even-toned skin, dark eyes. Hard to tell about her figure; she was wearing one of those long bulky sweaters. I noticed she was eyeing me back at the same time as I checked her out. She turned abruptly in the guise of grabbing a soda. Kinda of twitchy for a person who'd managed to score a job in this desperate economy.

"It is Rowlina Roth now. She has dropped the Holtzman," Carla Zimmer said with her head turned.

Kathryn and I went for the last slices and settled at the big round table to concentrate on fine dining.

Paul Ericson turned to me. "I've heard you and Kathryn are in quite a whirlwind romance? Is this leading to something serious?"

A silence fell over the table, until Kathryn sighed with amusement. "Really, Paul." Then she turned to me and said, "Paul has a college-wide reputation for being direct."

"Was that rude? I'm sorry," said Paul.

He seemed to genuinely want to know, but not in a gossipy way. I guessed he was Kathryn's campus version of my friend Farrel and my sister Sara, who'd each grilled Kathryn in their own ways to discover whether her intentions with me were honorable. Though they hadn't done it so publicly.

"To answer your questions, yes, yes, and no it wasn't rude," I said.

The tension eased. Kathryn smiled, looking down at the table. Dan Cohen, who had told me a while ago that he was a PFLAG dad, grinned broadly, and Bolton clapped once and said, "Great!"

Most of the others in the room looked up when they heard Bolton clap and smiled.

Only Carla Zimmer reacted with discomfort. She tried to cover her nervous expression by turning and coughing but I saw her wrinkled nose and deer-in-the-headlights eyes.

"I know you're all engaged in an important discussion, so I'll let you get back to work," I said. "Please don't keep Kathryn any later than..."

"No Maggie, don't rush off," said Bolton. We need your input on something we were talking about before the meeting. I was explaining to Paul how important it is to be *out*."

"Well, I just wondered why Gay people would choose to be out, if that meant they might experience discrimination."

"Are you married, Paul?" I asked.

"Yes, I am. I have the honor to be married to a wonderful person. I think you met Caren at the holiday party at the president's mansion."

"Oh, yes, I remember. She'd just done some major work reorganizing the doctoral program in Art History, right? What's she doing now?"

"Yes, it was a big job, and now she's getting ready to go on a tour with some grad students to Italy. Then she'll go on to France for a conference in..."

I was looking at him, smiling. He halted abruptly. "Oh... oh, I see!" He sat back in his chair with a look of complete comprehension.

"So, Paul, just to be sure you really understand this..." Kathryn said.

"Yes, I get it. It would be impossible for me to not talk about Caren. I'm proud of her; I love her. If I had to pretend she didn't exist... Yeah, I see. It would eat at me every day," he said. "OK, so then, do you think it's wrong to be in the closet? Is there any excuse?"

"People should keep their personal business to themselves. What people do in the bedroom has nothing to do with their lives," said Carla Zimmer with surprising sharpness. I couldn't help remembering that her boss Rowlina Roth, formally Rowlina Roth-Holtzman, had actually broken federal law to marry Holtzman in her own vain attempt to disguise her sexual orientation. Mr. Holtzman had failed at his beard job though. Among other flaws, he lived 3000 miles from Fenchester.

I nodded and said, "What people do in the bedroom isn't really the issue though is it? Civil rights is the issue. And sure, there are situations that make sense for people to remain closeted. People in the seventy-eight countries that still criminalize sexual behavior, people who were in the military under Don't Ask Don't Tell, parents going through tough custody battles in conservative jurisdictions, high school students whose parents would throw them out of the house if they found out..."

"I have kind of a hard time understanding why someone teaching at a liberal arts college like Irwin would hide. This college has full protections and even gives domestic partner benefits. Someone in the closet here, well, that would have to be an internal issue," said Bolton, shaking his head.

"You've always been out?" asked Paul.

"Even fifteen years ago, before I was tenured," said Bolton.

Paul turned to me and Kathryn. "And you?"

"Yes," we said in unison.

I went on, "But that's not to say... People have to come out when they're ready. It's a personal choice. I just hope people know that being in the closet actually makes you far more vulnerable."

"And why do you think that?" asked Carla.

"Because most people talk about their personal lives all the time. People who don't are suspect and vulnerable. So all some bully has to do is ask them if they're Gay," I explained gently.

"One could simply say, *That is none of your business*," insisted Carla.

"But the problem with that is..." I turned to Paul and asked, "Are you Gay?"

Paul shrugged and said, "No."

I went on, "See, ninety-nine times out of 100 a straight person would never say *It's none of your business*. So a person who does say that is probably Gay. The only other alternative for a Gay person is to lie, which Paul has just demonstrated would be demoralizing."

"You know," said Bolton, "bullies don't pick on people because they're Gay. They pick on them because they're vulnerable."

"No one is more vulnerable than someone who's living a lie," said Kathryn.

"So, so, you hate all people who are in the closet!" Carla said with a faint German accent, as she teetered on the transparent edges of panic.

The rest of the people clammed up in response to Carla's obtuse interpretation of the conversation.

Finally Bolton said, "Being in the closet calls for support not hatred. But I'm not wild about people in the closet who use their positions of power to spew anti-Gay rhetoric. All those far right preachers and legislators who vote against LGBT rights and then get caught with rent boys on vacation."

"Or in airport restrooms," laughed Paul. "OK, I know we have to get back to work, but one more thing..."

The pizza was gone, but these academics would stretch this topic into tomorrow if I didn't get out of the mix. I stood and said, "I'll let you all get back to work. Thanks for letting me join in the supper and lively conversation."

"I'll walk you out," said Kathryn, grabbing her coat.

On the way down the steps I said, "I kind of got you all off track there..."

"Maggie, an activist once told me that anytime you have a chance to explain discrimination to straight people, you have to take it. Most people don't even know there's no federal law or Pennsylvania law that bans employment or housing discrimination based on sexual orientation. I'm a teacher, and when the opportunity arises, I teach, and I'm happy to welcome guest speakers," said Kathryn, stopping at the bottom of the stairs."

"I'd really have a hard time if *you* wanted us to pretend you slept in the guest-room!" I laughed.

"To be honest, Maggie, I'm not wildly personal with my students. It's not my nature. But I'm proud to say that I've never shied from standing up for their rights and that's far easier to do out of the closet than in. Of course everyone has to come out on their own schedule. But here at Irwin? Good grief, we just went to full gender-neutral housing. This is a progressive institution. It's one of the reasons I choose to work here."

I smiled. This was one of the many things I loved about Kathryn, that her Lesbian identity is important to her and that she's passionate about civil rights.

"So what's the deal with Carla Zimmer? I mean, project much?"

"I know. She's always like that. Maybe she's in love with Rowlina Roth. Did you hear how her voice picked up a hint of Rowlina's accent when she got emotional? Perhaps Rowlina only hires people into the Architecture History Department who are deeply in the closet so she can continue to be comfortable in her own dark little walk-in. I wish there was something I could do to help her."

"It's a shame. It's all making her so unhappy and Carla's getting caught in the current. So, Bolton Winpenny is the steel drummer?" I said, considering.

Kathryn nodded. "Oh, here's a revelation. Remember when I told you it was Bolton's idea to end the retreat when that woman in the department became hysterical?"

"Professor Panic Attack?"

"Right. Well, it turns out that Bolton put her up to it. It was all an act so that Bolton could suggest we end the meeting and go home. Rather brilliant, really." Kathryn pulled her coat tighter and faced me.

I put my arms around her and we kissed. It made me hear music.

"Thanks for the pizza, but I'm still hungry."

"For more dinner?"

"Not that kind of hunger."

"I'll try to make them hurry so I can get back soon."

"Fat chance of that."

We parted reluctantly. She turned back into the building and I trudged off into the dark cold night to stop back at the library and retrieve the bag of sculpture, then head home.

Tomorrow and Tomorrow and Tomorrow I chanted to the musical steel drum beat that looped through my brain.

CHAPTER 11

When I got to the loft I dropped off the sculpture, which I'd been carting around all day. It was going to be a while before Kathryn would be released from academic purgatory, so I went down to my office to work on identifying the young man who was killed in the cemetery.

I checked my electronic calendar and found that Nora had made an entry with a note below it that said:

> *Tomorrow, about 8 in the morning, Mrs Henshaw wants a wee talk with you. Her number is below. -- Your faithful minion, Miss Lenderbee*

I smiled and made a note of it, while I silently wondered if Kathryn would come home in time to make me too tired for an 8 a.m., or if she'd come home so late we'd both be too sleepy for an evening assignation.

I sat at my desk in the empty office and booted up my desktop computer that has enough *gigs* to store the collective pasts of everyone in Fenchester.

Identification is one of those investigation jobs that has become much easier with each new generation of electronic apps. One of them is the excellent recognition feature that's part of my photo storage program. It matches faces.

When I interned for Seamus A. McFinn Jr. at Discreet Investigations, I hit upon the rather brilliant idea of scanning a decade's worth of every high school year book in the valley. It was an interesting project that I was able to do mostly online at a relatively low cost.

There are two high schools in Fenchester, Carlton Fen and General Merganser Hunterdon High. And there are a couple of dozen other high schools in other towns and small cities in Lenape Valley as well. I'd downloaded every senior picture. The matching program scans a face on one photo and matches it with another. The program could make mistakes and be confused, but all in all it worked rather well. I was the only one in town that had this kind of resource.

If the man killed in the cemetery had been a senior in any of the local high schools in the last few years, there was more than an eighty percent chance I could come up with a match. Of course he may not have been local or he may dropped out before his senior year... or he may have been absent on Senior Picture Day, but it was worth a try.

I downloaded the photo of the shooting victim into my desktop and ran it. Thirty-two similar photos came up. I went through them one by one, taking out the ones that really didn't match, and came up with six possibles. Then I ran the names though a variety of other searches. I ruled out three more. Of those, one now worked in a senator's office, one was a local firefighter and looked different in current photos, and one had died in Iraq.

The three photos left were of Anthony Rossi, Francis Kibbey, and John M. Williams. Rossi and Kibbey had gone to Hunterdon High and Williams had gone to Fen. I printed them and put them in an envelope. Their names were pretty popular so they were going to be harder to track down. I'd work on them tomorrow.

I closed up the office and went back to the loft. I changed clothes and went up to the top floor for a workout that would either take my lust-laden mind off Kathryn or greatly increase my preoccupation with her. It did both. Finally I ran two miles on the treadmill full tilt until my mind began to focus on what I was going to say to Lois Henshaw the next morning. I was leaning toward the direct approach.

By the time I was done with the workout I was sweating and tired and sorely hoping I'd find Kathryn slipping into her nightgown downstairs so I could slip her out of it.

But Kathryn still wasn't home. So I did some laundry and housecleaning. By midnight I was still alone and the worse for it. So I went to bed to read more of *Fenchester — A History of Love, Loss, and Generosity* by Gabriel and Suzanne Carbondale in case I met up with Amanda Knightbridge again and she quizzed me on it. It really was fascinating, though it didn't have as much about Victoria and Evangeline as I would have liked. I read carefully for an hour and then let myself drift off to sleep with the light on, until my phone chirped with a text.

It said, < Alas. Just to my budget now. Go to sleep. Profoundly sorry. >

Crap, I was profoundly sorry too.

The phone chirped again with another text that said simply, < Friday >

That cheered me.

Hours later I vaguely heard the door chime Kathryn in. Moments after that I felt her body, still chilled from the February night, slip next to mine. I put my arm around her and felt her relax into me.

She sighed, "It's nice to come home to you." And then we both fell asleep.

In what seemed like ten minutes later, I felt her leave the bed. The pale rays of winter dawn fought their way through the window. I turned when she came out of the bathroom dressed for the day. She knelt by the bed to put her arms around me.

"Come back to bed," I whispered in her ear.

"Do you really want me to?"

"Yes."

"Don't you want me to see Victoria's journal?"

"Yes, but can't you Skype or clone yourself or some other high tech thing?" I groaned.

"Um..."

"I'll get up and have breakfast with you."

"I don't have time. I have a meeting in less than two hours, and if I don't see this journal this morning, I may self-combust."

"*Ha!* OK, you can go, but when will you be back?"

"At 5 p.m. I'll be back to help the drywall crew. Farrel said they could all work until ten. That's not too late. Ten? And you know, Friday isn't that far away."

"Mmmmm, OK."

She kissed me goodbye. I got up to dress and have breakfast before beginning my one-floor trek to the office.

****

Nora wasn't due to come in until 9 a.m. Sara and Emma would come in about then if they didn't have a hearing or other off-site meetings. I had about an hour to get a few things done before office distractions slowed me down. I called Lois Henshaw and she answered before the first ring was through.

"Maggie, sorry to make ya call so early, but I'm the type who's up to catch the worm," she said distractedly. "I have more worms than I know what to do with." Then she laughed longer than there was anything to laugh about, then stopped without anything else to say.

"Lois, look, I read the reports. I know what you want me to do, but I can't figure anything out by retracing the other P.I.s' dead-end paths. So I have a suggestion that you're probably not going to like."

"What?" she asked warily.

"I'd like to just have a talk with Samson and ask him what's up. Maybe he'll tell me. Maybe he even wants you to know and he just doesn't have a way to tell you."

"Just ask him?"

"Yeah, that's my proposal. If you aren't interested I'll just give you your money back, because it's a waste for you to hire me or any other investigator just to do the same thing again. That would be throwing your money down the toilet."

"Gosh darn. Oh, gosh darn it. But what if he...."

"But what if I actually find the answer to his behavior?"

"Yes... no... oh gosh DARN it, Maggie. This is worse than my own cooking. How did I ever get into this fix?"

"Do you really want me to answer that?"

"Huh?"

"Was that something you want me to answer? Because it's pretty simple. You've lost communication with the person you love best on earth and you're torn between wanting to get it back and finding out something you'd really rather not confront."

There was a long pause. Finally Lois responded with, "I know it's not trendy, but I still like men. I really do love him, Maggie, with all my heart and soul. But I can't go on with things this way. I have to know. So go ahead; ask him. When are you going to do it?"

"I have time today."

"Oh, gosh da... Well, OK, I'll just hold my breath until I hear back from you. But don't tell me anything that will make me upset."

I sighed inwardly. "Is he home now?"

"No, he's running around doing errands. But he'll be at our apartment building remodeling one of the second floor units by about 11:30 a.m. It's at 1012 Washington near 10th."

"Lois, I may not be able to get back to you right away. So really don't hold your breath, OK? Give me a few days."

I had several more hours to work so I took out the three possible photos that might identify the man killed in the graveyard and did a series of searches to find more information on their names. Among other things, I tried Zaba and Nexis, scanned the public voter roles, went through literally hundreds of possible Facebook pages, and ran through public arrest records. After several hours and a dozen search engines, nothing came up. Their names were either too common or they just hadn't created an electronic trail since they'd left high school. It's sometimes hard to imagine, but there are some people who just aren't on the grid.

Ultimately I did some other office work, chatted with Nora for a moment, and at about noon I grabbed my coat and bag and walked the short two blocks to 1012 Washington. It had snowed in the night, not enough to coat the sidewalks, but the lawns in the Mews park were dusted with white. The sun was out and the air was clean and crisp. The day was much brighter than the task I was on for Lois Henshaw.

The apartment house the Henshaws owned was not just a converted single family home. This building, just a block down the street from Farrel and Jessie's, had obviously been built as some kind of commercial and multi-family dwelling in the 1930s. It was triple the width of all the other buildings on the block. The deco style tiles framing the door, the cut glass transom, and the marble front steps had been kept up nicely over the last eighty years. The building had a dentist's office and a CPA's office on the ground floor. Eight apartments, four on each floor, were in the two upstairs stories.

The apartments were accessed by a central entrance. Each key-locked mailbox had a doorbell button underneath. Number 2's box had no name-tag.

I turned to look back at the southeast corner of the Mews that was directly in front of the building. The trees lining the central walkway were leafless. Their twiggy branches looked like a spiky line drawing against the blue sky. There was an open section of ivy-covered yard that surrounded a military statue of none other than Merganser Hunterdon in his crisp Civil War general's uniform.

The Carbondales' book said Merganser had reached the rank of general in his twenties and that he was one of the youngest generals of the period. I'd been surprised to find out there'd been a thousand generals in that war. I briefly wondered what Merganser had done to get his commission. Some brilliant battle tactic, some heroic act of bravery? It hadn't said in the book. Merganser's likeness wasn't dashing and young though. It seemed old and tired, and the "unfortunate" quality of his features was more than apparent. I wondered if Victoria had created this sculpture too.

The statue faced west with its back toward the small houses on 10th street where Amanda Knightbridge and Gabriel Carbondale lived. I had a perfect view of the historic house from here. Fen House was where Evangeline had lived, and then after her death, where Victoria Willomere Snow had lived for the rest of her life. I imagined how the row would have looked in the 1870s when Evangeline and her family had had to move in. There would have been no park in front of the little houses then; they had been built for the lowest of workers. It must have been very embarrassing for Evangeline's mother, who was a descendent of three of Fenchester's most affluent families, to be living in a tiny home with stables as her front yard. As Amanda had suggested, the smell must have been awful.

How did Victoria Snow fit into all this? In her journal, she was on her way to rescue Evangeline from poverty with the help of Charlotte Cushman's directed commission. But history indicated that when Evangeline died, she was still engaged to Hunterdon and that he mourned for her for the rest of his life. Maybe Evangeline wasn't a "sister of the heart" after all. Maybe Evangeline needed more support than the comfort Victoria's single commission could buy. After all, Hunterdon was the richest man in the State.

These days the little row homes on 10th street were really quite charming. I wondered when the yew trees that flanked each front door had been planted. By 1900 the Mews Park had been fully installed and was probably quite a community showpiece, as it is now. Victoria had lived there then. She must have liked looking out on it, as much as Suzanne Carbondale had in the years she'd lived in Fen House. I paused and looked up at the front windows of the Henshaw's apartment house. I had a flash of enlightenment.

A tenant swung open the outer door and came down the steps. I took this opportunity to duck into the lobby without ringing. I went up the stairs and found number two, which was the front apartment on the left. While there's never a good excuse for rudeness, when I'm on a case I find that conventional manners can get in the way of sleuthing. The door was unlocked, so I walked in without knocking.

It was a nice apartment. Large, light, and empty of furniture. There was a small kitchen to the right, with room for a tiny table. To the left were two bedrooms and a 1930s tiled bathroom.

Samson Henshaw sat on a metal folding chair looking out one of the deep-silled windows. There was a folded tarp, a full plastic garbage bag, a sealed paint can, and some painting tools on the floor. There were several Brews on the Mews paper cups on the sill. The room looked like it had been recently painted. I sniffed; it smelled fresh and clean.

Henshaw spun around in surprise. He stood up and took two steps away from the chair as though he'd been caught peeping through a bathroom window. Maybe he had, but probably not.

"Maggie! How'd you get in?"

"Door was unlocked," I said as I made my way to the window to see what he was looking at.

Things clicked in place in my mind. Six weeks, the view, what Lois had said, what the other investigators had found. I looked into the garbage bag. It was filled with empty coffee cups and food containers.

I turned slowly and said to Samson Henshaw, "What are you doing here, Samson?"

"I just finished painting."

"Funny, there's no smell of paint in here at all. So, you're waiting for her to come back? Suzanne Carbondale?"

"I don't know what you're talking about."

"Yeah, you do." I sat down on the broad windowsill and looked back out the window. "Samson, this is a stupid place for surveillance. You can't even see the back door. Do you stand out there sometimes too?"

"Not so much, now that it's cold," Samson admitted. He deflated and plunked back into the folding chair.

"Were you in love with her?"

"Still am," Henshaw admitted.

"Have you seen her since she left Gabe?"

"What? No, I haven't seen her since right before she left town. That's when she told me she was going to leave Gabe. We'd been talking for weeks before that though. We'd talk about her work and about the house I wanted to build on speculation. The economy's rotten, but she made me feel like I could pull it off. She was working on a manuscript. We'd talk over coffee, usually at Brews. Sometimes take a walk." The floodgates in Samson Henshaw tore off their hinges and he spent the next two hours telling the entire story of his obsession with Suzanne Carbondale. Most of it had to do with his own life. I listened patiently.

When he stopped, I asked, "How intimate was this?"

"You mean, were we sleeping together? Well, no. I hadn't really thought about her that way. But when she told me they were going to break up, suddenly I just realized that I loved her, and then she left town before I had a chance to tell her. She wrote that book about Fenchester with Gabe and really Suzanne did almost all of the work. Gabe's really an asshole, you know? What a phony."

"What's her new manuscript about? Did she say?"

"I guess kind of a sequel to the book they'd done together, but it was all written by her this time. She was really excited about it. Maggie, when she told me she was going to leave Gabe, suddenly the path was clear, know what I mean?"

"Yeah, I know what you mean, but *your* path isn't clear. Did you forget you're married to Lois?"

At least Samson had the good grace to blush.

He said, "Lois is a good person and I loved her; I still love her. It would be unfair to pretend I didn't, but Suzanne was different. So different. She completed me. It was a whirlwind and we were riding it."

"But you never really told Suzanne you felt this way? Or did you?"

"No," he said forlornly. "She cared about me though; she said so. When she told me that, I couldn't think about anything else. I figured we could go away together and life would be perfect. As soon as she's back I'll tell her and we'll be all set."

"Samson, don't you think you're kind of putting all your eggs into a basket you don't even own?" I asked gently. I knew Suzanne Carbondale was the type of woman who sincerely cared about everyone. She was always a very nice person who developed close friendships precisely because she did care. But it didn't mean she was in love with everyone.

He whirled on me and his voice became sharp. "No, that's not the way it is. I know that when she comes back we can just talk for a while and then it will be her and me together."

The plan seemed like a house of cards to me. After all, Suzanne left without even telling him. "Do you hear from her? Phone? Email? Anything?"

He calmed down a little and replied, "I texted her and she said she'd spoken with her publisher and was going out of the country for some research. She didn't know when she'd be back, but that when she did she'd be in touch."

"That's what it said exactly?"

"Well, no, not exactly. Here, I have it."

Samson showed me the text he'd received from Suzanne after she'd left. It said, < Talked w pub. Going mexico - research. Back soon. Will call u then. >

"That's the only message you've had from her?" I asked.

"I've left a bunch of messages and texts, but she probably doesn't have a good signal in Mexico.

I knew that Jessie had gotten some texts from Suzanne from Mexico, which indicated Suzanne could get a connection at least part of the time. This relationship between Samson and Suzanne seemed to be mostly in his mind. But mentioning that to him, wasn't going to make him see the situation any more clearly.

"Samson, Lois is really concerned about you. Have you even thought about her?"

"I don't want to hurt her."

"You are hurting her every day by not talking honestly with her."

"I don't know what to do. I guess I'll just confess everything to Lois and move out. Hey, maybe I could hire you to find Suzanne?"

"Samson, when Suzanne comes back to the United States, what if she doesn't share your feelings?"

Samson looked like I'd thrown a bucket of water on him. He kind of woke up for a moment and gasped, but then he flickered back into his unrealistic world. He mumbled, "She said she cares about me."

"How long do you plan to wait for Suzanne? How long are you going to leave Lois in the dark?"

"I don't know. What do you think I should do?"

"I think you should be honest."

"To Lois?"

"I was thinking more about being honest to yourself. Once you're able to do that, then you need to talk to Lois."

CHAPTER 12

Samson had promised he'd talk to Lois in a day or two, and I'd figured that it would be in Lois's best interest if I let Samson talk to her, rather than telling her about Suzanne myself.

When I left Samson it was late lunchtime. I could go home for a dull nosh in my own kitchen or I could snag some fresh guacamole at La Casa Mexicana on 11th Street. Tortillas won out and I was on my way to molé.

La Mexicana Grill was bustling with a late lunch crowd. Mariana Estevez, the owner and family matriarch, was hard at work serving afternoon customers. She barely had a chance to wave to me as she sped by with a big tray. I not only got a little snack for myself, but I arranged for two large orders of fajitas to be delivered to the loft at dinnertime. We'd all be working on the drywall by then and would need the fuel.

Rafael told me at the cash register he'd call when he was about to bring the food over.

****

It was nearly 3 p.m. when I got back to my office. In the parking lot in front of the building was Farrel's full-sized van, two cars I didn't recognize, and Kathryn's little Mini Cooper.

I wanted to add a few quick notes to the Lois Henshaw file about my conversation with Samson. Maybe I should just get in touch with Suzanne Carbondale and ask her if she had any feelings for Samson. If she said "No," I'd let him know that the grass wasn't greener on the other side. He was living a fantasy, and Lois was the reality. I had a feeling that if Samson didn't choose reality soon, he was going to have to move into that apartment with no furniture in order to have a place to live.

Nora was at her new desk working on some kind of billing list that looked very dull. She perked up when I came in.

"What have you been doing since I saw you last? Catching criminals? Thinking up drag names?"

"Confidential things," I smiled.

"Discretion is still the better part of valor."

"Is Sara here?"

"In her office but..." Nora noted the flashing light on Sara's extension. "She's on the phone. Do you need to speak to her?"

"No, I was just wondering. Did Kathryn come by?"

"Dr. Anthony?" Nora's voice dropped to a whisper and picked up two degrees of brogue. "She was by a wee bit ago. Very dressed up she was, said she'd have to change her clothes tae work wit Farrel an some mates muckin' about upstairs and that it was faer chanking up there. I ken you'll both be stowed oot the rest o' the night. She wha swatchin for your ta come home."

"Why are you talking like we're in a pub in Glasgow?"

"Am I?"

"Aye," I smiled.

"Well, em, I get a bit flustered, sometimes."

"Kind of have a wee crush on her?"

"Just sussed that out, did ya? But dinna fas yersel." Nora cleared her throat and laughed, stepping it down. "She seems to bring that out in some people."

"Aye," I said.

****

"Lift it all the way to the ceiling. Push hard!" called Farrel, as I and one of her crew levered a horizontal sheet of drywall to the top of the wall frame. Farrel used her drill with the automatic screw-feed to tack the sheet into place. Then she and another crew member rapidly applied a line of screws to each edge, firmly attaching the whole sheet to the wall studs.

"Just three more sheets and we'll be done with this wall and we can take a dinner break," said Farrel.

Farrel and the crew had come in early and Kathryn had joined them. Three of the walls were just about done, but the last one, the one that had to fit around the open second floor, would take the longest. Kathryn, Jessie, and the other half of the young people in the crew were measuring and marking the irregular pieces that would go on that side.

I helped hold up the last two sheets, as Farrel and the others finished with the screws. When we were done, La Casa Mexicana called with the ETA on dinner.

"*Rafael llegará en diez minutos*," said Mariana.

Everyone was happy to hear that and went to wash hands and dusty faces in the top floor bathroom.

Kathryn came down with me to the loft to set the long dining table with plates.

"You don't realize how cold it is up there while you're working. Oh! I'm covered with dust!" said Kathryn, stretching her arms over her head and yawning. She looked at her watch. "Just a few hours ago it was a skeleton and now it's a room!"

She slipped her arms around me and gave me a dusty kiss and a hug that mixed joy with satisfaction. Her smile was so genuine I felt it too.

"Thank you for letting me do this!"

"We earned the money for it together. It's working out well, isn't it?" I asked.

"It's... it's very exciting," Kathryn nodded.

"Kind of a turn-on for you?"

"Well yes, as a matter of fact," she said in a low voice.

Jessie came down the big spiral staircase into the loft to help get drinks ready. She'd already set pitchers of iced tea in the fridge. We pulled some extra chairs around the table. We needed enough for the seven women and three men.

Farrel is always insistent that everyone dress safely for hard work. Long sleeves, long pants, hard hats if there's any overhead work. Respirators for toxic dust. Hearing protection if there's noise. Goggles. She'd even made Kathryn buy steel-toed shoes. Everyone in the room was wearing work boots and either denim overalls or jeans and flannel shirts. It looked like a cross between an Oshkosh commercial and an ad for the Michigan Womyn's Music Festival.

"Is there going to be anything for me to eat?" I heard one of Farrel's former students whisper.

"There are vegetarian fajitas along with the chicken, so yes, there will be plenty," nodded Farrel, just as the door bell rang. "Go help Maggie bring up the food, will you?"

He followed me down the two flights. We took the bags from Rafael's huge backpack.

"*Espera Rafael, déjame darte una propina,*" I said.

"*No, Maggie, no tienes que hacerlo. Está bien.*"

"*Pero quiero que lo cojas, por favor. Tú necesitas ahorrar para... cosas.*"

"*Está bien, de veras, y como quiera yo le doy todas las propinas a Mariana.*"

"*Bueno pues llévaselo a ella entonces.*" *

* "Wait, Rafael, let me give you a tip," I said.
"No, Maggie, you don't have to. It's OK."
"But I want you to have it, please. You need this to save up for... things."
"It's OK really, and I give all the tips to Mariana, anyway."
"Well take this to give to her then."

I gave him twenty percent of the bill and hoped that he'd keep some of it but knew he wouldn't. My stepmother Juana told me long ago that I shouldn't try to figure out the dynamic of the Estevez family. Everyone who worked there was related in one way or another.

"It's another culture that you can learn about, but you'll never really understand, so just roll with it as best you can and try not to get in the way," she'd said.

We toted the bags back up to the loft. Jessie transferred everything to large bowls, stuck in big serving spoons, then set them on the table.

Everyone dug in like Amish carpenters after a barn raising. Aaron Copland could have scored it.

I turned to Farrel to ask how long the next wall would take, but she just held up her hand and said, "Can't talk... eating."

"About three hours—we should get it done tonight. Then we can clear out all the drywall scraps and begin taping this weekend. Don't you think?" said one of the crew members.

Farrel nodded. Everyone else seemed fine with it. I'd forgotten how hungry young people eat. Most of the food was gone already. I looked at my watch and it was only a quarter after seven. I heard Jessie say quietly to Kathryn, "Vacuum cleaners."

Farrel filled everyone's iced tea glass. She said, "Let's move the scaffolding to the other corner for the taping. It will be faster." Everyone nodded in agreement.

One of the guys said to Kathryn, "This is the highest ceiling we've ever done. What is it? Twenty feet?" Kathryn and I nodded.

The two crew women, Shar and Dawn, had been working with Farrel for several years. They had their own business creating faux finishes and detailed woodwork, but times were tough in the construction world so they still did work like this with Farrel when it came up.

Shar was short, had close-cut dark brown hair, dark attractive eyes, a compact body, and more energy than everyone else put together. Farrel always said that when Shar was on the job, it would be done twice as fast. Dawn was the quiet one of the group. Introspective and methodical but very detail-oriented. Occasionally she'd point out something that everyone else had missed. She had long light brown hair that she wore in a ponytail, was tall and on the willowy side, and had an understated way of talking. She was local; she'd met Shar when they'd both begun working on Farrel's crew.

Shar said to me, "I saw you on the WFEN news about the shooting of that guy in Skeleton Park on Sunday. What was his name?" All of the crew was interested.

"I have a picture of him. Maybe one of you've seen him around." I pulled the photos out of my bag. "I just want to warn you, I took this after he died," I cautioned. This made the older women all stand up and begin to carry plates to the sink, but the young people crowded around to look at a dead man who was just about their age. I had the yearbook photos out to show them too.

Dawn held the post-mortem photo closer. She said, "I think I know this guy from high school. His name is, um, Frankie something, I think."

I pushed the yearbook photo of Francis Kibbey over to her.

"Yes, that's him!" She read the name on the back. "Yes, Frankie Kibbey, that's who it is. I was in biology with him. I was a Junior when he was a senior. This is so sad."

"Did you know him well?" I asked.

"No, just had that one class with him. Just an average guy... I don't really know anything else about him."

"Farrel, come here for a minute," said Kathryn staring at the high school photo Dawn had identified.

Farrel told the rest of the drywall crew to get to work and she'd join them when the dishes were all cleaned up.

When the young people were all upstairs, Farrel and Kathryn said in unison, "It's the dealer!"

"What?"

"It looks like the dealer we bought the sculpture from. It's hard to tell from the photo you took in the graveyard, but this high school portrait is more clear. The dealer had a scarf around part of his face, but it looks like the same guy," said Farrel.

"The eyes are just the same," said Kathryn.

"This was the person you got the Victoria Snow sculptures from?"

"He had a great deal of good merchandise," Kathryn nodded.

I sat down. "OK, so this means..." I considered for a minute, "I guess it means this Frankie somehow had a pipeline to some really good merch, and he had no idea how valuable it was."

"And he told me he'd have more merch for sale at Pesky!" said Farrel.

"When is that? Do you think somebody will take over with the sales? Perhaps the red-headed man in the hooded sweatshirt?" asked Kathryn.

"Peskeetotemburg Antique & Flea Market is every Wednesday morning," said Farrel. "That's tomorrow, and I was planning on going anyway. I suppose you two will be coming along? We leave at 5:30 a.m."

CHAPTER 13

At 11:30 p.m. all the sheetrock was in place and ready for taping, and the younger crew members had gone home.

"OK, I'll pick you up tomorrow at six." Farrel yawned. "Dress warm."

Jessie hugged us both, and she and Farrel gathered up her iced tea pitchers and left. The crew would be back Friday to do the drywall taping. Farrel had classes and other commitments until then.

Kathryn stretched with her arms over her head like a sleek young cat. My carnal smile caught her eye and she came toward me with an equally ardor-tinged expression.

She put her arms around my waist and said, "How early do we have to get up?"

"I'm thinking about now," I whispered.

"We should take a nice long shower to get all this dust out of our hair."

My phone rang. I pulled it out of my pocket.

"Yeah?" I tried not to groan.

"Maggie?"

"Yeah?"

"This is Samson. Look, this is important." The connection crackled and the signal was almost lost but then gained a little clarity. "Can you hear me?"

"What is it?" I asked.

"I heard her cell phone! Suzanne's. I heard it! She's here!"

"What? What do you mean? Where are you?"

"I'm on Hazel Street, behind 10th."

"Shit, Samson, you're stalking Suzanne's house again?"

"Well, you said it wasn't a good view from the front, and I just wanted to take one last look. But listen, I saw someone go in the back door. I couldn't see her very well. I was afraid to call out, so, so... I called her cell. And it rang! I could hear it as she went into the house!"

"Samson, that could have just been a coincidence. People's phones ring all the time..."

"No, no, it was my ring. The one Suzanne programed in for me. She did that for everyone. Mine was *If I Had a Hammer*. So it has to be her, right?"

"Well, Samson, if it is her, and I'm not saying that it is, she didn't answer, so, maybe she'd rather not talk to you right now."

"Maggie, come over here. Please? I'll wait here. Oh wait. There..." Crackle, buzz... nothing.

"Hello? Samson? Hello?" I looked at the phone. "Shit."

"What?"

"Well, that was Samson Henshaw and he thinks he just saw Suzanne Carbondale behind her house, and now I think he's going to do something stupid."

"Should you be telling me this? Is it confidential?"

"Huh? Well, no, I'm not working for him. But I was talking to him today. Oh crap." I looked toward the Mews through the dark windows.

"You want to go over there," said Kathryn simply.

I looked back at her.

"Go. It might be important. Do you want me to come with you?"

"No, no, you take a shower and I'll just run over there and then be back as soon as I can. OK?" I said.

"Yes, OK," Kathryn nodded.

"Are you sure?"

"Yes, go. I doubt you'll be as late as I was last night. We'll be even." She smiled.

I kissed her and picked up my bag. I got my Beretta from the safe and grabbed the minivan keys. I drove over because it seemed like I should. I figured there would be parking nearby on Washington because street sweeping on the north side would be early Wednesday morning, so there'd be few cars there.

I zipped over to Liberty, then down to Hazel, the alley street behind 10th. I didn't see Samson near the back of the Carbondale house, so I went all the way through to Washington. Along the way there had been no free parking spaces at all but I got an easy spot on the north side of Washington, which was completely car free other than a tiny Smart Car and one large white van.

I took handcuffs, pepper spray, and my gun out of my bag and stowed the bag under the front seat. I pulled off my jacket. It was still freezing cold in the van, because it hadn't had time to warm up in the three blocks I'd driven. I rigged my holster over my shoulder and stowed the gun in it with all the safeties on.

This was a lot of police gear for what would probably be nothing more than a minor mistake. There was no reason to think I'd need it, except that this whole thing could end up being a domestic dispute. A lot of cops will tell you those can be the most dangerous of all. Love or money are the prime motivators for murder. Domestic crime is often about both.

"Samson?" I called quietly from the narrow street behind 311 N. 10th.

There was a tall stockade fence across the back of the yard that stretched from the side of the garage at 309 to the garage wall of 313. Gabe didn't have a garage, which meant he always parked on the street.

In the middle of the stockade fence was a wooden door with a sign on it that said, BEWARE OF LARGE DOG, with a picture of a snarling bulldog in one of those spike collars.

I reached over the top of the door, unlatched it, and slid through. Buster, the behemoth Great Dane, crashed through his dog door and ran toward me at full cantor. One foot from me he skidded to a stop, bent his head, and slobbered my hand. If burglars were easily grossed out, they'd be no match for Buster.

"Wipe," I whispered.

I petted him lavishly with my other hand as I tried to shake off the slime, finally wiping it on my pants and making a mental note to put these jeans in the dirty clothes when I got home. Buster turned and headed back to his dog door, then stopped short of it, and turned back to invite me in.

I didn't need to go in. The house was dark. It was after midnight. Gabe was no doubt asleep and Samson had clearly gone home. Probably the whole thing had been a mistake. Maybe Samson's battery had just run down. Whatever.

I whispered goodbye to Buster and walked back down the alley toward my van. I took out my cell and rang Samson but the call went to voice mail. "Samson, this is Maggie. Where the hell are you? It's freezing and I can see why you left, but I'm not pleased that you didn't bother to tell me you'd gone. Gabe's is dark, so I figure this was a misunderstanding. Unless something earth-shattering happens, don't call to explain until tomorrow because I'm going to bed."

Back in the loft, I was happy to see that the lights were still on in the bedroom.

"Maggie?" called Kathryn. "You look annoyed. What happened?"

Kathryn was sitting up in bed waiting for me in a sheer nightgown that made me stop in my tracks. A smile flickered across my face. It wasn't simply lust, though that was certainly part of it; it was the pleasure of having her there. Here was a very beautiful woman and not only was she waiting for me in my bed, she wanted me to talk to her about things that had happened to me. And she was smart, so the comments she was about to make were going to be edifying. What fun. I felt very lucky.

"Maggie, you still have plaster dust all over you, and what's that gunk on your pants? Take a shower and I'll get you a glass of wine. Then lie down and tell me, and I'll rub your back a little. OK?"

"I can't imagine anything nicer, but Kathryn, if I lie there and you rub my back, I might fall asleep. In fact, I'll probably fall asleep. I wouldn't be able to..." But she just waved me toward the bathroom.

The hot water was relaxing. It was a relief to rinse the white pasty stiffness out of my hair. I toweled off, used the blow dryer a little, and slipped on a long t-shirt.

"He wasn't there," I said when I came back to bed. "That's the entire story."

"Did you call him?"

"No answer. I left a message."

"A stern message I hope?" Kathryn was far more indignant than I was about my being stood up by Samson Henshaw on a cold February night.

"I don't think I carry off *stern* very well. You're good at stern. I managed vexed. He probably figured out that it was all a stupid mistake and realized how freezing he was and went home to Lois."

"But why not call?"

"He's kind of off kilter."

"Because he... um. You probably can't tell me this so let me guess. Let's see, his wife has seemed very depressed lately. He is preoccupied all the time. He's been like that for awhile. He was stalking around Hazel St. behind the east end of the Mews." She paused to consider. "Well no one has really left that part of the Mews except Suzanne Carbondale. So I'm guessing he was in love with her, she left without warning, and he's been casing her house to see her again."

I smiled.

"Did he hire you to find her or something?"

"He didn't hire me. He's tangential to a case that someone did hire me for, one that's ongoing but almost over. I can't really talk about it. "

"If I was part of your company, *would* you be able to talk to me about it?"

"Well, yes, I think my company investigator license would cover you. It covers support people—secretaries, assistants, interns, that kind of thing."

"So maybe you should hire me. As your assistant or intern?"

"Are you serious?"

"I am, yes," she said earnestly. Then she smiled. "So I could be a shamus? A gumshoe? A PI? A... um..."

"A Sherlock, an operative, a sleuth, a bloodhound. But if you were my assistant, then you would be more like Della Street or Dr. Watson. That would work; you already have the doctorate."

"So we could work together? A crime fighting team?"

"A team with benefits, like Nick and Nora Charles, or Spenser and Susan."

"Or Jonathan and Jennifer Hart, or Troy and Roderick Alleyn."

"Or Tommy and Tuppence, or... Batman and Robin."

She snorted. "So my stalking skills might come in handy rather than just seeming pathetic?" She lay back on pillows propped against the headboard then turned toward me. We looked into each others's eyes and something strong passed between us. After a moment, we both exhaled.

"I could get a dragon tattoo," she said in a low voice.

"OK, I'll check with my legal advisors to be sure it's all kosher."

She nodded, then she said softly, "It's very late, and I think we should go to sleep now because I'm going with you tomorrow morning, and I want to be sharp for my first day of work. OK?"

"OK," I smiled.

****

Farrel edged her van into the boggy parking area under the Peskeetotemburg Outdoor Antique & Flea Market sign.

"People have been coming here to buy, sell, and trade every Wednesday morning since 1837," said Farrel to Kathryn, as she stuffed five empty canvas carrying bags into a larger one and slung it over her shoulder.

It was just getting light and it was freezing. The people who were still setting up their wares were sweeping a coating of light powdery frost from the crude tables that came with each fifteen dollar spot. Dealers and savvy collectors know the best buying at outdoor antique markets happens before dawn. Farrel was off and... well, not exactly running, but moving fast. In the antiques biz, you have to be quick and discerning to find a prize.

Kathryn and I were slower.

"1837," repeated Kathryn. "Do you suppose Evangeline or Victoria shopped here?"

I looked over the rows of tables that striated the gentle slope in front of us. At the bottom of the hill were two pavilions. They were really nothing more than roofs over concrete slabs, like giant carports. There were rows and rows of cardboard boxes on the concrete. Beyond was a large block building with a short order snack bar in the front that was open for business. I could smell the aroma of coffee and lard-fried Pennsylvania Dutch breakfast food wafting up the incline.

I tried to imagine Evangeline or Victoria, in warm furs and long skirts, hunting for bargains among the carts and boxes of produce, gimcrackery, and occasional treasure.

"I can't see Evangeline being here in the 1870s. After all, it's nearly twenty miles from Fenchester. Unless there was some kind of train, it took a day or two to travel this far in those days. If she shopped such places, she would have stayed closer to home. Victoria might have made it here. She had a driver's license in the 1920s. But even in a car, in those days it took a long time to travel forty miles round trip.

Several rows ahead I could see Farrel haggling with a dealer. A minute later cash changed hands. Farrel grabbed a clean blue underpad from her bag, wrapped the item, and moved swiftly along.

Kathryn was looking at some good quality costume jewelry. She pulled off her gloves to hold up a stick pin in the faint pre-dawn light. It was a gold toned oval with the embossed shape of a nude woman standing in a stream.

"What's your best price for this, please?" called Kathryn.

A woman dealer sitting on the tailgate of her hatchback peered at the pin Kathryn was holding up.

"What do I have on it?" she called back. Clearly she didn't want to expose herself to the cold by standing and shedding her blanket. Shopping through this market would take us about forty minutes, but this woman was probably going to have to endure this until about ten or eleven a.m., when most people would pack up for the day.

Kathryn looked at the tiny hang tag on the piece. "You have twenty-five on it."

"Cash?"

Kathryn nodded.

"I can let it go for twenty."

"I'll take it, thanks," said Kathryn, handing the woman the money.

"May I see it?" I asked as we stepped away from the table. I looked at it with the loupe I carry in my pocket. "It looks like real gold," I said quietly.

"How can you tell?"

"Well, you look at the very tip of the pin to see if the gold plate has worn off. If it's old and it's plated, then darker metal will show at the point. This looks all gold to me. Good for you," I said softly.

Kathryn smiled and squeezed my arm, then opened her bag, found an old business card and pierced the pinpoint through it, then wrapped it in a paper towel.

I could see Farrel in a pavilion, shifting the contents of one of the auction box lots. At 8 a.m. the on-site auctions would begin and all the boxes would be sold very quickly. Dealers used the auctions to turn the dregs of their inventory into a little cash. There was rarely anything good in the boxes, but once in a while an excellent buy would turn up. I hoped Farrel didn't find anything she wanted to bid on though, because 8 a.m. was almost an hour and a half away, and I was hoping I'd be somewhere warmer by then.

"Lots of empty booths. Is it always like this?" Kathryn and I were passing several wooden tables with nothing on them but frost.

"It's what? Twenty-two degrees? This is probably the worst day of the year to be here. On summer days the place is packed."

We came upon a double booth with full tables of a variety of real antiques. The vendor was still hauling out merchandise for sale. His huge brown coat had the furry quality of a matted old stuffed animal. As a matter of fact, it looked more like he was wearing an old bear costume rather than a plain coat. His hair was a cross between dreadlocks and Albert Einstein. He'd accessorized with a red and white striped scarf.

My inner monologue said, *Where's Waldo? He was eaten by a bear.*

Farrel joined us. She said, "I know this guy. He's not your man." She picked up a pair of dull silver-colored rings, covertly eyed them with her jeweler's loupe, then called to the dealer, "What can you do on these napkin rings?"

"For the pair?" growled the dealer.

"Yes."

"Two twenty-five."

"Can you take two bucks?" Farrel asked.

When he nodded, Farrel pulled out her wallet and gave the shag-carpeted man two one hundred dollar bills. He reached in his pocket with a frost-reddened hand, pulled out a huge roll of money and wrapped the Benjamins around it.

I heard Kathryn murmur a question to Farrel, and Farrel's quiet one word response. "Tiffany."

Near us was a pile of cast iron waffle irons, corn bread molds, and Dutch ovens. Kathryn uncovered two large black frying pans. She leaned in to me and said, "I think we should get a cast iron pan. Jesse uses hers for making corn bread and roasting vegetables. Do you know about the quality of these things?"

"Some. From the black patina, you can tell they've been well seasoned. They're both heavy and thick. That's good. Flip them over and read the maker's names."

Kathryn used two hands to turn each one over. "Um," she said peering closely at the embossed logos on the bottoms. "This one says Wagner Ware and this one says... Griswold Erie PA. Wagner and Griswold. Oh! The cats!" She laughed deeply. "I get it!"

Farrel came over to look. She spoke quietly so the dealer wouldn't hear. "The italic font of the Griswold company name in the large cross means it was made between the 1890s and about 1920. This Wagner Ware pan was made before 1922. Collectors like Griswold a bit more, but don't mention it to our cats; we try not to play favorites."

"Why do collectors like the Griswold pans better?" asked Kathryn.

"Mostly name recognition. Both of these pans were made when the quality was high for both companies," Farrel said softly. "This seller is pretty savvy. He'll charge more for the Griswold just for the name. So if you're buying this pan to cook in, get the Wagner."

Kathryn got the dealer's attention and asked the price of both pans. Farrel was right. His price for the Griswold was twice that of the Wagner. Kathryn made a counter offer on the Wagner of eighteen dollars, which was accepted. Kathryn paid the man, put the black pan in a canvas bag, and slipped the bag over her shoulder.

Another customer asked about a Lionel train engine on the table.

The dealer mentioned a large price, but the customer was unfazed. He must have been an avid collector. He made a counter offer. I heard the dealer say, "OK, you can have it for that, but I want a hug too, otherwise no deal." The customer said something else and the dealer shook his head.

I moved to the very end of the table to look at a pile of framed animation cels.

"I have authentication certificates for each of those," called the dealer as the train collector hugged him.

"Maggie," called Farrel, "see if there's a Daffy."

I knew Farrel already had a small collection of animation cels. These clear acetate sheets were generated by the thousands by animation artists, each one showing a slight movement and then photographed over a painted background. Jesse had given Farrel a cel of Bugs Bunny on Mars, as a present on Farrel's birthday in the first year they were together.

I don't talk about this much, but during the three years between the loss of my mother and the annexation of the Martinez family to my own, I spent each afternoon in front of the TV set watching a local small-town kids' show stream ancient mind-numbing cartoons for hours. I sat transfixed, trying to absorb the silliness and reconstitute it as the armor I needed to block out sadness and loss. It was bizarre that the station was showing cartoons that were thirty years out of date, instead of the cartoons produced at the time. I suppose it had something to do with the lack of cable TV in that part of NY State.

Like most cartoon connoisseurs of any age, I liked the Warners' best. I found the steely strength and mental fortitude of Bugs Bunny bracing and the sophisticated hysteria of Daffy Duck a hoot, but I loathed cartoons that featured moronic kids or redundant cat and mouse antics. Regardless, the memory of every one of them is etched in my brain.

I flipped through the cels on the table. No Daffy. These acetate paintings were all from 1950s and '60s cartoons. Two images of Speedy Gonzales, a cartoon I'd always found racist even as a child, and one of the Parisian King of sexual harassment Pepé Le Pew.

There was also a Casper the Friendly Ghost cel. As a child I was morbidly fascinated with Casper. After all he was a ghost who could communicate and even hug his *friends*. But I was also constantly disappointed by the incredibly insipid story lines that never had a laugh, and there was always at least one scene where Casper cried from loneliness. How could anyone find that amusing?

Kathryn came to my side while I was holding the Casper cel.

"I never understood Casper," she said idly. "He's a dead child, people scream when they see him, and he has to save someone from certain death just to get a little cordial conversation. Can you imagine some writer pushing the story line to a network executive by saying, *We'll make it a comedy cartoon for kids?* I liked *Animaniacs*."

"They didn't show *Animaniacs* in our neck of the woods. I didn't get to see them until I was a grown-up."

"Yes, well, neither did I," she smirked. "What are these?"

"Um... this is Cool Cat with Colonel Rimfire. Rimfire was the antagonist. Cool Cat was a groovier version of the Pink Panther. I really liked Cool Cat. He was just so... cool. I looked at the price for a minute and then put it down wistfully. "The rest of these are of Merlin the Magic Mouse and his sidekick Second Banana. Do you think less of me because I know this?"

"Do you think less of me after my theoretical discourse about Casper?"

"No, they were my sentiments exactly."

"Do you think less of me because I didn't recognize Cool Cat and Merlin? All I know is that Mel Blanc did all the voices," mused Kathryn.

"Mel Blanc didn't do these voices. He did most of the earlier Warner Brothers voices, but not these. He didn't do these." For some reason this hit me like a punch in the jaw. Why was it so important to me to communicate this? I did a mental tsk, tsk. I was still too wound up with these cartoons.

"I have to stay for the auction," said Farrel joining us.

"Did you find something interesting to bid on?" asked Kathryn,

"May I see?"

Farrel nodded as I took a look around the entire frozen field and didn't see anyone that could have possibly been the red-haired runner in the maroon sweatshirt.

"You and Farrel go and look at the auction lots. I'll check the booths inside," I said.

"Should we be watching for anything, Batman?" asked Kathryn evenly.

"*Victoria.*"

****

It smelled like old grease and industrial cleanser in the block building. There was some heat but not enough to call it warm.

At the front of the large space were two rows of permanent dealer booths. In the far end of the building, a large open area was available for one day set-up at a slightly higher cost than the outdoor booths.

Dealers who set up in one day antique markets in the dead of winter don't do it because it's fun. They do it to make cash. They often shop the markets too. Getting good merch to sell takes a lot more time than actually selling it. Dealers scour other antique and flea markets, garage sales, auctions, and even dumpsters for items of value they can resell for more than they paid. Dealers buying for resale really score when the seller doesn't know the real value of what they have, desperately needs cash, and doesn't have much financial investment in what they're selling. Frankie Kibbey fit that description. If someone else was now selling his merch, they were in the same boat.

My eyes adjusted to the dim light and there in the corner booth by the back door was a young dealer with ginger-red hair, wearing a maroon hooded sweatshirt and jeans.

I considered my options. It's legal to make a citizen's arrest when a person is in the commission of a crime, but though selling stolen goods is a crime, I didn't have any proof his stuff was stolen.

Of course, Red was wanted for questioning in a murder case. *Maybe I'll just encourage him to come with me for a cozy chat with the police.*

I meandered slowly down the line, pretending to be interested in booths along the way. I lingered at a booth full of antique postcards. Red was dragging a big cardboard box through a side door. He hefted it onto an undraped table, along with the three other boxes he'd already brought in. Each was uncovered and brimming with newspaper wrapping.

Red's lack of Pesky experience was working to my advantage. Had he set up outside where the aggressive buyers were, they would have swarmed his boxes before first light and bought him out in the shortest possible time. Inside there was less action.

A few of the dealers in the building now wandered over to his table, so I was able to join the small crowd without spooking the mark. Red unwrapped items and called out the prices when people asked. I watched the action. He pulled out a hand-embroidered keepsake pillow. It was clearly 19th century. Two of the dealers asked how much.

Red said, "Um, like, twenty dollars, cash?"

One of the dealers rapidly tossed a twenty at him and took the pillow in exchange. As Red pressed the cash into his pocket, I got a good look at his face. He was young—couldn't have been more than a teenager. Bright red hair. Curiously light blue eyes that were red rimmed and dark circled from lack of sleep. His most noticeable feature after his red hair was a pervasive look of fear lurking behind every one of his nervous expressions.

Customer service was not his forte. Red didn't know how to encourage cash flow. He ignored the questions of customers and kept twisting around to glance out the door and around the room. All the while he didn't realize his biggest problem—me—was standing right in front of him. This was exactly the way I wanted it.

Red pulled items out of his boxes and sold them slowly because he had no idea how much this stuff was worth. Things that Cora Martin would sell for $900 he was selling for $40. The low prices were making some of the potential customers nervous.

"Is it a repro?" asked one in disbelief.

I moved down the table peering at the still wrapped items. There were sculptural figures and drawings that were obviously by Victoria Snow. This was where it had to end, because though some of the objects of virtue were worth several hundred dollars, these items by Snow were worth thousands, and they surely belonged to someone other than this teenage desperado.

Time to act. I covertly pulled out my phone and texted Kathryn, < Need backup bring farrel >.

This was going to be a trial by fire for Kathryn, but Farrel had pulled my bacon out of the broiler more than once.

My cell buzzed back, < OK >.

Red was making a short sale on some silver candlesticks that was causing the guy buying them to sob at his own luck. Red didn't care. All he could see were the five twenties the customer was fanning in his direction.

I took out my P.I. badge and held it up. I shouted at Red, "The police have a warrant out for you for questioning on a murder, and I have reason to believe this merchandise has been stolen. You need to accompany me to the Fenchester Police Station."

I scanned the dealers who'd made major scores. The few shady ones were ducking out side doors, their bargain-priced loot in hand.

Red's head snapped up. He froze. The customer with the candlesticks dropped them on the table and snapped back his twenties.

Red tried for bravado but only managed a reedy squeak.

"Look, you're wanted for questioning all over the state. Come with me to speak to the police. It really will be safer for you if you do it this way." I said honestly.

In a weak spurt of misplaced self preservation, Red grabbed a beautiful enameled vase that was still partly wrapped in newspaper. It looked Austrian and valuable. As the newspaper wrapping dropped away, he threw it at me like a forward pass. The small crowd of antique dealers gasped. I caught it with both hands and carefully set it back on the table. The dealers cheered.

Red fumbled in his sweatshirt pocket and pulled out an old-fashioned straight razor. He slashed at me and then behind him at the other dealers in his way. They parted down the middle like a '70s hairstyle and he ran between them. I tried to run after him, but I had to sidle past the tables. I leapt to catch up, as Red slashed at another shopper, nearly nicking her hand.

But there was no need for me to grab him. Outside the door, Kathryn swung her new Wagner frying pan like a baseball bat, whacking Red squarely in the back as he tried to brandish the razor again. He pitched forward, sprawling on the gravel.

He continued to slash out with the razor as he scrambled to get up again. I kicked the razor out of his hand.

A second later I was on top of him, whipping my handcuffs from my belt in the back and snapping them on his wrists. "I'm making a citizen's arrest for attempted assault with a deadly weapon."

****

"I'm going with you," Kathryn said after Farrel and I had dragged Red to his twenty-year-old minivan and pushed him through the side door and shoved the rest of his boxes alongside him.

"Kathryn, you should go with Farrel," I said as she handed me the razor she'd picked up from the gravel a few feet from Red's hand.

"Not negotiable. I'm coming with you. As a matter of fact, I'm going to drive," said Kathryn. She folded her arms and looked at me steadily.

I sighed as Farrel snorted. Farrel said in a stage whisper, "You don't have a chance."

Kathryn winked at me disarmingly.

"This is serious, Kathryn," I said.

"I know. That's why I'm driving. Don't shake your head at me."

It probably would be smarter to have her drive while I questioned Red. We'd have to take him straight to the police station and once we got there I wouldn't have another chance to talk to him one-to-one. "Oh, all right. But wait outside for a few minutes." I turned away from her and slid into the Chevy Astro with Red.

All the seats were gone except the driver's. We had to use the sliding side door because the double back doors were tied shut with rusty wire and a chain with an old padlock that somebody had probably lost the key to in the last century. Dirt peppered the worn gray carpeting. Crumpled sheets of newspaper were ready to roll around like tumbleweeds when Kathryn took the wheel. Besides Red lying on his side, the Chevy held two used paint cans, an open cardboard box with a piece of painting tarp, some used paint rollers, and the four other dirty boxes that were filled with the fine antiques that Red had been underselling.

I pulled Red over on his back and got close to his face. In my best bad cop manner I growled, "You are going to lie quietly and behave yourself."

He whined in a reedy voice, "Who are you? You want money? Take the stuff. The van's a piece of shit, but you can have it too."

"I'm taking you to Fenchester Police Headquarters, where you're wanted for questioning in a murder investigation. You also just tried to slash a lot of people with a rusty razor, and that's grounds for a citizen's arrest just about anywhere. Why didn't you just come with me?"

He squealed, "Police! Murder? Is it Frankie!?! Is Frankie dead? Oh shit. Oh no," he sobbed.

"What's your name?"

"I didn't kill nobody."

"I didn't say you did. What's your name?"

"Red."

"Red? You're kidding. Well that's a coincidence, but it's not your real name."

He hesitated.

"You're in a lot of trouble right now, Red. And you don't have any friends. If you didn't help to kill Frankie, then I'll do what I can for you."

"I didn't kill him. I'd never."

"Real name... right now."

"It's Sydney... Sydney Kibbey, but people call me Red."

"Was Francis Kibbey your brother?"

"Yes... I didn't kill him! I didn't even know he was dead."

"You saw him get shot! They reported he died on the news. How could you not know? Did you just not *notice* he wasn't coming home for dinner?"

"I don't watch news." Red smelled like a clothes hamper in a men's dorm during finals week. And though he was scared, he didn't seem very upset about his brother's death.

"OK, keep quiet and don't move." I tugged the chain of keys out of his pocket and unclipped it from his belt, then crawled back out of the van and took out my cell to call Sgt. Ed O'Brien, but the officer on duty told me it was his day off. So I asked for Sgt. Marc Freligh.

I'd known Marc on the force for longer than I'd known Ed. We'd gone through the academy together. He was a good cop and an ally and often Marc had more imagination when investigating a complicated case than Ed did.

"Marc? I'm bringing in that guy wanted for questioning about the shooting in the graveyard."

"I didn't kill him," groaned Red from inside the van.

"Shhhh," I said.

"What?"

"Not you, Marc."

"Maggie, you mean the maroon sweatshirt perp with the red hair who shot that guy in the cemetery? The one that you and the Scottish woman saw?"

"Yes, right. His name is Sydney Kibbey and the one who was killed was named Francis Kibbey. They were brothers. Thing is, I don't think he did it. And neither does the other witness... the Scottish woman. Neither of us saw a gun."

"Yeah well, O'Brien does, and I was pretty much sold on him too. But, you say he didn't have a gun? Oh man. Well, I'll start processing his information either way. What's your ETA?"

"About forty-five minutes."

"What? Where the heck are you?"

"Peskeetotemburg."

"Pesky? That's not in our... Wait, forget I said that. In fact, forget we're talking. Just get him in here."

"He was selling stuff that was worth a boatload of money, and he has no idea where it came from. He also tried to slash me with one of those old flip-open razors in front of witnesses."

"Receiving stolen goods, attempted assault with a deadly weapon. Both felonies. Are you sure the stuff is stolen?"

"*Suspicion of.* I'll see you in a little while."

"Maggie, be careful OK? We're looking at him for murder, so be sure he's secure. You know what I mean?"

"OK. See you soon."

I turned to Kathryn, who had the heavy bag over her shoulder and a bright gleam in her eye.

I smirked and tossed her the keys. "OK, OK, let's go, Robin."

She angled behind the wheel and turned the engine over.

Farrel drives slowly and evenly. Even her cats like riding with her. With Kathryn at the wheel we'd get back faster than Farrel any day, but I was a little sick just imagining what it would be like.

"Kathryn, take it easy on the gas. There's nothing to hang on to back here."

"Gentle as a kitten," she said.

"Yeah, well, I had a kitten in grad school who knocked over a bookcase to get to the plants on the top shelf. As I recall she also used to pounce on me in the middle of the night and bite my neck."

"I could do that," said Kathryn, adjusting the mirrors and revving the engine. I heard the seatbelt click and her shift into gear.

It's a manual, I groaned inwardly.

The old van bumped over the uneven parking lot and out onto the main road. I was watching Red. What I didn't see was the full-sized white Econoline van with tinted windows fire up its motor and roll out of the parking lot ten car lengths behind us.

Even with gentle driving, this twenty-year-old engine would have groaned out a high-pitched whine. Going up South Hill, over a road that was potholed like a toaster waffle, the Astro's engine sounded like an old kitchen blender crushing ice on high. Kathryn took the winding back route to Fenchester. She held the road fairly smoothly through hardwood groves and past two-hundred-year-old farms.

Red groaned. "Can't you take the hand-cuffs off? I said I didn't kill Frankie."

"Look Red, you slashed at me with this," I said holding the razor between two fingers, "and you're a flight risk."

"I'm scared. Those guys are after me cause I took their van."

"What guys? Look, Red, I'm not a cop, and you don't have to say a word to me, but if you really didn't kill Frankie, I'm just about the only person who's willing to listen. The cops are looking for someone to lock up and throw away the key. *And* there are other guys after you too? Maybe you'd better tell me what happened in the cemetery on Sunday."

I stared at Red's face pressed flat against the dirty carpeting while he made up his mind.

"I'll talk about Frankie."

He didn't sound threatening or dangerous, but on the other hand he might be working with a murderer and he tried to slash me. This is the kind of situation that instructors at the academy caution rookies about. *Don't let your guard down.* There's nothing worse than having to explain how the perp got the upper hand when he'd been completely under control at the beginning of the interrogation. That was what Marc Freligh was hinting about on the phone.

But handcuffing a person is a risky thing to do, even in a citizen's arrest. As a P.I. I'm not really supposed to do it unless the perp is dangerous or I'd witnessed him committing a crime and he was about to flee. Among other things, I would be legally responsible if he got hurt in any way. Red didn't quite fit the profile of someone who had to be handcuffed.

I sighed and hauled him into a sitting position with his back against the side door as Kathryn slowed to rumble over the train tracks at South Fen Crossing.

"Don't make me sorry I'm doing this," I said to Red as I unlocked the cuffs and put them in my pocket.

"All this slow and even driving is wreaking havoc on my ability to travel at the speed of light," called Kathryn above the whine of the Chevy's neglected engine.

"What were you doing in the cemetery before Frankie got shot?" I asked Red.

"I... I had went there to meet him. To help get some stuff to sell."

"He had it in the graveyard? Where was it? Where did he get it?"

"I don't know," whined Red, flailing one arm to keep upright as we went around the corner. "We found it."

"You found it? You did? Where?"

"Well, Frankie told me he found it. He was with those guys that take things from people, but then Cue and Willie got arrested. So Frankie needed another job. He never went into the places like Cue and Willie. He just drove the van."

"Cue.... Cue?... like Cue Ball? Was he bald? Were these the guys who dressed up like they worked at the water company and stole from old people? All this stuff you were selling is stuff they stole?"

Red nodded. "Yes... No this is Frankie's stuff. Wait, they didn't really steal; they just took things when people weren't looking," said Red innocently.

"That's pretty much the definition of stealing, Red. So why are they mad at *you*?"

"Well, Frankie borrowed their van. And I still have it. See Frankie found a stash of some really old shit, like antiques and stuff. He didn't tell nobody but me. He took some and then borrowed Cue and Willie's van to go to a flea market on Sunday and it sold really good. So he wanted to get more and he needed me to help, so he texted me to meet him in Skeleton Park near that statue of the girl in the nightgown."

"So you met him?"

"Yeah."

"And? You went to get stuff?"

"Yeah, well no, see we started to. We went past these bushes and Frankie went in this cement house. It was dark... and he started to hold up his lighter..." Red began to shake. He swallowed a few times before he could go on. "But... there was somebody there in the dark. And Frankie freaked and yelled for me to run. There was a shot. I ran to the side and Frankie ran past me. Then there was another shot and Frankie *spinned* around, like he was doing a dance. He didn't look hurt, just like he was spinning around, you know like when you're a kid and you spin? And then he fell down. I ran over to him. There was blood and he whispered for me to run. So I did."

"Who shot him?"

"Didn't see."

"You didn't see? That doesn't make sense, Red."

"Frankie was in the way in front of me. He dropped his lighter. It was dark, like as dark as when you close your eyes at night."

"But how did you get out of the graveyard without the cops seeing you?"

"I was running like freaking hell and I didn't want to get caught, so I ran around and back past the bushes and to a little cement house. I hid behind a statue in the back of it. It was really tight, but I squeezed in and I waited there for, like, hours. I fell asleep and when I woke up it was dark and I was so cold. I pushed past the bushes and there was no one around, so I got out without no one seeing." Red was shaking again.

"Why would you go back to the cement house when there had been someone with a gun in there?"

"Well, well see, I heard the police and I have a warrant. I didn't want to run into the cops."

"You were more afraid of the police than of someone who had just shot your brother?"

Red nodded. "I guess that was stupid. Frankie had said there was stuff in there... but there wasn't nothing in the cement house to take, so I just hid. It was a good hiding place."

I shook the disbelief out of my head. I'd heard stories like this a hundred times when I'd been on the police, especially from teenagers. Red felt he had nowhere else to go, and he'd wanted to find more things to sell. Simple as that. I sighed. "What kind of a warrant?'

"Failure to appear, for a shoplifting charge."

"Doesn't seem like you always make good choices, Red. Where was this crypt? Can you show me?"

Red shook his head again and pushed his bright red hair out of his eyes. "I looked for hours on Monday, but all those little freakin' cement houses look the same."

"Well, how did Frankie find it? Did he tell you?"

"Probably followed somebody. That's what Cue and Willie do when they seen somebody old who looks like they had money. They just follow them to see where they live."

"So where did you get this stuff you were selling today?"

"Frankie already had it in the van. See, I knew Cue and Willie would come looking for the van, since Frankie took it on Sunday. So I had to sell the stuff before they found it. I couldn't bring stuff in the house or nothing because... well, it's not safe where I live."

I was thinking about a home that was less safe than an old van tied up with rusty wire and beginning to understand Red a little better when a huge crash lurched us forward. Red and I were sent ricocheting off the van's wall. I held on to the seatbelt dangling where the passenger seat had once been as Red rolled all the way to the back. .

"What was that?" yelled Red.

I saw a flash of white out the back window, then saw Kathryn glance in the rear view mirror, grip the wheel, and stamp on the gas.

"Brace yourself," yelled Kathryn. "We're going to be rammed again!"

There was another crash. I'd been ready for it this time. I held on to the metal legs of the front seat. I'd felt the jolt but missed the secondary recoil. Not so for Red. He bounced off the inside of the back door and three of his boxes slammed against his ass.

Red groaned at the sight of the van gaining on us again. "Shit! What the..."

I was ahead of him, way past *what,* I needed to know *who.* This wasn't a random act of road rage.

Kathryn was in her element. She took the curves, sped up, and left whatever was slapping our butts in her dust for a minute.

"Oh my! Hold on!" she yelled again. I heard the screech of tires and felt the van take a curve on two wheels. I managed to pull myself up to my knees so I could see out the back windows. A big white van with a dark-tinted windshield was racing up behind us, readying for another lunge.

Both Kathryn and I knew we were coming to the South Mountain cliffs that we had to skirt before driving down into Lenape Valley. Kathryn's eyes darted to the rearview mirror again, then back to the road.

"We're about fifty feet ahead of that van," shouted Kathryn over the din of the straining motor.

I hoped fleetingly that the transmission would hold out, just as it popped out of gear. Kathryn jammed it back in, double clutching like a pro.

"Red, is this some pissed off friend of yours?" I yelled over the squeal of tires.

"Hell no! I don't know anybody with a van like that. Holy Mother of God!" gasped Red as we hit a bump in the road and literally made air under all four tires.

The Astro's front end bounced up, and when the back wheels struck the pavement again sparks flew from the tailpipe hitting the road, and we had a full view of the white van behind us. I peered hard, trying to see through the windshield, but it was covered with some kind of mylar reflective coating. All I could see was the reflection of the dented rear end of the minivan we were in and my own face.

Huh. So that's what I look like when I'm in a life and death situation. My face looked far calmer than I felt.

We were now speeding along the cliff's edge. Kathryn was doing her best to hold the Astro away from the forty foot drop as the road curved up the mountain, but she was going twice as fast as the posted speed limit. And the big Ford van behind us was going faster than that.

"It's going to hit us again!" called Kathryn. Her voice was even, almost calm. Yet I didn't have time to dwell on how proud I was of her.

"Hold it steady, Kathryn. I'm going to kick out a back window."

"Hurry," yelled Kathryn. "Here it comes."

The back windows were hinged at the top. I kicked the lower edge of the one on the driver's side and the plastic lock popped open. The window swung from the top but crashed back down. I grabbed the scissor jack that was in the wall pocket of the van, hefted it over my head, and hurled it at the top hinge of the window. The window broke out and the jack sailed out as well. Both hit the grill of the white van, which swerved and braked, slowing it down for a short moment.

It was a good thing it did. I could feel Kathryn taking a sharp outside curve. If we'd been hit then, we would have gone over. I grabbed one of the paint cans and shook it hard. Paint sloshed inside. I thrust my hand in my pocket for my keys and used one to pry open the lid. Swirling the paint in the open can, I crawled on my knees to the window and holding the can like a water bucket I tossed the liquid out. It covered almost all the van's windshield in one broad splash. There was an immediate squealing of brakes as the white van desperately fought to hold the road.

"Kathryn, slow down. We're losing 'em."

The white van's powerful windshield wipers came on. I saw an arm stick out the driver's side. The hand held a gun. It fired one shot and then turned off on a side road. The shot from the white van had gone way wide over the cliff.

If Fenchester had had 500 police officers with nothing else to do, they could have combed the countryside for the slug. *So long, slug.*

CHAPTER 14

"Maggie says she found this guy Sidney Kibbey selling junk at a flea market..." Sergeants Marc Freligh and Ed O'Brien were briefing their team and I was invited to put in my two cents.

I sighed inwardly at so many shaved heads. Fenchester Police Department was still following a paramilitary model. The paramilitary model hires officers based on rigid physical fitness requirements most easily achieved by large-sized males. Women applicants can score 100% on the written test, have a black belt in Karate, an IQ higher than Steven Hawking, be able to run fast enough to win Olympic Gold, and have x-ray vision, but if they can't jump sixteen and a half inches from a standing position, they fail the entrance exam to the academy.

Now don't get me wrong, I fully support the Fenchester Police, and I know a dozen officers, including both O'Brien and Freligh, who are as smart and wily as any star on a fictional cop show. But the two big problems with the paramilitary police model is that it doesn't recognize that a diverse group of people with unique skills and attributes is a better team at complex problem solving than a group of people where everyone thinks, looks, and is even sized the same.

In ten years on the force, I never had to jump sixteen and a half inches from a standing position, but twice during a pursuit I squeezed through a tiny window to nab a suspect, leaving the rest of the bulkier police team behind. One time, when the rest of the squad was readying a battering ram, my smaller hand was able to reach through a mail slot and unlock a steel door, ending a hostage situation without anyone getting hurt.

The second reason the paramilitary model isn't appropriate is that it doesn't necessarily fill the police ranks with people who are the most likely to understand how to deter or solve crime. An applicant with a Ph.D. in criminal psych gets no more consideration than an applicant with nothing more than a lackluster high school education. Not saying that high school grads can't figure things out, but they haven't studied *how* to gather information from diverse sources. In my police experience, when it came to a complex case, uninformed preliminary conclusions were the biggest deterrent to solving it.

Cutting crime in a small city isn't like fighting a war. The two most likely reasons for violent death in a small city are gangs, or domestic violence in families. Fighting most crime has a lot to do with working on stopping it before it happens. Calming community tension, getting the confidence of citizens so they'll alert police to problems, getting young people to avoid gangs, figuring out how to stop gangs from forming altogether, gathering the best information in the fastest way, setting up programs to curb domestic violence, communicating with diverse cultures are not things that soldiers are trained to do. What's needed for police in small cities is a social work model.

You never see a team of young social workers who all just recently shaved their heads. *Just saying.*

Sergeant Ed O'Brien said, "Maggie thinks he didn't do it. I'm not so sure. I think we should hold him. Maggie, go ahead on your take..."

I pointed out something they were all still ignoring, that Nora Hasan had seen Red empty-handed when the second shot was fired and so had I. Since there was no evidence, they couldn't hold him on a murder charge. All Red could say about Frankie's murder was that someone standing in a dark crypt shot him. He wasn't even sure where the crypt was, just that it was near some bushes. I told them about Frankie's relationship to the home invasion crew of bogus water company workers, too.

Sgt. Marc Freligh said, "Forget about either Cue or Willie doing the shooting; they were both in custody at the time it happened. That's thanks to Maggie, by the way."

"But they're out now. One of them could have been driving the white van that rammed Maggie," suggested Tito Rodriguez, one of my old partners from vice squad.

"Maybe, but where would those guys get a van like that?"

"Boosted it?" said Tito.

"Why ram us though?"

"Maybe they wanted the stuff Frankie was selling...."

I thought about this, but it seemed unlikely that they'd even known about the merchandise Frankie was selling. Unless Frankie had stolen it from them and not told Red that. Hmmm, that was an idea.

"Might there be something else hidden in the van that they wanted? Money, drugs, jewelry from one of their home invasions?" asked Marc. He went ahead and assigned two officers to search it carefully.

That was more likely. But it still seemed wrong to me.

I'd given the police my information. I felt like I was done there. Earlier in the day, I'd dropped Kathryn off at the loft on the way to the police station.

Before I drove away, Kathryn had said, "I know you have to work, but I have quite a buzz going. I'd hate to waste it." I could see the telltale glow of adrenalin surge in her expression. The last thing I'd wanted to do was leave her to take Red in, especially because this was supposed to be a day we spent together.

Dealing with Red at the police station had stretched from the afternoon into the evening. I ached each time I looked at my watch and remembered that last searing glance Kathryn had sent my way.

"Maggie," said Ed, "you're going to have to go through this stuff with the evidence clerk to catalog it now. These old things are probably pretty valuable and we don't even know what half of them are called."

"Ed, that'll take hours," I sighed.

Ed smirked. "All you have to do is tell us what the stuff is called so we can look it up. What, you have some better place to be?"

"As a matter of fact, I do."

****

It had taken hours to catalog the impounded antiques Frankie had *found.* The police wanted exact values for all thirty-five items. Value determines both the severity and the punishment of a property crime and accurate descriptions are required in identification of ownership. The Austrian vase with its Russian enamel decoration that Red had lobbed at me, for example, was worth about $5000.

It was nearly 9:30 p.m. by the time I got back home.

I took the steps two at a time and fairly burst through the main doors of the loft when I got to the third floor. *Not being very cool here, detective.*

Kathryn wasn't there, though her blue and white mini Cooper was in the small parking lot. I could smell her perfume, but the whole place had begun to smell faintly of her all the time. I put my Beretta away in the gun safe and then went into the bedroom. No Kathryn in there, or the laundry room, or bathroom either.

I was figuring she may have gone for a walk when I heard the door at the top of the spiral staircase open. She came down the steps and crossed the room to the counter in the kitchen area. She had in her iPod earplugs so she didn't notice me. I could faintly hear the driving rhythm of the Gypsy

Kings. A hot dance tune was making her hips sway. She went through the mail on the counter, putting things addressed to her in a separate pile.

I came up behind her, pressed against her, and kissed her neck.

"Oh, are you still here?" she said. "You better get going before my girlfriend gets back."

I laughed. "Uh huh, very funny. Well, I deserve that for leaving you alone all day."

She reached up a hand and stroked the side of my face to my throat.

I turned her around and lifted her up to the countertop.

"Pay attention to me now," she said.

"Do you want to go to bed?" I asked in low voice.

"As a matter of fact, I do, but I think you should have dinner first and tell me everything that happened after you dropped me off. I'm Della Street, remember? Shall I fix you something to eat? Do you have more work to do or can I have you all to myself now?"

I kissed her again and smiled. "I had something to eat at the station. Um, I just have to make a few notes in my computer, and I have to charge my phone. It ran down."

"I know. I tried to call you and it went right to voice mail. Oh, and Lois Henshaw tried to call you. She said she's tried six times!"

"She said? Did she call *you*?"

"Indeed she did. She wants you to call her. She sounded desperate."

"I'd better call. I pulled out my little Mac and noted the details about Red in chronological order as I tried Lois Henshaw's number.

"There's no answer at the Henshaw residence," I said typing.

When I was done with the notes I told Kathryn everything that happened at the police station as I had a cup of coffee. She asked questions about procedure and the evidence impound.

"Maggie, are you sure about me working with you? If you don't want me to, then skip the formal hiring and we'll pretend I never asked."

"You're already hired. I checked with the insurance company, added your name to the rider, filled out the W-2 papers, and put you on the payroll as an intern. All done while I was waiting around the police station. You'll have to sign a few papers. By the way, interns only get out-of-pocket reimbursement."

"I promise not to get in your way. This is really just so we can talk about things and keep them confidential. If we were straight... we could have... uh."

I knew what she was thinking. If we were straight and legally married, we would have spousal immunity if either one of us was subpoenaed.

Same-sex couples lose out on that right, federally and locally, because even same-sex marriages from marriage equality states like Connecticut aren't recognized in Pennsylvania and no same-sex marriages are recognized by the federal government. Of course... we aren't at that stage, not yet anyway.

I said, "We haven't had a chance to talk about Victoria Snow's papers."

"Oh yes. Well, the Charlotte Cushman part is so frank! I would never have imagined that a thirty-year-old Victorian Era woman would have had the boldness to write down that graphic story even in her private journal. If someone had found it, I suppose terrible things could have happened to her. Still I've read that more than one of Charlotte Cushman's young devotees wrote *her* letters like that and she responded in kind. She got those women to promise to burn the letters, but of course they didn't and some still survive."

"So did Victoria and Evangeline hook up, or did Evangeline stay true to her rich fiance, Merganser Hunterdon?"

"I only had an hour and a half with the papers, but I managed to look everything over. There's nothing further about their relationship anywhere in the file. Whether her courage held up once she got to Fenchester or if she just had to be content to love Evangeline from afar is still a mystery."

"But I want to know whether she made that little sculpture while looking at that lovely woman in all her natural glory, or if Victoria just used her imagination."

"I do too. But this journal doesn't tell us. Anyway, I'm having the first volume of the journal made into a digital file."

"Uh huh, I heard about the young woman who is *devoted to you* in the media department."

"Devoted? I wouldn't say... Well," Kathryn paused to consider, then she smiled a little.

"And you're concerned about *my* fidelity?" I laughed.

"I'm sure she's just concerned about adding to her resume."

"Yeah, another notch on her resume."

Kathryn smirked. "But seriously, surely that journal is the first book of a set. Where are the others? There's so little historical information about Victoria's personal life, and she lived right here in Fenchester!"

"Well, it's a big archive. Maybe there are more files down there. How many miles does Irwin College say it is?"

"Not as big as some huge systems. The New York Library has eighty-eight miles of stacks. Bryant Park Library in Manhattan has over forty miles. Irwin's is more like twenty."

I stared at her. "Twenty miles of stacks? That would reach to downtown Wassailberg!"

"The stacks connect underground to the old library buildings as well, all the way to College Street. Expanding the stacks is really why they had to build the new Wellington Library ten years ago."

I imagined a cross-cut of the campus showing both above and below. Like a drawing of a tree showing both its branch and root systems.

"If we want the answer to the fruition of Victoria's and Evangeline's romance we may have to search for it."

"You could ask Isabella Santiago to help you find it. Did you see her while you were there?"

"I was hypersensitive, darting my eyes up every few minutes just to catch a glimpse of her. I didn't see her, though."

"Did you ask Amanda about her?"

Kathryn nodded. "I did. I called her. I didn't exactly ask if Isabella is alive. I just asked Amanda to tell me about her and she said rather calmly that she has spoken to Isabella several times and was lucky to have her help. When I asked her if she knew anything else about her, Amanda told me, 'Dr. Santiago was very private, so I find further research in this area is better left undone.'"

"Left undone?"

"Really Maggie, we may just have to leave this alone. What's that line from MacBeth? *Life's but a walking shadow.*"

"Why is it that Shakespeare keeps coming up? I feel like I hear it everywhere these days."

"Well, Victoria's journal certainly shows that Charlotte Cushman peppered her seductions with it. And Gabe Carbondale. And Nora!"

"Yes, Nora, I'd like to mention once again that though Nora's flirty with everyone, she's certainly in your devotional harem. Her voice hushes when she speaks of you. It's enough to make me into a green-eyed monster."

Kathryn laughed. "*Green-eyed monster* that was coined by Shakespeare, too. It's from *Othello*. Iago says:

> *O, beware, my lord, of jealousy;*
> *It is the green-eyed monster which doth mock*
> *The meat it feeds on; that cuckold lives in bliss*
> *Who, certain of his fate, loves not his wronger;*
> *But, O, what damned minutes tells he o'er*
> *Who dotes, yet doubts, suspects, yet strongly loves!*"

Kathryn thought for a moment. "But, maybe Portia uses it better in *The Merchant of Venice* when she says:

> *How all the other passions fleet to air,*
> *As doubtful thoughts, and rash-embraced despair,*
> *And shuddering fear, and green-eyed jealousy! O love,*
> *Be moderate; allay thy ecstasy,*
> *In measure rein thy joy; scant this excess.*
> *I feel too much thy blessing: make it less,*
> *For fear I surfeit."*

"Kathryn, do you *fear surfeit*? I thought you were a fan of passion."

"I am indeed. So I'll have to find another way to *rein in doubtful thoughts, and rash-embraced despair.*" Kathryn found something in her shoulder bag and brought it over to the table. It was a paper sack.

She said, "In pre-celebration of your birthday, I got you an early present from the antique market this morning, before all the excitement began. This is just one in a series of surprises I have for you. Oh, and Farrel and Jessie want to have a little dinner party for you on Friday evening."

"If it doesn't get in the way of your plans."

"I believe I can work around it," she said in a low voice.

Inside the bag was a small rubber mold for the kind of clay that always stays soft until you fire it in a kitchen oven. There was also a set of wooden clay tools.

Kathryn said, "Can you use that clay I gave you before in this?"

"Yes!" I went to a drawer in the kitchen and pulled out the set of small blocks of clay. I took the porcelain-colored one back to the table and began to knead it to make it soft.

Kathryn watched me, her eyes bright, her breathing deep. I pressed the ball of clay into the flexible mold and then popped the face out. It was detailed but not an expression I would choose. So I tore open the clay tools and began to reform the face.

After a few moments I looked up at her thinking at first that it would be fun to make this face look like Kathryn. Then I realized I'd been absorbed in this task for several minutes.

I said, "I'm sorry. I'm not paying attention to you. But you know what art supplies do to me!"

"Yes, they make you excited. I was counting on that."

"It's a science experiment?"

"In a way. But also the little mold reminded me of those decorated faces that Victoria made. I like to watch you. May we talk while you work?"

"Yes, always, but I think I'd like to work on something else now." I'd noticed Kathryn's shirt was open an extra button and it was giving me a different kind of artistic impulse that I didn't want to waste.

"Which do you think is more life affirming? Making love or falling asleep in each other's arms?" I asked.

"Does this have to be an either or decision?"

"No, it doesn't. You can also select all of the above."

The doorbell rang.

"Rats," said Kathryn. "Maybe whoever it is will just go away."

The bell rang again, continuously for the next twenty seconds. I knew who it was. "Betcha a backrub it's Lois Henshaw," I sighed.

"Lois is your client. If it is she, you must talk to her." Kathryn looked at her watch. "My dear, getting up before 5 a.m. has taken its toll on me. I'm going to have to go to bed. But I don't have any obligations tomorrow, so I'm available for a breakfast date."

"Will you be available for a pre-breakfast date?"

"Mmmmm, yes, even better."

****

"It's Samson. He hasn't come home for almost two days," said Lois.

I had let Lois Henshaw into the building and taken her to my office, because I was afraid if I took her up to the loft, I'd never get her out of it. She was wearing a goofy hat. It was actually in the shape of Goofy the Dog's head. She lifted it off by the ear-flap ears and plopped it on my desk. It stared at us as we talked.

"Lois, isn't the big problem between you and Samson that you *never* know where he is?"

"No, no, no, au contraire. Like I told you before Maggie, I always know *where* he is. See, he has one of those GPS things on his phone."

"You mean *you* put one of those GPS things on his phone... Does he know?"

"About the GPS? Well not exactly. See, I'm of the *what you don't know won't hurt you* school of thought."

"Uh, no, if you were really of that school, you wouldn't have hired me."

Lois's brows knit together in profound concentration. Finally she said, "I love him, Maggie. I've never loved anyone else. He's my everything."

"OK, so...."

"So, the GPS says he's in the cemetery and he hasn't moved. I even went to look for him, but he's not there. He disappeared and I'm very worried about him. I think something has happened to him."

"Maybe he went for a walk in there and lost it or something."

"Maggie, you said you'd find out about him. Right now I'd settle for you just *finding* him. I have a bad feeling about this. It's killing me."

It was nearly midnight, and my patience had worn thin, no thanks to unquenched randiness and lack of sleep. I wanted to yell at Lois that maybe Samson was tired of a relationship that included twenty-four hour satellite tracking. But one look at her face showed me that would have crushed her. Clearly she really did love him, and sometimes love makes people do desperate things. Right now, Lois Henshaw looked as desperate as a teenaged tech addict in a power failure.

"Lois, I did talk to Samson and he said he would clear this up in a few more days. He asked me not to tell you any more than that. But I'm working for you, so I'll tell you if you want."

"Yes, tell. No, don't. Yes... wait do, no... No don't tell me, no, I'd rather hear it from him... But... he's never been gone this long."

"Maybe he went away for a few days to figure things out." This might really be true, but I also wondered if Samson had just taken the chicken's way out and left town or if maybe he'd finally found Suzanne Carbondale and his dreams had actually come true. Either way, he was really being a weasel about Lois.

I added softly, "Look, I'll check around for him in the morning. Don't worry. Go home now and I'll call you tomorrow."

Lois left reluctantly and I went back to Kathryn in the loft.

Kathryn was nearly asleep when I came in. But she turned over and said drowsily, "What did she want? I guess you can tell me now that I'm your intern. I think I'm going to add this to my resume," she yawned.

I said, as I changed into a long t-shirt, "Samson didn't come home and the creepy little stalking program that Lois put on his phone says he's in Skeleton Park and hasn't moved for forty hours. She looked for him but there was no sign of him."

"He must have lost his phone."

"That's what I told her."

I got in bed and stared up at the ceiling, trying to work out something elusive. I said, "Lois said Samson disappeared in the cemetery, but really it's his phone, right? But I wonder why?"

"Why what?" whispered Kathryn.

"Why do so many people seem to be disappearing? I can't figure it out. I'm sorry Kathryn. I'm supposed to be paying attention to you."

She opened her arms and I settled into them. She whispered in my ear, *"Before-breakfast-date."* And then we fell asleep.

CHAPTER 15

On Thursday morning at 5 a.m. I woke with a start, already struggling to figure things out. When I'd spoken to Samson Henshaw last, it had been late at night and he was on Hazel Street. Obviously he had his phone then. Where was he now? If he actually met up with Suzanne Carbondale and finally ran away with her, why would he have gone into the cemetery?

I went up the spiral stairs to my studio and found a large block of white oven-bake clay and a box of seashells and brought them back to the dining room table.

I took out the little rubber face mold and formed six two-inch-tall faces. I went and got the bigger molded faces Victoria had made, unwrapped them, and lined them up on the big table. The shells Victoria had used with them didn't just decorate them; they acted as part of the form like hats and earrings and scarves.

I pressed some shells into the soft clay of the little faces I'd just made and then realized I wanted to change the nose, because it looked too cartoonish. I used the clay tools to do this. I molded some more faces and altered the features on each one, adding different shells, changing each face accordingly.

Victoria's molded faces watched me. I was struck by their similarity and the differences of each one as well. Obviously Victoria had also used one mold and then altered the features to make each face look different, just as I was doing.

"So, Victoria, I wonder how many variations you made of your angel," I said softly. "Whether she fell for you or not, when she disappeared from your life, it must have stung you for the rest of your days."

I thought about Frankie's murder. How the heck did Frankie's shooter get out of Skeleton Park without anyone seeing? I tore a large piece of drawing paper out of a pad I had next to the couch and laid it evenly on the large dining room table. Then I stared at it for a long time, visualizing the civil war cemetery from several angles. I drew the view I'd had from the top of the vault: *The Lost Bride*, the crypt behind her, the headstones, bushes, and trees. I drew the entrance gate, the ground, the shadows. It took an hour. I kept a very open mind as I did it. I was trying to remember everything.

I got up and walked away from it. I went to the kitchen and got a glass of orange juice; then I went back to the drawing and looked at it with fresh eyes. This is the way I work. It helps me see things from different points of view.

I thought about the other statues of Evangeline and sketched them into my drawing, and a bold symbol emerged. I stared at it and then into space. What about the parts I couldn't see?

I got my laptop and brought it back to the drawing. I booted up an aerial map program, the kind that shows satellite photos of most of the United States. I zoomed in to Fenchester, and then in to the two square blocks of the Civil War Cemetery north of Washington Mews. I magnified the image until I could clearly see a white dot that was the top of *The Lost Bride*'s head with the crypt beyond it. Zooming out one click, I could see the other five Evangeline statues, like a connect-the-dots picture—*The Lost Bride* to the east, the three others forming a perfect line to her, and the other two to the right and left. I rose and got a piece of tracing paper. I held it over the laptop screen and connected the dots of the five sculptures. They made a perfect arrow with *The Lost Bride* at its point. An aerial treasure map pointing to something else that I couldn't have seen from the ground. In a tight circle of yews behind *The Lost Bride* was another white dot, and a white square beyond that, big enough to be a small crypt. The arrow was pointing to it.

Now I knew why when both I and Nora were facing each other, we had both seen Red run *behind* a group of yews. He hadn't run behind them, he'd run into them, and hidden in the crypt in their center.

The Lost Bride beckoned me now. I stowed a strong flashlight in my small backpack, got my Beretta from the gun safe and tucked it into my shoulder harness, slipped on my warmest jacket, and went out into the predawn February morning. I figured I'd just have a look around and be back long before Kathryn woke up.

Farrel, who not only shops but occasionally sets up at early morning antique markets, always says that dawn or even a few minutes after it is the coldest part of the day. But I couldn't imagine how it could get any colder. My breath didn't just condense; it made frozen clouds that seemed to fall from the air and crack on the sidewalk.

The Mews was deserted. A frigid city wind whipped down the alleys, making small cyclones of frost-covered leaves in corners and doorways.

The wrought iron fence around the cemetery loomed. I followed it to the gate. It's funny how things look so different in the dark. The blackness of this space felt heavy but I didn't mind; it felt safer to me. I held my eyes shut tight for a count of sixty, to adjust.

I stood still and let all my senses send me signals. I thought about the sounds I was hearing, the shadows I could see, the smells, the feeling of the wind against my cheek. I opened my mouth and tasted the cold air. *OK, grasshopper, roll.*

Instead of taking the gravel road through the center, I went right and skirted the fence for a while. No one could have seen me. I was in the shadows whenever the moon peeked out. I made my way along the south side until I came to the corner; then I followed the east fence north until I was about three quarters of the way through the field of stones. I stopped and looked around, breathing softly as I patiently waited for the moon to come out again and show me the way. It did, and by now my eyes were so used to the dark I could see everything. I'll have to thank Jessie for all those carrots she froze for me from her victory garden.

I skipped using my flashlight. It would dim my night vision. I scanned about for any sign of Samson Henshaw, or his phone for that matter. I took out my own phone and called him. I could hear it ringing through my phone but not anywhere nearby. It was so quiet in the boneyard I could have heard it, even if it was only on vibrate.

I moved along the outer wall until I got a glimpse of *The Lost Bride*. There was no direct path to the statue from where I stood, but that didn't bother me. It was better to stay off the paths right now.

I moved carefully, staying low, weaving my own way through the stones, keeping undercover whenever I could. Finally I drew behind Evangeline's main statue. Tension had crept into my shoulders and neck the way it had that time in college when I realized I'd studied the wrong section of the text book in the middle of a major exam. Then, like now, I was flying by the seat of my pants. But why was I so edgy? There didn't seem to be anyone around; it was quiet. On the other hand, I was in a pitch-black graveyard where a guy had been shot just a few days before and the killer had magically disappeared. OK, yeah, I guess there was a reason to be nervous.

Butch up, I told myself.

A sliver of moon shone through the clouds again and cast a dim eerie light on Evangeline floating above the ground, waving me to her. She seemed more animated in the blue-gray moonlight. It was remarkable. I wished Kathryn was here to see her. Farrel once told me that soon after she met Jessie she stopped being able to fully enjoy things without her. "Now,

I want to share everything with her," Farrel had said.

At the time it seemed a little too codependent to be completely legit, but I understood it now. Funny how you never question someone's motives when you share them.

I moved east toward the dark shadows that were the yew circle I'd seen in the satellite photo. The yew trees were prickly and nearly thirty feet high.

I walked around the sweeping branches to the right. They were like the ones in our yard when I was a child. Fan-like branches brushed the ground. As a kid I'd found the perfect hideouts underneath them. When I needed to get away, no one had ever found me. Finally I'd shown the secret space to Sara and we'd used it as an exclusive hideout and clubhouse for years.

Suddenly I knew there was someone nearby. Before I even heard the other person's footsteps, I noticed a scent. I stood stock still as the other neared, stepping quietly but certainly not noiselessly. I'd be all the more visible if I tried to duck away. So I just waited. The element of surprise was on my side.

The footsteps neared. I stepped swiftly out and circled the person's body with one arm as I clamped my hand over her mouth. She tensed and took a breath to scream but I stopped her by saying, "It's me. It's me, Don't scream. It's all right."

It was Kathryn.

"Oh, you scared me," she said.

"Shhhhh. What the heck are you doing here?" I whispered.

"I wanted to call you but your phone is off. I didn't know how to project the Batwoman symbol on the clouds so I just came out to look for you," she said in a strained voice. "Maggie, I'm surprised you didn't pummel me," she whispered.

"I knew it was you," I said simply.

"How could you know?"

"Your perfume. I associate that lovely smell with the nape of your neck," I whispered back still holding her in my arms but facing her now.

"I'm not the only one who wears Chanel, Maggie. You could have had your arms around some other woman."

"Who else would be wearing Chanel in this graveyard just before dawn?" I asked. "How did you know I was here?"

"I went to look for you and found your laptop open on the table. I just looked at the browser history and saw the satellite photo. I could see the arrow, so I took a chance that you were out here. I'm honing my detective skills. Remember the Tommy and Tuppence plan?"

"You checked my laptop history? Geez. Good thing I erased the Lesbian porn sites."

"I can't believe you came out here without telling me. It could be dangerous."

"I have a flashlight."

"Oh, well, if you have a flashlight."

"I have a gun, too. But I'd rather not have to use it so let's keep our voices down. I might point out that *you* coming out here completely on your own could have been quite a bit more dangerous than my being here."

"Have you found anything? Do you really think there's someone else lurking around?" said Kathryn, ignoring my concern.

"I'm still looking for an entrance to this yew ring and so no, I haven't found anything, and I don't know if there's anyone else around. Shall we go home?"

"I didn't come out here to take you away from your work. I'm here to be Harriet Vane." She whispered that in my ear too.

"Are you sure? It's very cold."

"I bet the opening is back there," she said pointing in the direction I'd come. We circled back beyond where I'd started and Kathryn stopped at a space where the branches wove less tightly together.

"Here goes," I said softly as I pressed into the scratchy boughs. It was just one layer of branches filling in the opening to this little grove. Kathryn was right behind me. We stumbled into the open space just as the clouds parted and the crescent moon made another appearance.

There in the middle of the clearing was a lyrical statue of the same white marble from which the others had been carved.

"Oh my," exclaimed Kathryn. "Who is it?

"It's not Evangeline Fen," I said immediately. In many ways I was far more drawn to this figure than that of Evangeline. It was a 19th century woman, but she was a woman with a purpose. Her sleeves were rolled up, her hair was pulled back into an efficient bun with stray strands across her forehead and curling around her ears. She was crouching on one knee, a cold chisel was carved into the marble at her knees, she had a mallet in her hand, and she was wearing a smock. Her other hand was raised in a welcoming gesture and her head was cocked to one side. Her expression was hard to read because the flashlight beam flattened her features, but there was an amused devilish quality to it. In fact, the loose hair strands popped up hornlike which gave her expression a demonic flavor.

"I know who it is. It's Victoria." I stared at her, shining the light all over the form. "She's hiding in these ancient yews, watching over her work." I knew it, sure as I know how it feels to be an artist who had to part with her best pieces.

"Are you sure? Is it signed?" Kathryn went closer to scan the base for some kind of signature. "There's some lettering here but I can't quite read it. Let me have the flash." She reached back for it.

Kathryn crouched at the base of the three-quarter-sized statue. In a low voice she said, "It's too long to be a signature. Oh, there, it says: "MAN MAY ONLY CHASE THE DEMON MESSENGERS OF GRIEF WITH UNBOUND CHARITY.""

Kathryn stood, using the light to view the form again. She whispered, "Her arms are very strong. Not a beautiful face, I think, but she has character. And," she flashed the light lower, "an ample bosom. It's Victoria Snow alright."

"It's hard to make a self portrait beautiful," I said from experience. "Well Gauguin did, and maybe Rembrandt when he was young, but most artists don't try to. Frieda Kahlo made herself ugly."

We walked around the statue of Victoria Willomere Snow and all her serious worker-like presence and went to the crypt behind her. I peered in, expecting to find the same square room with a low ceiling and stone coffin as the others, but I was surprised. The room was wider and less deep. The coffin lay perpendicular to the door and just a few feet out from the back wall. There were two cement angels on pedestals guarding the coffin, one attached to the wall on the right and one on the left.

"People have been in here," said Kathryn, following the beam as it swept over the floor. "I guess these footprints could be decades old. If there was nothing to disturb them."

I didn't say anything. Footprints are evidence. There was a set of handprints too. They were near the coffin. Two hands about eighteen inches apart with the finger pointing at us. I went closer and shone the light along that spot. Then I turned and faced Kathryn.

"What?" she said.

"Well, I don't get how these could be here. The position of these hands is so unlikely." I looked at them again. Kathryn came to my side.

"I see," she said.

"And look at the footprints," I went on, "They come in and go out, but they don't really turn around. Maybe..." I pushed on the lid of the coffin with one hand and felt the solid immovable weight of a thousand pounds of marble.

"Oh, really that would be too fantastic," said Kathryn.

I didn't answer. I played the light over the floor again, following the footprints that seemed to step to the right and then back to the center. I scanned the angel on the right. She had a sturdy posture, as though braced to fight anyone who got in her way. And her face was dirty. I flashed the left one. Her face was clean. I moved to the right and reached up. I pushed on the dirty face of the angel and she tilted back an inch. I handed the flashlight to Kathryn and used both hands to push the angel harder. She tipped backwards, leaning the entire pedestal with her as though there was a counter weight below the floor. At the same time, the coffin made a grinding noise and then with a low rumbling moan it slid back to reveal a large opening in the floor.

CHAPTER 16

"Oh for heavens sakes, Maggie, this is like a Nancy Drew Mystery! *The Secret of the Old Crypt*," said Kathryn incredulously.

"If the frock fits."

"Does this kind of thing happen to you all the time?"

"In a word, no. Most of the things I do job-wise are about as boring as being on hold for tech support. But this particular adventure seems to be afoot, literally. Are you game?" I asked, stepping into the opening. It was the beginning of a steep ramp that angled into the darkness below.

"Certainly I'm game. I wouldn't miss this. But why on earth would this hole be here?" she asked.

"Um, maybe Underground Railroad? There were other tunnels in the Valley. Fenchester was a stop for runaway slaves. The area was full of Quakers in those days. That might explain it. Not sure if this crypt was built that early though. And this system"—I glanced back at the now fallen angel—"seems like a cross between Harry Potter and a gothic romance."

"Could it be a prohibition tunnel?"

"Could be both. The tunnel could have been here to help slaves and then the crypt was built over it to make it more secure to run liquor."

Kathryn arranged her scarf and tugged her gloves on tighter.

"Are you sure you want to do this? Farrel would never go down there."

"Why? Is Farrel afraid of the dark?" asked Kathryn, following me.

"No, no, she has an irrational fear of rodents, and under a graveyard would be a prime hangout for them. Especially if this connects to any old sewer lines. How do you feel about that? Do you have any irrational fears?" I asked, stepping carefully into the darkness.

"I'm not sure this is the perfect moment to discuss my innermost fears, irrational or otherwise. For now let me just say, I'm not wild about snakes, though not irrationally so, and heights are often the subject of my bad dreams. I can handle most other tangible things. We'll discuss the intangible fears another time over wine or something, shall we?"

"OK then, let's have at it. If you get scared, just pretend it's a nightmare," I suggested.

Kathryn seemed remarkably amused considering we were probing a dark passage under a coffin. This was an interesting thing to find out about her. Kind of a thrill in itself.

Focus on the task at hand, I told myself.

We edged along the incline slowly until the stone ramp leveled out. There was a large oak lever there. I pulled it. It rattled and moaned and moved the coffin back in place. My flashlight showed a passage ahead that went east and one behind us to the west.

The floor of the passageway was rough stone. The walls were packed earth. I stood still and listened. It was oppressively quiet. I took off my backpack and fished out my little compass. I wanted to know exactly where we were going, so we could be sure to find our way back out. It was a little warmer down here; there was air movement but no breeze and no feeling of frost. Just that constant sixty-degree temperature you read about in heat pump ads.

This was how the shooter had gotten out of the cemetery without being spotted by me or the police. I was mildly glad that was cleared up, but I was far more concerned that a person with a gun had access to this tunnel and might even be down here with us. Though why someone like that would stick around I couldn't imagine. Even if there were valuable antiques down here, the shooter was now facing a murder charge.

On a hunch, I took out my phone and redialed Samson Henshaw's number. A note of ring tone made us both jump. A light flickered on the tunnel floor and went out. Samson's phone was right at our feet. I picked it up.

"Well, that clears up that mystery," said Kathryn.

"Some of it, but the *Where's Samson?* part is still wide open." And that worried me.

We made our way along the eastern passage that angled downhill. In about fifty yards the relatively narrow passage T-boned into a larger tunnel that had a fitted cobblestone floor, walls, and ceiling. In the larger tunnel were cracked pipes made of molded clay running along the wall. I shined the light around, then looked at the compass.

"We must be under 10th Street now," said Kathryn. "I guess this access was built when they fitted all the houses with gas lighting. These look like very old gas pipes. Or do you think this was the sewer main?" she asked.

"The sewer pipes are at the backs of the houses. But at one time the Mews *was* at the back of the big stately homes. I guess it might have been the sewer then and they refitted it for gas at the turn of the century. I think we're below the contemporary water and gas lines now." I took out my phone. Apparently the streets of this part of Fenchester were made of kryptonite, because I had zero bars.

"Kind of creepy down here," said Kathryn softly.

I couldn't have agreed more, but I was trying to act tough. So I just nodded in the dark. Kathryn took out her phone to use as a flashlight. Then she sniffed. "It must have been very unpleasant smelling back in the days after it was built."

"Of course in those days, when horses were the mode of transportation, the streets stank of horse shit and most people still used chamber pots that they emptied into the gutters each morning. So maybe those who had to work down here didn't notice it as much," I said.

"It doesn't smell bad now, though," she sniffed again. "It smells like..."

"Lavender."

"Yes. How could that be?" she asked.

"I don't know. If this were a fiction novel, it would be a plot point. But maybe we just stepped on some dried lavender bushes outside the crypt and because there's no breeze we can smell it now?"

"Or maybe Evangeline Fen's ghost is lurking here in the dark. Now that you see ghosts we should consider..."

"Let's *not* consider that right now," I said.

Kathryn snorted.

We headed right, toward the Mews. It felt as though we'd gone about half a block when Kathryn said, "There are steps up there to the left." When we got a little closer, she said, "When is a door not a door?"

"When it's ajar," I answered.

Three stone steps led up to a heavy wooden door that was open a few inches. The knob was big and old-fashioned, like Alice's after she shrank.

"Where are we?" asked Kathryn. "I've lost my bearings."

"Still under 10th. I'd guess the middle of the 500 block.

The door swung out and we climbed a steep staircase. On a landing at the top of the stairs was another huge oak door on strap hinges. It had a heavy wooden bar wedged through supports. The bar was held in place by an old padlock on a wrought iron hasp.

"Hmmmm," said Kathryn, touching the lock. "It's been oiled." She rubbed her fingers together.

The lock was the type that an old skeleton key would open. On a hunch I took out my keys and selected the old-fashioned brass key that went to one of locks on Farrel and Jessie's house.

"What, no utility belt?"

"Accessories do make the outfit, but I'm traveling light. I can pick locks, too." But I didn't need to; the key popped the lock in one twist.

As we slid the bar out of the supports, Kathryn said, "So this would be that breaking and entering I've heard so much about?"

"We didn't actually break anything," I said. "We're following clues."

"Lesbian College Professor Arrested in Attempted Burglary," mused Kathryn.

"Do you think they'd really say Lesbian?"

"Well, if it was Fox."

I turned the big knob and we pushed the creaky door open to another set of stairs.

"Why are we carrying that bar up the stairs?" Kathryn asked as we reached the top.

"Because I don't want one of the undead living under the graveyard to trap us by putting the bar back in place while we're sleuthing for clues."

I swept my flashlight around and spied electric wires snaking down one of the walls to an old-fashioned light switch. I went to it and tweaked the Bakelite knob gingerly between two fingers. I twisted it, hoping I wouldn't electrocute myself.

Light flooded the room from large clear bulbs in rows near the high ceiling. Some of the bulbs were out, but the light from the rest allowed us to see the whole room.

It was huge and had a faintly unpleasant smell. Thin horizontal windows lined the very top of the twenty-foot brick walls. On one side was a row of stacked wooden boxes.

But it was the rest of the large room that really caught my attention. It was an artist's studio. A sculptor's. And except that some of the metal tools were rusty from disuse, the place was ready to produce art.

There were five huge porcelain vats against one wall, each the size of a hot tub. Two of them had their lids pushed off to expose a vast quantity of dried clay. Clay-shaping and stone-carving tools stood ready in racks on the shelves that lined another wall. There were armatures, small wooden mannequins, and calipers of all sizes. Sketches were tacked to large bulletin boards above long tables and heavy stands.

On the wall of shelves to one side was a vast number of finished and nearly finished sculptures. Full bodies, busts, torsos, heads, studies of shape and movement, all formed of clay or carved from stone. There were mold forms and literally hundreds of clay faces decorated with shells, pebbles, and other found objects.

To the left of the shelves were two narrow doors. At the back wall was a steep wooden staircase that went almost to the ceiling. I swept my flashlight beam to the top of the brick wall, but there was no door up there. The stairs ended surreally at nothing.

Also at the back wall was a refrigerator-sized block of partly carved white marble with a full set of cold chisels and several heavy wooden mallets on a table next to it. I was drawn to the stone sculpture like a pin to a magnet. A nude female form was emerging from the marble as though the stone was both giving birth to her and she was struggling to free herself from it. As though she was stepping out of a wall of churning water, her face, breast, hand, arm, knee, thigh, and hip, seemed to break through the rough surface.

Kathryn joined me as I touched the sculpted arm.

"This is Victoria's studio," whispered Kathryn.

"Certainly is. And this... this is Evangeline. Look at this. Victoria had to have loved her to make her look like this. It's like Michelangelo's *Four Seasons*, yet so feminine. But still strong. I bet... I bet Victoria never intended to finish it. It's a masterpiece. I could look at it all day."

We stood at the sculpture for a very long moment and finally I broke the silence. "I wonder if anyone else has ever seen this?"

Kathryn walked back to the boxes. "Well, Frankie saw it, if he was paying attention. This is where he got his merchandise. There was a another box here. See the outline of it against the wall?"

I scanned the room carefully. "And he took the sculpture and molded faces from those shelves. You know, he even had an old-fashioned house key that probably worked on the lock on the stairs."

Kathryn was drawn to a bookcase where folios of prints and drawings leaned against nine or ten books.

"Oh, look! Look, it's Victoria's other journal," said Kathryn. "See? There's a two on the cover... and here's a third one!" She pulled her gloves from her jacket pocket and lifted the journals from the shelf. "Maggie, there's no reason for me not to take these is there? I'll turn them over to the Irwin library for them to copy. I would hate to leave them here."

"I can't see any reason for you not to take them if you're turning them over to Irwin. Amanda said Victoria left everything to the college, so I suppose this all belongs to Irwin."

"My sculpture that I bought at the antique market?" Kathryn asked, taking off her scarf and wrapping it carefully around the journals to slide them into her shoulder bag.

"Probably."

"Rats."

Kathryn walked back to the boxes. "They're packed so well. Wrapped in oil cloth. Fitted joints." She glanced around at the walls. "It's fairly dry in here, though who knows how it is in the summer." She touched the very edge of a sketch pinned to the board on the wall. It didn't crack or fall away.

I was scanning the boxes. There were splinters on the floor where one had been opened and then removed.

"So, Frankie follows someone here. When they leave he sneaks in and opens a box," I said. "He had an old key that would have opened the lock, figures it's all salable, so he takes a box, grabbing a few sculptures and some of the head molds on the way out. It must have been heavy. No wonder he wanted Red to help him with the others. I wonder why only one of them was opened..."

"But the killer found out? Perhaps we should call the other person X?"

I snorted. "OK, we can call the person X. So Frankie repacks the stuff into a few cardboard boxes and takes the loot to Adamstown, where he makes what seemed like a mint to him. He still has merch left over, and he knows there are fourteen more boxes down here and all these figures. So he plans to come back for the grand haul with Red."

"But X gets wise to him... I'm so liking this detective talk."

"Yeah, OK, X gets wise. X is no slouch. X figures out Frankie is stealing the private stash and gets very angry. X checks around down here." I pointed to the floor. "See here are X's footprints. Sensible shoes, about a men's size 7 or 8, I'd say."

"So X waits for Frankie in the crypt the day before the next flea market and when Frankie goes to open the passage, X shoots?" said Kathryn.

"Right, but misses with the first shot. Frankie spins around and pushes Red out of the way and from the crypt X shoots again and hits Frankie. And then X just melts back into the earth, undiscovered. We all heard the rumble of the passage closing." I considered for a moment. "Probably surprised X that Red was there. Had he not been, X probably would have followed Frankie to be sure he was dead."

"It's so cold-blooded when it's about one person killing another," said Kathryn.

I nodded. "Stay here a minute." I stepped back from the boxes and gently walked back to the door. I got down low and held my flashlight so the beam swept over the floor surface at a low angle. There were many footprints. I could see Frankie's sneakers and X's sensible shoes. I could see ours and at least two others.

I scanned the whole room again. I said, "We're in a basement. So..."

We both said, "It's the Majestic!" in unison. We were below the old theatre that now shows art movies and hosts the community playhouse.

"How could dozens of volunteers not know this studio is down here? After all, there are windows to the outside," said Kathryn.

I looked up at the windows and then glanced at my watch. It was 7 a.m. but the windows were still black. "Maybe they're covered up. And... I guess we could be in the back of the building, on the side they just use for storage. Ya know, the Carbondales' book mentioned that there was a speakeasy in the basement of one of the town theaters. That could explain the tunnel here. Somebody could easily roll a keg or a cartload of bottles down that ramp."

I flashed on the footprints again, then followed them past the wall of shelves toward the two narrow doors. As I walked past the large clay vats I noticed a whiff of something that made me hesitate.

It was then that we heard the voice.

CHAPTER 17

Kathryn and I froze. Human sounds were coming from behind one of the narrow doors. I reached in my holster, drew out my Beretta, and clicked the safety off. I waved Kathryn behind me. She slipped silently back behind the vats.

I moved closer to the door. It had a pull handle and it was fastened shut with a thick old barrel bolt.

"Who's in there?" I called, but I already knew the answer.

"Maggie?" croaked a dry voice. "It's me."

I slid the bolt over and pulled the door open. Samson Henshaw tipped into the room. He'd been sitting in the door frame at the top of a steep staircase, leaning against the door. He blinked in the light, shading his eyes with a shaky hand. He had a two-days' growth of beard and he stank.

When his eyes finally adjusted, he saw Kathryn and flinched back. "Oh, it's you," he said, recognizing her. He looked around the room like he'd never seen it before. "Do you have any water?" he rasped.

Kathryn went to the old sink on the side wall and twisted the handle.

The pipe gurgled and groaned and suddenly a gush of rusty water flowed out. Samson pulled himself up and dove for it.

"Wait for the rust to clear," Kathryn cautioned, and in seconds it did. I didn't mention to Samson the probability of lead pipes, because the fact that he'd gone without food or water for two days was the priority. He drank and drank until his stomach was distended.

"How'd you find me?" he finally croaked.

"More to the point, how the hell did you get in here?"

"I don't know. No... wait, yes I do. Oh God I really stink. I'm sorry."

"What happened?" I asked in an even voice that calmed him.

He went on slowly, breathing deeply between every few words, "Right, well, I was waiting outside Gabe's and I saw Suzanne go in. I'm sure it was her, because you know, I told you, I rang Suzanne's phone and I could hear it ringing *If I Had A Hammer* as she went into the yard. So I called you. Geez, it seems like that was years ago."

"What happened then?"

"In just a few minutes, maybe four or five, I could hear Buster barking.

She came out, so I rang the phone again. You know, just to be sure it wasn't a fluke coincidence. It rang again. Same song. This time Suzanne turned her phone off, but I followed her. She had a flashlight, so it was easy to see her from pretty far away."

Samson stopped to get another drink, then splashed the water over his face. "She went fast. I worked hard to keep up, but I didn't want her to see me yet."

If Samson was so sure Suzanne loved him then why not just speak to her? Obviously he was afraid of what he might find out.

"She hurried out to Washington Street. I could barely keep up. I was just coming around the corner when I saw a light go on in a big SUV or something, so I ducked back. The light went out and I thought she was going to drive off, but she pulled something onto the sidewalk and when she got under a streetlight I could see it was a big hand truck. She rolled it in front of her, north along 10th Street, then up Fen, and then into the cemetery. It was so dark in there I could follow closer. I was almost ready to call out, but then she just disappeared. But see, I heard branches moving and I figured she was hiding in some bushes, like maybe she'd seen me."

Samson considered a minute, then said, "I used my phone to see. Inside the bushes there was a vault. Just as I got in there I saw this hole closing up in the floor and Suzanne's light was gone. When the floor finished closing, this tilted over statue sprang back up. So I just tried pushing on it and the hole opened and I went down. But at the bottom I dropped my phone. The screen went to sleep. It was so dark I couldn't find it."

"But, you could still see the light ahead of you, right?"

"I didn't want to lose her. I started to run and she went around the corner. When I made it to the corner, I could see the light going up the stairs. She left the door open so I followed. When I got in here I saw something kind of flickering. I got to that door." He pointed to the narrow door we'd found him behind. "There was a candle a few steps down. I stepped in and someone hit me on the head." He touched there and winced.

Kathryn looked at the back of Samson's head. "You have quite a bump there." His hair was sticky and matted from the blood that had come from a cut on his scalp.

"Did you fall down the stairs?" I asked.

He nodded. "I guess so. I don't remember that part so well. But I woke up at the bottom. My knee really hurt and my arm and, well, *everything* hurt and everything was dark. At first I just couldn't figure anything out. Then later I thought I might be... blind. I kind of panicked and passed out, I guess."

Samson shrugged loose his jacket and pulled his collar over to the edge of his shoulder. He was black and blue over most of his skin.

"I could feel the steps, so I dragged myself up, but the door was locked. I tried to rest and I think I passed out again. When I woke up, I could see some kind of purple light coming from round spots in the ceiling. I was glad I wasn't blind, but it was still so dark. What day is it?"

"It's Thursday morning." I looked at my watch. "It's nearly 7:30."

"Oh shit, Lois must be out of her mind. I told her I'd be back in an hour on Tuesday night."

Now he's thinking of Lois? Do people still use the word fickle?

"Samson," I said, "we need to get you to the hospital."

"Yeah, there's this ringing in my ears and I have a headache. But mostly I'm really hungry. Why would Suzanne push me? She must be out of her mind."

"Did you see her face?"

"Yeah, I saw her.'

"Her face? You're sure it was Suzanne? What was she wearing?"

"A dark red coat and a scarf over her head. Shit, it was cold out. It was her Maggie... The ring tone."

"Samson, all you saw was a shadow with a scarf. If it was Suzanne, then you're saying she pushed you down the stairs and left you in there to die?"

"No, no. I'm not saying that..." His voice trailed off. He'd been thinking this already, but he didn't want to admit it out loud.

Kathryn edged over to the top of the steps. "What's down there?"

"I dunno. I was afraid to go back down there and get lost."

I pulled my flashlight back out of my pocket and went over to the narrow door. I flashed it around the walls just to see if there was a light switch. That would be a kick in the pants.

Just like the steps we'd taken up to the studio, there were about twenty steep steps down to an irregular stone floor. It was a miracle Samson hadn't broken anything. It was a miracle he hadn't died.

In fact, whacking him on the back of the head with... I looked around. There was a broken face mold with a small dark flaky stain on it on a shelf near the door. The big hunk of plaster must have sent Samson arcing into space before he began to roll. I didn't say *attempted murder*, but I thought it so loud, Kathryn looked at me pointedly.

Halfway down the stairs a thin chain dangled from a ceiling fixture. I could just barely reach it with the tips of my fingers. I pulled gently and a low wattage bulb bathed the brick-walled room in yellow light.

There were flakes of the plaster mold and some *lack of bathroom* stains under the steps. Well, it had been two days.

I went carefully down the stairs, trying to breathe minimally. The space was the beginning of a rough tunnel that went... I took out my compass... east. But it ended in a pile of rubble that filled the tunnel to the ceiling only about twenty feet along.

It looked as though Victoria had used this space for storage. There was a wide door under the stairs. I opened it and swept the flashlight around. A large room that extended far back under the studio held dozens of pallets with stacks of canvas bags. The first few pallets were marked PLASTER, but the rows beyond were all marked Red, Porcelain, and Terra Cotta CLAY. I lifted one of the heavy bags near the door out of my way. It tore open, puffing plaster dust into the air. I made my way carefully between the stacks toward the back of the room just to be sure no one was hiding there or that there wasn't another door that led out to the street or something. No luck. I tried to avoid stepping in the plaster dust, but I was tracking it all over.

I marveled that Victoria had amassed so much material. Of course the clay pieces in the studio would have taken hundreds of pounds to make. I wondered what would happen to this stuff. Using Victoria Snow's clay to make a sculpture would be inspiring.

I stepped out and closed the door. I could see marks where Samson had fallen in the dust on the floor. Some of the step edges were freshly splintered and scraped. There were also marks that looked like someone had dragged something from the storage closet to the steps.

The rubble that blocked the other end of the room seemed new. There was rebar in it. It must have been some kind of cave-in that happened after Victoria died. When she was alive, this tunnel probably connected to the main one. There was an old-fashioned four-wheel cart against the other wall that Victoria could have used to bring in all this material.

I couldn't understand why Victoria would choose a workplace with no daylight. It seemed unnatural. She had to get here by climbing under a coffin in a graveyard through a sewer tunnel. Yet Victoria had created some great works here. There's a moral in this somehow.

She must have been pretty spry to have worked this space into her later years, I mused. Maybe she'd had a helper, perhaps a younger woman who was Victoria's able right hand, just like the young man who lived with Georgia O'Keeffe as she painted into her nineties. Maybe Victoria hadn't been as reclusive as everyone supposed.

"Maggie? What are you doing? I think we should get Samson out of here." Kathryn came partway down the steps.

"Just looking around. Is he OK?"

"I'm OK," croaked Samson. "I just needed a drink. I want to see where I was. Holy shit, I can't believe I sat in the dark for two days when I could have just reached up and pulled on the light. Oh crap and there's a faucet over there too. Do you think that works. Seeing this is making the whole thing worse," he groaned.

Kathryn said, "We should take him out. He's still shaky."

The three of us went back into the studio. Kathryn said, "There's a strange odor in here. Is it sewer gas?"

"No, that's not a sewer smell." I'd noticed it when we first came in. It was faint but I'd smelled that odor before and just like the gawker who can't turn away from a highway accident, I was drawn to it despite the sense of dread it stirred up. I'd hoped it was just some dead sewer animal that had crawled up the steps. An alligator maybe.

I sniffed again and knew it wasn't an alligator. I went to the nearest clay crock with a lid on it. It was glazed cast-iron, like a big round bathtub. The cover, a four-foot disk of white glazed earthenware, served to prevent the clay inside from drying out.

I pushed against the lid, lifting its slight lip over the edge. It was heavy, but the smooth glazed surfaces slid against themselves easily. The lid had a good seal. That's why the smell had been faint. As soon as the top was pushed back, the dusty clay and plaster smell of the studio was replaced by the odor of death. The overhead bulbs cast light into the open vat. The three of us looked in.

Samson barked a short scream. Kathryn took two giant steps backwards and I felt a rush of sadness that filled my eyes with white and then a rim of tears.

"Oh my lord," said Kathryn. "It can't be Victoria Snow." She put her hand over her nose and mouth. "Who is it?"

"It's Suzanne. Suzanne Carbondale," I said softly.

Samson roused and rushed forward. Then he turned, vomited the quart of the water he'd just drunk, and crumpled to the floor in a dizzy faint. He roused in a second and began sobbing, "No... Oh no."

"We have to get out of here. It's a crime scene. I need to call the police," I said firmly.

Kathryn came closer again and looked over my shoulder into the vat. "Crime? Are you sure? She might have just fallen down the steps like

Samson and hit her head, or... broken her neck." Kathryn whispered the last part. The closeness to sudden death was sinking in, but she was trying to be analytical. I found myself pleased by that, but Kathryn was missing a key point.

"Kathryn, she didn't die naturally and then crawl into this vat and pull the lid over herself."

I leaned in. Suzanne's body lay on its side with knees drawn up nearly to her chest. She was wearing a red and green sweater with reindeer on it and a green enamel wreath pin. Her head was against the side of the vat. There was a lot of blood on her shoulder. It had stiffened the collar of her shirt. I took out my flashlight and played it over Suzanne's body slowly, then closer to her neck and the area around it. I took a pen from my jacket pocket and pushed back her collar. There were two wounds at the base of her neck. Suzanne's blood had stained the side of the vat wall and pooled on the surface below.

I turned and swept the flashlight around the outside of the vat. There was plaster and clay dust on the oak flooring.

I looked back at Samson, who was sitting on the floor with his head in his hands, his head nodding as though he was dizzy again. He looked so white he seemed opaque.

"Um..." I whispered.

Kathryn took the hint and came closer. I said in a voice inaudible to Samson, "Looks like she died in there. Which either means someone forced her in there and then killed her, or she was knocked out, put in there and then finished off. There are neck wounds. That's where the blood came from."

"How do you know she was killed in there?"

"You can see footprints and drag marks but no blood stains on the floor. It's clean but not washed. If it had been washed, the dust would be smeared and caked. It's murder."

Kathryn turned toward Samson, then back to me. "I doubt he did it. There's no blood on him. Well, I guess he could have fallen down the stairs when he was trying to leave the crime scene."

"He could have, but she's been dead a long time, not just the last two days. Look, she's wearing a Christmas sweater and pin. I think she's been in here since just after Jessie saw her on Christmas Eve. If he did it, he's the stupidest murderer in the world. Coming back down here and getting locked in with the corpse so close by? And he's been pining away for her for the last six weeks."

Kathryn whispered back, "What if he came down here to hide the evidence, wipe up the fingerprints. Maybe tried to hide the body and then he fell down the steps and couldn't get out?"

"Possible. But then we're posed with a pretty big question. How did he manage to lock himself in?"

"Oh, yes, there's that," said Kathryn, looking at Samson.

"So if he wasn't following Suzanne, who *was* the person he followed?"

"The killer? Maybe she was trying to implicate him?"

"Maybe. But we really have no evidence it was a woman." Another look at Samson's chalk-white face changed my tone. "Samson looks very shocky. People can die of shock. We don't have time to get him down the steps and out the tunnel. We have to get some EMTs to him fast."

I took out my cell and tried to get a signal. No bars. I climbed the steep steps that ascended from the basement to the ground floor of the Majestic to see if I could get a signal near the windows. At the top was an archway blocked by a wall of newer brick. The opening had been sealed long ago but long after the original building had been built. No secret passage through it though. Victoria had probably walled this door frame up herself. Kind of a dramatic way to ensure privacy.

Holding the railing tightly, I leaned over and held the phone near the ground-level windows. One bar. Not enough to make a call. Probably enough to send a text but how could I explain this all in a text message?

I surveyed the studio from this aerial view and spied the tools I needed. I climbed back down, grabbed a big cold chisel, an extra heavy ball-peen hammer, and an eight-pound sledge. You don't have to be MacGyver if all the tools for the job are right there. There were even some old-fashioned goggle-like safety glasses to protect my eyes. Farrel's insistence on safety gear had successfully rubbed off on me. I also hoped that none of these things had anything to do with the murder because if so I was destroying evidence, but I really didn't want Samson to die from shock and dehydration; he needed an ambulance.

I carried everything back up the steep steps, wiped off the glasses and put them on. I took a moment to balance myself. Then I pounded the chisel into the mortar and wished for only one course of bricks. I loosened a four-brick square pretty quickly. I called down to Kathryn and Samson to stand back in case any bricks fell into the studio.

Of course the other side might be a big tank of water or a room full of pea coal. The flow of either would knock me right down the stairs. *Ah well, Carpe Diem.* I moved down a step, drew back the sledge, and slammed the middle of the loosened bricks.

The sledge crashed through the bricks so easily that it almost flew out of my hands through the wall. I threaded it back to my side and smashed at it again less forcefully, making a larger opening. The wall *was* only one course thick and seemed to be more for show than security. After all, nobody really questions a brick wall.

A few more whacks and I had a hole I could squeeze through.

Kathryn called up to me, "Where does it come out?"

I took out my flashlight, leaned into the hole, and looked around. "Looks like a prop room."

I crawled through the opening then poked my head back. "I'll be right back."

****

"How do you know it's Suzanne Carbondale?" asked Sgt. Ed O'Brien.

"Hair color, clothes, wedding ring, that bracelet, and honestly, Ed, her face, even though... How long does the Coroner think?

"Maggie, it always amazes me that you can stand this stuff. Makes me want to toss my cookies."

"I worked highway patrol."

"Oh yeah, right."

Truth was, though, seeing someone like this whom I'd known and cared about was not settling well in my stomach, much less my soul.

O'Brien answered, "Being in the airtight vat is making it tougher, but the Coroner's saying about six weeks. Might have been more. Couldn't have been much less."

"It couldn't have been much more, Ed. People saw her six weeks ago."

"Must have been a pretty girl. Yeah, Henshaw said he saw her." O'Brien paused to look around. He said idly, "Sure have been a lot of witnesses barfing lately."

"He just drank a lot of water."

"I see that," O'Brien said, scanning the floor.

"I thought Marc Freligh was taking over this case," I said.

"What do you mean *this* case? Marc's on the Skeleton Park case."

I explained about Frankie, the antique market sales, and the crypt.

"Jesus, Mary, and Joseph, I'm betting the brass aren't going to believe this connection. But I'll call Marc in. It's his case now. Kind of interesting though; maybe we could work together on it."

"When you do call Mark, you and he might consider keeping the fact that Henshaw's still alive a secret for now. Tell Henshaw and his wife to lie low for a few days. I'm betting whoever clocked him believes he's dead and that can be an advantage sometimes."

"Yeah, OK, I see your point. For a few days anyway," said O'Brien.

"How did she die? Could the M.E. tell?"

"Major bruise on the back of her head. Probably knocked out here, dragged into the vat and then stabbed. Killer could have thought she was already dead when he put her in, but then she moved or something and... Well, you can see where the blood is," said O'Brien.

"You know, someone's been making it seem as though she was still alive. My friend Jesse got an email from her last week. And someone's updating her Facebook page, saying she's in Mexico researching a new book."

"Really? Talk about a virtual world. I'll have the tech guys trace back the updates to the person making them."

"Hard to do. They'll just show that *she* was making them."

Ed sighed. "Age old question, Maggie..."

"Who profits?"

"Uh huh."

"The husband to some extent, though there isn't much to inherit. They rented their house from the college. They weren't rich. I guess he'll get their book royalties, but how much could that be? Still... the best motives are money and love and I think Suzanne was about to leave him. So he may have been engulfed by a jealous rage, though he really wasn't the type." I thought for a minute. "Problem though, Ed..."

"What?"

"Carbondale was in England presenting a seminar on US Civil War history during the holidays. And people saw Suzanne after he left. Heck, I even saw her after Gabe left on the 20th. If the Coroner is committed to six weeks or more..."

O'Brien sighed again. "So the husband didn't do it? That's a novelty."

Fenchester's finest smashed a larger hole through the brick wall in the Majestic's prop room and cleared the bricks away. Using that access was easier than the underground tunnel.

EMTs took Samson Henshaw to the hospital. He was back on the verge of dehydration, having lost the water he'd drunk to *chunder,* as Nora Hasan would probably say.

When he was stable, Samson used my phone to tell his faithful wife Lois he'd be at Fenchester General in a few minutes. She wailed with joy and relief when she heard his voice, then told him to thank me for finding him. O'Brien suggested to them both that they avoid talking to the press and stay under wraps for awhile.

I guessed my finding Samson a few hours from death counted rather heavily on the pro side when it came to Lois's evaluation of my work. With Suzanne out of the picture forever, Lois would probably be stuck with Samson again, which seemed to be what she wanted. I thought about that carefully as Samson tried to get Lois off the phone.

Kathryn was shaken by the sight of the dead body but braced up to say she'd stay through the crime scene investigation.

"No, Kathryn, don't stay here. They probably won't let you anyway. It'll be grim and tedious, and besides... I think you should go and tell Jessie and Farrel about Suzanne."

"And Gabe?"

"The police will send someone to tell him."

"Do they think he did it?" she said quietly.

"They always think the spouse did it. But he has an alibi."

Kathryn left for Farrel and Jessie's. I promised to meet her there.

By the time Sgt. Marc Freligh arrived, Ed O'Brien and I were surveying the sub-basement storage area. When the CSI team had finished with it, they confirmed that Henshaw had been in there for two days. I really didn't want to know *how* they'd figured that out.

"Hi Marc," I said to Freligh. His crisp uniform and carefully combed dark brown hair were in direct contrast to O'Brien's rumpled raincoat and nearly bald head, yet they were both skilled at their jobs.

"Henshaw says he thought he was blind until he saw light coming through those sidewalk prisms," I said, pointing to the ceiling.

"Huh, I never even noticed... What are they, like glass stuck in the sidewalk or something?"

"Yeah, exactly. They're solid shafts of glass about the length and shape of cardboard wrapping paper tubes, standing on their ends in the cement. They used them at the end of the 19th century to cast a little bit of light into underground spaces. City engineers are careful not to cover them over when they replace the sidewalks. They're all over the city, but I always thought they just let light into basements. They must light all the tunnels."

O'Brien pointed his flashlight at the rubble blocking the tunnel.

"Can't get through there anymore."

"It must have been a sinkhole," said Sgt. Freligh.

"Remember that one back in the '90s? Big water main, size of a semi, broke in the center of town. Washed away tons of dirt underground. Street fell in. Swallowed half a building at Hamilton and 7th and ruined the foundations of six others. So much water gushed out of the main, the reservoir went down three feet," said O'Brien.

"Too much limestone. It wears away and then the pipes break. Now, any time the street cracks the city digs it up, pours fill in, and cements it over. This one caved in the alley behind the Majestic's parking lot. It closed the theater for a week. The chief of police's wife was in a community production of *Fiddler on the Roof* and no one could park for the play." Freligh grinned.

"They just filled one down on 5th Street near the art museum the week before Christmas," said O'Brien.

"I remember. It detoured traffic for days," I said idly, but I was too busy thinking about death, love, and friends to pay much attention to small talk. I blinked my eyes to will away emotions.

Kathryn had said just before she left, "This is the downside of the private eye business, isn't it?"

"Want to quit?" I'd asked.

"No, no, I'm your sidekick. I'll stumble through," she had said sincerely.

"Gonna show us how you found all this?" O'Brien asked me.

I took O'Brien and Freligh back up to the studio, down the other stairs and all the way underground to the stone ramp. I pushed on the oak lever, and the hole in the tunnel's ceiling opened up.

"Holy mother of God," O'Brien said climbing up into the crypt.

Bright daylight made us cover our eyes.

"Huh, looks like we're going to have six more weeks of winter," said Freligh, blinking at the ground.

"Nobody would ever believe this! I better call the street department to put one of those big metal plates over the door here, we have to seal this off as soon as possible. We'll seal off the Majestic, too. Can't get down into that basement from the theater anyway. We had to break down a door," said O'Brien punching in numbers on his phone and arranging it.

"Are you guys going to talk to the husband?" I asked.

"We've sent someone. They took him to the station. We'll question him, but with that alibi, unless we find out he took a round trip red-eye, we sure don't have anything to hold him on," said Freligh.

After O'Brien had made sure the steel plate would be covering the crypt opening within an hour, he and Freligh disappeared back into the floor of the crypt.

I stood marveling at the ingenious hidden entrance. No slap-dash affair. Masterful craft, probably done in secret too. *Must have cost a fortune to build.*

******

"Jessie feels terrible," whispered Farrel at the door.

We went into the kitchen where Kathryn and Jessie were drinking tea at the table by the window.

It was late afternoon. The sun was going down. In its last rays I could see the backyard koi pond was rimmed with ice. It would have been solid but a tiny heater kept a round section liquid. Dozens of different kinds of birds flitted around the only open water in the city. Jessie watched the birds silently as they queued up to take a bath.

"What's going on with the investigation?" asked Kathryn, taking my chilly hand. She didn't want to upset Jessie, but both she and Farrel were desperate to know.

Jessie exhaled and shifted in her seat but didn't turn from the window.

"They sent someone to take Gabe to the station," I said.

"She was killed?" asked Jessie, turning red-rimmed eyes to me.

"It seems that way. The last time you saw her was Christmas Eve, wasn't it?" I asked, "Did she have a reindeer sweater on?"

Jessie nodded. "Yeah, she had the sweater on. I can't stop going over it in my mind. She came in the morning to drop off some empty cookie tins. She said... she said she had presents for us, but that she would bring them by Christmas morning. She was working on her new book... She'd found something significant and she wanted a second opinion. She said she'd tell me all about it but she was late for an appointment. She was only here a minute."

Jessie paused to think back. "Gabe had already gone to England. With him gone, she had a lot of time to work. Later in the afternoon, I got a text from her saying she was at the airport because she had to go out of town and would I take care of Buster." Jessie stopped speaking abruptly and turned toward the window again. Farrel stood up and put her hands on Jessie's shoulders. Jessie pulled Farrel's arms down to wrap around her.

"We ended up taking care of Buster until a few days after Gabe came back in mid-January," said Farrel. "Gabe didn't seem worried that she'd gone away. She'd done this before, just going away on a trip."

"Suzanne emailed from her phone," said Jessie. "Her message said something like: *Thanks for Buster. Research breakthrough. Don't know when I'll be back. Important.* So, we ended up just bringing Buster here."

"Much to Griswold and Wagner's chagrin," added Farrel. "The email also said the signal was weak in Mexico."

"When we brought Buster back to Gabe," said Jessie, "he said Suzanne had dumped him. He sure seemed like the wounded husband, but in a week he was redecorating and was moving on with his life. I bet he pushed her in a fight or something." Jessie hesitated, then shook her head.

Farrel peered carefully at Jessie. "You think Gabe could really do that? He's a weasel, but to kill her on purpose?"

"He could have done it." She faltered, then said, "Jealously, passion?"

"Really? Gabe's never seemed to care much about anyone other than himself, Jessie. It's not like he's going to inherit a ton of money or anything," said Farrel. After a moment she patted Jessie's shoulders. "OK, I'm going to make a big plate of nachos."

"I'll do it, Farrel," said Jessie moving to stand up.

"No, Jessie, take a break. I'll make the food. Maggie, you can open some wine."

"I'll help," said Kathryn.

I found a bottle of red wine in their rack. Kathryn found some olives, fresh red peppers and green onions in the fridge and began to chop them up. Farrel put full-sized tortillas in the oven and while they baked she grated cheese. When the tortillas were crisp she spread salsa and mounded on chopped peppers, cheese, olives, and onions, then topped it all off with cilantro leaves. She pushed the tray of tortillas into the huge oven. Within ten minutes we were digging in.

Two bottles of wine and a few toasts later the sadness yielded to sweet stories about Suzanne that made the mood a bit lighter.

When there was a pause, Jessie said, "Please, someone, tell me another story."

"I know," said Kathryn. "The journals. We found them in Victoria's studio. They're parts two and three of Victoria's set. We could read them. Oh wait, you don't really know about the first one, do you?"

Kathryn unfolded the story of Victoria's adventures. There was a lot of low-pitched snickering as Kathryn read from her notes about the Charlotte Cushman encounter.

"I studied Cushman when I team taught art history," said Farrel.

"Forget about her. I just want to know what happens when Victoria comes to Fenchester. I need a happy ending," said Jessie.

"Um, Evangeline only has two years before she falls from her horse in the forest," I said.

Jessie groaned.

Farrel said, "But do they hook up or not? That's the question."

"Let's see what Victoria has to say. I'm used to her handwriting." Kathryn took the thick little journals out of her bag, then hesitated. "I could use some latex gloves."

"I have a supply in my bag." The three of them stared at me. "For crime scene investigations, there's such a thing as fingerprints, you know. Honestly... minds in the gutter."

Kathryn pulled on the gloves and gently flipped to the end of the third journal. "Oh my, it ends in the 1930s. That's decades after Evangeline died. But the second one continues right on from the first volume. I'll read from that. Um, here are some things about travel arrangements to Philadelphia to present her piece for the Centennial Exhibition and all these pages are about getting ready for the opening of the exhibition. She talks about how many people were there on opening day. It was in Fairmount Park on the Schuylkill River and she says over 180,000 people attended the opening. And here she talks about the Women's Centennial Exhibition Executive Committee honoring her work in a special gallery along with Edmonia Lewis's... "

"Kathryn," said Jessie, "history is fine in its place, but could we hear about something a little more... uh..."

"Erotic?" suggested Farrel.

Kathryn laughed. "Ah, here's something about Fenchester." And then   .
in her most sexy bedroom voice Kathryn read from the flowing script:

May 18th, 1876
The train to Fenchester was horribly late. My journey did not end until past midnight when the locomotive pulled into the station in the dead of night. The city was silent save for a crew of gandy dancers working by lantern light far down the track, where it curved out of the city.

"What's a gandy dancer?" asked Farrel. "Sounds like a group of hoochie koochie girls?"

"No," I said, "the gandy men were train track workers. They had to shift the track back in place at sharp curves. They used big long bars called gandys and they sang songs that helped them all push at the same time."

"You know everything," said Kathryn, winking at me.

"I wish I did," I said softly.

"Read, read," said Jessie.

Kathryn resumed,

When the train pulled to a stop I was not surprised to see the station deserted, but then to the delight of my heart, my angel appeared from a dark corner and rushed to meet me. When she was just a few feet away, she stopped short in profound hesitation...

until I lifted my arms. She flew into them and held me fast, bringing me increasing joy.

I was deeply aware that this bold demonstration of emotion was unlike the Evangeline I had known in Rome. Although her letters over our three years apart had been quite personal and increasingly affectionate, while we had been together in Rome she had been all the more reserved than the other women at Charlotte's house. Even when we had had tea tête-à-tête, she was shy to look in my eyes, and when we walked together through the ruins, she did not take my arm. Upon our final parting, she simply offered her hand, though the tears in her eyes told me what I had hoped was more.

But, now, here she was, wrapped in my very fond embrace, which I sorely hope is quite more than a simple greeting from someone lonely and fearful of dire personal events.

I said simply, "My dear."

She said softly in my ear, "I have dared not beg you come, but I cannot express how glad I am that you are here, dear Victoria."

"Her embrace loosened finally and I held her at arm's length to look at her in the moonlight. She seemed tired, but her beauty has increased five-fold since we have been apart. Her sweet young features of three years ago have become the definition of grace, elegance, and allure.

My Evangeline had come to the train station to meet me with her sisters and had stayed the lengthening hours when she found the train lacked time. When her sisters grew faint-hearted and left for home as twilight fell, Evangeline stayed, chatting with the station master's wife and when that good lady left for home, Evangeline tarried alone save for a porter asleep on the platform next to a baggage carriage.

Evangeline woke the porter and I gave him directions to bring along my larger bags to Evangeline's home in the morning, whilst I carried my carpet bag by my own hand. I found myself guiltily pleased that her income had been reduced, so that likely there would be no guest room and thus I would be required me to sleep in a bed warmed by her entrancing form.

Alas, when we finally arrived at her small home, not really more than a tradesman's townhouse and yet curiously charming and comfortable, I found that indeed we would be sharing a bed. But also sharing it was her sister Adelaide, who woke when we *opened the front door and flew to the front room to ask me all course of questions about my travels.*

Addy is a kind and well-meaning girl of 18, though sharpness of wit is not her forte and she has only the merest shadow of Evangeline's striking features. (Same can be said for the youngest sister of the family, Geraldine, who shares a small alcove with Carlton, their young brother). When I finally was allowed to retire, Addy insisted on sleeping next to me, and indeed snored in my ear for the rest of the night.

I must see if there is a suitable hotel in town... Perhaps Evangeline might see her way clear to join me there. Yes, I shall commit to make that a certainty.

"I bet," said Farrel. "This is... um..."

"Remarkably frank for the Victorian era?" said Kathryn

"Well, I was going to say *hot,* but I agree it's also frank."

Kathryn was gently flipping through the pages of the journal."Don't skip any of the good parts!" said Jessie.

"Well, this is all about retrieving her luggage, which was lost for a while. So much for things being different in the olden days. And this is about sending for her tools and supplies to be brought to Fenchester to begin her commission for Irwin. It even has the name of the company that she hired to bring them. This is really a find."

"You're going to write an article about this aren't you?"

"Farrel, I'm going to use this as a basis for a significant book. It's a gem..."

"I wonder..." I thought for a minute. "I wonder if Suzanne found the first book in the library stacks. That would have made her excited."

"She might have been excited about any sort of research."

"Yeah, but she was found in Victoria's..."

Jessie sighed.

"Keep reading Kathryn," I said.

May 21st, 1876

Today, Evangeline and I had the entire afternoon together. I confess I am both elated and distraught. She told me quite directly of her serious financial problems, but I would have felt them not insurmountable, were I to help.

However, Evangeline also said, "Victoria, when a woman such as myself, who has no real skills and no family protection, and who has admittedly the serious responsibility of a family far less capable and far more desperate, it's simply a matter of making a good match. Surely my mother insists it is so and it seems to have been so, because I have consented to accept the proposal of General Merganser Hunterdon and having done this, I have secured future financial relief for my family."

I confess that when she said that to me today, I felt as though I was falling from a great height and it took me several moments to recover.

Finally I was able to ask meekly, "Do you love him?"

And much to my relief she replied, "My dear Victoria, I not only do not love him but I have an odious dislike of him. In fact, his advances have been unpleasant. He seems only interested in the most lurid aspect of matrimony, perhaps shadowed only by the support my family name can lend to his respectability."

"Oh no!" said Farrel, "Evangeline Fen's about to sell her virtue. Is this a romance novel or what?"

"Farrel, stop interrupting," said Jessie. "Go on, Kathryn."

"Hmmm, this is more about her luggage finally arriving and she's sending it to the Hamilton Hotel where she secured a suite. OK... Here's something. It's three days later..."

I have taken it upon myself to embark on serious research as to the root of Evangeline's financial problems. Whilst certainly true that the entire country has suffered from the bank panic and indeed many have been ruined, as far as I can see, a significant amount of the Fen family holdings are not only intact but flourishing. Particularly the farms and lumber mill.

Evangeline insists that her financial advisors, Auerbach, Shilling & Scand, have presented her with reams of papers showing crippling debt and she has carefully reviewed them. She really is quite astute when it comes to numbers, yet I fear she trusts these advisors far more than is their due. After all, whilst the dollars and cents add up to a loss, one does have to ask where the numbers have come from. It is not as though Evangeline is actually in the cornfield counting the bushels. The sums are brought to her for her review.

Debt comes from unlucky speculation and there is no indication that the shares Evangeline's family held were on margin. While overhead is a concern, the profits from the production areas of her holdings are clearly more than double the costs involved. So where, indeed, is this debt coming from? Who is doing the borrowing, and why? Are her advisors nefarious or just fools? Perhaps there is more than an obvious reason why they deign to use their initials in their signage.

Funds are certainly not overspent for the upkeep of Evangeline's family. They own this little house outright. It would surely be an ample and charming town home for one or two, plus housekeeper, were it not for the stable odors. Yet it is quite cramped with Evangeline, her mother, her aunt, and her two sisters and brother, along with the scullery who lives in the below-stairs quarters.

Evangeline has been told by Messrs. Auerbach, Shilling & Scand that two substantial notes are due at the end of next month. And that payment of those will reduce her family income to near zero and turn them out of the house. Yet I cannot see how this is possible.

I have wired Franklin and asked him for the loan of an auditor to accompany me and Evangeline in the meeting two days hence with her financial advisors. Franklin, ever the doting and supportive brother, has wired back that he will also attend the meeting and in the meantime will look into the Fen holdings through other channels. He is arriving on the four o'clock train, tomorrow.

"Who's Franklin?" I asked.

"I looked him up," said Kathryn. "He's Victoria's younger brother, Franklin Cedarbrook Snow. He was a major Philadelphia lawyer even at the young age of twenty-eight. He ran for office and ultimately became a Senator and then a cabinet member under McKinley."

"Read more," said Jessie.

"OK, this is later that day."

It is quite late and I have just sent Evangeline home in a hack. The rooms I have taken at the Hamilton are comfortable but seem empty the moment she leaves. I have asked her to stay but she insists that her family feels more comfortable in the house when she is there.

I took these rooms not because I felt the need to leave the tiny Fen family home. In fact, I would gladly stay there regardless of the discomfort if only to be near my angel, but I needed a place to spread out the papers and financial records to elucidate the Fen family holdings.

Evangeline and I have found several significant discrepancies between actual shares and profits. I must say that Mr. Auerbach seems nothing more than an American Uriah Heap to me. Unctuous is quite the understatement and I caused Evangeline to laugh when I said so.

I ordered an intimate supper for the two of us to be delivered in my rooms. I found her looking at me with a brightness that warmed me. I was nearly seized with a passion to take her into my arms, but that wouldn't solve anything, and both of us seem to know it.

As yet she is guarded. Perhaps that is so because I offered to cover her debts. I was in error. She is not the sort to be indebted to a dear friend, much less one she... well. It is perhaps a condemnation of our era that a woman would hastily enter a loveless marriage for security, but would never encumber a friend.

Kathryn turned the page and said, "This is after the meeting."

June 1st, 1876

I don't suppose this meeting could have gone better. It is gratifying to have Franklin here and he has taken to Evangeline. My brother knows me far to well to misunderstand my commitment to Evangeline. Like two children scheming as one, he is always on my side and I am glad to see he approves of my obsession. Franklin and his faithful accountant Mr. Purrit were able to lay plain the figures of Evangeline's so-called advisors, 'Asses Three,' as Franklin calls them privately.

Franklin threatened them with criminal prosecution. They relented under his brilliant 'cross examination style' questioning and indeed I pride myself in that I was able to add quite a bit of enlightening information from my examination of the Fen family books, which I have reviewed without ceasing for the last several days.

Mr. Purrit easily confirmed that Evangeline is due several large sums from share investments that will not only cover any debt but will allow her family to live comfortably. Under pressure of prosecution by my formidable brother, the asses have admitted that..."

"Oh my God," said Kathryn scanning the page.

"What, what!?!" we all said in unison.

"...have admitted that... General Merganser Hunterdon had pressed them and indeed paid them to create this financial debacle for the Fen family. Franklin has already sent for the police and telegraphed state banking authorities."

Kathryn sat back in utter amazement.

"So, *Ersatz, Shamming, and Scammed* sold out the General!" said Farrel.

"But I'm afraid to ask what happened. Hunterdon was so wealthy and powerful he could have just had Brother Franklin and Mr. Pruitt thrown in jail or worse before they got out of town," I said.

Kathryn was gently flipping the pages to find out the future of the past.

"No, that's not what happened! Here, listen to this, just a few days later,"

June 7th, 1876

My brother is even more powerful than I had imagined!

Under further pressure the dastardly money counters who nearly ruined the fortune of my angel admitted they had caused the ruin of several <u>other</u> families and businesses in the district by simply confusing the books and presenting fraudulent bills. They did this under the direction of Merganser Hunterdon, to his financial advantage.

Via a series of telegrams Franklin has called an informal meeting of a wide range of powerful men from Harrisburg. They arrived by train this morning. Of course, I was not permitted to attend, but Franklin recounted everything to us later.

The problem, it seems, is that the General controls so much of the financial infrastructure of the state that he has effectively stalled his own indictment. The gentlemen from Harrisburg fear that the rocky economy that has been shored up since the panic will collapse if the richest man in the state is prosecuted. And while he may be a crook, his own businesses are actually sound. It has been revealed that Merganser was instrumental in a great deal of the slave trade and purchase in the years before the war. As heinous as that surely is, he has a great deal of information about other key people in the Northern financial world who were also part of these nefarious dealings. He threatened to expose them if he is indicted.

So the government regulators have agreed to make a back room deal, as Franklin would call it. The majority of Merganser's corporation will now be run by a closely regulated network of new board members. Merganser will remain at liberty but he will be powerless. He'll draw an allowance and I suppose he will continue to control a small part of his own accumulated wealth. But for now, his Scrooge-like grasp is loosened on those weaker than he.

"It's always about money, isn't it?" I sighed. "So does this mean Evangeline doesn't need Victoria anymore, or is this where the doors open?"

"I'd hate to think money ended their relationship. Let's see, this is also from that day," said Kathryn.

I confess that the vast majority of my concern has always been for Evangeline and now everything has changed. I have already taken rooms for her family at the Hamilton Hotel, where they will reside until a more suitable residence can be arranged. Meanwhile I find myself oddly drawn to the little tradesman's row home on Washington Mews. I believe I may purchase it and rebuild the inside with modern convenience. I think I shall reside there while I work on my sculpture commissions for Irwin College. I'll plant lavender in every free inch of earth in order to overcome the mephitic odor.

Yet, dear journal, what this means for Evangeline and... me... I do not know. I can at least rest assured that any question of marrying that criminal general is out of the question. Yet... the Harrisburg power brokers have asked that Evangeline's engagement continue for a suitable period, because as it turns out, Gen. Hunterdon's engagement to one of the state's oldest families has helped to stabilize the state's banking system even more than his money has done.

"Well, how long is she going to have to pretend she's engaged to him?" asked Jessie.

"Well publicly, 140 years or so," I said.

"Hunterdon must have been furious. Oh look, it goes on to say here," said Kathryn.

Franklin tells us that Merganser is near to spontaneous combustion. Certainly Evangeline and I will not escape his verbal curses, but they are impotent in our world.

Evangeline has agreed to keep up appearances until all danger of the state's financial instability has passed. She wants none of his money for herself but has already planned a series of public works including a vast public library, a network of schools for children, an education program for poor mothers, and a modern hospital with a nursing school for women on the edge of the city.

"Until all danger of the state's economic instability has passed? Well, no wonder the myth of their devotion to each other has survived for 140 years," Farrel said.

"Well, well, doesn't this cast a different light on the city of Fenchester?" said Kathryn, pausing to sip some more wine. "Now, these next few pages are all about the allocation of various monies. They did leave Merganser with control of a few things—the funeral home, the Majestic, some land holdings... an office building. Based on what Franklin said about a board controlling Hunterdon's money, how was it that so much of the city's philanthropy is attributed to him?"

"Well, he did have some money left, but why did he throw himself into commissioning all those beautiful sculptures of Evangeline after she died? He must have hated Victoria Snow, but he ended up giving her twenty dollars every day for the rest of her life for those commissions? Why?"

"Yeah, hard to explain, but can we get back to the romance?" asked Jessie. "Isn't there anything else?"

"Yes, here, about a week later." Kathryn read,

June 17th, 1876,

The heat wave that is lowering the attendance at the Centennial in Philadelphia has hit Fenchester. The weather is oppressively hot, nearly 100 degrees in the shade at not even ten in the morning. These steamy days are giving me second thoughts about living so close to a vast stable.

Evangeline has suggested we ride into the country. I confess I am not the horsewoman she is, but I would ride an elephant if that were the key to finding moments alone with her. I must bring forth the spirt of Charlotte Cushman and not be complacent. Though being with Evangeline as dear friends has been a pleasure, I can wait no longer. What would Charlotte do? Yes, well, I know exactly what Charlotte would do!"

Kathryn scanned the rest of the page and the next two, then she said, "OK this was written the next morning:"

Were I not tethered to the earth by the heavy garments my sex must endure, I would fly over the rooftops. Today may well have been the best day of my life, but I place hope in that it is just one of a lifetime of happy days to follow.

"Oh no, this is so sad," said Farrel. "Knowing what happens to her is like being able to see into the future."

"Focus on the present," I said. "Go on, Kathryn."

Kathryn looked up at me briefly and our eyes locked. She nodded slightly, then she went on reading:

When my beautiful Evangeline and I rode out of the city, she said in her most confidential voice as we mounted the horses, "I have something to share with you. I've never shown anyone this secret place before. But I find I have a fondness for you, Victoria that... that surpasses my sisters, when it comes to secrets."

The enchanting look in her eyes quickened my heart, and I found myself wishing I was riding astride to ease a tension that began to build in my nether regions. It turned out, however, I was glad I had saved this physical sensation to share with my angel later in the afternoon rather than relieving it at a canter.

When we reached the middle of a lovely green glade, she dismounted and I did as well.

"I think the horses do not need to be tied. The grass and water in the stream will meet their needs. You know, Victoria, I'm quite successful at knowing what horses want, but I find that skill fades when it comes to..." Victoria turned and looked at me for long moment as I held my breath and hoped she would come to me on her own, without my bidding.

Instead she drew from her horse bag a large parcel she tucked under her arm. It was quite hot in the sun and our heavy riding clothes added to our discomfort. I was desperate for relief from the heat and desperate for a different sort of relief ever since I had first felt Evangeline in my arms at the train station.

"Come along," she beckoned.

I followed her between low yew branches out of the glade. A wall of yews in a broad circle made a private outdoor room. (I may note here that I will henceforth find a circle of yew trees a meaningful and deeply comforting place to me, always.)

In its center was a rock pool that the clear stream swelled and eddied. Birds darted around it, but it was unspoiled by any human presence. It was ours alone.

"Fancy a swim?" said Evangeline softly and then she smiled the most provocative of smiles and I was quite ready to swim with her for eternity.

She put down her parasol and opened her parcel. In it was a large blanket that she spread on the ground. "There is no one around, Victoria. I have come here fifty times and never been disturbed." And then... she began to disrobe.

"Jiminy Crickets," I said.

Kathryn paused here and I shifted in my seat. Kathryn glanced at me in a way that made me desperately glad that we were sharing this moment. I saw Jessie lean against Farrel's shoulder.

Kathryn read:

I stood stock still, hoping the moment was not a mere figment of my imagination and then with a smile upon my lips I undid the buttons of my shirtwaist and slipped my dress up over my head. The extra padding we both wore at the back was soon discarded, petticoats and the rest of our fashionable trappings were cast aside into two large heaps. I thought briefly that the fabric from our ensembles would have clothed a dozen needy children.

My angel's modesty was now protected only by her summer chemise and drawers. Their light linen fabric was sheer, and for the briefest of moments I reflected that her modesty would be protected by nothing at all when this fabric was wet.

She took my hand and we stepped down into the small rock-lined pool. The water was warm but refreshing, and we hastened to submerge ourselves in its liquid embrace.

"How did you find this lovely place?" I asked her as I paddled to the center and dipped my head under the water.

"When I was a girl, my pony led me to it. I was supposed

to ride near the house, but I'd travel for hours letting the pony choose the trail. That was when we could afford to keep horses."

"You could keep a horse now, Evangeline, if you wished. Your finances would more than bear it."

I swam back to her and we moved to sit near the edge of the pool, still with the water to our shoulders but resting on the rocks beneath.

"Victoria," Evangeline began, "my mother and sisters and... I are eternally grateful to you for all you have done. When I received your note saying you would come to Fenchester, I had looked forward to your caring sympathy but had never dared believe you would so adroitly solve all our problems."

Evangeline's voice caught and she turned from me in the throes of emotion. The full meaning of her family's gratitude was clear to me, but at that moment I cared for nothing but the knowledge of where her own heart lay.

I said, "It makes me very happy to be able to grant you peace of mind. I hope you know that I would do anything... anything, I could to make you happy, my dear."

"Would you, Victoria? Could you know, when you left me in Rome, I thought I would die from the loss of you. I cried for days, though I hid it from the others at Charlotte's house. I made up my mind to tell you the next time we met. But then my circumstances were so reduced, so desperate, I thought it unfair to burden you with more than a request for advice. I didn't want you to think I wanted you to... financially encumber yourself. Now that those troubles are a thing of the past, however..." She reached for my hand and drew me closer.

I said earnestly, "But don't you know, darling Evangeline, that I would have given my last breath to ease your cares? I would have... I will... if you but allow me..."

And with that, she kissed my cheek, then slipped up the water's edge until she was only waist deep, and as I had suspected, the soaked fabric that covered her had become as clear as glass, thus revealing a vision that is etched on my very soul for eternity. I was ready to act, but it was she who reached forward.

With hands on both my shoulders, she drew me to her slowly until I was very close.

I managed to say, "Evangeline, dare I ask?"

She answered my question with a kiss on my lips. It was not the type simply between dear friends. Indeed my Angel became a tiger burning bright. Her meaningful kiss grew ferocious as I responded. She forthwith rent the linen fabric from my eager form and tore hers away as well. We pressed together, feeling each other not with gentle fingertips but with every inch of sensitive flesh.

I confess that I had imagined this moment a hundredfold and taken pleasure from the planning of my actions, yet it was clear that Evangeline had not only done the same but had all the more skill in her stratagem. The pond had a perfect place for one to recline while a water sprite found a dozen spots to suck and stroke.

I grew desperate for a spend and moaned my need in a primal way which was somehow not foreign to this ancient spot. She parted me and clove me with her tongue using skill that would have rivaled Charlotte's, but driven with an ardent force that would have put Charlotte to shame.

I felt my body grow ready and she felt my readiness as well, using it to excellent advantage. She concentrated on building my urgency until I begged release, which she achieved with surprising boldness, using her entire hand in a way I had not experienced previously. Indeed, I doubt such a sizable... stimulation would have been as intensely pleasurable had I not been so perfectly prepared and desperately desirous, and, indeed, so in love with my Angel. In fact, when the primal sounds of my release had ceased to echo against the yew trees, I found I was ready for it yet again.

I was joyously exhausted by Evangeline when she finally allowed me rest. But the merest sight of her fueled me, and I took her in similar ways, slowly working her to peak again after each culmination. We spent hours taking turns bringing each other delight. Speaking strictly for me, I could have spent the rest of my life in that circle of yews, making love with my Angel.

I am very glad my skillful mentor Charlotte Cushman had taken me... well, shall we say under her wing... And based on my experiences of the afternoon, I wouldn't be surprised if one of Charlotte's disciples took Evangeline under her wing whilst in Rome. Because my darling had delivered to me pleasures many times my wildest imagination. If indeed Evangeline developed her skills from her own imagination, then she is as inventive as the entire White Marmorean Flock (as Mr. James described us) grouped as one.

When we finally drew back to rest as the sun dipped below

the trees, she said, "It has always been you. There has never been another."

I am sure, dear journal, I will always consider those ten words the sweetest I have ever heard. I told her I felt the same.

As Evangeline lay back against the pool's edge that a million years of swirling water had etched, I suddenly saw her as a siren, a naiad, a Rhein maiden. She is my muse, the one for whom I will make every sculpture, every work, from whom every inspiration will come. I know, as sure as the sun will come up tomorrow, that this will always be true. If I were never to behold another woman, or even another beautiful thing of any kind, it would not matter because the vision of Evangeline at that sweet moment will be enough to sustain my commitment to art itself and will inform my every work for the rest of my life.

Kathryn stopped reading and looked up.

Finally Farrel said, "Can't beat the 19th century for poetic license."

Jessie said with amusement, "That's how you feel about me, isn't it, Farrel?"

Farrel replied, in a remarkably serious voice, "Yes, it is."

Kathryn saw I was staring at her and she smiled.

So that was how Victoria was able to create a thousand sculptures in a windowless cave. The memory of Evangeline was her inspiration. She didn't need anything else.

Kathryn scanned the next page, then she read:

We are now together. She is mine, I am hers. And I count the seconds until I shall be with her again.

There was a pause in the room that was filled with heavy breathing and considerable shifting in seats. I had a feeling that everyone was thinking about being alone with the woman who shared her bed. I certainly was.

"My, my," said Kathryn.

"Talk about Uhaul Lesbians! One afternoon and it's a lifetime commitment," said Farrel.

"It happens that way sometimes," said Kathryn.

"Yes, it does," said Jessie.

Kathryn was looking at me with that half-smile that thrills me and makes me weak at the same time.

Jessie's head snapped up. She looked at the clock on the wall. "Do you think the police still have Gabe or that he's back home?" she asked insistently.

"I don't know. He has that alibi, so they won't hold him long."

"It's Buster's dinnertime. Not eating will make him sick... Remember that time?" asked Jessie turning to Farrel.

"Uh huh, he got dehydrated and had to go to the animal hospital."

"Can you find out?" Jessie asked me.

"I'll check."

I reached Sgt. Ed O'Brien on my cell in a minute.

"No question she was murdered, Maggie. Stabbed twice in the neck close together. Looked like a vampire bite, but they were kind of square holes. Do they make, like, sculpture tools like that?" asked O'Brien.

Kathryn, Jessie, and Farrel were following my every word. I hated to shock them, but I had to respond. "Yeah, there are all sorts of things like that. Handmade icepicks, files, even old-fashioned flooring nails. Any one of those could have been within reach in the studio."

"Well, whatever it was, it's not there now. The guys checked everything for bloodstains. There's nothing. If the perp used a tool from the studio, then he took it along."

Or she, popped into my brain. It always does when people presume it has to be one gender or the other.

"No way Carbondale could have done it, unless he hired a hit man. We're getting ready to send him home in a squad car right now," said O'Brien. He told me a few things about Gabe's interview and then asked me to let him know if I found out anything else.

I turned to the group after O'Brien hung up. "They're bringing Gabe home in a few minutes. Sgt. O'Brien says Gabe's alibi is pretty solid."

"He said something else, didn't he?" asked Kathryn.

I nodded. "Gabe told the police investigators that Suzanne had already left him *before* he went to his conference. She'd moved out her clothes, office papers, her best kitchen tools. Everything she really cared about she packed up and took away a week before he left for England."

"I wonder why she didn't tell me," said Jessie softly.

"She didn't have much, but what she had was pretty fine. All the art was original. Her kitchen stuff was top of the line. She had one Remington chef's knife she paid $75 for at an auction. But everything she valued would have fit into a couple of boxes. Wouldn't you say, Jessie?" asked Farrel.

"I don't know what to say... Oh Maggie, I thought she left without telling me goodbye. Now it turns out she's been lying at the bottom of that thing all this time. I hate to think..." Jessie sobbed and Farrel went to her to hold her in her arms. Jessie hugged her back tightly.

Kathryn reached for my hand. I held it and saw the glistening tears in her eyes.

Then Kathryn said, "What was that last thing... about the tools?"

Nothing got by Kathryn.

I took a breath. "The Coroner confirms it was murder."

"You already figured that, Maggie. What else?" said Kathryn.

"She was stabbed twice in the neck by something pointy, like a square skewer."

Farrel nodded saying, "A needle file could look like that, or a horseshoe nail, or an eighth-inch mortise chisel, even the tang on the other end of a chisel. Did they find it down there? The murder weapon?"

I shook my head. "It's not there."

Jessie got up from her seat and walked to the other end of the kitchen, out of earshot. "You don't have to stop talking. I just don't want to hear this," she called back.

"So how do they think it happened? Was it like you said?" asked Kathryn.

I nodded. "The Coroner said it hit a vital artery when she was stabbed. That's why there was so much blood. She probably didn't regain consciousness."

"That's a tiny bit of comfort," said Farrel softly.

"So the murderer grabbed a tool to use as a weapon and killed her, and then took the weapon along?" asked Kathryn.

"Looks like it. Or I guess the killer could have brought the weapon into the basement..." I mused.

"Unlikely that someone would be carrying a mortise chisel in their pocket or purse. Even I don't do that," said Farrel.

"True, unless..." I said, thinking about the lethal wound in Suzanne's neck.

"I'm going to call Gabe. I'm worried about Buster. I don't trust Gabe to take care of him," said Jessie coming back to the group. She dialed but got no answer.

"He dropped his cell phone in Buster's dog dish. He probably hasn't replaced it," I said.

Jessie said slowly, "If she died right after I saw her... then where is all her stuff. If she moved it out, where did she put it?"

"I saw some boxes in the mudroom of the stuff she left there. Gabe must have shuffled the remainders of her things into boxes so he could do his macho remodel. Suzanne did always say she traveled light. You would have had a lot in common with her Kathryn. Traveling light," I said.

"I have more than I thought, though. Mostly books, and now I have my Victoria Snow sculpture and a baby grand piano. So I guess my light traveling days are behind me," said Kathryn

I smiled at that. "You have that nice little watercolor... um..." Something flashed into my brain. I said, "Farrel what did you say about original art?"

"Huh? You mean about Suzanne? Well, that she had some pieces she loved. Small things, but great."

"No repros? None?"

"No, Gabe had some, but all of Suzanne's things were original."

I thought back to the day I'd fixed Gabe's lunch. I asked, *"Everything* she had was original?"

Farrel and Jessie nodded.

"What is it?" asked Kathryn.

"I think... I think I better go over to Gabe's."

"Why?" Farrel and Kathryn asked in unison.

"Because when I was at Gabe's, Buster knocked over a box in the mudroom and I saw what was in it." In my mind I saw Gabriel Carbondale packing those boxes and putting them there. Then I thought back to Nora Hasan saying, *'And now, all the world's a stage.'*

"Kathryn, all those pompous things that Gabe is always saying, they aren't just random are they?" I asked. "Giving short shrift, bag and baggage, meat and drink to me, good riddance, vanish into thin air... He's not just making those up, is he?"

"No, of course not," said Kathryn. "It's all Shakespeare."

I stood up and grabbed my jacket.

"What's this about?" - Farrel.

"It's about Gabe lying. Lying a lot and having the acting skills to pull it off. It's time I got some answers from Gabe."

"I'm coming with you," Kathryn said, getting her coat.

As we left, Jessie called, "Be sure Buster has his dinner!"

And I distinctly heard Farrel say the word, "Team."

"What did you see in that box that is making us rush over to Gabe's?" asked Kathryn as we walked swiftly along the darkening street.

I was still putting things together in my mind. When I hadn't answered her for a block, Kathryn said, "I'm supposed to be the steadfast partner. Enlighten me about the evidence."

"OK, Suzanne had a small Matisse cutout. It fell on the floor when Buster tipped over a box."

"A real Matisse?"

"I think it was a book plate print. But if it wasn't a repro...."

"I priced one of those once. The ones from *Jazz* are worth around seven thousand dollars!" said Kathryn.

"I know. It's hard to believe someone would leave that behind when they moved out and Gabe must have known that when he packed it away. I'd like to get a better look in those boxes."

As we made it to 10th Street we saw a squad car pulling up to Fen House.

A uniformed officer and Gabriel Carbondale got out of the idling car and walked to the door.

"OK, are you up for some team work?" I asked Kathryn.

"Consider me your able-bodied apprentice. What are we going to do?"

"As soon as the police car drives away, ring the doorbell. Then chat with Gabe to get him to stay in the front of the house while I take a quick look around the back."

"You can't just break in. Oh rats, we're back to that again."

"I'm going to get Buster to *invite* me into the mudroom. I just want another look at those boxes before I talk to Gabe. Ring my phone as soon as he stops talking to you."

"Just don't shoot the dog," said Kathryn.

"Jessie would kill me with her bare hands if I did that."

"Wait, Maggie... um... When Carbondale came back from England and found Suzanne's expensive Matisse still on the wall, surely that was suspicious. Why didn't he tell you or say anything to the police? Why didn't he act more concerned?"

"*Act* is the pivotal word. He didn't act concerned because he's an actor. Get ready."

We gripped each other's hands and looked into each others eyes and then Kathryn moved closer to the front door to be able to swoop in as soon as the police left. I ran around to the back alley. I reached over the top of the backyard gate, slid the latch back, and swung it open enough to slip through and edge into the yard.

Buster burst through his dog door, bounding toward me like a bull charging a matador. He reared up, landing his snowshoe-sized paws on my shoulders. Dog slobber whipped my cheek. I lifted him down and wiped my face with my sleeve."

"Hi buddy," I whispered as I patted him into a tail-wagging frenzy.

"Shhhh. OK, calm down."

He immediately turned and charged back through his dog door into the kitchen.

I cupped my hands around my eyes and peered through the window into the mudroom. There was a low light on in the kitchen. Nobody back there... Not a creature was stirring except a dog the size of a small pony. Buster paced the room, swinging his beer-can-thick tail like a dull scythe.

I could faintly hear Gabe and the cop talking in the vestibule. Then I heard the front door close and the police car pulling away. As I waited for the doorbell, I admitted to myself I had no good excuse to sneak into Gabe's house.

I tapped on the glass. "Buster... Buster... gimme a reason." He tilted his head, then he ran out of view in the direction of Suzanne's old office. A minute later he came back to the mudroom doorway, sat down, and looked at me. Then he looked toward the office, then toward me, then toward the office. He ran to the office again, his frying-pan-sized paws were surprisingly quiet. He came back to the door, sat down, and looked up at me, doing a great imitation of every fictional dog in media history trying to tell the main character something important. Buster yawned and shook his head, jangling his tags and chain collar like sleigh bells.

I took a step back into the dark yard because Gabriel Carbondale suddenly walked into the kitchen from the living room hallway. He shrugged off his jacket to hang it on the hook next to the back door. He moved slowly, like a man who had way to much on his mind. Not a surprise, since his wife had just been found murdered.

Gabe noticed Buster, who ran out of view to the left. Gabe watched him and then followed. I faintly heard him say something. A light went on to the left in Suzanne's office. Buster ran back into my view and sat down, looking left then at me, then left.

Then suddenly a gunshot split the night and Buster reared back and howled like a horror movie werewolf, just as the doorbell began to ring.

CHAPTER 18

Before I was even conscious of moving, I was squeezing through Buster's dog door, glad I still had my gun with me. I pulled it out of my shoulder holster and flattened against the wall. Buster continued to howl until I told him to stop.

Buster pranced ahead of me and I slowly followed in full defense mode, with my left hand teacupping my right hand that held my gun, pointed down but ready. Somewhere close was a person who had just squeezed a trigger.

I turned the corner. Gabriel Carbondale was slumped over Suzanne's office table. There was a small neat hole in the side of his head and the small gun that had made it lay on the floor below his dangling hand. A red pool was rapidly leaking from Gabe's head and spreading over the tabletop. I moved toward Gabe. Buster held back, politely letting me go first.

I inched into the office and uselessly felt Gabe's neck for a pulse. I scanned the room. The other door that faced the hall to the living room was open. The hall beyond it was empty.

Buster padded back into view and sat in the doorway.

"Is there anybody in here?" I whispered to him.

He cocked his head to one side, flipping an uncut ear over his eyes. He leaned toward the rest of the house as if to listen. Then he shook his errant ear back in place, exhaled like a person, and yawned.

Either that meant *no*, or it was just comic relief.

I listened intently. There was no noise. There didn't seem to be anyone in the house. It looked pretty conclusively like suicide.

I called the police, told them simply that there was a dead body at Gabe's, and it was Gabe. I could hear the sirens before I'd even finished giving the information on the phone.

Kathryn texted me while I was talking to the police.

< Sirens? >

I texted back, < Gabe's dead >

****

The police swarmed the block. In minutes Kathryn joined me in the backyard and Sgt. Ed O'Brien was on the scene again.

"You've been drumming up a bucket of business for us lately, Maggie," said O'Brien, meeting me in the backyard.

He brought me back into the house and Kathryn tagged along without asking. As Jessie always says, *It's easier to get forgiveness than to get permission.*

"Maggie, you want to tell me how you got in, or shall we just overlook the little issue of the back door being locked."

By way of explanation I glanced at Buster's dog door.

"Usually people leave notes, but there's no note. So, help me out here... Carbondale just killed himself because he was upset about his wife being dead, or because somehow he flew over here from England and killed her and felt remorse?"

"I don't know about that, but there *are* a couple of things I do know. For one, he hid his wife's possessions that she certainly would have taken with her if she'd left him. We also know someone was making it look as though she was still alive by sending electronic messages. It might have been Carbondale doing that to cover up her murder."

"There's no way anyone in here could have gotten by you?"

I shook my head, looking into the office. The crime team was going over it. In the hallway an officer with a police dog came out of the door under the stairs that must have led to the basement. He called, "All clear."

I swear Buster's brows furrowed when he saw the other dog.

"No one got by me," I said, turning to Kathryn.

She said, "I was at the front door and no one came out of it."

O'Brien heard what Kathryn said but didn't acknowledge her.

"Here's another spanner in the works, Ed. Looks to me like Carbondale was a trained actor. He quoted Shakespeare without thinking, and he seemed to fall back on quoting the Bard when he was lying. I think lying was a skill he'd learned. The sadness, shock, and innocence over Suzanne's death and that guy Frankie getting shot in the cemetery may all have been an act."

"Geez," said O'Brien, running his fingers through his thinning hair. "So suppose he *had* his wife killed. Why?"

"Perhaps to get his hands on the antiques and sculpture in Victoria Snow's studio. They're quite valuable," said Kathryn.

O'Brien looked over to Kathryn then back to me. He deadpanned, "New partner?"

I hesitated. From the corner of my eye, I saw Kathryn's eyebrows lift. "Ed, this is Dr. Kathryn Anthony. She's working with me on this case. Kathryn, this is Sgt. Edward O'Brien. He's leading this investigation."

Suddenly Buster crashed through his dog door and rammed Ed into the cabinets, interrupting further elucidation.

"Maybe your *partner* could get this dog outta here? Have the guys taken *his* footprints?"

Buster sat down, looked at each of us, and then lifted his paw.

I whispered to Kathryn, "He's an orphan now, so I guess we'd better bring him to Farrel and Jessie's." I went to the cupboard next to the sink and found a bag of Buster's food.

O'Brien agreed to let Kathryn take the sealed bag. She grabbed a leash and left reluctantly with her new best friend.

"I'll see you in a little while," I called after her.

"Partner," O'Brien muttered, smirking.

We watched the team going over the crime scene. I ran through the case in my head.

O'Brien told me to stay while he went over the area. Then he came back to talk to me. He said, "So, whadaya think?"

I said, "Carbondale was ready to spend his own money to seal up the crypts. He tried pretty hard to keep people from going down there. Maybe Kathryn's right. He could have been trying to get that stuff for himself."

"What was it worth?"

"Well, if you count all the sculptures on the shelves and the huge one of marble in the back, millions. But nobody could have converted those things to that much cash. It would be worth more to Gabe as a historical discovery. Suzanne was working on a book. She could have capitalized on the sculpture find for book publicity, but they probably belong to the college and couldn't be sold off."

"How much cash *could* someone get out of that stuff on the sly?"

"Hmmm, I guess if you had the right connections you could probably get between 500K and a million. But no one could do that who was actually known in the field, and Carbondale was. He'd need to use some kind of go-between or agent."

"Like Frankie Kibbey?"

"No, no way. Kibbey blew out $50,000 worth of stuff for $500. Frankie was working on his *uneducated*-own. And Carbondale was in England, Ed, how could he..."

"Maybe he found a way to come back in the middle of the conference."

"You think he flew back here and killed her and then flew back to England? C'mon Ed, there are so many holes in that, even the Chief wouldn't believe it."

"No, see I figure he and the wife both found the antiques in that basement. He goes to England but knows she's going to leave him and might turn the stuff in to the college before she goes. At the conference he lifts somebody's passport and uses it to get a fast round trip ticket. He gets here, gets her to go to the studio, kills her in the vat, then flies back and no one's the wiser. After the conference he goes to get the antiques but Francis Kibbey follows him. Carbondale figures out Frankie is stealing the goods and might find the wife's body, so Carbondale shoots Frankie in the cemetery. Then when we find the wife's body, Carbondale knows he's in for it, so he offs himself."

"Doesn't work, Ed. Red said the shooter was in the crypt. Why would he make that up?" I thought for a minute. "Try this. Gabe knows about the antiques in the studio and wants the money. He's angry at Suzanne and doesn't want her to surrender the antiques to the college, so he hires someone to kill her. Maybe Frankie himself. Then one of them kills Frankie to keep him from talking. That would have scared Gabe into hurling, but he'd still have to use his acting skills to cover up what he knew. After that Gabe thinks Red knows about the contract he'd put out on Suzanne, or he might have just been keeping Red from telling anyone where the studio was, so someone like me wouldn't find her body. So he tried to kill us with that van. Wait. The van. *Oh shit.*"

"What?" asked O'Brien.

I held up my hand and squinted into space. "Ed, I'm a fool. I... I saw that van the night Samson Henshaw called me. It was parked out on Washington." I pointed north toward the side of the house.

O'Brien clapped his hands. "Great, it fits then. You know, Henshaw probably saw Carbondale himself get that hand truck from the van. It was *Carbondale* that Henshaw followed to the studio. I'll get the investigation team to find that white van. If it's Carbondale's, it'll be in the neighborhood and a little splashed paint on the front'll clinch it. Course, if we don't find paint on the front, then it's not the van that chased you up the mountain."

But I knew in my bones it *was* the same van.

Sgt. Marc Freligh joined the conversation. He said, "The body's in the bus. We're going over the crime scene now."

"Ed, I'm really not sold on this thesis, there are so many holes. For one thing, down there in the studio only one of the boxes of stuff had even been opened. How would Carbondale have even known the stuff in the other boxes was valuable? For all he knew, they could have all been family photos," I said shaking my head.

"Whoa, it's *your* theory and it's not bad. Give it a rest, Maggie. Carbondale got somebody to kill her, then he killed himself. Maybe just for the sculptures. You said they were valuable. We're searching the house now. It's a small place. Bet we find evidence of a hit. Go on and give your formal statement to one of the team and then you can go."

****

It was late when I got home. I stepped quietly into the bedroom. The reading lamp was on. Kathryn was in bed propped up against pillows. Her book had fallen to her side and she was asleep. The covers were pulled low enough to see she was wearing nothing. It took a minute for me to realize I was staring at her. The sight of her soft skin, her faint smile, the sheet just barely covering her breasts made me breathe deeply.

She said without opening her eyes, "Well, you won the bet. It was Lois, so I'll give you a massage."

"Aren't you kind of tired from getting up before dawn, chasing around a rabbit hole... and all the other things that happened today?"

"Yes," she yawned as she opened her eyes languidly. "But a bet's a bet. Of course maybe I should punish you for leaving me alone for the last few hours."

"I really didn't have a choice."

"Maggie, I think you enjoy helping with police investigations, even when it isn't your case."

"Not unlike you giving so much of your time to Victoria Snow. I think she's going to be *the other woman* in our relationship."

"Perhaps we should both be punished," she said archly.

"Hmmmm... Then I think I should get ready for bed."

"I do, too."

When I came out of the bathroom, Kathryn was asleep again. I couldn't blame her; she'd had very little rest in the last two days.

I got into the bed next to her and she stirred again, opening her eyes even more slowly.

"You've made promises you can't keep," I said gently.

"You may be right, but Friday is your big day. We should rest up for it."

"Sounds like a deal, querida."

****

Suddenly it was 9 a.m. I yawned and stretched. The covers were warm and the bed was soft. I didn't want to get out of it until I realized Kathryn wasn't in it.

I sat up. "Kathryn?"

She came to the bedroom door, fully dressed in form-fitting jeans and a loose scoop-neck sweater. She leaned against the jamb with her arms crossed and a half-smile.

She sang, "They say it's your birthday!" She came over to the bed and kissed me. "Happy Birthday, my dear," she said sweetly.

I smiled and flipped the covers back. "Come back to bed?"

"Tempting, but I let you sleep late and now the drywall team will be arriving upstairs in fifteen minutes and you told Farrel we'd help. Nora's going to lend a hand too. I saw her in Sara's office when I went down to borrow some coffee filters."

I stretched like a cat then hopped out of bed. "You know, Kathryn, I bet if you played your cards right you could get a whole crew of young Lesbians to build your office for you at no charge at all."

As I closed the bathroom door she called, "Yes, well regardless of that, remember that Farrel and Jessie are having a little birthday party for you tonight. Then I'll have some rather exciting... presents... for the rest of the weekend celebration."

"I'll try to be patient," I called back. *Maybe I should take a cold shower,* I said to myself.

****

The Carbondales' deaths were all over the news. Fenchester's current police chief had called them a murder/suicide. The drywall team was talking about it the whole time we worked.

"Isnae this the end? Squire found some dodgy way tae come back, skelped his lass in that fusty studio, then kilt that bloke in the cemetery because he wis afeart Frankie ken where her body wis hidden, and he wis afeart Red had be keeking about doone there too?" asked Nora.

Nora's brogue had clicked into overdrive due to Kathryn. They were sanding drywall compound near the office door. I heard Kathryn snort softly. Maybe it was just the dust.

At one point I took Kathryn aside and whispered, "Stop using your magic super powers on Nora. She's beginning to sound like a road company of *Brigadoon.* Be gentle or you'll have to pay extra when it comes to my birthday present."

"You're right. I've been teasing her too much. I'll stop. But regarding your present, I have a platinum card and I can't wait to use it."

I smiled devilishly and she did too.

Farrel said to everyone, "OK, we're just about done. Maggie, Kathryn, and Nora will finish sanding this part of the wall. The rest of you can begin cleaning up and packing up the drywall tools. I have to hurry. Jessie expects me home before five."

"Farrel?" I beckoned her out of the others' earshot. "How late is this party going to go?"

"Why? Are you hoping to get lucky later?"

"Well, as a matter of fact..."

"I'm thinking no later than 9 p.m. Farrel's eyes strayed to Kathryn. I could see her imagination working. She turned back to me, fanned herself with her hand and said, "I'll ask Jessie to make espresso!"

After the crew left, Kathryn and I stood in the middle of her new office space and appreciated the transformation.

"I was afraid when all the walls were up it would seem small, but it doesn't. It's spacious. And there's so much variation. The library part at the top of the spiral stairs, the quiet intimate part under the second level. I think I'll put a couch and chairs under there, and I'll put my desk in the big open part facing the windows. Oh, I really love it, Maggie! I've never designed my own space before."

"It's a great space. It really works," I said looking around.

Kathryn checked her watch. "Oh crikey, we only have a few minutes to hurry and clean up and then get over to the party. I'm sorry I'm not paying more attention to you on your special day."

"Crikey?" I said as we rushed down stairs to shower and change.

Minutes later, as we made our way down the dark street to Farrel and Jessie's, Kathryn stopped outside their house. She said, "Maggie, before we go in, I want to... uh..."

Normally Kathryn was so rooted and sure of herself, but at the moment I could tell her vulnerable side was causing her to hesitate. I turned toward her and took her gloved hand.

"Go ahead."

"I just want you to know... uh... I..." She put her arm around me and pulled me into a deep kiss and then she leaned back. "Happy Birthday Maggie, I... I care so much about you. These last months have been the best in my life." She paused, searching for the right words.

This was our moment. I took a breath.

But then out of the darkness appeared Cora Martin and Mickey

Murphy, the young man who lived in the upstairs of Cora's house. Mickey, who'd been troubled and at sea when he was on his own, had found a safe harbor with Cora, and Cora had found a new purpose in life taking care of the quirky but endearing Mickey.

"Hi, Hiya, Hi!" said Mickey gleefully.

"Well, here's the birthday girl," said Cora. "Babies, it's cold outside. Come along before we all freeze to death."

Kathryn and I both smiled. I could see in her eyes that the moment wasn't lost, just deferred. *Calm down, time is on our side,* I thought. On the other hand, Victoria and Evangeline had probably thought that too.

Everyone was in Farrel and Jessie's living room. In the gallery was a table full of my favorite foods, which included but was not limited to: mini flautas filled with chicken, stuffed mushrooms brimming with crab and cheese, tiny spinach balls with sweet mustard sauce, huge chilled shrimp, figs with stilton cheese and crushed toasted walnuts, sun-dried tomato tapenade on toasted French bread rounds, and cornhusk-wrapped tamales filled with masa, fresh corn, and roasted sweet red peppers.

Can Jessie throw a party or what?

Everything was small and easy to arrange on a little plate. All the people I cared most about were in this room. And a few new people I was just getting to know.

The minute we came in, my younger sister Rosa rushed up to me and hugged me like a little kid. She's in her late twenties but she has the joy factor of a child at an amusement park, which makes her so much fun to be around.

The woman we call Mom, the enchanting and irreverent Juana Martinez, grabbed Kathryn by the hand and drew her into the kitchen where Jessie was managing the food. Kathryn and Juana began to help.

I'd told Farrel that I didn't need presents. Instead I'd prefer contributions to the Lenape Valley grassroots community organization advocating for the civil rights of Gay, Lesbian, Bisexual, and Transgender people.

Sara came up to me looking festive and smart. She hugged me and put a hefty donation check in my hand. Buster the behemoth galloped between us, insisted on a pat, and then trotted back to his spot in front of the fireplace, where he lay down with a plop, grunt, and jingle. He looked like a Holstein rug with a lot of the Holstein still in it. Buster sighed in his eerily human voice.

"I bet he can't wait for all of us to go home so he can get out of that dog suit and hit one of the corner bars," said Sara.

Nora Hasan came in the front door and right behind her was Amanda Knightbridge. I scanned the room. The gang was all here.

Emma Strong, Sara's law partner, showed them where to put their coats and then Nora came over to me and Sara. She said, "Did you set this all up just to hear me say, 'This is the best food I ever... *ett?*'"

"I find your accent delightful, everyone does. But I also think you're a little too awestruck by my... *novia.*"

"I'm doing my best to rein meself in. But she's formidable."

I saw Kathryn back in the kitchen getting a stack of plates and handing them to Rosa. She tossed her head back and laughed with my family. I exhaled. "Yes, she is formidable, in every sense."

Amanda Knightbridge suddenly appeared at my side. "Maggie, have the police ended their investigation? Are they attributing *all* the crimes to Gabriel Carbondale?"

"Do you have another theory?" I asked sincerely.

"Do you, Maggie?"

"I don't feel right about all this, Amanda, but I don't have another theory."

"Don't you?" Her piercing eyes actually turned from China blue to midnight blue. It was so remarkable, I couldn't look away.

Finally I said, "I'm fairly sure that Gabe didn't kill Frankie."

"Ah!" she said this as though I was on the right track. Though I had no idea where the track would lead. "Who do you think killed Gabriel?"

"It looked as though he shot himself," I said slowly.

Farrel came in from the kitchen and told everyone it was *birthday girl blowing out the candles* time. Since I was the subject of the gerund phrase, I moved to the dining room, where they sang to me. I made a selfish wish and blew, and then dished out pieces of deliciously rich chocolate cake.

"There's espresso in the icing," said Jessie in my ear. "Have a big piece and give one to Kathryn." I laughed and hugged Jessie.

Cora handed me an envelope and then said, "Mickey has something for you, too. He made it himself."

Mickey's present was a drawing of the superhero Storm from the X-Men. Mickey calls almost everyone but Cora by cartoon names. The first time he met me, he gave me the name Storm.

He said, "Storm controls the weather and she's strong."

"I like this, Mickey, thank you very much. I'm going to put it in my office."

My stepmother Juana came up and put her arm around me. She was wearing a black suit, a mauve blouse, and a Mexican silver broach from the 1950s pinned near the neckline. Her hair was tied up. It was dark-chocolate-colored like Sara and Rosa's but had hints of silver. She smiled warmly, her dark eyes twinkling. She kissed my cheek then tilted her head to the side and said: *"El mundo es de los audaces y amor no respeta ley, ni obedece a rey, querer es poder,"* as she gave me a card.

Sara and Rosa shook their heads laughing. Judith and Amanda said, "Yes, true." And Farrel said, "Um, was that: The world is for the audacious. Love doesn't respect the king... um."

"Love doesn't respect the law or obey the king... And so the point is, *Go boldly,"* I said

"Roughly correct," nodded Juana.

Kathryn blushed. I did too when I realized what Juana was getting at.

"Mom, ease off the proverbs. They're verging on eccentric and it's not as though you're some old bruja at the edge of town," said Sara.

"When have I said anything even remotely eccentric?" said Juana.

Rosa said, "What about last week when you told me, *Con paciencia y saliva, un elefante se tiro a una hormiga."*

I heard Kathryn laugh and saw Sara roll her eyes.

"The ant punched the elephant with patience?" asked Farrel.

"In other words, *Oops there goes another rubber tree,"* I explained.

"Little strokes fell great oaks," said Juana. "Nothing eccentric about that!"

It took me a few minutes to stop laughing. When I did, I noticed Kathryn's half-smile and that she was looking at me more than fondly.

"I'm very lucky to have all my friends and family here in one place. It's kind of amazing that I've been able to lure you all to Fenchester!" I said happily.

"It was fate, perhaps," said Amanda.

"More cake anyone?" asked Jessie. Everyone groaned, though several offered their empty plates.

"Maggie, along with my contribution I wanted to give you this. Amanda asked me to locate it when I went to pay a bill at the county court house yesterday. It's Victoria Snow's will," Judith said, handing me a sheet of legal paper.

It was a very clear copy of an old-fashioned printed and typed will form. I began to read it over.

"Look, she not only owned Fen House, she owned the Majestic. Huh, I thought that belonged to Merganser Hunterdon. Um... It mentions a financial trust she'd previously set up to benefit some individuals, but... it doesn't say whom. Oh and here's the part that gives any additional cash or worldly goods outside the trust to the Irwin College Fen Scholarships. And she left her art to... ah, here, listen to this:

> *I prefer to imagine my studio work stay untouched by time, but if it is found, the entire contents are a bequest to Irwin College. Given by me in the name of my dear friend, Evangeline Lavender Fen.*

At the very end there's something in her own handwriting next to her signature. It says:

> *I declare, that there is joy in the presence of the angels of God over one sinner that repenteth. Until only then, when the last piece of silver acts in unbounded charity, I vow to let the demon messengers of grief continue their torment and I shall not rest until that day, though I confess that the torment is as sweet as the charity. Luke:15-8.*
> *Victoria Willomere Snow June 17th, 1926*

"Huh, is she talking about herself tormented by the grief of losing Evangeline? Everyone thought it was Merganser tormented by the loss of Evangeline that caused him to put all that money into public works. But now we know that wasn't what made him do it. Certainly the statute of limitations would have run out by the 1900s, yet he kept on paying her. I wonder what she had on him and why she didn't just leave Fenchester forever and go back to Rome or Paris," mused Kathryn.

Kathryn handed me a package and said, "I thought you should have this now. Mickey thought you might like it," she said.

I tore off the wrapper. It was a framed cartoon cel—the one I'd been looking at at Peskeetotemburg.

"It's Cool Cat and Colonel Rimfire!" said Mickey immediately. "Cool Cat is cool! Is he, like, your hero, Storm?"

"Yes! He's one of them, Mickey. Kathryn, when did you buy it and how did you get it framed so fast?"

"I managed to buy it at Pesky and have Farrel take it with her. I thought you'd like it."

"I love it. I wanted to go back. I love it." It was the symbol of my childhood healing and Kathryn had captured it for me. It was perfect. I hugged her very hard and then I briefly told the rest of my friends how important Cool Cat had been to my childhood.

Nora said, "Did someone famous do his voice, like in Disney movies?"

"Mel Blanc did all those Warner's voices," said Jessie.

But Mickey and I said in unison, "No, it was Larry Storch."

I nodded at Mickey and said, "Larry Storch did both voices."

"Yeah, yeah, he was the bad guys and the good guys all at once," added Mickey.

Buster trotted into the room with his leash in his mouth and sat down in front of Jessie.

Jessie said, "I have to walk Buster."

"Is it hard to do so?" asked Amanda.

"Well no, he's very easy to walk. He'd carry his own leash if I let him. We walked by a cat yesterday and he didn't even turn his head. It's just when we get to the lower end of the Mews, he wants to go back into his old house, so he pulls on the lead and he's amazingly strong." She looked at him. "Well, I guess it's not so amazing."

"Griswold and Wagner will probably never *merf and ow* to us again," said Farrel. "What are we going to do with him? We can't keep him with our show schedule. I mean, it's one thing for Cora to *feed* the cats..."

"I don't clean up after livestock, dahlings," said Cora joining us. She reached up to pat Buster on the head.

"At least he doesn't bark all the time like little yippy dogs. Maybe you can find someone to take him. He's really very smart and he's serene," said Sara.

"Perhaps I could take him?" mused Amanda. "I'd need a few days to Great Dane-proof my house. I'll have to move the Rookwood vases... Could you give me a few days?"

The relief on Jessie's face was so palpable that Farrel smiled automatically. Jessie and Farrel hugged Amanda.

As we got ready to go, Amanda took me aside and said, "I feel that Victoria's will is rather interesting. I think this is a bit more complicated than what shows on the surface, Maggie. I don't know the solution, but I think *you* will be able to figure it out. You will do so with Kathryn's help." She fixed me with that eagle stare of hers. Buster sat up and tilted his head and gave me the same stare.

I resolved to look over the will again.

CHAPTER 19

I'd kissed, hugged, and thanked everyone.

"I'm so grateful you had this party for Maggie," Kathryn had said to Jessie before we left. "Is there anything I can help you with?"

"Really?" Jessie had said. "I *do* need your help. We'll just have to take Buster on a few more walks and then we can deliver him to Amanda. But right now, he really does seem desperate to run toward his old backyard and I can't always hold him. I could use some help tomorrow morning, because Farrel has to go a weekend department meeting that will be over by 11:00, but she won't be able to help me at 10, when he has to go. I'm sure he'll calm down about this house thing in a day or two, but I really need you tomorrow."

Kathryn readily agreed to walk with Jessie and Buster in the morning around 10 a.m.

Back in the loft, Kathryn hung up her coat and slipped out of her shoes, which were wet from another dusting of snow. She said, "I'm glad I don't have to get up too early to help walk Buster. Want some coffee?"

"Yeah, and some cake," I said distractedly. I'd propped my beloved Cool Cat cel at the end of the table and was alternately looking at it and reading over Victoria's will.

"Kathryn, this *Luke 15* reference in the Bible, do you know it?"

"Not without looking it up."

"But you went to Catholic school."

She brought coffee cups and a small plate of cake over to the table.

"Catholic school didn't teach me anything about the Bible. I wish it had. It's quoted as frequently as Shakespeare."

"This part that Victoria wrote about repenting sinners. You don't think she meant because she was a Lesbian?"

Kathryn was looking at her iPhone. "Luke 15:8 is the parable of the lost coin. It's in the section that also talks about the one lost sheep. The King James version says:

> *"Either what woman having ten pieces of silver, if she lose one piece, doth not light a candle, and sweep the house, and seek diligently till she find it."*

"Ten pieces of silver? Victoria got twenty pieces from Merganser to pay her for the commissions. Twenty dollars a day for life. It sounds like a lottery prize. I wonder if she actually had him bring her the money each day? I don't see why she's referencing Luke 15:8. That passage sounds more like it's about being careful and diligent, rather than repenting. What does the next verse say?"

"Let's see. It says:"

> *"And when she hath found it, she calleth her friends and her neighbours together, saying, Rejoice with me; for I have found the piece which I had lost."*

"Because a lost sinner returns to the fold? I wonder who she meant?"

"Do you really think it's that important?" asked Kathryn.

I shook my head, distractedly staring at the "Cool Cat" cel. Both Cool Cat and Rimfire looked back at me smirking.

"Why do I keep thinking of the steel drummer on the subway. I guess because Larry Storch was on the subway and he did the voices for Cool Cat and Rimfire. He did them both..." Suddenly, I had an urge to make a drawing or sculpture.

"Maybe you should focus your attention on something else for awhile." Kathryn said this in the sexiest voice I'd ever heard. I felt heat creep along my body from the floor up.

"Yes," I said, noticing that Kathryn's shirt was open an extra button. Suddenly I wanted to go to bed with Kathryn and use that urge to both our advantages.

"What shall we talk about?" asked Kathryn.

I exhaled. "Let's talk about sex. How easy is it for you to talk about sex?" I asked cheerfully leaning back in my chair.

She shook her head. "Maggie, I grew up in a strait-laced northern New England family. It didn't exist. We didn't even hint about it. Even when my brothers were randy teenagers, they didn't talk about it. They probably thought about it. But talk... no."

"I was asking about you, not your family," I chided.

"I'm the Ice Queen, remember?" she said evasively, but there was a provocative challenge in her voice.

"Well, that may be what your grad students call you, but querida, they don't know you the way I do. Based on original research, there's nothing icy about you," I whispered. "That first night after I gave you a massage, I liked it when you told me to undress you."

"You're never going to give me another massage like that again are you?" she asked wistfully, rotating the chair slightly from side to side.

"Wait a minute, where did you get that idea?"

"You just did that to break down my defenses."

"Kathryn, would you like me to give you a massage right now? I'd love to spend a couple of hours touching you and rubbing your shoulders and making you feel relaxed. I'll even do it to you with your clothes on, although warm massage oil on your skin would be much more fun for both of us."

She'd swiveled her chair to face me. She looked right into my soul without saying a word. Then she slid her foot over to me and brushed her toes up my calf and along my inner thigh. I grasped her lightly behind the ankle, then reached and lifted her other foot into my lap.

"You're a tease, Kathryn."

"Why?" she replied innocently, but with a spark in her eye and a voice as deep and full as Evangeline's warm spring pool.

"Because you say you won't talk about sex but you bring up massage. And you've implied more than once you don't like to be tickled but... But now you're teasing me with your magnificent legs and very sensitive feet. Too bad they're covered with fabric." I held her ankles, pulled each sock off with a little tug, and then touched the sole of her right foot very lightly with my finger.

"Oh, no," she gasped, trying to pull away.

"Oh yes," I said, holding her firmly. "Tell me about your sexual fantasies. Come on Kathryn, it's my birthday. I want to know everything."

She faced me steadily without saying anything. She held the arms of the chair as though bracing herself, ready to do battle. The look on her face was full of erotic encouragement. She breathed deeply.

"You know," I said, "I can make you tell me your secrets the same way your brothers did. Didn't they used to tickle you to get you to tell things?" I gently stroked from the base of her toes to her heel. She leaned her head back and breathed in sharply.

"You want me to, don't you?" I asked in a low voice, repeating the caress.

"Oh, God," she moaned, closing her eyes. She arched her back. I watched for signs of arousal and was rewarded with the delightful contour of hardening nipples stretching the soft fabric of her shirt.

"Tell me what you fantasize about when you masturbate," I insisted. But I didn't stroke her this time. I wanted to hear just what this strait-laced northern New Englander would say.

Her face flushed as she collected herself and answered, "For the last few months, I've thought about you."

I shook my head. "Too easy. You have a fertile, passionate imagination. Tell me about your wilder scenarios. What happens?" I asked resuming the caress and watching her every move.

"Please." She strained to keep control.

I was painfully hot, but this was way too interesting to end.

"We can't interrupt this now. You don't honestly want me to stop, do you?" I asked sincerely. I didn't really want to force her. She didn't speak, but she shook her head no, then she challenged me with a direct stare and lifted one eyebrow.

The she-devil on my shoulder smiled so wickedly I felt the heat of her breath.

"Hmmm," I said stroking her again, "didn't you once ask me about my interrogation techniques? Is this what you imagined?"

Kathryn laughed in spite of herself.

"You're dodging me." I became merciless, tickling her slowly and gently but relentlessly. She could have pulled away easily. One hand is no match for two legs. But she didn't stop me. She let me go on and on until she was groaning and begging.

I stopped and said, "Tell me. Or shall I start again?"

"No, no," she pleaded, catching her breath.

"Then tell me about your wildest fantasies. Where would you be?" "In the bed," she confessed.

"Just in the bed? Well OK, who else would be there?"

"You."

"Anyone else?"

"No."

"Would you be undressed completely or..."

She nodded.

"And then? What would happen next?"

She shook her head not willing to tell me everything, but clearly wanting me to figure it out.

"OK, then tell me what my motivation would be." She didn't understand so I said, "What would I be trying to achieve?"

"You'd be doing this."

"You like *this*." I thought about it, considering what was actually happening between us. Finally I said, "I'd be *making* you give up control?"

She gave a tiny nod.

"What would it take? What would I have to do?" She wouldn't say, but I thought I knew. Maybe I should try a simpler route.

"Tell me what you would NOT enjoy."

"Pain."

"I would never want to hurt you. Now tell me, what's the highest number of orgasms you've had in one night?" I quizzed, beginning to stroke the sole of her foot again.

She wriggled and gasped. Finally she said, "Um, five."

"Five in a row over a few hours?" I asked curiously.

She nodded. "I was younger."

"And that lover made you give up control?"

"Almost," she admitted.

"What stopped her from being successful?"

"I did."

"I see," I said, thinking.

"Do you?" she whispered.

"Kathryn, is this a matter of spending days and days in bed?"

She smiled and said, "I like the idea of spending days and days in bed with you. May we do that sometime?"

"As soon as possible, but you promised to help walk Buster tomorrow, so let's concentrate on this evening. It's a time thing then?"

"Well," she said cryptically.

"Appliances? Strap-ons, vibrators, that battery operated rabbit thing?"

"What rabbit thing?" she asked with confusion.

"I don't know, some kind of vibrator that straight women like. They sell them at those sex-toy parties. A vibrator then?"

She gave a tiny shake of her head to indicate I wasn't quite on the right track.

"Fine, we'll save that for another time. So... What then? Tell me." I began to stroke her feet again but she wasn't going to give it up. So I started to list every kinky toy I could think of, to see how she'd react. She was totally turned on and amused. I was getting a heck of a load of information and was desperately trying to remember everything, but I hadn't hit on her fantasy yet.

Finally I suggested the category I'd thought she'd meant all along. Her provocative half-smile and a single raised eyebrow confirmed it.

"Just tie you to the bed? Shall we do it right now? Oh, and is this something you imagine doing to me as well?"

"Would you enjoy it?" she asked with interest.

"Of course. Are you surprised?" I replied.

"May I do it to you first?" She seemed to think I was going to say no.

"We have all night. There's plenty of time for this fantasy to play out with each of us as the main character. And yes, I'd love to be first. By the way, when I was twenty-two, I had eleven orgasms in one night. But we can reserve that goal for the multi-day bout."

Kathryn was making that humming noise that made me as ready as a revving race car. "Well, it *is* your birthday... but eleven? We may need the appliances after all!" she chuckled.

I thought to myself, *With the way I feel right now, I doubt it.*

She stood up and undid her hair clasp, shaking out her hair in a sensual way. She said seductively, "I need a little time, so wait out here until I call you. Would you build a fire?"

While she walked slowly across the room, I wondered if I was actually going to get my hedge clipped a dozen times. That'd be something to write home about. Wouldn't Sara be jealous? Not that I'd tell her.

As I was building the fire and pushing the logs from the main room side to the bedroom side of the fireplace, I went over what had just happened and realized Kathryn had played me like a harp. She'd been in total control and managed to engineer the entire outcome. Had she wanted to do it to me all along? Geez, she'd finally found a way to beat me at wrestling. And she'd made me think I was figuring her out! Had she really planned this whole scene or did she just seize the moment? I shook my head in wonder.

Wow, I smiled, *formidable may be an understatement.*

When the fire was burning in the grate I went into the guest bathroom for a quick shower. When I came out, she called me into the bedroom. I was beginning to crave hearing Kathryn call me to the bedroom. The room was warm. Firelight made dancing patterns on the walls.

I sat on the end of the bed and looked toward the closed bathroom door with growing anticipation. This must have been how Victoria Snow felt when she realized Evangeline was shedding her inhibitions along with her riding habit. My mind wandered to Fen house and how Gabe had looked just minutes before a bullet had ended his life. He really hadn't looked like a person who had given up hope.

Kathryn pushed the door open and I forgot about everything but her.

She was leaning against the doorframe in the sexiest outfit I'd ever seen. It was cream silk, sleeveless, and tailored to fit her perfectly. The neckline plunged to show the sides of her breasts. The hem touched the floor but there were side-slits to her thighs that showed her lovely legs. She held a little glass jar in her hand.

"Oh, Kathryn," I breathed. She'd brushed out her hair so that it curled gently around her face. Her expression held the promise of all sorts of delightfully dangerous things. Shadows from the flames in the grate accented the contours of her body. I was fully ready to let her do absolutely anything she wanted.

"Where did you get that outfit? It was made for you," I asked in awe.

"I love it when you look at me that way," she laughed. "I've been saving this for a special occasion. It does fit rather well, doesn't it?" She turned around in place to show me every angle.

I stared at her for a full minute and she just stood there and let me. Finally I said, "But... you know Kathryn, what we're about to do, you could have just asked me directly. You didn't have to make me think I'd figured it all out on my own."

She snorted. "Honestly, you're too smart. You caught me again. Look, Maggie, I'm not as sure of myself as you think I am. I didn't plan every word. Does it spoil it for you? Are you still... willing?" she asked, crossing her arms and walking toward me.

"Yes, yes," I said exhaling and nodding.

"Ready?" she asked in a very low voice, stepping closer.

"Just what are you going to do to me?"

Kathryn took a very deep breath. She dumped the jar on the nightstand. Twelve pennies fell into a pile. She said in a low voice, "I'm going to keep count until the pennies are all back in that jar. Stand up."

I glanced at the bed and noticed she'd set it all up. This was way more exciting than Christmas morning to a six-year-old. I could barely stand it. I made one of those gulping swallows and did my best to stand despite a heck of an ache that needed to be relieved very soon. I hoped she wasn't going to tease me too long.

She came close to me and ran her fingers under the collar of my shirt lightly. Then she stepped back again and said, "Take off your clothes."

She crossed her arms and watched as I did as I was told. She didn't move closer when I was done. She just looked me over from head to foot and said, "Lie down on your back and reach for the corners."

She had me secured and stretched out in no time. If I'd really wanted to, I could have pulled my wrists out of the velcro cuffs. But I didn't want to. She stood and looked down at me with an incredibly satisfied expression.

"I feel surprisingly powerful," she said.

I felt more vulnerable than I would have imagined. I said, "Are you going to punish me for all the bad things I did the first week we were together?"

She just smiled in a predatory way and a tiny thrill of fear tingled through my body like low voltage electricity. The ache between my legs now verged on charlie-horse. "I can't stand to wait much longer," I admitted in a low whisper. "Please."

Kathryn sat between my legs near the end of the bed looking at me. I could see the flashing firelight in her eyes. She slipped her fingers between my legs and stroked. The sudden sensation was startling and made me strain unconsciously against the cuffs. The bonds were loose enough for movement but not loose enough to resist.

"Yes, that's what I want to see you do, but not so easily," she said watching me. She stopped stroking, leaving me so close to the edge I nearly whimpered. She went to the top of the bed and tugged on a strap. It pulled my right arm straight toward the corner. She did the same to the left. Then she went to the bottom of the bed and tugged both leg straps at once. The slack was taken up; my movements were reduced.

"You know, you kept me waiting quite a bit this week. Perhaps I *should* punish you," she said rather wickedly.

"Please," I whispered urgently.

"Shhhhhh." When I stopped making noise she began on me again with long and full strokes that were perfectly aimed. They rapidly brought me to a rocketing climax that astounded me. She reached over and dropped one of the pennies in the jar. She did it to me again, and then another time with the perfect application of pressure and friction. They happened quickly, like she'd flipped an electrical joy switch that jolted sensation through my body. Just the sound of the next penny dropping was a total turn-on.

"Feel better now?" she asked me, shifting to my side. She propped her head up on one fist and reached for my breast, idly teasing my nipple to hardness again.

"Uh huh..." I squeaked as she traced her finger along the inside of my thigh. I was already feeling arousal again.

She moved to lie on top of me, holding my face in her hands, kissing me lovingly. They were wonderful caring and exploring kisses that made me want her to go on forever. She slid down my body, nipping and sucking at tender areas, until she settled between my legs. The velvet caress of her tongue pushed me up the ladder. It took longer than the first times, but the feeling of her was exquisite. I was peaking again and groaning at the pleasure of it.

Finally she rolled to my side. She whispered candidly, "Is this all OK for you? Is it too kinky?"

I turned to look at her.

"Honestly, is it too much? Are you uncomfortable? We can stop if you want. Shall I stop?" She was caressing my cheek with the back of her figures with such a look of genuine concern.

"Don't you dare stop," I whispered back. "It's been great. Very exciting. I feel wonderful, not uncomfortable. But... um... well, I'm up for anything you want to do. Don't you have some wild oats you're dying to sow? Sow them!" I looked deeply into her eyes, smiled salaciously, and challenged, "I dare you!"

Kathryn responded to this invitation with astonishing delight. It was like a green light at the races. The firelight infused her entire expression and she became a panther. She kissed my neck just at the base near my collar bone and then bit me hard enough to feel it.

"Vampire," I groaned and shifted my body.

She purred while beginning to rub my breasts with both hands. "So you feel all right then?"

"Yes, very fine. What are you going to... Oh!" I began to ask, but before I could get out another word she'd lightly drawn her fingernails along my side, near my waist. *Oh no*, I thought wildly. She'd found the part of my body that was the most ticklish. I squealed and strained to pull away.

"Ah, ha!" she said triumphantly.

I was in trouble now. She touched me in the same way and this time I convulsed, arching off the bed.

"Now I can get you to tell me all *your* secrets," she said with supreme amusement.

"Oh geez, no, stop, please... oh... a..." I was reduced to a series of unintelligible noises of desperation as she plied this sensitive place more firmly. She seemed fascinated by what it made me do.

Suddenly I was her x-rated science project. Simulation: Cause and Effect. And it wasn't just the tickling sensation that was the problem. The ache between my all-too-open legs had galloped back and was making me strain for relief. I really needed to be laid not teased, but I could see Kathryn was having too much fun with me to change directions. She was controlling me completely, and I wasn't stopping her, and that's what she wanted.

I had a lot less willpower than Kathryn when it came to tickling. She began to whisper intimate sexual questions about what I enjoyed in bed and forced me to answer. I was panting out anything I could think of just to get her to stop tickling me.

"Well, isn't this entertaining?" she teased fiendishly.

When she finally let me breathe, I gasped, "I thought you said you couldn't talk about sex?"

"It depends on the context. About myself, yes, that's very hard to do, but I'm not finding it hard at all to ask you about your desires. This is a new experience for me." She seemed very pleased. Kind of liberated.

"It's new to me too," I said, marveling at the vast, if somewhat old-fashioned, sexual vocabulary she had.

"Oh come now, I know enough about S. Peck Fuller to be sure she didn't let you off too easily," Kathryn laughed throatily, recalling a visiting college professor I'd admitted to knowing when she'd been at Irwin several years ago when I was on the police force. Professor Fuller had quite an erotic reputation in the academic world, but I hadn't admitted to Kathryn that I actually had a short but intense affair with her that had focused on her fascination with my police handcuffs.

"You slept with her?" I asked incredulously.

"No, I didn't, but I know some women who did. They were eloquent and unstinting in praise regarding her talents and demands. A bit of a modern day Charlotte Cushman from all reports. Would you care to tell me what you two did together?" she asked, sliding her hand from my hip to my breast. She fluttered her fingers against my side again. I squirmed desperately

I couldn't help flashing momentarily on some of the practical aspects of my relationship with Dr. Susan Abigail Peck Fuller. She was a professor at the Slade School of Art in London and the daughter of a Duke, though she eschewed the aristocratic title of Lady Susan in favor of her academic one. In intimate situations she often dropped her first name and said that they didn't call her A Peck Fuller for nothing. She had a doctorate in art history, but she also had a master's in physical anatomy. She'd explored some vitally important biological secrets that intensify sexual sensation with me. She was not the type to fall in love with, but a skilled teacher. Yes, she was a great deal like Charlotte Cushman. I certainly was planning on sharing what I'd learned from her with Kathryn, but this wasn't the time to be talking about other women, so I said, "What you're doing to me is erasing my memory of anyone but you."

"What a flattering answer. You deserve something nice for that." Which she gave me leisurely and intimately with her tongue while both of her hands massaged my breasts. I could just barely hear the pennies clinking into the jar. *So, this was Nirvana.*

"Don't you dare fall asleep," she commanded, firmly patting my cheek. I snapped my eyes open.

"What we're going to do now will be a little more... aggressive." She knelt on the bed close to me and whispered seriously in my ear, "Do you want a safeword?"

"Will I need one?" I asked in surprise. "Um, I'm not fond of pain either."

"If it hurts, say so and we'll stop, I promise," she told me gently. Then she produced a round-handled paint brush. It had long soft bristles and a wooden handle that was about the diameter of the shaft of a heavy shovel. The wood was smooth and polished; the end was rounded. I had a stirring feeling that I knew just what she was going to do with it.

She began by drawing the brush over my skin. Along my sides, under my arms, over my breasts. It tickled and heightened my senses. I was highly aroused all over again. I was amazed that a profound need was returning. I shifted my body and drew my legs together a few inches trying to ease it.

"Stay still," she demanded.

"Make me," I whispered.

She checked the velcro cuffs on my ankles to be sure they were secure and then tried to pull the ends of the straps at each bedpost to draw me wider, but I resisted. She climbed over me and sat straddling my hips. She looked at me intently then traced her fingers firmly up my sides and over my stomach. I felt a shock of sensation. I arched off the bed involuntarily, lifting her with me.

"Ooh that was rewarding. Do that again," she said, tickling me in the same way. I couldn't help arching and raising her off the bed again. "Mmmm, no more," I groaned.

But I hadn't said anything about it hurting, so she ignored my pleas. She tickled me again. This time saying, "Reach for the corners." I did it. She tightened the straps mercilessly. Then she did the same thing to my legs until I was totally splayed and unable to move an inch. "Yes, very good. Now," she said in a satisfied voice, "I'm in charge."

I laughed. She did too.

"You're going to be sorry you're doing this. Remember, you're next."

"You're in no position to make threats right now."

She began to do just what I thought she was going to do with the paint brush handle. First she parted me with her fingers. The light tickling touch drove me wild, especially because I couldn't move. She went ahead slowly, but without hesitation. I was so wet and ready there was no resistance. Just the penetration nearly brought on an orgasm.

"I saw a print of this very situation in a book of ancient Japanese erotic art. The Edo period produced many painted scrolls of beautiful women in tight bondage being taken in just this way," she said, as though we were having a casual conversation over coffee. In reality she was slowly pumping the thick handle of the brush as she stimulated me. I heard the sounds of each penny dropping into the jar but I'd lost the ability to know what they meant.

Kathryn shifted again and leaned close to my ear to say, "There's one more penny left..." As she pumped the brush handle slowly, she lightly stroked with her tongue, holding me on the edge for what seemed like eternity, and then when she finally let me come, she wouldn't let me stop. When I thought I couldn't possibly go on, she redoubled her efforts and I experienced a wave of sensation that made the room black and my mind devoid of everything but the ecstasy of her touch. As I floated over the edge of a churning, satisfying waterfall I could hear someone making a sex charged howling scream. It was me.

When she finally stopped, I was shuddering with pleasure.

"Shhh," she said kissing the side of my neck and stroking my hair. "Shhh, relax. That's all... for now." She pulled open the velcro cuffs at my wrists, then undid my ankles.

I groaned, moving my arms and legs slowly. I was breathing hard and shuddering intermittently with little earthquake aftershocks.

Finally I said, "Oh, Kathryn, that had to be some kind of magic."

"What time is it? Shall we have some wine or something to eat? Jessie gave me some wonderful cheese," called Kathryn, going into the bathroom.

The clock said it was only 11:30.

"I'm getting the feeling that Jessie catered this sex fest intentionally. How much did you tell her about your little plan? Oh and by the way this break is just the half time show. There's still the second act of this fantasy."

When Kathryn came out and went into the kitchen, I moved slowly to the bathroom, stretching my legs.

When I finished in there, I put on my bathrobe and joined her in the kitchen area. She was putting something into the oven. "This just has to warm a bit. I think we'll like it." She kept her back to me and avoided looking at me. She seemed nervous.

I caught her in my arms and held her to me. "Why are you shy all of a sudden?" I said trying to look into her eyes. She turned away a little.

"What is it?" I asked.

"Was it too much?" she asked, still not quite looking into my eyes. She put her arms around me and rested her head on my shoulder.

"Look at me, Kathryn," I whispered. "It was wonderful and fun and exciting. The best sex I've ever had. I liked it. I hope we do this kind of thing again, many times. I loved it... OK?"

She finally looked into my eyes in her searching way and then she smiled, "Really?"

"The best. I'm still smoldering. You're not feeling residual guilt from those years in Catholic school, are you?"

She laughed, shaking her head, and kissed me. I hugged her and she firmly hugged me back.

"Are you trying to distract me?" I asked as I went to the refrigerator for olives and pickles.

"What do you mean?" she replied, putting crackers on two plates.

"You know what I mean. And I'm not sure stopping to eat is the right thing to do in the middle of this wonderful adventure."

"Maggie..." The broiler bell chimed and Kathryn moved to take a small wheel of brie cheese encased in phyllo dough out of the oven. The flaky crust had turned a light brown and the cheese was bubbling warm.

"Jessie's homemade strawberry jam is inside this," said Kathryn.

"Are you nervous about what's going to happen next? Is that why you're having a hard time looking at me?" I asked.

She smiled, but there was a hint of something in her eyes that didn't shout self confidence. I brought a bottle of wine, glasses, and corkscrew to the table. I opened the bottle, poured two glasses, put the bottle down and took up her hand in both of mine. I kissed her palm and then kissed the soft inside of her wrist.

I wasn't sure exactly what she wanted me to do, and I might have been about to make a big mistake, but I took a breath and said softly, "You seem a little nervous and apprehensive about what we're about to do next. So let me reassure you right now..." I let my voice become stronger. "I'm not letting you off the hook for a second, even if I have to pick you up and carry you back in there. And I can do it too."

She sat back and blinked at me and then began to laugh that deep hearty laugh, just the kind Farrel had mentioned. It made me laugh too, but it also sent a vibration through me that recharged me from the ground up. I could barely wait to get her back to bed.

"Oh dear, what have I gotten myself into? I may need two glasses of wine," she said.

"I think we should leave the snack until later. I'll give in to the wine but just one glass. Then we'll go back into the bedroom. I don't want you to dull your senses. I promise you'll enjoy it," I said kissing her hand again.

"Uh huh," she said dubiously.

"Let me remind you, Kathryn, *this was your idea.*"

"Be careful what you wish for?" she asked.

"Uh huh."

As we drank the wine, Kathryn said, "Maggie, do you really think this whole issue is over? About Frankie, and Suzanne's murders?"

I didn't have to pause to consider this. "No, I don't. There are too many things that don't make sense."

"What?"

"Well, why was Gabriel Carbondale so keen on cementing up the crypts?'

"Because he didn't want anyone to find Suzanne's body?"

"Well, maybe, but if he was so worried about it, why not just go down there and get rid of the body? He had plenty of time to think of a way."

"I suppose, but when he got back from England he suddenly found out that Frankie was stealing from the studio, so Gabe shot Frankie and figured something had to be done to stop anyone else from going down there?"

I shook my head. "Even if he hired someone to kill Suzanne, why go down *there* to kill her, instead of just doing it at her house by making it look like a break-in or something?"

"Maybe they were afraid of Buster?" said Kathryn.

"Oh, right," I laughed wryly. "Buster didn't even know what a gun was until Gabe shot himself. Dogs have to be trained to attack people with guns. Suzanne had friends over all the time and Buster always loved company. I don't think the issue was fear of Buster. I just don't believe Gabe would kill her for money and then turn around and kill himself the second someone found out she was dead. He had an alibi."

"So love then? Maybe Gabe wanted to marry someone else?"

"But who? There's no one else around."

"No one's around Gabe. But there is someone who had love as a motive to kill Suzanne."

"Yeah, I know who you mean," I said. I said the name.

"That's what I was thinking," said Kathryn. "Are there any other suspects? Or... What if, what if Frankie killed Suzanne?"

"Yeah, I've considered that. It could have gone like this: Frankie is stealing the stuff. Suzanne surprises him, he pushes her and she's knocked out, then he tries to hide the body. He sees she's still alive, he panics, and stabs her. But then, who killed Frankie? I don't care what anyone says,

Gabe didn't have a gun, and Red said the shooter was in the crypt. And why was only one of the boxes of Victoria's stuff open if that was Gabe's motive? And how did those boxes of Victoria's things even get in her studio?" I said, tapping my fingers on the table. "Why weren't those boxes in her house when she died. Do you suppose the people whom she left her trust money to moved the boxes? How? When? For that matter, I just don't see how Victoria even got to her studio to work. Every time she went there she had to go into the cemetery through the crypt? Pretty unlikely."

"Maggie, you just leapt back in time more than 100 years. It's not like they're the same mystery."

"I keep feeling like they are," I insisted.

"Maybe I can get some answers from the second journal," said Kathryn. "I've only had a chance to read a quarter of it. I tried to skim the rest but her handwriting is much smaller after Evangeline died. Shall we read the journal? We could look at it now."

"Absolutely not. You're not standing me up," I said, pushing back my chair. It's time for act two." I reached out my hand and led her back to the bedroom.

"I thought you said you'd carry me," she said with a half-smile.

Before she could react I caught her up in my arms and tossed her onto the bed. We were both laughing but got quieter as we began kissing. I moved on top of her, softly touching her lips with my tongue. She had both her hands on my shoulders responding in a wonderful way to each kiss. I slowly reached for her wrists and held them up over her head, allowing my full weight to pin her to the bed. She made a gentle sigh of resignation underscored by that hot feline hum she made when she was excited.

This episode in our lives together was symbolic and we both knew it. I had given total control to Kathryn and with that comes complete trust. She readied to give up total control to me; implicit in that was her total trust.

So now I was on. I undid the velcro cuffs from the straps, slipped her wrists into them and clipped her wrists together. Then I threaded one of the straps through the slats of the headboard so her hands were securely fastened above her head. I slipped down her body and used the other cuffs to bind her ankles together. I knelt on the bed, looking down at her.

"You look just like a medieval damsel in distress," I said suggestively, putting a pillow under her head so she could watch.

"Are you the good knight who saves me, or the evil sorceress who ravishes me?" she whispered.

"Definitely the sorceress and probably evil, but I'm not sure about ravish... Let's say the evil sorceress who offers you pleasures beyond your imagination, though I have a feeling you've been imagining this for a long time," I smirked.

I ran my hands over the satiny material stretched over her lovely body. I played with her nipples through the fabric, running my thumbs across them until they peaked and hardened against the silk. She was feeling the same ache I'd felt at the beginning of her efforts on me, but she was getting relief by rubbing her legs together. I didn't think that was fair.

So I began to slowly lift her hem. Sliding it up her legs, feeling her soft skin underneath. When I'd raised it to the top of her thighs, I stroked down her legs and lightly touched the sensitive soles of her feet. She squirmed deliciously.

"I know we've done this already tonight, but I'm not sure we really finished. I think it would be best without your clothes though. You'll enjoy it more. That's part of your fantasy, isn't it?" She didn't speak. She had her eyes closed but a slight smile curved her lips. So I lifted the gown above her waist, exposing her hips. I pushed the fabric past her breasts and shoulders, over her head and up to her bound hands, uncovering her completely.

"Don't you look lovely and aren't we going to have fun?" I said, appreciating her beautiful body stretched out before me.

I trailed my fingertips back down to her feet. Then I seized up the paint brush and held her ankles firmly to the bed while I lightly tickled her right sole. She stiffened, trying valiantly to resist giving over to uncontrolled sensation. I stroked firmly, observing the layers of resistance falling away. I brushed her harder and she squirmed involuntarily, so I held her in place and tickled her until she was shrieking.

As soon as she said, "Stop!" I did immediately. I really didn't want her to be afraid or feel powerless. I wanted her to trust me.

"Do you really want me to stop?" I asked. "I'm going to give you a safeword. Or maybe a phrase, and all you'll have to do to make me stop is say it." I whispered a string of four letter words that would yank a cable FCC license.

"I can't say that," she laughed, still out of breath.

"That's what I'm counting on, but it's the only thing that will make me stop." I said it again. "Say it and I'll stop and let you go right away. But if you do, then you'll have to miss out on the hours of pleasure I have planned for you. Understand?"

"Oh dear."

"I'll take that to mean you understand."

I tickled her again for just a minute or two. She twisted and begged, "No, no please stop."

I eased for a second but didn't stop completely. Lightly running the tip of my finger along her sole. Her body flushed pink and her nipples became impossibly erect.

"Now let's do some exploring. By the way, begging for mercy might work so you can always try that, but I may not yield. Might just encourage me to work you harder. Just saying..."

"Mercy," she laughed. "Tell me your plan," she said in a soft voice.

"I'm going to figure out what you want. And then I'm going to do it to you, and probably quite a bit more."

"Is this all part of your interrogation technique?"

"Yes, as a matter of fact it is. I think you'll especially enjoy the thorough searches," I teased. I hooked the ankle cuffs to the corner straps again, then pulled on the straps slowly.

"Oh!" She shifted, as I opened her legs wide.

"This is going to be very exciting. Relax. Now, *I'm* in charge," I said slowly. She made an amused noise and stared at me with darkening eyes.

I looked at the glistening dark red hair between her legs, then reached and lightly touched her there. This tickled her too. She tried in vain to pull away, but she unconsciously nodded her head.

I stroked her and she arched in the restraints immediately, trying to press against my fingers in search of relief. I gave in to her in exactly the place that would make her climax, and she did immediately, groaning in evident release until she fell back against the pillow.

"This is fun, isn't it?" I said provocatively. She nodded, watching to see what was next.

Of course this wasn't the first time I'd made love to Kathryn. We'd had a number of wild nights and she'd shown me how to satisfy her. But now I wanted her to reveal things to me she hadn't ever told anyone else. Time to go where no one had gone before.

The bondage made everything so much more intense. She climaxed harder each time as I extended the sessions a little longer, not letting her relax in between.

After three strong orgasms one right after another, she pleaded between deep breaths, "I don't think I can do it again."

"Oh don't be silly, of course you can. Those were all just foreplay."

I got a hand towel from the bathroom. Then I took a bottle of massage oil from the drawer by the bed and poured an ample puddle of it in my hands. I rubbed it slowly over her hips, stomach, and breasts. I concentrated on her breasts for a long time. I rubbed up her arms, along her shoulders, down her thighs to her knees and savored each touch, watching her face carefully to detect which areas were most sensitive. She had her eyes closed. She breathed deeply, and still had the pleased smile.

I leaned to suck her nipple to hardness as I stroked her stomach. She convulsed, trying in vain to move her hands and legs. She was ticklish there. Maybe more than her feet. Panic briefly showed in her face.

"Ah," I said, "here's another one of your not-so-secret places."

"No, no... Oh!" she inhaled sharply. I licked her stomach. The tickling made her thrash around, I could tell by the tautness of her body that she was ready again. I bit her gently just below the navel and she cried out, not from pain, but from sensation.

"When you start to come, strain against the cuffs; it will heighten the moment." I placed the palms of my hands against her inner thighs and gently pressed her open just a little bit more. I used my thumbs to stimulate her. Then I began to slowly penetrate her, first with one finger, then two.

"Do you like this?"

She gasped out a surprising four-letter demand. "More."

"Finally a gratifying response to one of my questions." I added another finger and felt inside her, moving slowly. She moaned and began to lift her hips rhythmically. She was impossibly wet. She tried to move against me, pushing me into her. With my other hand, I reached to the left and pulled the ankle strap just a little tighter. When I did it on the right side, she groaned in magnificent pleasure.

I pressed into her, slipping my hand back and forth rhythmically. I leaned to her again, this time drawing her clitoris between my lips as I teased the tip of it with my tongue. She began to strain against the tightened bonds. Every muscle of her body tensed. She was feeling the surge build. Sensation gathered in her like dark clouds before a storm. Her body became rigid with anticipation. Then suddenly she arched, lifting her body and me from the bed in one intense rush of pleasure that stiffened her every muscle. I rode the wave with her as it reached the perfect moment of pure satisfaction. She came harder this time, differently. She yielded a series of *yeses* in a primal voice that surprised her as much as me. When she relaxed, her face took on a sublime expression.

"You look mighty smug."

She smiled broadly at this. I undid the ankle cuffs and she drew her legs in. I helped her, massaging her thighs and calves as I brought her legs together.

"Undo my hands?" She flexed her fingers and moved her head to glance at her arms still held tightly above her head.

"Not yet," I said in a voice that wouldn't tolerate dissent. "We have more to do."

She shook her head just a little.

Now I was the one with the predatory smile. I said, "Yes, Kathryn, remember, I'm in charge." Putting one hand under her thigh and one under her shoulder, I turned her over on her stomach.

Her breath quickened and she moved her head to see me. "Really... I can't."

"Let's see what you *can* do, querida."

I ran my fingers lightly over her skin, waking all the nerve endings, stirring her desire, rekindling her flames. "You have a great ass, Kathryn. In fact, your whole body is stunning." I lifted her to slip a large pillow under her hips, raising her for more access.

The little devil on my shoulder was cheering me on. I slipped my forefinger along her tailbone and massaged it slowly. She stretched involuntarily, an erotic sex stretch that left her legs farther apart. I took this as an unconscious invitation.

I stroked from the nape of her neck to her tailbone. After a nice long caress, I slipped the oily fingers of my left hand around and over the sensitive spot. Then I reached up and undid her wrist cuffs.

"I don't think I... I've never..."

"Shhh," I insisted. "Nothing to be nervous about. You've liked everything up until now haven't you?"

"Yes, yes, everything... but..."

"I'm going to show you a magic trick, Kathryn, that I really hope you haven't seen before." I rubbed down her back again, then began to massage her thigh with my left hand.

"Open up," I whispered. She squirmed and groaned and opened her legs further as I pressed my knees against them. The pleasure in her voice was evident. I wondered for a moment if I should get my rather powerful vibrator from the closet and make her have a very long continuous orgasm. She was just in the right mood for something like that, but then she was in the right mood for my original plan, too. I'd use the vibrator some other time... soon.

"Maggie," she said, "is this going to hurt?"

"When I'm done with you, I doubt you'll describe this as hurting. Now relax and don't hold back."

I repositioned so I could reach her clitoris with my right hand. I stroked with my thumb to arouse her while I put the towel in place, and then penetrated her vagina again with my forefinger.

I searched both inside and out at the same time with my right hand, while I teased and massaged the tighter opening very gently with my left. I could see her biting the pillow in anticipation.

Inside her, I made a few small firm circles, finding her spot. Kathryn gasped. Then suddenly she felt a lightning bolt arc to my thumb. She literally roared with release as I continued. Bucking and twisting she called out again and again. She pounded the bed with her fists. I didn't ease up until she finally let go, calling my name, wetting the towel. Then she froze, holding the highest moment of ecstasy inside her and with a deep primal cry into the pillow she peaked and then collapsed back on the bed.

She was taking very long breaths. Her face was totally flushed. She was damp with sweat and staring at me in disbelief.

I drew her legs together, rubbing them sweetly and making soothing noises as she regained her power of speech. I helped her turn to her side and she caught my arm and pulled me close.

My mind was already reeling with pleasurable things we could do together. I filed them away for next time and kissed her neck as she luxuriated in sexual afterglow.

"Are you OK?"

"More than fine." She turned and put her arms around me. "You're the greatest detective of all time. I can't quite remember what you did, but I have the urge to spout cliches. For example: I didn't know it could be like that."

"Kathryn, I hope this wasn't... I hope we can... um..." I said. Suddenly I needed reassuring. The little insecure being that lives in the back of my head was peeking out. I'd done some of my best work and if that wasn't good enough for her...

"You're not done with me now, are you?" I laughed making it a gentle joke.

"Done with you? Are you kidding. Ha! I'll never let you go, now." She took me by the shoulders and looked right into my eyes for a long moment. We both grew very still. Volumes passed between us, without speaking a word.

Finally she said, "If you were thinking I might be one of those women who becomes bored after, after she gets exactly what she wants, I promise you I'm not like that, Maggie, I'm really not. And I don't require, or even desire, that we do this kind of thing all the time." She looked into my eyes steadily again.

I smiled and exhaled a little bit of nervous relief.

"Or were you wondering if we can have this kind of adventure again? Oh Maggie," she said in a deep low voice, "I'm already thinking of new... uh... *things*... we could try."

I'm sure my expression became raptorial for a few moments, which perked the same on her face. "Shall we? Right now?" I asked. I looked at my watch. "It's not even that late."

"Well, OK. I'll do my best, but I have to admit to exhaustion. I think I used more energy in that one moment at the end than all I've spent in the previous month. I need to use the bathroom again and then I'd like to fall asleep in your arms.

We took turns in the bathroom and then she snuggled into me.

"You know, Maggie, being with you is one adventure after another," she sighed. "Happy Birthday."

We held each other and Kathryn fell asleep. But I lay awake for a while. I felt kind of different. We'd created a framework in which each of us became the steel drummer chasing away the problems we needed to defeat. We had made this good thing happen together and I was pleased by it.

As I drifted off, I thought about the crazy quilt of the last week and realized lazily that the threads were all wound together. I fell into a deep sleep and slept for many hours abstractly trying to untie them.

And then, I dreamed.

CHAPTER 20
THE DREAM

I was in Amanda Knightbridge's living room at a Neighborhood Watch meeting. Amanda was talking to me. There was another woman with her. After a moment I realized it was Dr. Isabella Santiago. I tried to look closely at her to see whether she was a ghost or a real person, but I couldn't get her in focus.

Amanda said in her precise voice, "Man may only chase the demon messenger of grief with unbound charity," as though I should understand. Both she and Dr. Santiago nodded.

I tried to ask them what it meant but they drifted into the crowd and I couldn't find them again. Frustrated, I left the house and found myself standing in the cemetery alone. It was getting dark. I started to weave through the graves.

I came to The Lost Bride clearing near the stand of yew trees. Suddenly Frankie Kibbey stepped into view. I remembered that the last time I'd seen him he'd been shot to death in the cemetery. I tried to move and tell him to run, but my feet were stuck in clay and nothing came out of my throat.

I gasped because Frankie already had a big hole through the middle of his chest. I could see trees through it. He walked toward me like a horror movie zombie. I realized I wasn't afraid of him though, just sorry he was dead. At that, he fell on the ground and didn't move again.

Mist enveloped the Evangeline statue. When a shaft of moonlight sliced through the clouds, the statue began to grow larger and change. The blurry Lost Bride finally took the shape of Suzanne Carbondale. I could see Samson Henshaw standing near the edge of darkness, staring at Suzanne. Suzanne had one hand covering her throat. She waved to Samson with her other hand and he reached out to her, but she looked me in the eye, then turned and pointed toward the yews.

They parted. Inside was Gabriel Carbondale with a big tub of mortar and a trowel. He was cementing up the crypt's entrance. Then he wheeled around and staggered away from the building like a drunk on a jag. He retched and nearly threw up, but it was only a dry heave. Mortar dripped from his trowel onto the ground, punctuated by steel drum beats. He heard the drum and looked around nervously.

The steel drum notes became a rolling tune. The music got louder. Suddenly the steel drummer wailing on his drum burst out of the cement Gabe Carbondale had troweled over the crypt entrance. Gabe saw the drummer, drew back, and staggered away. Just before Gabe disappeared into the night he turned around so I could see his face. He had a gunshot wound in his head, and he now looked just like Larry Storch.

The steel drummer came toward me in an ominous way. His terrifying expression mixed homicide with greed. But suddenly Kathryn appeared by my side.

The drummer froze. I felt stronger. I stepped in front of Kathryn and she put her hand on my shoulder. The steel drummer laughed grimly and patted his stomach. The drum suspended in front of him became a plate of fruit. He speared a piece with one of his mallets which had changed into a long two-tined fork. He pointed the fork at the statue that looked like Suzanne Carbondale. Then he brandished the fork toward us aggressively. He put it in a bag hanging from his drum and morphed into a cartoon. First he was Colonel Rimfire, and then Cool Cat, who finally became a puff of smoke that wafted into the leafless trees.

Buster trotted into the clearing. He shook his head, rattling his dog tags like coins in a bag. He dropped something from his mouth on the ground. Kathryn picked it up. She held it out to me. I reached for it. A stream of fine white dust shifted between her fingers onto the ground.

A frightening figure came toward us along the path. I tried to gasp out some words but before I could say anything, I realized the hideous face was nothing more than Lois Henshaw, garishly costumed as the bizarre clown in the painting on her wall.

Lois spun around in a spot of moonlight and capered over to the Evangeline statue that still looked more like Suzanne. Lois stuck her tongue out at it, then pirouetted back to speak to me.

Her voice had that surreal low tone that dream people have. Lois shouted slowly, "Where's Samson?"

Before I could answer, her clownish figure slipped backwards out of the main gate. She passed in front of a truck coming down Fen Street. I could see a lamp go on in a second floor apartment on the other side of Fen. Samson Henshaw sat there looking out. He stood up when he saw Lois. Seconds later I could see them together. Lois wasn't in her clown costume anymore. Samson was cooking. He handed Lois a spatula. Lois hugged Samson. Samson pulled the shade.

I turned to Kathryn, but she and Buster were gone. Back across the street the shade went up again. This time Kathryn and Nora were there. Nora had a teapot and Kathryn had a cup. Kathryn gave me her half-smile and Nora waved and winked. I beckoned them out; they nodded and pulled the shade again.

Piper Staplehurst, dressed to the hilt in her expensive burgundy coat and a Gucci scarf, drove a truck with glaring lights through the cemetery entrance. She stopped it near the crypt in the clearing. I tried to wave to her but she got out of the other side and couldn't see me. When I went around the truck, the steel drummer in a Hawaiian shirt with a burgundy background, was there. Now <u>he</u> had the face of Larry Storch. He tilted his head back to laugh, but thought better of it. He dragged a huge wrought iron gate out of the truck, lifted it over his head and disappeared into the crypt.

The truck shrank. Now it was the old Chevy Astro van. Cue and Willie in their fake water company uniforms carried boxes out of the van. The Lost Bride statue altered again into the beautiful form of Evangeline. Her normally serene features were those of a fury.

The two thieves ran toward the yews where a duck fluttered around quacking. Red appeared and joined them. I ran after them calling at Red to stop, but he ignored me. Judith Levy came out of the trees and managed to trip all three of the gang. They dropped the boxes and scrambled away.

Mausoleums and monuments began to loom up out of the shadows like scenes in a shaky camera mockumentary. I went into the crypt, through the floor, and into the underground passage.

When I got to the main tunnel I heard a rumbling that got louder and louder. The tunnel took on the shape of a subway platform. Cool Cat was there waiting. A subway train pulled up. The doors opened. Inside the car was Col. Rimfire, Gabe Carbondale, the steel drummer, the religion-spouting drunk, Larry Storch, Piper Staplehurst, Lois Henshaw, and the duck. Cool Cat got on. Lois and the duck got off and the train pulled away.

Lois Henshaw stood on the platform forlornly. She looked at me with tears in her eyes. She dropped her spatula. It clattered on the stone floor.

Farther down the tunnel a door flew open and out stepped Victoria Snow in all her glory; sleeves pushed up, wild hair pinned back, with an intense expression of purpose on her face and a hefty wooden carving mallet raised high in her hand. Victoria moved rapidly down the tunnel toward me, then turned and reached out her arms into the darkness. There Evangeline was moving swiftly toward her, but the quacking duck got in her way. She stopped short.

The duck grew larger and more grotesque and finally expanded into Gen. Merganser Hunterdon on a big black horse. He was angry and menacing. He reared the horse up in front of Evangeline, but Victoria shouted, "Man may only chase the demon messenger of grief with unbound charity," and threw her mallet with all her might. It struck Merganser and he fell to the ground and began to age hideously. Then he shrank back into a weak little duck.

The duck flew over Victoria, who was now standing in her studio. The duck dropped twenty silver coins into her hand. She closed her fingers but one of the coins dropped to the floor. She searched for it. Then she looked directly at me, pointed to the floor, lifted her foot and under it was the coin. She picked it up with a nod and then we were both back in the vast tunnel again.

Victoria saw Evangeline and swept her into her arms in a triumphant moment that made me feel as though there was hope for the world. But Merganser's riderless horse, big and dark, with fire in its eyes, snorted back into view. It was charging Evangeline.

I moved to warn her and suddenly I was being chased by the threatening animal. Its eyes were murderous, just as the steel drummer's had been.

I heard Kathryn's voice calling me. She was standing on the steps to the studio, high above the tunnel floor. She reached out and pulled me up out of the way of the charging horse. Kathryn had something in her hand. She gave it to me; it was her cup.

But then we saw the crazed beast. It didn't look like a horse any more; it was just a terrifying mass. It was chasing Suzanne Carbondale. She screamed as the dark cloud bore down on her. She changed into Frankie Kibbey, who turned to run. But the mass fastened to his arm dragging him along with it. I could see Frankie turn into Gabe Carbondale, who yelled and struggled as he was being carried off. And then Gabe changed into Evangeline, who turned to look desperately at me. She held out her hand. She called, "Help us...."

I jumped down and ran after them. The cloud of darkness was moving away along the tunnel faster than my leaden legs could go. I saw the face of the victim again; it was every victim I'd ever tried to help, and I couldn't reach them. I called out as darkness surrounded me, "Stop..." But my voice was so soft I couldn't hear it myself. I desperately tried again...

"sssssSSSSStop STOP!" I groaned.

I tried to claw through the darkness but it was like climbing a ladder through mud, near the edge of panic. Then I heard Kathryn's voice calling me and I could see a tiny light overhead. I felt stronger. I drew oxygen into my lungs. Her voice got clearer. And suddenly I was awake and in her arms.

"Oh, Kathryn..." I said, shaking my head to rid myself of the last gripping vision. I looked at the clock. It was 10 a.m. I shook my head again.

"No, no," said Kathryn, holding my head still. "Tell me, tell me what you were dreaming about, before the dream slips away!"

"I need..." I grabbed a drawing pad from the nightstand drawer and furiously began making sketches of the scenes in my dream. After a few minutes I stopped to look carefully at what I'd drawn, and then I drew in some more details.

When I finally stopped, Kathryn looked at the drawings and said, "Tell me."

I told her each person, each thing, each place, and every action I could remember using the sketches as prompts. I added more details as they came to me. She listened without speaking.

When I was done, I stared at her and she stared back.

"Do you know what it all means?" she asked.

"I think," I squeezed my eyes shut and sat still with my hand raised. I'd known some of it already, but now the rest of the pieces were fitting together. I nodded, slowly.

"Man must chase the demon messenger of grief with unbound charity," I said. I put my hand on my forehead, trying to make sense of it. Then I looked up. "Either what woman having ten pieces of silver, if she lose one piece, doth not light a candle, and sweep the house, and seek diligently till she find it?"

I could feel Kathryn watching me.

"You know, don't you?" she asked.

"Victoria wasn't repeating a parable. She was giving us directions. Yes, I have the motive and it's a good one. The same for all four murders. A few parts of it are still alphabet soup, but I think I know, almost everything."

"Four murders? Who else was killed?"

"Evangeline."

"But that doesn't have anything to do with what's happening now," insisted Kathryn.

"Yes, it does. It has everything to do with now."

"Maggie, who did it? Who killed Suzanne?"

"It was the steel drummer."

"I'm not clear on this. That wasn't Gabe?"

"No, he was the drunk. And she wasn't stabbed twice with an ice pick. She was stabbed once."

"But who is it? Who is the killer?" asked Kathryn.

I opened my mouth to tell her who I thought it was, but her phone rang with a text. She looked at it impatiently, then glanced at her watch and said, "Rats, it's Jessie. I have to walk Buster with her. I really should go. I'm already late."

"You go help Jessie with Buster. I'll call the cops and try to convince them of my theory. You'd better leave or Buster will take a dump in Farrel and Jessie's living room."

Kathryn kissed me goodbye and hurried out the door.

I sat down with my laptop to wade through the rest of the alphabet soup and put into order a series of events that began with Victoria Snow rescuing Evangeline Fen from financial ruin and ended, I hoped, with a single shot to Gabriel Carbondale's head.

Just as I entered the part about Victoria Snow becoming a grief-ridden artist in an underground studio committed to creating hundreds of images of Evangeline Fen, my head snapped up.

"That's how she did it. Oh shit... Buster!" I said after a lucid realization slapped my forehead like a hard-swung sea bass. And then my phone rang with a text from Jessie.

<Buster ran into suzannes. kathryn went after. help.>

Oh, no. This is bad.

I threw on clothes and opened the gun safe in record time. I stowed my gun in my shoulder holster and pulled on a ballistic vest. I hit the street at a run and made it to the back alley behind Fen House in minutes.

Jessie was at the back gate. Farrel had just joined her, out of breath. She'd run all the way there, as soon as Jessie had texted her.

"Where's Kathryn?" I asked panting.

"Inside," said Jessie. "She followed Buster into the house and then after a few minutes Nora went in too. Who knew Buster could open this gate by ramming it with his head?"

"Nora! How did Nora... And why doesn't Kathryn just come out?" asked Farrel.

"Kathryn and I saw Nora on our walk and she came along. Kathryn just texted that she thinks there's someone else in the house and to tell you that. I'll just call her," said Jessie.

"NO! Don't call! The killer could be in the house and hear Kathryn's phone. Kathryn is texting because she doesn't want anyone to hear her voice. You and Farrell go around to the front and ring the bell. I'm going in."

"Wait. Killer? It wasn't Gabe?" asked Farrel.

I shook my head, straining to see into the upstairs windows.

"But who? And why be in there?" asked Farrel.

A huge Baskerville howl rose from inside the house. It made birds flit from the trees.

"Oh crap, go to the front. NOW. Ring the bell and then move back. And call the police!"

I slid through the gate and into the backyard. I waited until I heard the front doorbell ring to peek through the backdoor glass. Buster barked when he heard the bell. There was no one in sight. I heard the bell ring again and then, faintly, a door creaked in the middle of the house.

I squatted and squeezed through the dog door. The barrel lock on the inside was snapped off. There was a dog-head dent in the middle of the oak panel. Buster had broken into his own house because he knew something was wrong there. I could see his fresh paw prints and some human knee-scuffs following after him.

Where *was* Buster? Surely he'd have heard me. His ears were as big as satellite dishes.

I decided to chance that if Kathryn was hiding, she would have put her phone on vibrate.

I texted, < Im in house where r u >

Kathryn texted back, < 3rd fl. Someone else in house. I think it's X.>

I stood up, reached in my holster for my gun and listened. No sounds.

I took two steps through the mudroom and pushed open the door to Suzanne's office. I peered through the other office door for a better view into the living room. Everywhere seemed empty.

If there was anyone else in the former home of Evangeline Lavender Fen and Victoria Willomere Snow, they were either hiding on the upper floors or had headed into the basement via the steps under the main staircase. I scanned the floor in the little hallway between the office and the living room and found a clue that I didn't even need a big magnifying glass to see. Dusty footprints headed from the basement door into the downstairs powder room and back. Kathryn was right. The dust clinched it. X was probably in the house.

I moved silently up the steps to the second floor. It had a large bedroom toward the front of the house and a smaller room at the back.

No sign of anyone on that floor save muddy snowshoe-sized paw prints on the hallway rug leading to the third floor staircase. Buster howled again. I could hear Kathryn shushing him. I ran quietly up the stairs.

There was a large open bedroom on the top floor. It had one window on the right, facing the street and two windows facing the back. All three windows were covered by thick curtains. The room was dark.

There was no one in there, but I could smell Kathryn's perfume. I crept up to a large oak closet door, taking those big toe-pointing steps that should have been punctuated by sneaking around music.

When I got near, I heard Buster scratch the door, shake his dog tags, and then *woof* softly. Kathryn shushed him again.

I cupped my hands to a crack and said, "Kathryn." I tried to open the door, but it was locked.

I heard the key turn inside. It was a large walk-in. A front window overlooking the street allowed in sunlight. It picked up Buster's white spots and the rich shine of Kathryn's hair.

"Fancy you hiding in the closet," I whispered.

"It doesn't suit me," Kathryn whispered back.

Buster flipped his ears. He was listening.

"Am I about to be fired or is this something Dr. Watson always does?" said Kathryn.

"Where's Nora?"

"I left her outside. Did she come in too?"

"Wait..." I was listening along with Buster and I heard what he heard. There was someone moving around on the first floor again. I heard a door creak and some steps heading toward the kitchen.

"Maybe it's just Nora?" said Kathryn.

"If it's Nora, then why doesn't she call out? I'm guessing she's hiding from who's walking around down there, making dusty footprints."

Kathryn nodded.

Suddenly Buster jumped up, barked, and ran full speed past me, nearly knocking me over. He rocketed down the steps, crash-landing on the ground floor.

Kathryn tried to call him back, but he wasn't interested.

"What the hell," the killer mumbled downstairs. I heard a scuffle and then a gunshot, a yelp, a strangled scream. And Buster rapidly padding two flights back to us with something in his mouth and a few dots of blood on his ear. He'd been grazed, but not deterred. He was very happy with himself.

"Bring that back, you fucking mutt!" grunted the voice.

"Uh oh," whispered Kathryn.

I nodded, clicking the safety off my gun.

We could hear footsteps coming up the stairs.

Buster said, "Woof." In full voice this time.

We all backed up. Buster turned to face the stairs. The silhouette of an angry figure with a scarf wrapped to the eyes burst into the dark room. We couldn't see a face clearly but I was pretty sure it was the person I'd suspected since the first moment I saw the wound in Suzanne's neck. And somehow even before that.

Buster tinkled his dog tags, just as the killer flashed a small silver gun in our direction.

"Stand back," I said to Kathryn, waving her deeper into the walk-in. I took a deep breath, bent my knees to make a smaller target and raised my gun, holding my other hand under it to steady it.

Buster leapt up and charged the enemy's weapon, and his tree-branch tail whipped my gun and sent it flying across the room, under a low couch against the wall.

"Oh crap," I said, wildly calculating plan B, as the intruder who had murdered three people skirmished with Buster to regain hold of a shiny little automatic. Kathryn came to the closet door.

"Back up!" I shouted to Kathryn. "Get back in there! Buster, come!"

"Buster rolled over and cantered into the closet with us. I slammed the door and turned the key. The gun looked like a Stuhtline .25 ACP. A peashooter like that could kill you but probably couldn't pass a bullet through a thick oak door.

"I thought you said Buster didn't know about guns," said Kathryn as we ducked to the back of the closet.

"He learned when he saw Gabe get shot," I said as I pushed past the hanging clothes to unlock the double window and swung both panes in. "Kathryn, go. Now!"

She hesitated. "Maggie, remember when I told you about my irrational fear of heights? Aren't we safer in here?"

"Only until the realization that any key in the house will open that door. Then we'll be fish in a barrel."

Kathryn took a deep breath when she heard the doorknob rattle. She hurried through the window onto the roof. Her feet slid over the cold slate shingles, but one of the metal snow birds stopped her and she was able to half-stand, half-crawl toward the next house.

I reached in my pocket to pull on my gloves, hoping they'd help me climb down off the roof.

Outside the closet, the lock held. I heard a shot thud into the door but the bullet didn't go through. Another slug came after, but nothing made it to the other side. Here's to the mighty oak.

I whistled at Buster to jump out and dove after him, holding onto the sill to keep from flying out into space.

On the street, Farrel and Jessie looked up at us. They were supposed to have called the cops but as yet I couldn't hear any sirens. A second later I heard Farrel yelling into her cell that shots were being fired. That would get them here in a hurry.

Buster scrambled on the shingles, then slid down the roof and right off the edge. I heard Jessie cry out. I stared transfixed as Buster plopped down onto the second floor roof, stood up, and gracefully leapt toward the yew tree next to the front door. He landed on a big branch that dipped under his weight and swung him lightly to the street, where he calmly stepped off and trotted up to Farrel. He dropped what he had in his mouth at her feet. It made a metallic ring when it hit the pavement.

I didn't have time to shake off my disbelief at Buster's Disney-style escape, because the killer was yanking open the other front bedroom window.

Kathryn was two houses along, inching her way north over the steep roofs. I followed, wishing she would hurry up. Kathryn's foot slipped but she grabbed the sill of the dormer on the next house and righted herself.

I looked back and saw an arm reach out the window and begin to level a gun at us, trying to rub out the witnesses.

Just ahead, the dormer window Kathryn was steadying herself on swung in. Arms reached out, grabbed Kathryn by the collar, and hauled her out of sight.

A shot rang out. It skittled over the dormer's roof, sending shards of slate into the air.

With Kathryn now out of the way, I crouched and ran along the roofs at top speed past two more houses. A moving target is very hard to hit with a small gun like a .25 ACP.

When I got to the last house, there was nothing but a three-story drop to the sidewalk. I looked back. The killer, with scarf wrapped high to avoid identification, was taking aim again.

There was a telephone pole about four feet from the roof corner with a streetlight a yard below. The pole had a heavy guy wire angling down to the sidewalk. In moments like this, it's best not to spend too much time thinking. The pitch of the roof was too steep to walk to the edge, so I gauged the distance, took two giant steps and jumped. A shot whizzed over my head.

I caught the arm of the streetlight with both hands, then swung over and slid down the guy wire to the street, ripping the palms out of my gloves as I went.

I ran to the front and looked up, but now there was no one brandishing a gun in the window.

Amanda Knightbridge had scooped Kathryn into her third floor window. I realized that it was her house we'd been climbing over.

Amanda and Kathryn came out of the house together. Before I was conscious of moving, I was holding Kathryn in my arms and she was hugging me as though the pressure itself would wipe the last fearful moments away. I looked over Kathryn's shoulder into Amanda's eyes. She nodded once, then turned and focused on the door of Fen house.

"*Now* you're going to fire me?" asked Kathryn, softly.

"Ow," I squeaked.

She held me at arm's length. "Are you hurt?"

"Only because you're squeezing all the toothpaste out of me."

Jessie said to me, "Now you know how I feel when Farrell is on one of those stakeouts with you."

Jessie spied Buster as he ambled his big waggie-dog body up to her. She stooped down to hug him like a giant Teddy bear.

"How did he get down to the ground?" asked Kathryn.

"Well, you may not believe this..." began Farrel. As she described Buster's flight, I looked around the ground to find the coin he'd dropped, then picked it up.

It was a 1910 Morgan silver dollar in average condition. Not particularly rare, but not something you get in everyday change.

Kathryn was looking around the group.

She and I said in unison, "Did Nora come out?"

"I believe she is still inside, with the killer," said Amanda Knightbridge in a measured voice.

Buster woofed quietly.

"We should wait for the police. They'll be here in a minute," insisted Jessie. "It's a small house; there's nowhere to go. Who is it anyway? I thought Gabe was the killer. Whoever it is probably doesn't have any more bullets.."

"The gun was a .25. From the shape, it was probably a Stuhtline. They have six shots and..."

"And five shots have been fired," said Kathryn. "Once at Buster when he went downstairs, twice into the door, twice out the window at us... So that's five. There's probably one bullet left."

I nodded. "We can't wait for the police, because there's a passage out of the basement.

"Passage?" said Jessie and Farrel.

Kathryn was nodding her head. "Of course! That's how Victoria got to her private studio. Not through the cemetery, through her own house!"

"If Nora's been taken hostage, I have to go after her now. There are miles of passages and we're talking about someone who's killed three people already,"

"I'm going with you," said Kathryn, following me into the backyard.

"We don't have time to argue," I said firmly.

"Then don't. I got Nora into this and I feel responsible. I have to help you. And we're a team." She said the last part softly, but she meant it. It was a pivotal moment.

I turned to face her with the furious look of a warrior. She stepped back in surprise. Her eyes widened. She'd never seen me so much like a virago before. I reached out and held her shoulders at arms length. I said evenly but with a tone that was flint and steel, "We're up against someone who is desperate and armed, who might have one shot, or could have a dozen more magazines. I have a gun and a bulletproof vest. You won't be helping me if you're down there. There is no further discussion."

Kathryn nodded.

I said seriously, "Look, I need you to convince the police that a murderer is running around somewhere under the streets of Fenchester with a hostage. And I need you to try to figure out where they might surface."

She nodded again, fully understanding the situation. We hugged fiercely for less than a second, and she ran off.

CHAPTER 21

I crouched through the dog door. The house was still. I ran upstairs, dragged the couch away from the wall, found my gun in a dark corner and came back downstairs.

The door to the basement was wide open.

I held my gun in front of me in *cop search* fashion, snapped on the light switch, and moved slowly down the old cellar steps. They were steep and a little uneven. Each one was fastened securely to the oak handrail that was attached to a row of four floor-to-ceiling upright posts the size of telephone poles.

There was nothing down there but some empty stone shelves built into the wall, a straw broom leaning in one corner, and some clay flowerpots on the floor. One of the pots was broken.

A light film of white dust had been brushed into a small pile in one corner. The sweeping had obliterated any footprints.

I centered myself by chanting, *Think fast. Think Fast. Think Fast.*

I considered the scene as though it was a puzzle. Question: Why are the pots on the floor when there are empty shelves? I went over to the wall of slate shelves. They were inset in the whitewashed stone foundation. I tapped on the wall under the middle shelf. It felt like solid rock but it had to move back somehow.

If it was anything like the coffin that moved in the crypt, there would have to be some kind of heavy counterbalance.

I went back to the stairs and inspected the railing. One of the posts wasn't attached to it. I climbed halfway back up the stairs and pushed the post toward the middle of the room. It tipped, tilting a section of the stone floor underneath it. At the same time the whole inset of the shelves lurched back into the wall revealing a very narrow, dark passage at one side. It opened much more quietly than the crypt. No wonder I didn't hear the killer use it after Gabe was shot. Of course Buster was also howling.

I had to push an oak lever out of the way to get into the space, which closed the opening behind me. My pocket flashlight showed there were two sets of dusty footprints in the passage. One had been made by sturdy work shoes, and they matched the prints I'd seen in the studio. The other set was irregular and scuffed, and in the shape of Nora's winter boots.

"It's showtime, folks," I said softly as I plunged into the passage.

****

The narrow, thirty-foot passage descended in a series of shallow steps. No one could have carried anything through it. I had to squeeze through by turning my body sideways, and even at that my front and back brushed both walls. Lucky claustrophobia wasn't one of my irrational fears.

The passage ended in a narrow opening into the main tunnel. Its wood door was propped open with a bag marked plaster. The outside of the door had a faux stone texture. It was probably invisible when it was closed.

I swept light over the floor. There was an empty metal hand truck leaning against the wall and beyond it traces of white dust leading north. I followed the dust to Victoria's studio under the Majestic. The police lock on the studio stairs had been broken off. A length of pipe with the broken lock still hooked over it lay on the floor. The door was open and the lights were on.

I moved swiftly and quietly to the top of the stairs, crouching low. There was no one in the studio. I looked up to be sure the police had resealed the wall I'd broken down. A large sheet of plywood was secured over the hole. The light over the steps, where Kathryn and I had found Samson, was also on. I crept down them cautiously. Things were different down there. It was empty of people but the killer had been there recently. Dust was scuffed all over. The door to the clay storage area was open. Someone had pulled one of the bags marked clay to the bottom of the steps. I checked around quickly. No one had been knocked out and been left behind a crock or anything. No Nora anywhere. The whole search of the studio took less than four minutes.

Back out in the tunnel, I was keenly aware that the person dragging Nora along as insurance was a rat in a maze who was focused on getting out. If the murderer didn't know the crypt exit was sealed with the steel plate, I might be able to catch up.

I remembered what Samson Henshaw had said about waking up at the bottom of the steps. He'd thought he was blind until he saw the faint purple light from the sidewalk prisms when the sun rose the next day.

I switched off my flashlight and closed my eyes tight for a few seconds to get them used to the dark. I could see dots of light in the tunnel ceiling where the ends of the glass shafts poked between the fitted stones. I started off at a careful trot, touching the tunnel wall as a guide.

I was almost to the intersection of the tunnel under Fen Street. Just a little way beyond would be the side tunnel to the crypt. I heard someone shout a single word, "Nae!"

Suddenly a flashlight beam appeared, coming toward me along the side tunnel. I flattened myself against the wall. The beam didn't even sweep in my direction. It turned left and went west under Fen Street. The sidewalk prisms helped me speed to the tunnel intersection. I stopped and peered around the corner. Far ahead was the bobbing beam. Adrenaline coursed through me as I followed the light, breaking into a jog. Luckily the noise of trucks and buses rumbling along Fen Street above me covered my echoing footsteps.

I was closing on the light, so I slowed. With each bounce the flashlight took, I heard the distinct jingle of pieces of metal and an occasional grunt of protest from Nora.

Where are they going? I counted the blocks in my mind. Two more and we'd be under the Irwin College campus. As far as I could tell in the dark, we hadn't passed any doors or branch tunnels.

The tunnel got wider and the flashlight beam began to rise. I heard the sound of shoes going up a metal staircase. At the top of the stairs were two illuminated yellow door signs that said *Danger Radioactive* between black triangles. This was the lowest level of the Irwin Library Archives. The bogus warning signs were to keep people away. Inside those doors were miles of stacks and people who could be causalities. Either the killer was going to keep Nora as a hostage or toss her down the stairs. I ran for the steps.

When I clanged onto the staircase, the flashlight whirled on me from a few steps above. My quarry pushed Nora toward me, dropped the flashlight on the landing, and reached in a shoulder bag.

A shot rang from the .25. I swung Nora around so she was behind me, but the unaimed bullet missed us both.

There in the dim light from the signs I saw the gun pointing more carefully in our direction. The trigger clicked but there was no shot. Now the gun *was* out of bullets.

"Hide," I said to Nora as I raced up the stairs.

"She only had one bullet? Crikey!" said Nora incredulously.

"She might have another magazine. Get going."

I made it to the top landing as the person who'd just shot at me got to the first door. I grabbed for an arm but a swing of the heavy bag knocked me back.

The first door flew open, flooding the scene with nearly blinding light.

The killer screamed, because Samson Henshaw stood in the door with blood running down his face. The killer had thought Samson was dead.

The light from the open door illuminated everything. The killer stumbled, staring at Samson with mouth agape, then tripped back along the walkway toward the next door, grasped the handle, and pulled it open.

A cloudy white light seemed to seep out. The killer screamed like a squawking crow at what was in the doorway, then staggered backwards, hit the metal railing and teetered over the three story drop.

"No!" I shouted as she toppled over in slow motion. She caught onto the railing with one hand, dangling over the dark space.

"Let go of the bag!" I shouted when I got to her.

She shook her head, her hand slipped, and she dropped the bag. Silver coins pinged and jingled all over the floor of the tunnel. Her free hand snatched at the railing. Her flailing legs swung wildly.

I reached over and grabbed her coat collar, twisting to lever her back over the rail. When I turned, I saw what had frightened her in the doorway. The cloudy white light made the figure blurry, but I was sure it was Suzanne Carbondale and the red stain on her shoulder didn't just look like blood. It *was* blood. The light got blindingly bright again and morphed Suzanne into Evangeline Fen. I distinctly smelled lavender. I was shocked into immobility for a second and wondered if everything that was happening was just another one of my dreams.

I tried to shake it out of my head. I fought to keep the struggling figure from falling to her death. Her weight, along with the extra weight of my bulletproof vest, made my feet leave the floor. She was pulling me over the edge with her, and there wasn't much I could do about it other than drop her. I felt a flare of panic.

Suddenly somebody grabbed my belt and heaved me back. I was balanced again. I dragged the killer over the railing and onto the walkway floor. I flipped her over and kneeled on her back.

I swiveled around to look back at the door. There was no one in the doorway, but at my side was Kathryn. She'd saved me from going over the rail.

Kathryn whispered in my ear, "I saw her! Just now, at the door."

"You saw her, too? Was it Suzanne or was it Evangeline?"

Kathryn shook her head in surprise. "No, no... I saw... Isabella Santiago!"

****

Down in the tunnel the bright lanterns of the slightly late cavalry lit up everything. A puffing Ed O'Brien and an agile Marc Freligh joined me on the platform. Nora was with them.

"You daft, barmy..." said Nora addressing the killer who'd kidnapped her and dragged her through the tunnels as a hostage. "Really Maggie, she's crazy, totally lost the plot. Be careful with her; she'll kill you if she gets the..." Nora's voice caught in her throat and she began to cry softly. She said, "Oh, my, I'm a wee bit jeeked."

"Nora," said Kathryn. "Come in here." Kathryn reached out her hand to lead Nora into the library. I'd noticed once Kathryn was done rescuing me, her discomfort with heights had caused her to move away from the edge of the high platform.

I realized I was a little jeeked as well. I took a deep breath. Then I dragged the quivering figure through the archives door.

The killer turned from her fetal position and saw Samson Henshaw wiping ketchup off his head. The killer was shocked. She looked wildly around and then shouted at me, "Is Suzanne alive, too?"

Samson lunged, but I held him back.

Sgts. O'Brien and Freligh came through the door.

"Sorry we're late. It took a while to figure out how to open that passage at Fen House," said Freligh.

O'Brien took one look at the woman on the floor. "Who is it?" he asked.

I hoisted her to her feet and pulling off her scarf I said, "It's Piper Staplehurst, from the museum."

CHAPTER 22

"It smells like Turkey Day," said Sara as she hung up her coat.

It was Sunday morning at Farrel and Jessie's. Buster lolled at Amanda Knightbridge's feet. Cora Martin and Judith Levi were in their usual places. Nora were there too. The air was heavy with the aroma of wonderful food.

"We felt like we had a lot to be thankful for," said Farrell. "Where's Emma?"

"My dedicated law partner is meeting a client," said Sara.

"Pretty?" Farrel asked.

"No that wouldn't be enough to miss a brunch like this. It's a serious case. Pro bono. And she's going to have to clean up a lot of the mistakes the previous lawyer made," said Sara.

Jessie brought a squash filled with cornbread and pecan stuffing to the table, while the rest of us helped carry in a casserole of praline-topped sweet potatoes, a basket of homemade rolls with Jessie's special honey butter, a huge salad, and a big platter of roasted vegetables.

Cora couldn't contain herself. "Tell us everything, Maggie. Everyone is asking me, dahling. From the TV news, I couldn't tell anything."

"In Jane Austen's time, this would have been a story all of you could have dined out on," said Judith Levi. "You as well, Amanda."

"I was merely in the right place at the right time. Yes, do tell us, Maggie, has Piper Staplehurst confessed?"

"My police contacts say Piper's made a deal. She'll get life in prison rather than the death penalty," I said. "She's confirmed all the details. I don't think the Fenchester police have ever dealt with anyone like her before. She has a criminal history that's as staggering as her list of aliases. She's had a dozen different hair colors in as many years and her heavy make-up was far more disguise than fashion statement."

"Explain how you knew it was Piper Staplehurst all along. And why *she* was the steel drummer," said Kathryn.

"Well, ever since Farrel told that subway story about the steel drummer, the drunk, and Larry Storch, everything kept reminding me of it."

"Yes, I felt that somehow that story held the key," said Amanda.

I nodded. "Then Kathryn gave me that animation cel of Cool Cat and Colonel Rimfire for my birthday."

"What did all that have to do with anything?" asked Sara.

"Because Larry Storch did the voices for Cool Cat and Rimfire. Larry Storch was doing all the voices. That's the point. He did *all* the voices. As Mickey said, he did the good guys *and* the bad guys. Get it?"

Everyone looked confused except Amanda Knightbridge, who was nodding at me contentedly.

"See, the cel was just a reminder that the steel drummer and the drunk were working a classic scam together. People might be ambivalent about loud steel drum music on its own, but if it's chasing away a threatening drunk, it's suddenly worth a lot of tips," I explained. "And Kathryn, when you told me about Bolton Winpenny arranging that other professor's hysterical fit so that Bolton could suggest you all end the retreat. Well, it was the same kind of plan. You even *called* Bolton the steel drummer."

"The steel drummer suggested the wrought iron gates," explained Amanda.

"Yes, exactly. There was real concern about gangs in the cemetery but Gabe's reactionary idea of cementing up the crypts was offensive to nearly everyone. Then Piper Staplehurst shows up with the wrought iron gates plan. People might have balked at the gates if they'd been just presented on their own, but in contrast to Gabe's ugly cement idea the period gates were brilliant. Of course Gabe and Piper were working together. The hero and the villain were the same team, kind of like Larry Storch doing the voices for all the characters," I explained.

"The drunk was a fake?" Farrel laughed shaking her head. "And he went right on into the next car and then the steel drummer followed him. They must have made a fortune that day!"

"But what happened with Suzanne?" asked Jessie.

"Suzanne was working on a book about Victoria and Evangeline. She found Victoria's archived papers in the library. There was information about Victoria's studio and the money. Suzanne had also found the passage under Fen House too. After all, Suzanne lived in Victoria's house and it wasn't hard for me to find the passage, once I began looking for it."

"But then Suzanne made her fatal mistake. She consulted the wrong expert," said Farrell sadly.

"Uh huh. Piper Staplehurst came to Fenchester Museum looking for things she could cleverly steal and turn into cash. That's her M.O. She even lucked out by having a door to the underground tunnels just a few feet from her own desk. I'm sure she figured they would give her access to all sorts of lucrative places. But then a sinkhole cut off her easy access to the underground infrastructure just a day or two after she arrived in town. That must have frustrated her. All that was left was a small hole at the top of the pile of fill the city had dumped into the sinkhole. It was just big enough for her to squeeze through, but not a space she could have moved anything of any size back out.

"She was hoping for a big score, but not having much luck when suddenly Suzanne Carbondale shows up right in Piper's office, happily telling her exactly where Victoria's studio and money were and that there were passages to it under Fen House and under the crypt."

"Suzanne showed Piper the studio on Christmas Eve. And Piper killed her so she wouldn't tell anyone else and just left her there," Jessie said softly.

"You knew Piper was the killer all along, didn't you Maggie? How?" asked Kathryn.

"At the neighborhood meeting *she* was the one yelling out about gangs from the back of the room. I thought that was strange. When Farrel told us about the steel drummer and the drunk I knew they were a scam team, and everyone was saying that Piper was like the steel drummer. I began to think of her as someone with an ulterior motive," I explained. "Her silver sucket fork was the murder weapon. When I saw that the wound in Suzanne's neck looked like a square-toothed vampire bite, I thought of Piper's two-pronged fork. She'd told us she carried it with her everywhere. Even in my dream, the steel drummer was eating fruit with a long fork. That's exactly what you use a sucket fork for. But there just wasn't enough motive and I certainly didn't have proof.

"So Piper wanted the gate over the crypt entrance to keep people from finding Suzanne's body?" asked Farrell.

"That's one reason."

"But what about Gabe? How did he get mixed up in all this?" asked Sara.

"Gabe was the one person who would know Suzanne hadn't just gone away. She'd have never left her dearest things behind. Piper didn't want Gabe searching for Suzanne and she also knew there was an entrance to the tunnels in Gabe's basement, which she needed. So she decided to use Gabe. The minute he got back from England, Piper took him to the studio and showed him the sculpture and boxes of antiques that could be turned into money. They opened the first box and looked at what was inside.

That's what Frankie found when he followed Piper's trail to the studio.

Piper made sure Gabe left his fingerprints on anything that could implicate him in Suzanne's death. Then she told him Suzanne was dead and that her body was in the studio, and he'd be blamed. She made Gabe help her arrange to gate up the crypt and I think she promised him some money too. So Gabe went along with Piper in sending emails and Facebook messages to make it seem as though Suzanne was still alive. Piper had already used Suzanne's phone to send texts to Jessie and Samson right after she'd killed Suzanne," I said.

"I'm pretty sure Gabe was afraid of Piper too. I don't think he realized that Piper had ruthlessly murdered Suzanne herself until Piper shot Frankie in the cemetery. Gabe wasn't acting when he threw up there. It took all of his Shakespearian skills to convince me and the police about what he'd seen. He was especially frightened after Piper phoned and threatened him later that day, when I was in his house. What Gabe didn't realize was that by being in England when Suzanne was killed he had a solid alibi for her murder."

"That daftie Piper was maniacal whilst dragging me through the rabbit hole," said Nora. "Maggie, I don't think I've really thanked you for saving my life." Nora bowed to me like an actor taking a curtain call. I smiled.

"So the motive was Victoria's money?" asked Sara. "Are we talking about actual hidden cash or simply the value of the art and antiques?"

"Oh, there was cash. Remember the twenty silver dollars a day that Merganser had to pay Victoria? Well, that's what Piper was looking for, and she found it. Victoria had been stashing those coins away for sixty years."

"Where?" asked Farrell incredulously.

"In the plaster and clay bags. It hit me in my dream when Victoria found the coin under her foot in the studio. The money was in the only place it could have been, under her studio in the storage room. The bags in front had real plaster and clay in them, but farther back were over 600 seventy-five-pound sacks of dimes, quarters, fifty-cent pieces, and silver dollars. Buster nabbed one of those dollars out of Piper's hand at gunpoint. And all along I was finding Piper's dusty footprints."

"Explain about Frankie and Red," said Kathryn.

"OK, Piper was trying to turn some of Victoria's silver into working cash while she arranged for trucks to bring in the wrought iron gates and then take out the bags of coins. By the way, that was her main reason for gating the crypts, so that trucks under her control could legitimately be in the historic cemetery. All those bags of coins were very heavy. Anyway, she saw Frankie at a flea market peddling Victoria's possessions. She went back to Victoria's studio and found that one of the boxes of antiques was gone. She figured correctly that Frankie had followed her into the tunnel through the crypt, and she knew he'd be back to get more for the next market. There's one in Gloversville on Monday morning, isn't there?"

Farrell nodded.

"So she hid in the crypt on Sunday, ready to kill Frankie the minute he showed up. She really is ruthless. She was also the one in the van chasing us. The police found it near her apartment. She was trying to get rid of anyone who might have known about what was in the studio."

"How *many* silver dollars?" asked Cora.

"Over 500,000," calculated Farrel.

"Crikey!" said Nora.

"500,000 dollars, Maggie? I know it sounds like a great deal of money, but in today's economy it isn't such a huge amount," said Judith.

"I agree, Judith," said Kathryn, leaning back in her chair. "All that planning, arranging that grant, getting the van, three murders, staying in Fenchester when she was on the verge of being discovered. The risks were so high. I just can't see why Piper Staplehurst would go to this much trouble for five hundred thousand dollars. She could have converted some of Victoria's sculptures into cash. She couldn't flood the market with a *blizzard of Snows*, but she could have sold a few and made half a million from them. So much work for such a small amount of money."

Everyone was nodding, except Farrel and me.

"No, Kathryn, you're forgetting something important," I said.

"What?" asked Kathryn.

"That Victoria saved over 500,000 dollars in *silver*, based on the face value of the dollars, quarters and dimes," I said pointedly. "But each silver dollar is close to an ounce of silver. And in the current market silver has been fluctuating between 30 and 40 dollars an ounce. So... it's not 500,000 *dollars* we're talking about; it's over 500,000 ounces of silver. That's well over sixteen million dollars!"

Awe settled over the room.

"For a professional thief, sixteen million dollars of stolen merchandise, or even hot paper money, probably has a cash value of less than ten percent, and even that's hard and dangerous to get. But these silver coins could be cashed in at any one of those *We Buy Gold* shops. There are a dozen of them just in Fenchester. Some of the good shops even pay ninety-five percent of the current market value. This silver wasn't hot either. She probably would have taken most of the sculpture as well. She had the trucks for it. It would have been the perfect crime, if she hadn't had to kill three people."

"Piper also nearly murdered Samson," said Sara.

"Right, but that wasn't quite as pre-meditated. Piper used Suzanne's cell phone to fake texts from Suzanne to her friends. But then Gabe broke his cell when it dropped into Buster's water dish. So Piper gave him Suzanne's phone to call her in case anything was up. Later she took it back to send more fake Suzanne texts. Samson thought he saw Suzanne leave Fen House. When Samson dialed Suzanne's phone he heard his own ringtone coming from Piper's pocket and followed her," I said.

"He followed Piper into the crypt and along to the studio," said Kathryn. "Samson told us he'd seen someone get a hand truck from a van and take it into the crypt. Piper must have wanted to use it to move the heavy bags of coins and couldn't fit it through the narrow passage under Fen house. In the studio, Piper heard Samson coming. She set up a candle on the steps to decoy him and then hit him with a plaster mold."

"Kathryn, you're catching on to this private eye stuff," said Sara.

Kathryn shook her head. Then she said, laughing, "Not exactly, Sara. I got the motive wrong, and up until Maggie pulled down Piper's scarf, I thought the killer was Lois Henshaw!"

"Couldn't have been Lois. She has coffee with Shelly at Brews on the Mews every morning, rather than chasing around flea markets," I explained.

"I missed that point," sighed Kathryn.

"But when the going got rough, you saved my life at the library archives. Kathryn, how did you know where Piper was going?"

"Well, Nora uses one of the office phones. I tracked the GPS on it. It showed Nora's phone was going west. In the 1800s when the tunnels were built, there was nothing out there but the college. Everyone at the college knows that the library archives have underground floors. I headed there. On my way, I saw Samson Henshaw. He insisted I tell him what was happening. And I felt I needed some back-up. It was his idea to use a ketchup pack for the blood. He was brave."

"It was risky," I said.

"Maggie, I don't see how Suzanne found Victoria's studio so quickly. There's no studio information in Victoria's archive box. Nothing about where the money was hidden or a passage under Fen House either," said Kathryn ignoring my concern.

"*Now...* There's nothing in there *now.* I think there were some papers there about the studio and money that Suzanne found and told Piper about.

They were probably fairly cryptic, so that the average researcher wouldn't have understood their implication, but to Suzanne they were clear. There could have been a bill for the cost of having the secret passage built and receipts for having supplies delivered to the Majestic. Suzanne could have known that Victoria owned the Majestic if she'd seen the public posting of Victoria's will. I'm guessing Victoria paid for the passage herself, but I think Merganser was the one who set up the crypt passage, to run all sorts of black market items through.

"After Piper killed Suzanne she had plenty of time to remove those papers from the library archives, smuggle them out in a pocket or something and delete all the references to Victoria Snow from the computer files when a librarian was away from the terminal. In that way no one else could ever find Victoria's information again."

"Except Isabella Santiago!" said Amanda brightly, then shook her head at my questioning glance.

We were eating apple pie. Jessie was passing around the coffee pot. The meal had taken most of the day. It was getting dark out. I heard Wagner and Griswold merfing and owing on the stairs, hesitating because that giant dog was in their house again.

"Kathryn has uncovered something else in the journals," I said.

"Victoria gave money to various charities and traveled quite a bit, especially to South America. Though she was reclusive in Fenchester, she was selling in a number of galleries, so the income from her work easily paid for all her expenses. Everyone knew she was getting the twenty dollars a day commission fee from Merganser Hunterdon, but there was only about thirty thousand dollars in her bank account when she died. Even at the time, people speculated where the rest of the money was," said Kathryn.

"She wanted it to all go to Irwin. That's what her will says. But if you ask me, I think she wanted to have Merganser's silver in one place before she finally gave it away," I said.

Kathryn nodded. "The interesting thing, though, is no one has really wondered *why* she was paid so much. Victoria made Merganser pay her for the rest of their lives and they both lived into their nineties. It was as though each of them was trying to outlive the other. It turns out the key is the line Victoria carved into the wall of the crypt: Man Must Chase The Demon Messenger Of Grief With Unbound Charity.

"What do you think it means, dear?" Judith asked Kathryn.

"I think Victoria was talking about Merganser chasing the demon, but the demon of grief *was Victoria herself*," said Kathryn simply.

"I just don't understand. Why would that misogynist, crooked, thieving, weasel Merganser consent to give Victoria so much money?" said Farrel. "He must have hated her!"

"He gave her the money because General Merganser Hunterdon murdered Evangeline Fen, and Victoria could prove it."

Everyone gasped.

"He cheated all those people out of their money, and he was a murderer, too?" asked Sara.

"I'm afraid so," said Kathryn. "Victoria had evidence that proves Merganser Hunterdon hired a trio of... well, *ruffians* is too gentle... they were thugs, to head off Evangeline's horse and make sure she had a fatal *accident* that broke her neck.*"

"Oh no," said Jessie. "It's so sad. I'm not sure I want to hear this part."

I thought about my dream. The frightening riderless horse chasing Evangeline. It hadn't needed Merganser to ride it, because he'd hired someone else as the hit man.

"Jessie, Victoria didn't write much about the accident. She didn't even write about the funeral. I think she was devastated. But she finally got a grip on herself and found a renewed purpose. Shall I read some? "

Everyone nodded. So Kathryn opened her bag, put on her white cotton gloves, and carefully drew out Victoria Snow's second journal.

"This was written about a year after Evangeline died," Kathryn began.

Date, July 4th, 1879

Three years after the nation's centennial, and I find myself alone and independent. Demons have haunted my dreams and crushed my spirit. I have felt little since the passing of my beloved Angel.

I had seriously considered taking my own meaningless life, but now my beloved brother Franklin, who has been my only rock, has brought me the evidence of the horrible deed committed by the devil incarnate, Merganser Hunterdon. Perhaps anyone else would have kept the truth about my beloved's death from me, yet Franklin has understood that my sense of justice could overcome my grief.

Yet I drew out a volume of Anne's poems and found:

I dreamed an angel, Angel twice, through death,
Wrought us another "Night." A stately dream,
Where reconciling Infinites did seem

To fold round life's perplexities, and wreath
Its ancient glooms with stars: — a marble breath
From Art's serene, fresh, everlasting morn,
Where the dull worm of earthly pain is born
To winged life thenceforth, and busieth
With golden messages its mortal hours.
O the Divine, earth would have wronged and slain!
Its pangs are rays above her falling towers
 Of lovelier truth — breaths of a sweet disdain
Shedding strange nothingness on meaner pain,
Drops of the bleeding god that turn to flowers.

And so this very afternoon I visited our rock pool and there I experienced an epiphany accompanied by a ray of blinding light that struck the deepest regions of my soul. I fully believe it was sent to me by my Angel.

My two glorious years with my beautiful Evangeline were filled with passion and the brilliant light of the most generous and giving woman in the universe. She had humor and intelligence unparalleled. She was kindness personified. Though I fancy myself a competent artist, my contribution to society pales to a puny flicker in comparison to what Evangeline was able to do in just a mere twenty-four months.

My dear brother has brought me the sworn statements and indeed the witnesses who would bring swift justice upon this evil man. Yet, I will not seek the arm of the law. It is too lenient, too gentle.

Today I commit my life to honoring Evangeline and punishing the minion of Satan who took her away from this world.

My dear brother has compelled this evil murderer to sign a complete confession and consent to act as an instrument for good and generosity. Some would say I was committing acts of blackmail, and perhaps it is so. But those leaders of the State still seek to compel me, and indeed the memory of Evangeline, to allow Hunterdon to act as a financial figurehead to ensure the stability of the economy. And they too do so with the action of threat and coercion based on the evidence of his evil deeds.

I will see to it that every cent of this evil man's money goes toward the civic projects Evangeline envisioned. I will allow him liberty as long as he suffers everyday. Especially as I shall act as the demon messenger of grief, pricking his horrible soul with a pikestaff dipped in brimstone as punishment for his most evil deed. Every plan he makes for his own wealth and fame I shall foil, every misstep he takes, I will cause him to stumble and fall. I myself cannot emulate the sweetness and light, and indeed forgiveness of my beautiful Evangeline. Yes, I am the antithesis. I shall act as an earthly devil and shall dedicate myself to creating the hellfire in which this man must burn.

Perhaps I shall create a statue of him with his back to me, to symbolize his inability to know how I contrive to torment him.

And I shall be sure that I take good care of my safety, for I will live a long life fueled by my mission. I shall celebrate everything about my Angel in my work, and I shall use the devil's wealth never for my personal benefit, but to do good in the world. The contract he signed yesterday shall require he pay me twenty dollars in silver a day. He will bring them to me each evening in supplicatory penance, a daily reminder of his sins, and of the one who holds his reins. Further, he must spend every discretionary cent beyond, to make this City a better place.

My hollow life now has new meaning. And though I take on the pitchfork of the devil, I am sure my Evangeline will understand, and will surely delight in the good works I shall bring to fruition. And while I shall not find joy ever again, the action of my pitchfork shall bring me satisfaction.

"Well, this is quite a turn of events. Victoria Snow fueled by vengeance and Merganser Hunterdon compelled by nothing more than fear. No doubt it was the tip of Victoria's pikestaff that caused him to drop out of the Senate race after he had won the primary," said Amanda. "Is there anything that can confirm Victoria's condemnation of Merganser?"

"Victoria notated a legal document that should still be on file. The Philadelphia law firm founded by her brother is still in existence. All I have to do is request to see the document," said Kathryn.

EPILOG

Piper Staplehurst was convicted. No one had to testify because she took a plea. For someone so calculating, Piper had made many foolish mistakes. She'd left a huge amount of incriminating evidence around her apartment. Everything from the big gun that had killed Frankie to the sucket fork were in plain sight in her kitchen. She even had a bag of silver dollars and one of Victoria's sculptures under her bed. And though the fingerprints on the gun that shot Gabe were too smudged to incriminate anyone, the powder blowback from the shot was on Piper's hands. She was sentenced to life plus 200 years.

Suzanne's sister claimed her body for a funeral in Illinois. Jessie and Farrel hosted a local memorial for her in their home that ran all day. Hundreds of people attended.

Gabe's memorial was more complicated. He'd been blackmailed into crime, he hadn't killed anyone, and he had no family to claim his body. Yet Gabe had covered up Suzanne's disappearance at least partly from greed. Perhaps if he'd spoken up, Frankie and Gabriel himself wouldn't have been murdered. Ultimately, it was Jessie who took charge of Gabe. She and Farrel paid for his cremation and spread his ashes in the Washington Mews Cemetery.

"It's what Suzanne would have wanted," Jessie explained.

Red Kibbey disappeared after getting probation for conversion of property. He left Frankie's remains to the city to deal with. Frankie's older and more dangerous partners in crime, Cue and Willie, went to prison for home invasion and robbery, for five years. They got out in eight months.

The millions of dollars of Victoria's money rightfully went to the Irwin College Fen Scholarship Fund as Victoria had directed. The more than one hundred Snow sculptures in her studio went to the college as well. The college created a spectacular traveling exhibition of her newly found work. Kathryn wrote the catalogue notes for it. The large work of Evangeline emerging from the stone traveled with the exhibition and then was installed as the focal point in the grand foyer of the fine arts building. It further established Victoria Willomere Snow as one of America's greatest 19th century sculptors.

Irwin College was so happy I'd found the sixteen million dollars and the Snow sculptures they wanted to give me the standard finder's fee. I suggested quite a bit less if they let Kathryn and Farrel keep the Snow sculptures they'd purchased from Frankie. The college agreed as long as those works could be part of the traveling exhibition for a year. The reduced finder's fee still paid off my entire home improvement loan.

Kathryn located Merganser Hunterdon's confession at the Snow, Platt, Raymond, and Fen law firm in Philadelphia. When she got back from visiting their offices she told me, "One of Evangeline's great-great-nieces heads the firm."

"Evangeline's great-great-niece? What's her first name?"

Katherine answered with her sexy half-smile, "Lavender."

"Uh huh," I nodded, "and what does she look like?"

"Well, I'd say she looks like. Hmmm, how shall I put this, like... *Victoria's heart's desire.*"

"I'm surprised you're back so soon," I said wryly.

"My dear," Kathryn returned, putting her arms around me, "Victoria's heart's desire is not my heart's desire."

When she got all her notes together, Kathryn applied for a grant to produce her book about Victoria Snow. She received confirmation of it in record time. With part of it she hired Nora to be her part-time research assistant, which extended Nora's educational fellowship.

Nora continued to work part-time for Sara and Emma and continued to hold Kathryn in awe despite her best efforts to lighten up. I suspected Kathryn was teasing her by using her academic voice in its lowest register whenever they spoke. And I suspected Nora kind of liked it.

Amanda and Buster seemed to understand each other. She took Buster to her office at Clymer House at Irwin each day. He became a favorite fixture at the college.

The vandalism of the Civil War Cemetery stopped. Apparently it had been committed by Piper Staplehurst and Gabe Carbondale themselves to justify covering the entrance to the crypt. The grant for the wrought iron gates turned out to be real, however. Amanda Knightbridge oversaw the implementation of it. The Victoria crypt was secured within a few weeks, cutting off access from there to the tunnels.

Before the college rented out Fen House to someone new, it sealed the basement tunnel. Yet I couldn't help believing that there were quite a few other entrances to those tunnels around the city.

Samson Henshaw went back to Lois and they tried to make a go of it. A few months later they divorced, and Lois left on a cross-country trip that ended up in Sarasota, Florida. She met a professor at the Ringling Bros. Barnum and Bailey Clown College, and they lived happily ever after.

****

Right after the brunch, Kathryn and I went home to the loft. We shrugged off our jackets and scarves. I put the bag of Jessie's leftovers in the refrigerator.

Kathryn stretched her arms over her head. "Mmmm. You know, if I keep eating as we do at Jessie and Farrel's, I'll lose my girlish figure. How do you manage?" she smiled, coming near me.

"I work out two hours a day and only eat there once a week. The rest of the time I eat watercress," I said, reaching for her.

"I've never seen you eat watercress," she said, beginning a slow kiss that made my toes curl.

"Kathryn, are you really serious about working with me? Doing investigations? Are you sure?"

Kathryn walked over to the couch and sat down. She patted the place next to her and I sat, waiting for her answer.

She leaned her head against her fist with her elbow on the back of the couch. Her voice became higher and slower. "I'm not just playing detective. Though there are parts of it I do like. You know, the part I really love about historical research is finding out about things, and figuring out connections, and there's a great deal of that in detective work. But it's more than that." She paused for a moment. "Maggie, intellectually I know your job is an inseparable part of who you are and that I cannot ask you to change that."

"I appreciate that you understand that."

She took a deep breath and said, "I can't just stand at the sidelines and watch you do these dangerous things. I need to share them with you and you seem to like talking them over with me. I'm very good at research, and I like to do it. I think I'd really be able to help you when it comes to that kind of thing. So, if you let me, and if you promise not to talk down to me, I'll be the rookie. And by the way, I'm not particularly used to taking that role."

"I would guess not," I snorted lightly.

"Now you're teasing me."

"No, I'm impressed, but Kathryn, if you're going to do this, even if it's just behind-the-scenes research, there are things you really need to learn."

"What kind of things?" Her eyes were twinkling.

"Like how you have to identify yourself, and what you're legally allowed to say and do. How to preserve evidence. First aid. Martial arts. The search engines that find out the best information. That kind of stuff. If you really want to be in on things, then you could take a few courses at the community college."

"You're serious about this? You'd let me do this?"

"Kathryn, I don't know if you're ready to make this... um... kind of commitment, but it would be safer for you if you learned the skills."

"I see, yes, I could do this. After all, I'm good at school. I could take some summer classes; I'll have time then. Are you sure you want me to? Because I know I'm asking for a great deal of you. A great deal..." she said, shaking her head, then glancing around the room. "I'm asking you to share every part of your life. It's quite a presumption."

"I've never been in this type of relationship before, but... um... I'm game." Then I realized that what I'd just said was pretty insensitive and an understatement. I was more than game. I was just kind of nervous about admitting it.

Kathryn's face held consternation and I felt like crap for putting it there. It was time for me to do something outside of my comfort zone.

"I'm uh... May I tell you a story?" I asked softly.

Kathryn nodded, seeing my serious expression. She reached for my hand and held it in her lap.

"OK, but I have to preface it."

"Go ahead."

"Jessie was hit so hard when she found out about Suzanne. It reminded me that there can be all sorts of reasons a person leaves the ones they love, and they don't always do it by choice. But the problem is that that feeling of abandonment happens regardless of why, especially for kids. Um... I told you before that I'm not *issue free*. That's my issue. Well, one of them. I haven't really told anyone this before... not even Sara or Farrel... See, I'm really laying myself wide open, and its scares me."

"I'm not sure what you mean."

"Oh Kathryn, I just want you to understand that this is the one thing you cannot tease me about. You can tease me about many things, but this is where I draw the line," I rambled.

"Maggie, I understand," said Kathryn in a gentle whisper. "You're about to tell me something very personal and you don't want me to use it as ammunition in the occasional disagreements we might have."

I turned toward her and laughed. "I'm certainly making this dramatic."

"Trust me..."

"OK, yes. Well, it's about my mother. She died when I was eight years old and it was pretty painful."

"I can imagine."

"Maybe you can, but probably not," I said honestly.

"You're right. I'm sorry, go on."

"I loved my mother. She was smart and fun and spent a lot of time with me, helping me learn new things and to see the world as a wonderful place. She was a painter. She traveled a lot. She was always going away to have shows of her work in faraway places. I only have one painting she did. The rest were sold in shows and galleries."

"The abstract of Mexico?" Kathryn nodded toward the big abstract of a Taxco cafe. The colors subtly carved out the forms of the street, buildings, and trees. "It's very good."

"Yes, I love looking at it. Here's my story:

> One day my mother was getting ready to go on a trip to New England. I remember it so well. She was packing her big suitcase with her clothes. She already had her painting gear in the car. I had to go to school, so I went into her bedroom to say goodbye.
>
> My mother was wearing jeans and a sweater like always. She hugged me hard, and I remember her looking sad, but I may just be projecting that. That's what the child psychologist said to me for the few visits I had with her after this happened.
>
> Anyway, I kissed her goodbye and went off to third grade, and then after lunchtime the teacher got a call and left the room to get a teacher's aide to watch the class. I walked through the empty hall with my teacher.
>
> One of our neighbors was there. She tried to smile but her reddened eyes and crying sniffle probably frightened me more than if she'd just told me what was wrong. She drove me home.
>
> My father met me at the door and hugged me and took me into the kitchen to explain that a car accident in a faraway place had taken my mother away forever and that she wouldn't ever be coming home. There was a bluebird sitting on the bird feeder outside the kitchen window. We hardly ever had bluebirds there. I wanted to tell my mother it was out there, but she wasn't there, so I couldn't.

After that, for what seemed like weeks, I'd come home from school expecting to find her there. When someone came in the door, I'd absently expect to see her.

Then one day I was alone in the house and I saw a bluebird on the bird feeder, and I cried for two days. And then I idled for about three years just trying to get through each day.

"Three years? Oh Maggie," said Kathryn with a soft sigh.

I don't really remember much about those years except that I drew pictures and I watched cartoons every day.

At night I'd dream that my teddy bear had disappeared and I'd spend hours looking for it in places that were impossible to get to. Images jumbled together. There was always at least one scene of my mother leaving with her canvases. It usually happened when a bluebird appeared. It was like one big Dali dream sequence.

In many of those dreams, my mother would talk to me. And sometimes she'd help me look for my toys, but we could never find them. As I got older, I would realize in the dream that she was dead, and she couldn't really be there. Then I'd know it was a dream, and I'd even tell her so.

And... and she'd say, 'Well if it's a dream then maybe you can fly!' So I'd step back and jump in the air and fly."

Kathryn said, "You could fly on demand? That's a pretty exciting thing. Do you know when you're dreaming now? Can you still fly on demand?"

"Sometimes, and sometimes I just go and kiss some random girl."

"In your dream..."

"Yes, Kathryn, in the dream, not in real life. I don't fly in real life either."

Kathryn laughed, but then said seriously, "That's how you felt for three years... and then?"

And then my father married Juana. And Sara and Rosa saved me from a life that was out of my control.

Sara was a riot right from the first day. Rosa was only two years old, but she was very funny too. Sara was eight, and she looked up to me and challenged me at the same time. I taught her things an eleven-year-old knew. I started doing martial arts then too. Pretty soon I was speaking Spanish like a native, and I had someone to play with, and a new mother who'd listen to me and hug me and tuck me in.

But I was pretty slow to trust that they wouldn't disappear. I finally got over that. It helped a lot that there were three of them and my father. Better odds.

"Did you have a hard time when your father died?"

"It was just a few years ago. He'd been sick for a long time and he kind of prepared me for it, but yes, I miss him very much..." I paused and then said, "So...." And then I couldn't think of anything else to say.

"So, this is the baggage you were talking about?" asked Kathryn.

I gave a slight nod.

Without a word Kathryn took me in her arms. She said, "I'm not going anywhere." She held me close until I felt the warmth of her body and relaxed into the strength and message of her embrace and felt safe.

****

I woke up with a start to a dark room and a digital clock that glowed 3:30. Kathryn wasn't beside me. I got up and went into the big room. Kathryn was sitting in an easy chair by the wall of windows, gazing out at the moon over the Mews.

She turned when she heard my footsteps.

"Did I wake you?" she asked. "I'm sorry."

"Is there anything wrong? Would you rather be alone?"

Kathryn shook her head. "I'm glad you're here, but I don't want to keep you from resting."

"Come and sit with me on the couch in the bedroom. It's warmer in there." I drew her by the hand to the bedroom couch. Kathryn curled up and I spread a soft quilt over us both.

"Can't sleep?" I asked, putting my arm around her.

She shook her head. Kathryn had told me early in our relationship that she'd had occasional bouts of insomnia all her life.

"It's so frustrating. It's not as though I'm not tired." She stifled a yawn. "But I think I've figured out something rather significant by reading more of Victoria's journal. It's really full of interesting things. When I write the book, I'll have to research every part of it, but I like doing that."

She yawned again. "After she lost Evangeline, Victoria frequently traveled to South America. Even when she was quite an old woman. Early in the century she spent time in Chile, in the capital. She would have been in her late sixties by then. There was significant political unrest. She met a young woman. She was Chilean, but of German descent. Did you know there was a large German population in Chile in the early 1900s?"

I shook my head.

"I didn't either. Here, I'll read it to you."

May 12th, 1914

This morning one of the Rothmeyers introduced me to a charming 20-year-old girl named "Gisa." It's a shortened version of Gisella. Her family was part of the old regime and, I gather from other sources, not particularly well regarded. Some sort of allegation of fraud attached to her grandfather.

Her mother is no longer living, and had no people, her father disappeared years ago, so Gisa is at sea. She is quite well educated and capable. She speaks a number of languages, far better than I, and is talented in art as well. She drew a picture of me with which I was quite impressed. And frankly, it takes a great deal to impress me in that area. She can draw perfectly, but she has the boldness to go beyond.

Gisa's drawings reminded me of some of the drawings in Etta's collection. I saw them in Paris the last time I was there. Etta bought them from Gertrude for a song. Gertrude is clearly growing bored with Etta now that Gertrude lives in Paris full time. Yet Etta is still young enough to attract someone and she is certainly rich enough to do so.

I honestly think Gisa's drawings are much more striking than the drawings I saw in Etta and Claribel's collection the last time I was in Baltimore.

Gisa has asked me to hire her as an assistant and apprentice, and I'm seriously thinking of doing so.

"Wow... She's talking about the Cone sisters and Gertrude Stein!"

"I know, and the drawings Etta bought from Gertrude Stein. I wonder whose they were... Picasso? Matisse?"

"All those famous artists really did all know each other, didn't they."

"Yes, that's not the least of it though. You see, she brings this young woman home with her, to Fenchester."

"Really, hmmm. A June-December romance? Twenty?"

"Gisa was twenty-one by the time they came back to Fenchester.

She seems to have lived with Victoria for the rest of her life, but, though Victoria mentions her often and fondly, she never says anything..."

"Romantic about her?"

"Exactly. Yes. They were not lovers. Gisa was more like a daughter. It's so funny Maggie, but now that Victoria is writing in the 20th century her written voice is much more contemporary. She does say something else very important; wait until you hear this. It's five years later."

August 15, 1919

 Gisa says she wants to have a child. I feared at first she was telling me she was preparing to leave with some man. Men certainly do find her attractive. However she assures me she means nothing of the kind and has no intention of leaving. She wants to bear a child to complete our unconventional family.

 She has planned this rather carefully and seems to know the steps she must take to... make it happen. She was willing to explain what they were but I confess I didn't have the stomach for it. This proves I suppose, that I am a woman of the era that bears my name. Though, of course, I have had experiences beyond those of the average Victorian woman.

 I prefer to think of it akin to Ruth in the benefit of Naomi. Whither thou goest... Though I've always suspected those two to be more than adopted mother and daughter. The latter describes our relationship more precisely than that of the two women in Ruth.

 Gisa will "put her plan into action" on the sea voyage we shall take to Europe in a few days. In that way, we shall not have to worry that the... father... as it were... might become an albatross. She has explained to me that if she can find a young lad without "experience" she is assured that disease cannot be a problem.

 My anxiety with her decision underscores my love for her, my dear child, whom I could not bear to lose. Ah well, I suppose the medical practices of today are much advanced to those in my younger days when women regularly died in childbirth, and Gisa is young and strong. And of course, her mind is made up, so I have no hope of changing it. I fear for her nonetheless.

 And perhaps I fear for myself, having to share our small home with a crying infant now that I have nearly reached my three score and ten.

"There is a great deal of other information in here about a show of Victoria's work in Philadelphia and then the preparations for their trip. After the trip there are references to Gisa's *condition*. And then, this is the last entry in this journal."

Date June 17th, 1920

After a frightening night which hosted a midwife and nurse, we have a baby! Gisa insisted that she did not need to go to the hospital. In fact, I suspect the lack of a physical father may have prejudiced the staff against her. But we conferred with the midwife a number of times preceding the blessed event and she posed no protest.

Gisa has now appended a new surname for convention's sake. I suggested Fen, but she chose the name of the city of her birth in Chile. Probably just as well.

I am surprised to find a roaring fondness in my heart for this newborn babe. It's rather shocking I feel this way, but there it is. Interesting, is it not, that my maternal instincts have lain dormant for decades until the waning years of my life. They now present themselves with the ferocious attitude of a lioness... Fancy!

The connection of the birthday of this child and the day Evangeline and I first shared ourselves in the spring-fed pool touches my heart all the more.

The baby is quite beautiful and remarkably tiny. Gisa insists that we shall name this lovely child after beauty itself. I see now, more than ever that these are my daughter and granddaughter. And they are, indeed, beauty itself; they have replaced the perfect beauty from which I was parted so long ago. When I pass on to reunite with my perfect Angel, I will leave these beautiful beings behind to fill her void and make a difference in the world in their own way.

I stared at Kathryn as she lay the journal on the table and pulled off her gloves.

"That's all there is in the journal? That's the end?"

"It's the last page. She had to squeeze the writing in. I suppose there might be another book somewhere in the world, but we don't have it now. So, they had a baby. It's so remarkable. I wonder what happened to her?"

"Kathryn, I think we know what happened to her... think about it."

"Hmmm?"

"Think about it! Her last name is the name of the city of Gisa's birth! Victoria met her in the Capital of Chile! Santiago... And they named her after beauty."

"Bella? Isabella Santiago?" Kathryn sat back with her mouth open. "I didn't think of... Maggie... she'd be..."

"Very old. But the question is, is she alive or is she a ghost? I didn't tell you that when you saw Isabella in the archives, I saw, well, I saw a ghost, and it wasn't Isabella. In fact it was two ghosts." I told Kathryn who I'd seen in the doorway.

"Maybe you were lightheaded and the stress and bright light made you see something that wasn't there."

"Well, maybe. I have considered that, but I think Piper saw them too. Because when she saw that Samson was alive, she asked me if Suzanne was alive too."

Kathryn shook her head a little bit. We sat together looking at each other, then finally she said, "Is this something you're going to investigate?"

"I'm not sure, but either way, I'm glad we're sharing it."

She smiled and kissed me and said, "I may never sleep."

We both laughed.

"Here," I said turning to the side and putting a pillow between us.

She leaned into the pillow and I put my arms around her. I touched her cheek, feeling the warmth of it with my palm.

She turned and looked deeply into my eyes. I suddenly knew what she wanted, what had been keeping her awake, and what I needed to do.

"I should sing you a lullaby, but I'm not very good at singing, so I could recite something." She nodded, still searching my eyes.

I thought for a minute, took two giant steps and then a flying leap.

I recited:

> *I love your lips when they're wet with wine*
> *And red with a wild desire;*
> *I love your eyes when the lovelight lies*
> *Lit with a passionate fire.*
> *I love your arms when the warm white flesh*
> *Touches mine in a fond embrace;*
> *I love your hair when the strands enmesh*
> *Your kisses against my face.*

Not for me the cold calm kiss
Of a virgin's bloodless love;
Not for me the saint's white bliss,
Nor the heart of a spotless dove.
But give me the love that so freely gives
And laughs at the whole world's blame,
With your body so young and warm in my arms,
It sets my poor heart aflame.

So kiss me sweet with your warm wet mouth,
Still fragrant with ruby wine,
And say with a fervor born of the South
That your body and soul are mine.
Clasp me close in your warm young arms,
While the pale stars shine above,
And we'll live our whole young lives away
In the joys of a living love.

"It's kind of a sappy poem, but the point is, I love you, Kathryn," I said softly.

She said gently in a high sweet whisper, "I love you too, Maggie."

The Poems

The poems appearing in this book were all written and published before 1923 and so are in the public domain. The author is deeply grateful for the creation of these poems and to the brilliant women and men who created them. The reader is encouraged to read more of each of these poets' works.

Love Song For Alice B
Written by Gertrude Stein

A Darting Fear—A Pomp—A Tear—
Written by Emily Dickinson

Dim Eden of Delight
Written by Anne Whitney

O, beware, my lord, of jealousy;
It is the green-eyed monster which doth mock...
from *Othello*
Written by William Shakespeare

And shuddering fear, and green-eyed jealousy!
from *The Merchant of Venice*
Written by William Shakespeare

I Dreamed An Angel, Angel Twice, Through Death...
Written by Anne Whitney

I Love You
Written by Ellen Wheeler Wilcox

AUTHOR'S NOTES

The author firmly believes that the words Gay, Lesbian, Bisexual, and Transgender represent a culture of people, not simply an immutable orientation and identity, and so throughout this book those words are capitalized in the same way one would capitalize Latino, African-American, Hispanic, or Black, which each similarly represent much more than an accident of birth.

The author thanks real life people Bolton Winpenny and Marc Freligh, who both generously bid at a charity silent auction to benefit Pennsylvania Diversity Network, for the opportunity to have their names as characters in this book. Neither of them are in the profession of their character and their characters' actions and behaviors are a product of the author's imagination. Both of them in real life are active supporters and leaders in the GLBT community.

There are references to real historical figures, events, and places in this novel. While Victoria Willomere Snow and Evangeline Lavender Fen and all their families and circumstances are the complete invention of the author's imagination, the author has made an effort to fit their stories into the historical timelines of real women artists and poets of the late 1800s and early 1900s, many of whom were Lesbians.

The Centennial Exposition in Philadelphia, the bank panic of the 1870s and the sailing of the Bothnia and Scotia referenced in Victoria's journals did take place, however the interaction of the characters in them is a product of the author's imagination.

Charlotte Cushman, the brilliant Shakespearian actor who played Hamlet and other men's and women's classical roles, was a real person who lived in Rome and the United States in the late 1800s. She was a Lesbian and wealthy patron of the arts. She was in historically documented long-term relationships with writer Matilda Hays, artist Emma Stebbins, and actor Emma Crowe, and quite a few other women. Hays actually sued Cushman for support when Cushman began her secret affair with Emma Stebbins. Cushman died of breast cancer when she was 59 years old.

Laura Keene was a contemporary of Charlotte Cushman. She established, for the first time, regular matinees that ladies could attend without the company of a man. Keene's theater company was performing when President Lincoln was shot. Lincoln's head did rest in her lap as he died. Her blood-stained petticoat continues to travel the world as part of exhibitions about Abraham Lincoln's life and death, long after people remember Keene's work. In other words, her underwear is now more famous than she is. Charles Busch's play *Our Leading Lady* is a fictionalized account of how this event affected Keene. Actor Kate Mulgrew played the part of Laura Keene in the play's first production.

Lesbian sculptor Harriet Hosmer wooed Charlotte Cushman's partner of ten years, Matilda Hays, away from her in Rome in 1854, which created quite a drama between the three women. Hosmer was one of the premiere sculptors of her day whose primary patron was Wayman Crow, the father of Emma Crow, who was one of the two Emmas with Charlotte Cushman at the end of her life. Many young male and female apprentices learned their trade in Hosmer's sculpture studio in Rome.

Edmonia Lewis, who was of African, Haitian, and Ojibwe decent, really did study art at Oberlin College in the 1860s and worked in Harriet Hosmer's studio in Rome. She also had a studio in the same building as Anne Whitney in Boston. She did have a major piece in the Centennial Exposition in Philadelphia titled *Death of Cleopatra* that was lost for over one hundred years and then found, restored, and now resides in the Smithsonian.

Sculptor and poet Anne Whitney and her life partner Abbey Manning were also part of the circle of women artists in Rome. They lived in Boston in later years. Whitney really did apply for a commission to do a monument of abolitionist Charles Sumner by presenting drawings and sculptural studies. Whitney was awarded the commission, but it was revoked when the judges found out she was a woman. She did indeed do the sculpture of Sumner anyway and it is still in place on the grounds of Harvard University.

History does indicate that Edgar Allen Poe married his wife Virginia Clem when she was thirteen years old, and he was twenty-seven. They were first cousins.

Gertrude Stein regularly sold drawings and paintings by Matisse, Picasso, and other famous artists to Etta and Claribel Cone, often for just a few dollars. The Cone sisters' collection is a major feature of the Baltimore Museum of Art. Historical sources hint that Gertrude Stein was fascinated by Dr. Claribel Cone and had a romantic affair with Etta, which ended when Gertrude began to live with Alice B. Toklas in 1910. In 1921

Gertrude Stein wrote the poem *Love Song For Alice B*, in reference to the woman she referred to as her wife for the rest of her life.

Mannerbach, the coin silver spoonmaker who created urn-back and bird-back spoons, practiced his craft in Reading, Pennsylvania, in the early 1800s.

Shakespeare coined dozens of sayings and phrases that are part of today's everyday speech; a list of some of those phrases can be found at the end of these notes.

Actor Larry Storch, who lives in New York City as of the writing of this book, really did the voices of Cool Cat and Col. Rimfire and was Corporal Agarn on *F-Troop* in the 1960s. He began his career in 1949 and is still working today.

In 1986 the author boarded a subway car in New York City and at the next stop Larry Storch and a woman got on. Soon after, a reeling, Bible-spouting drunk came into the train car, followed soon after by a steel drummer. The author remembers it well and wonders if Larry Storch does too. They both gave the steel drummer some money.

The term Coordinative Biography was coined by this author who firmly believes that one's life cannot be separated from one's work. The author also firmly believes that to end homophobia, bullying, and intolerance, students must be taught about the important contributions that Gay, Lesbian, Bisexual, and Transgender people have made to history.

The author encourages the reader to seek more information about these important figures in history and their interesting lives, especially the Lesbian artists, poets, and actors. For extensive information about Charlotte Cushman and the Lesbian artists and writers in Europe in the second half of the 1800s, the reader may find interesting: *Across the Untried Seas: Discovering Lives Hidden in the Shadow of Convention and Time* by Julia Markus (Knopf - 2000) and/or other works about Charlotte Cushman's life, including her collected letters to Emma Stebbins.

AN INCOMPLETE LIST OF EVERYDAY
PHRASES COINED BY SHAKESPEARE

A dish fit for the gods
A fool's paradise
A foregone conclusion
A ministering angel shall my sister be
A rose by any other name...
                    ...would smell as sweet
A sorry sight
All corners of the world
All the world's a stage
All's well that ends well
And thereby hangs a tale
As cold as any stone
As dead as a doornail
As good luck would have it
As merry as the day is long
As pure as the driven snow
At one fell swoop
Bag and baggage
Come what come may
Discretion is the better part...
                    ... of valour
Eaten out of house and home
Exceedingly well read
Fair play
Fancy free
Fight fire with fire
For ever and a day
Foul play
Good riddance
Green eyed monster
Heart's content
High time
Hoist by your own petard
I bear a charmed life
I have not slept one wink
In a pickle
In my mind's eye,
In stitches
In the twinkling of an eye
It is meat and drink to me
Lay it on with a trowel

Lie low
Love is blind
Make your hair stand on end
Milk of human kindness
More fool you
Much Ado about Nothing
Mum's the word
My salad days
Neither a borrower nor a lender be
Night owl
Off with his head
Out of the jaws of death
Pound of flesh
Primrose path
Rhyme nor reason
Screw your courage to the sticking place
Send him packing
Set your teeth on edge
Short shrift
Shuffle off this mortal coil
Star crossed lovers
Stiffen the sinews
Stony hearted
Such stuff as dreams are made on
The crack of doom
The Devil incarnate
The game is afoot
There's method in my madness
Thereby hangs a tale
This is the short and the long of it
To-morrow, and to-morrow...
                    ...and to-morrow
To sleep: perchance to dream:
                    ...aye, there's the rub
Too much of a good thing
Truth will out
Vanish into thin air
Wear my heart upon my sleeve
We have seen better days
Wild goose chase
Woe is me

(photo by the author)

LIZ BRADBURY

ABOUT THE AUTHOR

Besides her work as the author of the critically acclaimed Maggie Gale Mystery series, Liz Bradbury has written and had published over 400 nonfiction articles and essays on Gay, Lesbian, Bisexual, and Transgender issues. She has had regular columns in several publications and web sites including the *Valley Gay Press*, PA Diversity Network's web site: www.padiversity.org, *Panzee Press*, *Diversity Rules*, and *Gaydar Magazine*. She is a founder of the *Medusa Literary Society for Fiercely Independent Lesbian Publishers*, has been a co-editor of *Sinister Wisdom Magazine*, and was a judge in the 2012 *Kissed by Venus* short story competition.

Liz Bradbury is also a founder and the Executive Director of Pennsylvania Diversity Network, the largest GLBT advocacy organization in PA. She has been the publisher of the Valley Gay Press newspaper for 14 years. As an advocate for the GLBT community, she has worked to successfully pass pro-GLBT legislation. She speaks frequently on GLBT rights and is an expert on same-sex marriage equality (and the lack of it) in Pennsylvania.

Her earlier careers include teaching woodworking, furniture design, and art history at State University of New York, and antique dealer.

She lives in Allentown, Pennsylvania and Amelia Island, Florida with her spouse Dr. Patricia J. Sullivan.

Liz is currently at work on her next Maggie Gale Mystery:
C-NOTES AND SKI NOSE

Liz invites readers to friend her on FACEBOOK
and invites readers to:
Join the FACEBOOK group:
MAGGIE GALE MYSTERY READERS
For discussions with the author and other readers, and special inside information.
and
Join the FACEBOOK group:
MEDUSA LITERARY SOCIETY
For discussion and information on independently published Lesbian literature.

If your organization or book club would like to arrange a reading, book signing, or workshop event with the author, contact the author through Facebook or through Boudica Publishing Inc. For the fastest response call Boudica Publishing at: 610-820-3818. See further information at www.boudicapublishing.com or at www.lizbradbury.boudicapublishing.com.

BOUDICA PUBLISHING INC.

For more information about
Boudica Publishing Inc.
or its imprint
Lesbian Mystery Books
see www.boudicapublishing.com
or call: 610-820-3818

LESBIAN MYSTERY BOOKS

Made in the USA
Charleston, SC
27 March 2013